SCARS

A KILLERS NOVEL, BOOK 5

BRYNNE ASHER

SCARS

A Killers Novel, Book 5
Brynne Asher

Published by Brynne Asher
BrynneAsherBooks@gmail.com

Keep up with me on Facebook for news and upcoming
books
https://www.facebook.com/BrynneAsherAuthor

Join my Facebook reader group to keep up with my
latest news Brynne Asher's Beauties

Keep up with all Brynne Asher books and news. Sign up
for my newsletter http://eepurl.com/gFVMUP

Edited by Hadley Finn
Cover by Haya in Designs

ALSO BY BRYNNE ASHER

Killers Series

Vines – A Killers Novel, Book 1

Paths – A Killers Novel, Book 2

Gifts – A Killers Novel, Book 3

Veils – A Killers Novel, Book 4

Scars – A Killers Novel, Book 5

Souls – A Killers Novel, Book 6

The Tequila – A Killers Novella

The Killers, The Next Generation

Levi, Asa's son

The Agents

Possession

Tapped

Exposed

Illicit

The Carpino Series

Overflow – The Carpino Series, Book 1

Beautiful Life – The Carpino Series, Book 2

Athica Lane – The Carpino Series, Book 3

Until Avery – A Carpino Series Crossover Novella

Force of Nature - A Carpino Christmas Novel

The Dillon Sisters

Deathly by Brynne Asher

Damaged by Layla Frost

The Montgomery Series

Bad Situation – The Montgomery Series, Book 1

Broken Halo – The Montgomery Series, Book 2

Betrayed Love - The Montgomery Series, Book 3

Standalones

Blackburn

CONTENTS

Prologue	1
1. Beeps	9
2. A Wager	19
3. The Moment	31
4. Prison	43
5. Red	55
6. Unless You Piss Me Off	67
7. Where Dreams and Fears Collide	79
8. Tou-fuckin'-ché	89
9. The Ghost	103
10. Complicated	115
11. Checkmate	129
12. I Look Fucking Good in a Tux	139
13. Rules	151
14. Exoneration	161
15. Rage	175
16. Like Old Times	193
17. Next to Me	209
18. Money	219
19. Do You Trust Me?	233
20. Plans	247
21. The Bella Lottery	257
22. Lost Time	265
23. Welcome to Crew's Fucked-Up Family	275
24. Up Your Game	287
25. Open Season	297
26. Flirting Sperm	309
27. Windmill	317
28. Treasure Forever	329
29. Macpussy	337
30. You Were an Arsehole	349
31. Kills Me	359

32. Stampede	363
33. Gray	371
34. Dog Years	377
35. Catch My Breath	383
36. A Second	393
37. Charlie Daniels	403
38. Brilliant Babies	411
39. Simple Man	421
40. Shatter	431
41. Coinci-fucking-dentally	441
42. Sentry	451
43. Double	461
44. Cocky Self	471
45. Bloody	475
46. Diversify	489
Epilogue	495
Thoughts and Acknowledgements	505
Also by Brynne Asher	509
About the Author	511

CONTENTS

Prologue	1
1. Beeps	9
2. A Wager	19
3. The Moment	31
4. Prison	43
5. Red	55
6. Unless You Piss Me Off	67
7. Where Dreams and Fears Collide	79
8. Tou-fuckin'-ché	89
9. The Ghost	103
10. Complicated	115
11. Checkmate	129
12. I Look Fucking Good in a Tux	139
13. Rules	151
14. Exoneration	161
15. Rage	175
16. Like Old Times	193
17. Next to Me	209
18. Money	219
19. Do You Trust Me?	233
20. Plans	247
21. The Bella Lottery	257
22. Lost Time	265
23. Welcome to Crew's Fucked-Up Family	275
24. Up Your Game	287
25. Open Season	297
26. Flirting Sperm	309
27. Windmill	317
28. Treasure Forever	329
29. Macpussy	337
30. You Were an Arsehole	349
31. Kills Me	359

32. Stampede   363
33. Gray   371
34. Dog Years   377
35. Catch My Breath   383
36. A Second   393
37. Charlie Daniels   403
38. Brilliant Babies   411
39. Simple Man   421
40. Shatter   431
41. Coinci-fucking-dentally   441
42. Sentry   451
43. Double   461
44. Cocky Self   471
45. Bloody   475
46. Diversify   489
    Epilogue   495

    Thoughts and Acknowledgements   505
    Also by Brynne Asher   509
    About the Author   511

To my Beauties

May you kick arse in everything you do.

PROLOGUE

One year ago
London

Bella

If my blood could boil, it would.

When this nightmare began three weeks ago, I never imagined I'd end up here. I thought they'd realize their mistake, kiss my arse in apology—as they should—and we'd share a glass to laugh off their epic levels of stupidity. It's a fuck up on their end that should've been smoothed over in a blink. Someone else's fuck up—not mine. I don't fuck things up, at least not at work, and never anything as royally as this.

My personal life is a different story.

"Bella, you can sit there and chew on this all day. Doesn't change the facts."

I want to shift my feet, drag my sweaty palms down the sides of my denim, and then drop kick his arse across the room. But I don't allow myself any of that. Instead, I tip my head, narrowing my eyes. "I dare you to call me Bella again. Only those I love or trust get that side of me and you certainly don't fall into either category at the moment."

His jaw hardens and he sucks in a breath. "Let me call your father. You're a Donnelly. We owe it to him—to his legacy and that of your grandfather. He can acquire proper counsel. You're going to need it."

I open my mouth when I shouldn't ... but that's nothing new. Holding my tongue has never been my strong suit. But this man, whose generation in British Intelligence falls somewhere between my grandfather and father, should be castrated—he's that piss poor at his job. "I wouldn't need a solicitor if you knew how to perform a bloody investigation. My grandfather is surely rolling in his grave knowing he once believed in you."

His voice lowers. "Isabella, do yourself the favor of taking me up on my very gracious offer of calling your father—"

"You call my father and, I swear, he'll bust your nuts for incompetence until you're forced to beg him for mercy."

This beanpole of a man hasn't always been an imbecile, but he's worked too long and has seen better days. He hasn't kept up with technology or the gym, and should've handed over his credentials years ago.

Even so, this isn't good.

This is leaning on the side of catastrophic.

If *this* were simply not good, they would have

summoned me to Vauxhall. Instead, they cornered me here, a bogus meeting in an abandoned warehouse in Hackney under the guise of needing to discuss a case. My car is four streets over. One of me, five of them. I'm an operative, and an unarmed one, at that.

I also know if they drag me in from here, there's no way I can prove they're bloody fucking *wrong*. Whatever they've done, they did a bang-up job of framing me.

"The money trail doesn't lie, Isabella. We've been following it for weeks."

"It's bogus," I snap. "Someone set me up and you know it."

He shakes his head and his minions, who'd dance a jig upon order, step in beside him. With muscle at his sides, he stands straighter and keeps spitting his poisonous lies. "We've got two in custody and they're being transferred to the city as we speak. It's not looking good for you. You need a solicitor, and from the evidence I've seen, a good one."

Fuck.

From my periphery, the door is too far. I have no idea what's behind me or if there's another way out, but from the way they've arranged themselves, I highly doubt there is. Just because they're minions, doesn't make them dim-witted.

All I can do is talk. Lucky for me, I'm brilliant at that.

"They're my targets and you've already shot my cover to hell. I'll interrogate them myself and get to the bottom of this."

He shakes his head and has the nerve to smile. "That's not going to happen."

"Then, please, do me the honor of telling me what *is* going to happen."

He takes a step toward me but I don't flinch. If we were alone, I would have been out of here twenty ticks ago and he'd still be writhing on the dusty, gritty floor. "You know what's going to happen."

I know exactly what he means, but I keep talking because, at this point, my best chance is to rile him. "Have we traveled back a century where the boys with tiny balls take care of business in back alleys instead of Vauxhall where an asset can get a fair shake? Or are you still rubbed raw that my father was bigger, better, and more brilliant than you?"

"Thorne has nothing to do with this."

"Like hell," I toss back. "He's hailed as one of the most integral operatives in British Intelligence history and has been traveling the world signing books with my mum while you're here, creating your own fiction and trying to lay it on a woman because you think I'll go down quietly for something I. Did. Not. Do." When I take a step in his direction, I see it in his eyes—he braces. Well, he fucking should, even though I have no idea what I'm going to do next. "Do not expect me to fall on the sword for upper brass. Donnellys don't give up and they don't bow down. I don't kneel for anyone, certainly not you."

He waves his hand and the man beside him starts for me. I turn fully to him and flex my fingers but don't have a chance to move.

Glass shatters.

Noise fills the wide-open space.

The air becomes so heavy, it's tangible.

I look to the side, but can't see a thing. My eyes burn

like a flaming brimstone and I blink away tears that form in an instant.

All but one of the men threatening me shuffle for the door. The big one comes after me even through the gas-filled air. When he gets close enough, I hope to hell my instincts have my back since I can't see for shit when I swing my leg around.

I hear a humph when I make contact and then move for the perimeter. I'll feel my way out.

That's when arms circle me from behind.

Before I can do what I'm bloody best at, I hear breathing and feel a hard shell pressed to the side of my head.

"Sweetness, don't fight me today. You won't win."

I freeze.

I know that voice, even through a gas mask. I'd recognize it until the day I take my last breath. It's my nemesis—and the man who's also my bedmate when we're in the same general vicinity.

Then, even though my lungs beg for clean oxygen and my mascara is running down my face like a drippy faucet, he has the nerve to lift his hand and maul my left breast.

"You're in a fuckload of trouble, baby."

I cough and sputter and spit, but he doesn't move. If he's here to play the hero, he could get a bloody move on.

"Time to do what I've been trying to for years—get you out of this country once and for all."

I squeeze his arm with all I've got because my stomach starts to roil from the tear gas.

"And this time, you're not running from me."

Damn him.

When I think I **might** pass out from lack of oxygen, he moves.

Cole Carson.

The man who will surely be the death of me.

When he's not giving me orgasms, that is.

1

BEEPS

Fairfax, Virginia
Present Day

Cole

Beeps.

It's all I hear.

They echo and roll around my brain. Slow ... methodical. They're sure to drive me insane.

But I'm clinging to them.

They're the only thing reminding me she's alive. Cutting through the room as sharp as the figurative knife I took to the gut when I got the call. Hollingsworth knows our history and told me. I got here as fast as I could and haven't left her side.

Bella.

I had no idea she was even in the damn country.

"Documents are on the way and hospital records

have been changed." I listen to Hollingsworth peck away on a keyboard.

"You're sure no one who matters heard her name?" I ask. I've worked with Asa Hollingsworth long enough and know he's solid but I don't know everyone who was in the waiting room when I arrived after finding out Isabella Donnelly took a bullet to the gut. Asa assures me no one there is a threat. I keep barking orders. "While she's here, she's Isabella Carson. I'm sure she covered her tracks on her way to the U.S., but we need to be sure. I have no idea when she'll be well enough to run away from me. Because I have no doubt she'll try."

Asa is smart enough not to ask further about my laying claim to her.

I keep talking. "I want to know who she was here to meet. Do whatever it takes. The more I can find out before she wakes up, the better."

"Already on it. But if you, of all people, don't know why she's in the States, I'm not sure who else will. Bella can work alone and has proven she doesn't need anyone at her back to survive. Your best bet is the source herself. She'll wake up and the ball will be in your court. Don't fuck it up. I'll tell you, her being here was a surprise to all of us—even Crew—and she contracts for him."

That shit is about to change. Crew Vega had better get used to it and find someone new to be his eyes and ears in the Middle East. He and I only speak when it's absolutely necessary. If I see Vega's face again while Bella is lying unconscious in the ICU, I'll rip him to shreds. Hollingsworth, however, knows this and is my go-between. He'll do anything for Vega. He'll also do most things for me.

I turn my attention back to Asa. "I didn't fuck it up last time, asshole. Until she wakes up, I'm counting on you."

"Right. And I need to go so I can hit it hard. Worming my way into these systems takes time. You're lucky to have me."

I shake my head and don't answer, never taking my eyes off her chest.

Rising ... falling ... rising ... falling ...

I need her to live and I need my employer to *not* know she's here. And since she's lying in ICU and I work for the Central-fucking-Intelligence Agency, that might be asking for a miracle. "Don't call me until you have answers."

I hang up and stare at the woman who's been circling the revolving door of my life for years. She was twenty-three when she rocked my world. I thought she was too young and too reckless to maneuver the underworld we swam in on a daily basis. It didn't matter what her last name was or how much weight that name carried, I didn't trust her. That was my first mistake when it came to Isabella Donnelly. She's a force and anyone in her line of sight would be foolish to underestimate her. She's proven it and continues to do so by contracting on her own while staying hidden all this time. And still, I'm the idiot who can't tie down my wild Brit.

I don't take my eyes off her. The fire inside her is gone—the fire I loved so much that burned under my skin for years. I've tried to quench it and smother it. Hell, I've even tried to ignore it. I had to make the hard choice and walk away from it when shit got real at home. Little did I know, quitting her would be harder than dealing with the shit circling me in the States.

Now, she's pale and lifeless despite the damn beeps filling our space and I'd do anything to have her fierce flame back. That's what happens when you take a bullet to the gut from point-blank range. She inserted herself into a situation that wasn't her problem or her business. She saved lives but that doesn't change the fact she is where she is.

My phone vibrates.

Asa – No one at our camp knows why she's here. Crew is digging and I will too.

Shit.

I'm surprised Vega doesn't know. He and I might not see eye-to-eye at times, but he's no liar. At least when it comes to the good guys.

Somehow she snuck back into the States without even him knowing. Given her status, her stepping foot onto U.S. soil is riskier than dancing into a bullfight dressed in crimson. But I'd bet my security clearance she didn't give a shit.

"What are you chasing, sweetness?"

I get nothing but those damn beeps. How can I despise them while my gut hangs on every single one at the same time?

I stand and move to her side.

"Sir, visiting hours for ICU don't start for another two hours."

I look up and find a new nurse. They must've had a shift change because I went through this with the last one but I'll do it as many times as I have to.

I pull out my credentials. "I'm not leaving."

"Oh." She chews on her lip and looks from my ID to

me. "I might need to talk to my head nurse—"

"You can talk to the Attorney General for all I care. I'm here until she wakes and I'm not leaving until she does. You're stuck with me."

She looks down at her tablet and scrolls across the screen. "Isabella Carson. You're her husband?"

Good. The records have been changed.

I glance down and for the first time am grateful the woman who haunts me is heavily sedated. If she knew I was spinning this, she'd try to wrestle me to the ground.

She'd lose but I'd still enjoy it. I always have.

I answer honestly because you never know when you might be hooked up to a polygraph. "Her last name is mine on the paperwork, isn't it?"

"Yes, sir, it is. I'll speak to my manager and I'm sure she'll make an exception. For the next twelve hours, Isabella is mine. I promise to take good care of her."

I don't argue that she's wrong. Bella will always be mine and has been from the start. "I appreciate it."

Bella

OXYGEN.

My lungs are begging for it.

Who knew breathing could be such an arduous task?

I've never felt heavier. Like the world is sitting on my chest and I've lost all control.

I'm surrounded by death. This room reeks of it. Or something close to it, which is fitting since it's how I feel.

I try to move or shift or stretch but it's impossible. Then, like a freight train ... it hits me. Why I'm here—*how* I got here.

And I cannot be *here*.

Vega's man Jarvis was in a squeeze that he didn't know was coming. My contact got word to me when my flight landed in Washington. I'd been poking around and he knew I'd pay for the information, which I did. It got ugly and I'm sure I'll own the even uglier scar as a souvenir from my first trip out of the Middle East since I was forced to go dark.

I was supposed to be in and out of the country in less than a day on a completely separate matter. One that was risky but nothing more than what I normally pull off on any random Wednesday morning.

Okay, fine. It was more. On the importance scale, it was off the bloody charts. So much so, I was willing to set foot into the western world for the first time in years.

No one plans to catch a bullet and this couldn't have happened at a more inopportune time or place.

"You're awake."

What little breath I've managed freezes in my lungs as memories hit me hard.

No.

It can't be.

I'm not sure how much worse this can get, but that deep voice cutting through my groggy state makes it really, really bad.

I could pick that voice out of a crowd cheering on the World Cup. It's the same one that caresses my dreams and plagues me in consciousness—both in equal measures.

I can't help myself. I drag my eyes open and angle them toward the nightmare sitting a meter from me.

He's no dream and I don't think I'm hallucinating from the good stuff they're surely pumping through my veins. I'd definitely be feeling like a crock after taking one to the belly if I weren't medically snockered.

There he is, in the flesh. As red, white, and blue as Abe-fucking-Lincoln, only he's not wearing the ridiculous top hat. He's sporting one of those ball caps Americans like so much. It's turned to the back, giving me full access to his eyes that are burning into mine, reminding me of everything I've tried to wipe from my brain.

Which only reminds me of all the reasons why I've tried to forget him, which, in turn, only reminds me why I shouldn't bloody be here.

Right now, my list of troubles is so long, the man sitting at my side is at the bottom of it.

Cole Carson.

My everything and my heaviest burden. The one who torments me and who I can't shake despite my brain warring with the stupid organ that always comes out the victor.

Stupid, stupid heart.

If I could dropkick it, I would.

He stands, towering over my bed, and picks up a cup as his voice fills my sterile space. "You've been through it. A bullet lodged next to your spinal cord. Internal bleeding. Two surgeries. You've been out for almost two days."

I try to swallow but my tongue might as well be sandpaper. I squeeze my eyes shut, and not only because the dim light burns like the pit of hell, but it also hurts to look at him. When his touch hits my lips with the ice chip he drags across them, I wince. It's been too long since I've had his touch.

The melting water drips over my cracked skin and feels so good, I want more. I snake my tongue out for more relief. It's as refreshing as a spring, helping me swallow over my raw throat. But I also crave his touch.

"I need..." I hardly recognize my own voice. Not that it matters since he doesn't allow me to speak.

"Shh," he hushes and not gently, either. "I know exactly what you need and it's taken care of. While we're alone, I'll explain how this is going to go. Everyone here thinks you're my wife. Records have been changed and a new ID, passport, and VISA are on their way. Once you regain some strength, we're going to get this shit straightened out once and for all. I'm done fucking around, Bella."

Cole. It doesn't matter if I'm lying here stitched up from a gaping hole. He has no subtle or sympathetic or sensitive bone in his Adonis frame.

Leave it to me to hook a chump made solely of muscle and brazen cheekiness.

My mum would have words for me.

"Sleep," he demands as if he rules the world. Okay, fine. He might have a heavy hand in some realms, but not with me. He never did. "You need your strength so you can sit up and eat. You're wasting away before my eyes—I don't like it."

I clear my dry throat. "God forbid you dislike something."

"There's a lot not to like right now, baby. No one can change that but you."

"Go away," I mumble. It feels like a brick building is taking a nap on my chest.

He *tsks* me and shakes his head. "That's no way to talk to your husband."

Husband.

I should never have chanced this trip, no matter why. The stakes are too high. I should have left well enough alone. So what if I live in Pakistan with an occasional holiday to Kuwait? It could be worse.

I could be in prison.

I don't care how much I struggle, I lift my heavy lids. The beautiful arsehole is smiling down at me and I have a feeling it's because he finally has me right where he wants me. He knows I can't do a damn thing about it.

"And you thought I never wanted to settle down. *Isabella Carson.*" My name mated with his drips off his lips like honey. So sweet it's sticky, in a way that promises to be delicious yet messy as hell. He tips his head and his tongue sneaks out—it's tasted every spot of my body—lapping his bottom lip I was once obsessed with. "Fucking kills me to see you like this but I could get used to having you in the country. In fact, I already am. And if you think I'm going to let that change anytime soon, you're crazier than I gave you credit for."

Exhaustion is eating me alive. Any other day or in any other situation, I wouldn't allow him this song and dance. No one can put Cole Carson in his place like I can. Even he's admitted it. But I'm no match for him in my condition.

I start to drift and his tone turns to a mumble. "Who knew it would come to this to get you back, sweetness."

Cole is as cracked as ever.

One can't be back if they were never *there* to begin with.

2

A WAGER

Five days later

Cole

When you spend a majority of your career working clandestine operations for the CIA and traveling the world, downtime is a hot and rare commodity. Even after I benched myself at a desk job at Langley because life took a turn, I was still busy as hell, but for other reasons. Back then, I was always searching for my next high—a high I could only seem to find working as an operative.

Well, that and a certain MI6 blonde who's currently pissing me off and making me hard, all at the same time.

Long story short, I don't have time to sit and do nothing. Fucking ever.

Aside from running home to shower a couple times, I've been at the hospital since Bella got out of surgery. I followed her from recovery to ICU and about did myself in when she was rushed back into the OR because of internal bleeding. Back to recovery, ICU—a-fucking-gain—and, finally here, to a private room where the oxygen is stagnant.

And it has not one thing to do with the lack of fresh air.

I almost lost my shit for the umpteenth time when I walked in to see one of Crew Vega's top soldiers sitting next to her as she slept. Outside of her doctors and nurses—who've gone through my extensive background checks—Jarvis is the only other person who's seen her. He got in when she was still in ICU where no one was allowed. The only reason I held it together was because Jarvis announced he's "*Team Spice Girl* all the way."

He's one of the best, if not the cream of Crew Vega's crop. And since I have no idea what the future will whack us in the knees with, I added that motherfucker to my speed dial. I know for a fact there's not much he won't do.

When I met Isabella Donnelly years ago, she was as tough as she is today. But when we were alone, she was different. She was funny. She was soft. And she was sexy as fuck when she'd melt under my touch. We would fuel each other until we lit up the night—at least when we could find time between assignments, or hell, sometimes during one. Those might've been the best since she and I get off on the same high.

Being a spy isn't for the faint at heart—especially for the brute American and the beautiful, cunning Brit.

It's been too long since I've seen her. Months ago, I engineered an unnecessary trip to the Middle East. It was my last of many attempts to get her to quit and allow me to finally do what was needed to get her out of her bind. My plan was to do what I'm doing now—create her a new identity. It would mean putting herself out to pasture like I had to do. It went against everything I am to work at a desk job, but I did it because it was the right thing to do and she could too, if it were important enough to her.

If *I* were important enough to her.

But because we are who we are, and like all my failed attempts before, I crashed and burned.

She's the only woman I've ever wanted and I can't tame her. I've tried everything. She thinks she's got something to prove to the world.

She does have something to prove to the intelligence community, but it's not how she can take down any man who dares come at her or how resourceful she's proven to be. She's got something bigger to worry about and it has everything to do with her freedom.

Then she snuck back into the western world, got blown to pieces, and they almost weren't able to put her back together again.

I swore I was done. I've been a glutton for punishment too long.

But here I am—back for more.

For the first twenty-four hours I sat and stared at her, I was pissed. Pissed at her, pissed at the world, and pissed at myself because I can't let this shit go and move on like a grown-ass man. I have every reason to step back and focus on my life here.

But the longer I've sat in this damn room, my anger

has only multiplied ... at myself. Because quitting Isabella Donnelley has proven impossible.

Over the past few days, I've taken every advantage of the situation. I'm not even sorry that it includes her barely being able to stand up straight or her not able to communicate outside of these four walls.

What I've done might lean toward disturbing. This is me and I have no boundaries. But that doesn't mean I'm not paying for it.

And I'm learning when it comes to Bella Donnelly, the price for doing disturbing shit is steep.

"Mrs. Carson, here are your discharge papers with directions for recovery. Your husband has your prescriptions."

For the millionth time since Bella became alert, she throws me a glare when the nurse addresses her as *Mrs. Carson*. I give zero fucks as to how she feels about her new alias.

She might be irritated but she's not stupid and looks to the nurse. "He's my soon-to-be ex. I appreciate all you've done for me. You've been lovely and I'll never forget you."

The nurse's eyes widen and dart to me but I shake my head and try to reassure the older woman who's been assigned to Bella. "She has a sensitivity to artificial food coloring and gets this way when she eats too much red Jell-O. It'll work through her system with the stool softeners. No one is getting divorced."

Bella's blue eyes ice over and I see that fire inside her flicker. "I do not have a sensitivity to anything. I could eat a unicorn laced with pesticides and still kick your arse to kingdom come."

I'm pretty sure a lazy smile settles on my lips—one

only she can put there. I look to the nurse and shrug. "See? Once she gets back on an organic diet, she'll be fine."

"An orderly will be in shortly to wheel you out." The nurse drops the papers on the table and is gone in a flash.

The door barely hits the nurse in the ass when Bella turns, standing as straight as she can. "I've made arrangements. Crew is on his way. While your constant supervision has been thoroughly irritating, I have to admit, I appreciate the alias. Being extradited to England is not on my bucket list."

I gloss over her talk of extradition as well as her shitty thanks for taking care of her. "Vega is on his way?"

She turns again and throws what little clothes I brought her into my duffle. "Yes. I spoke to him this morning while you were in the loo. He said he and his wife have a spare bed for me and I am welcome to recuperate there until I can get on my feet to do what I came here to do."

"You're not going anywhere with Vega," I grit. "And you know better than to use a landline."

"Do you really think after all I've been through, I would risk communicating with anyone that would alert authorities? Please, Cole. Give me a shred of credit. I know how to communicate safely. Not to mention, he said they live on a vineyard." She turns to me and hikes a brow. "Do you know how long it's been since I've seen a vineyard? Let alone had good wine?"

I narrow my eyes. "Let me guess. Tuscany when we were able to steal two days between your assignments?"

She exhales before planting her ass on the side of her bed with a groan.

"I'm right. I remember it like it was yesterday. We had that B&B to ourselves. The food was good, the wine was better, but the sex was the highlight."

She looks away and shakes her head.

"The beginning of the end," I add. "Had I only known, I would've talked you into running away with me forever."

She might not be able to stand straight easily on her own yet, but she levels her eyes on me and her tone is as strong as ever. "You didn't have the luxury then just as you don't now, Cole. You have responsibilities, that's not changed."

"You used to understand my responsibilities." I pull out my phone and press go on a number I've called way too often over the last few days. I listen to it ring and don't take my eyes off the biggest challenge of my life. And that's saying something. "Not only did you understand, you insisted I put them first, which I did and will do until the day I die. But it doesn't mean I can't have other things as well."

Hollingsworth answers but his greeting is as frustrated as I feel. "You've already called for an update today. I swear I'll reach out if I find out why she's here."

The frown that has marred Bella's face ever since she came to and saw me sitting next to her deepens as I speak into the phone. "If Vega thought I was pissed the night of the shooting, it's nothing compared to what he'll have to deal with if he shows up here today. He's not taking Bella anywhere. She's been discharged and is going home with me."

"Damn you," Bella hisses.

Asa keeps talking and I hear voices in the background. "Well, since I'm watching my boy Crew go at a new recruit on the mat, I don't think he's heading your way anytime soon. Don't worry, if anyone is going to kidnap your woman, it won't be us."

I exhale and am grateful for at least one less speed bump to maneuver.

"Good luck taking her home to Red." Asa has the nerve to laugh even though he isn't wrong. When I told Red what was going on, he looked about as happy as Bella does with me right now. "I'd pay to see that show."

"I don't need any visitors, especially any of you. It was bad enough Jarvis got into her room when he did."

"Jarvis." Bella's face lights up and it pisses me off. "He owes me his life—he said so himself. I'll ring him to come get me."

I hold my hand up. "Of all people, you're not talking to Jarvis."

"Tell her she's out of luck," Asa adds. "He's in Ohio with Gracie. But they'll be back tonight. Gracie couldn't stop talking about Donnelly before they left. She's going to want some time with your spy."

"Nobody is getting time with Bella unless I allow it." The topic at hand glares at me right before she rolls her eyes. "I wanted to make sure there wouldn't be a scene to deal with before we left the hospital. Call me if there's anything I need to know. We're headed home."

Asa laughs again. Despite our friendship, he pisses me off like everyone else these days. "Good luck, brother."

I disconnect before he can say anything else and cross my arms. "I know this goes against every grain in your beautiful body but I need you to cooperate. Being at my house is the safest place for you right now. I have my ear to the ground and don't think anyone who matters knows you're here. It needs to stay that way."

She shifts where she's sitting and pain cuts through her features. "I'm not safe anywhere and haven't been for a long time. We both know this, but what you can't seem to get through your thick skull is, I'm accustomed to it and have proven I can operate within it."

My eyes narrow. "That wasn't the case last week."

"That was different and you know it. I'm an operative. I can make my way around a gunfight if I have to, but it's not my specialty."

I nod. "Exactly why you shouldn't have inserted yourself into one."

"How many people would be dead right now had I not?"

I lean in and put my hands to the bed, caging her in. She's makeup free. Her long, platinum hair is pulled back with a tie. Even though she's still a little pale and needs to gain some weight—some fresh air and vitamin D wouldn't hurt, either—she's as beautiful as the day I met her.

Our lips are inches apart when I lower my voice. "I'm not worried about *people*, sweetness. I'm only worried about you."

"I'm fine."

"Not quite," I rebuke. "But you'll get there and you'll do it under my thumb. It'll be interesting but there's no other choice."

Her eyes fall and her exhale fans my skin.

"See? Even you know. The sooner we quit arguing, the sooner we can move forward."

She opens her eyes. These have to be the most honest and productive words we've exchanged so far. "It doesn't mean I have to like it. As soon as I'm well enough to travel, I'll be gone."

"You wouldn't have to be gone if you told me why you're here. You underestimate my desk job, Bella. I have contacts who have friends who have cousins who have step-siblings in dark places. The *CIA* logo might be on my business card, but that doesn't mean I don't wade around shit here in the U.S. when I have to. I just don't do it on the record."

She hikes a brow. "Good on me. I'd be disappointed in myself for hooking up with a rule-follower."

I reach up and swipe a piece of hair out of her face. She doesn't flinch at my touch, but her eyes flare. "I'll make you a deal—you give me one month. If your name isn't cleared in the next thirty days, I'll personally stuff you in a crate and ship you back to Pakistan."

Her comment bounces back. "And if you do the impossible?"

"*When* I do the impossible," I correct, "you do what I want."

"I refuse to stop working, Cole."

I shake my head. "I'm done asking you to quit. It's in your blood. I've learned that and will respect it. I swear I will. There are many ways for you to work that don't include you living in Pakistan."

"Name your wager."

I pause, allowing the stagnant hospital air to hang between us and get a good look at her. Her blue eyes I'll never get enough of. Her fair skin that I can't wait to taste again. And her sheer, utter strength I feel, even now, though her body is broken and weak.

I never want to forget this moment.

It's why, when I say the words, I know I'll go to the

ends of the earth to make them happen, despite every molecule in the universe working against us.

"You'll marry me."

Her quick intake of air is enough for me to know how she feels about my wager. I want to lean in and kiss her. Bury my hand in her messy long hair and my cock in her pussy—absolutely the sweetest I've ever had. It makes my insides do things it's never done for anyone else.

And I look forward to having it again. Soon.

She loses a hint of her attitude. "I've answered that question too many times, Cole Carson."

I shrug. "Which is why I didn't ask this time. Today, I'm demanding it. I clear your name—you marry me. We'll figure out the rest after the fact. I'm not fucking around with details anymore."

She pulls in a big breath and I can tell she's almost due for a pain pill. I see it in her eyes but I can also see her mulling over my offer. Which is why I don't give her a chance to accept or reject it. She's too proud to admit she needs my help.

She's also too scared to admit she wants me as much as I want her.

"Bella."

Her eyes meet mine and they're stormy with indecision.

I choose for her. "It's a deal. Get ready, sweetness. It's game on."

She pulls her bottom lip between her teeth.

Oh, yeah.

Game.

Fucking.

On.

3

THE MOMENT

Bella

"Do I look like I'm in the mood to babysit your fresh-out-of-the-box operative? This is not the case to toss your newb into the fire. I get why we need to partner on this, but I'm not going to be the bodyguard for your MI6 princess."

I look at the tall, dark, handsome, yet broody beast of a man standing opposite me in the briefing room. "Would someone please inform the foolish American my CV speaks for itself?"

Cole Carson ... his name alone sounds like an Old West character or a teeny bopper groomed by Disney to become the next pop-music sensation. He's wearing trousers and a crisp, white linen button-down, rolled at the forearms. He's got at least six or seven inches on me and I stand flat-footed at five-nine. But unlike my slight frame, he's broad and looks like he could smash boulders with his ape hands and thick, veined arms. If I didn't know better, I'd think he'd been on holiday, lounging on the beaches of the Mediterranean for the last month. He's clearly going for the wandering tourist and friendly bloke look.

I grew up around covert agents. My family's love affair with British Intelligence started with my grandfather. Then my father followed in his loafers. My older brothers—who put me through hell but also taught me hand-to-hand combat—are currently deep under and have been for some years now. My family was only moderately surprised when I announced my ambitions at the ripe age of eighteen. I'm not sure what else I would have done. I'm a Donnelly—this work pumps through my veins.

I turn to the man who's bloody scowled since our introduction. It's time I put him in his place—we have a case to focus on. "For your information, I'm not new, nor do I need a nanny. I have two completed cases tucked in my garter. They need a lovey-dovey couple on this and I fit half that bill. I know my part and will play it well—I'll garner all the attention so you can play the superhero. You can go ahead and thank me in advance for making you look good."

He narrows his eyes. "I don't need anyone to make me look good, but I do need a partner who won't crack under pressure and one I can count on to have my back. I highly doubt you're that person."

"Well then, I'll take that as a compliment as to how skilled I am. If I can fool a cocky bastard into thinking I'm not a threat, our target will have no clue."

His square jaw hardens as my words sink in. I've never let anyone fuck with me and the arse standing across the room will not be the first. I take a step and offer him my hand. "Carson, a pleasure, I'm sure."

Carrying out our little chat as though there isn't an army

surrounding us, he finally gives in. Shaking his head once, he moves, his hand swallowing mine as if he's the whale and I'm the helpless guppy. He holds tight but I stand my ground, as I always do.

He raises one thick, arched brow. "This will be interesting. What should I call you while I'm playing babysitter?"

I tip my head. "Since we're supposed to be lovers, I suppose you should call me Bella."

His hand squeezes mine tightly, no doubt trying to prove some idiotic point that he's superior because he was born with a cock. "Fine. Do me a favor and don't get me killed ... Bella."

"Bella."

I look over from where I've been staring out the window. We've driven through the city and sat in a load of traffic. I forgot how the western world can get so congested. Now, the lush, green countryside rushes by and vines snake their way up tree trunks, strangling them—which is fittingly symbolic. I'm feeling sympathetic to those trees right now and bring my hand up to my own neck, forcing myself to breathe as my figurative noose tightens.

I met Cole Carson when I was so green I might as well have been a female leprechaun, fit to live in the thick forests we're driving through. It seems like a lifetime ago. So much has shifted since that day.

He's changed. I've changed. But our circumstances have changed more than anything. Our situations were barely compatible to begin with, but now the thought of being together seems utterly impossible, which is why his wager is as crazy as the man who's basically taken me hostage. And the shitty thing about it is, I have no other options right now.

Talk about being stuck between a rock and a hard place—though my place happens to be between an alpha male and being falsely accused of treachery. My situation is as stinky as dirty-donkey balls.

I ignore him and ask, "Are you taking me to the countryside to put me out of my misery and dump my body? Because I might not argue at this point—if you hit another bump in the road, my stitches may pop."

"You might be begging for that by the time the day's over," he mutters. "I need to tell you something."

I don't take my eyes off the forest racing by. "I'm clearly here, Cole. If you have something to say, spit it out. As much as I want to, I'm too sore to jump from a moving vehicle today."

He sighs. "Lucky me, since I know you'd actually do it."

I turn to study his profile and can't help but reminisce about the many times we've been like this—while working or stealing time between assignments. We knew our time together would end and we'd have to go our separate ways. Most of those times we never knew when we'd see the other again. It would make those moments electric with energy, deep with desperation. Not like we are now. I might talk a big game but I feel like complete rubbish. I have no idea when I'll be strong enough to leave the States undetected, but it needs to be soon—much sooner than a month.

I change my mind. "You know what? Don't tell me. I

don't need to know any more than necessary for the few days I'm here."

"Days?" The word snaps me like a whip. "Sweetness, you agreed to a month."

I hardly agreed to a thing. I couldn't. His *deal* brought back too many memories. Plus, he didn't ask me to marry him. He *informed* me—a trait in Cole Carson that usually pisses me off, but at that moment it did something completely different. I don't scare easily, but sitting on my hospital bed surrounded by the man I might want but with whom I know it will never work because of life circumstances ... it cut deep.

Looking back at him, I decide it's time to stand strong and do what I planned when my private plane touched down in the US of A—take charge of my life and get shit done on my own. "I did not. You're the one who came up with that horrendous deal. And, for your information, I don't need your help clearing my name. I can bloody well do it on my own. I was on the path before I had to step in and save Jarvis."

He shakes his head. "A wager's a wager. And I never lose. I'm remedying what should have been done years ago."

"You know what you can do with your wager," I mutter.

"I'm trying to do you a favor and explain some things, baby. Some shit went down and I had to make some changes since the last time we were together." He steals a glance before looking back to the road and flips the signal to turn.

"Fine. Tell me. I don't know what could be so important that I need to know now. It's not like we didn't just spend a long week together in the hospital."

He shakes his head as he slows for an upcoming turn onto a narrow drive and drags a hand down his face. He's frustrated, and since I know for a fact Cole manages international crises on a daily basis, this is not good. "It's a long story and I wanted to fill you in before we get to the house."

"House?"

"Like I said, things have changed."

I've never spent time with Cole in the States, never been to his home, or met his family. It was my choice. I knew our real lives would mix like oil and water, and there was that other little tidbit that I knew I was guarding my heart.

But now I wonder if he slipped me an extra pain pill because I realize this doesn't seem right. "Where are we?"

He doesn't answer, but creeps around one more bend when an old farmhouse appears.

My eyes widen. "I thought you had a condo in Alexandria?"

He says nothing and flips off the ignition, gets out, and rounds the car in a wink. He opens my door and holds out a hand. "Let's do this."

That hits me in the gut. Those three little words might as well be Cole Carson's tagline. If he's said them once, he's said them a million times. He'd say it on assignment or when we were alone in bed.

Or in the shower.

Or even once in the back of a cargo van.

Then there was that one time at a gala in Berlin.

Shit. I need to put that out of my mind.

I pull in a breath as I carefully release my safety belt.

Cole is pulling me to my feet, when the front door to the weathered house bursts open on its rusty hinges.

Cole doesn't let go of my hand and his other arm comes around to steady my weight when we turn to the noise.

That's when I see her.

I gasp.

"Damn you, Cole," I bite under my breath and my eyes shoot to his. "You have some bloody nerve. I never thought you'd bring me here if she was with you. There's no way I'd have agreed to this."

"I know. It's why I didn't tell you." His arm around my waist tightens. "It'll be fine."

It won't be fine. I'm suddenly grateful for my pain killers because I cannot imagine how my insides would feel right now from them twisting in my gut.

I look back to the house, to *her*. Pictures haven't done her justice over the years because she's even more beautiful in the flesh. Seeing her for the first time is too much and I reach out to grip Cole's shirt. He instantly returns my squeeze.

I can't tear my eyes away and decide I'd rather take another bullet than walk into what's waiting for me.

Because she does *not* look happy.

Cole

THIS IS THE MOMENT.

The one I've been dreading and craving. For years, I've tried to convince Bella this would be okay. How it might be bumpy at first but I'd make sure to smooth it over in the end. And I would've been able to pull it off had I brought Bella into my life here years ago. Back when I merely had regular drama.

Back before that drama grew into a shitstorm.

The storm started five months ago—the worst of it parked on top of me and not budging. Life's timing has never been on my side.

But then again, my actions in the past haven't helped much, either. This is one more reminder how fuckups keep coming back to slap me in the face.

She doesn't run to me, doesn't call for me, and definitely doesn't crack a smile. I've tried to explain over the last few days how I'm bringing a friend home. She asked me a million questions, as she always does, but none of them were about my *friend*.

They were all about her mom.

"Abbott." The moment I call for her, Bella rips her hand away from me and tries to push from my side. My hand on her hip flexes, keeping her close because I'm done with her putting space between us—the tangible and figurative distance I've come to despise. I hold her tight and call for my daughter. "Come here. I want you to meet Bella."

Abbott leans into Red and shakes her head, her long dark curls swaying around her shoulders and arms.

"You've kept a lot from me," Bella mutters under her breath. "Don't think you're not going to pay for this later when we can speak privately."

I push her toward the house and lean in to whisper, "Abbott is with me all the time—I have full custody now. That's not changing—ever. And because I can't manage her on my own with work, Red moved in with me. I'll explain the rest later."

I let go of her waist and collect her hand, pulling her forward. We come to a stop at the bottom of the porch where my daughter's dark, leery eyes haven't moved from the woman at my side.

"Well, here she is," Red growls.

I instantly narrow my eyes on my father. He was told to be on his best behavior, at least to be a good example for Abbott. I don't need to deal with him on top of everything else right now. "Bella, this is my dad, you can call him Red. Everyone does, including me." I let go of Bella's hand and move to my daughter, swinging her up into my arms and planting a kiss on the side of her head. "And this is my Abbott."

Bella might be tough as nails but one thing she's not is rude. "Abbott. You're more of a beauty in person than any picture your father has shared. It's lovely to meet you. You, as well, Red."

Abbott wraps her arms around my neck tighter than she normally does. "She talks funny."

I pull her to keep her from choking me. "Bella is British. She's from England. I explained yesterday and showed you on the map how far it is from Virginia."

"I'm English," Bella corrects me the way she's done from the day we met. "I'm from England, so I'm English."

Abbott goes on like Bella isn't standing here in front of us. "She still talks funny."

"It's okay," Bella excuses Abbott. "I suppose I do sound funny."

Red pipes in, "My granddaughter is used to redneck speak."

I sigh even though it's the truth since Red is helping raise her.

"Let's get Bella into the house. She needs to get off her feet." I set Abbott down and she turns for the front door, her hair flying after her as she runs away. Despite my attempts to prepare her for this moment, she's just as pissy as I expected.

"Well, this is going to be loads of fun," Bella mumbles.

I shake my head. The bullet didn't seem to nick her sarcasm. It's as strong as ever.

"She'll come around." I hold my hand out to help her up the stairs. She takes it, which means she must need a pain pill.

"Give me a couple of days and I'll be out of everyone's hair," Bella says.

"Good to hear," Red belts. "Cole told me this could be a permanent thing."

"I've had about enough of you." I glare at Red as I get Bella through the door. If I didn't know better, I'd think she was casing the place to break into later. I should know, I've done it a thousand times—at times with her by my side. Those days were the best—way better than today. "I'll get your bag after we get you settled. You can wear my T-shirts and sweats until I can get you some clothes."

I veer Bella to my room on the main floor and Red heads to the kitchen where he grunts, "I'm doin' it up special for the Queen tonight. Weenies and beans!"

I barely get Bella to the threshold of my bedroom when she grits under her breath, "*The Queen*? He hates me, Cole."

I lean in and put my lips close to her ear. "He doesn't hate you. I swear."

She yanks her hand from mine. "That's hard to believe, but I hate you right now. I need a bed and a damn pain pill so I can get better and get the hell out of here."

Bella

Bangers and beans.

I'm sure it's the worst post-surgical meal—
even if it is a step up from Jell-O. I could only
stomach a bit.

Between the pain, the meal, the company, and the
setting, I think I'd fare better if I were captured and
tortured behind enemy lines.

I never thought I'd be here—in Cole's home, his
room, his bed. The times he and I were together were
the best. I was doing what I loved and had the company
of a man I was trying my hardest not to fall in love with.
It was all I could do to live in the moment because
looking to the future was not an option.

And this is why.

I knew his story and how I'd never fit into it beyond
our stolen moments between assignments. Doing what
we do for a living is complicated enough without a
child's wellbeing at stake. He's a single father, doing his

best to navigate the rocky relationship with Abbott's mum for the good of their shared daughter, no matter how that child came to be in this world of horrid adults.

Cole was always upfront and honest about Abbott's mum. Tabitha Malley is proof Cole Carson isn't as powerful as he seems. The man whose home I'm currently held hostage in usually has instincts as sharp as an ax. But it turns out he's a mere mortal like the rest of us, and over seven years ago—long before I was in the picture—he was swindled by a horrible woman. She wanted more than the casual relationship they agreed to and trapped him, purposefully getting pregnant.

One pin prick in a condom and he was tied to an eighteen-year prison sentence—Tabitha, not Abbott. Only desperate and truly deranged women pull stunts so horrendous.

Cole explained that no bind he's ever gotten himself into while working as an operative for the CIA has ever made him feel as claustrophobic as when she announced they would share a child.

Plain and simple, he didn't believe the child was his. But once the beauty he helped create entered this world, a paternity test sealed his fate.

I know this to be fact because before I hopped into the sack with Cole. I was nosy enough to run a full background on him. What can I say? I am an operative at heart—I trust no one until I know for certain I can trust them with my life.

Cole took responsibility for his daughter, both financially and emotionally. It's the type of man he is. One thing I know for certain is his love for Abbott. I feel it in my bones every time he speaks of her.

But he's cut Tabitha out of his life. The only contact he has with her pertains to their daughter.

Tonight, when I was nibbling on bangers and beans while propped up in Cole's big bed, he told me *why* he now has full custody and how it won't change ... ever.

Recently, Tabitha found her arse in the hot seat with the law during the time my arse was in its own sling. As a side note, my arse is in hotter water than hers was, legally speaking. But since I'm not guilty, nor did I leave my child home alone while on a drinking binge for over twenty-four hours followed by a DUI, I shall ride my high horse proudly.

I know for a fact Tabitha Malley is something you'd have to scrape off the bottom of your shoe after a long day of work in the slimiest of regions, but what she did is beyond horrible. When her days are over, I hope she rots in hell for being the worst kind of woman, human, and mum.

Cole was immediately awarded full custody. Abbott's mum was charged with child endangerment, driving while under the influence, and a slew of other charges I might remember if my brain weren't foggy from painkillers.

If Cole's reality could be any worse, poor little Abbott isn't dealing well from having her mum disappear from her life. I'm not sure what six-year-old would, but from Cole's explanation, his daughter refuses to believe her mum is gone for good. My heart breaks for her. Every child deserves two loving parents.

So, apparently, that is that.

Abbott isn't happy I'm here. Red is clearly less than thrilled with my presence. And Cole thinks I'm going to marry him in a month.

Which is why I'm in bloody, fucking hell.

The sun has set over the Carson home. Besides Cole explaining what he's been living through the last few months, I've spent most of the time since we arrived by myself, and I'm thankful for it. But, the door creaks, followed by the floorboards protesting even louder under his feet. I had a feeling this would happen. Cole's house isn't small but it's not Kensington Palace, either. His bed is big and soft and I'm sure he wants to sleep in it despite my being here. My back is to the door, even though it hurts to lie on my side. My goal is to avoid whatever conversation he thinks we're going to have next.

But my seclusion from the rest of the house hasn't hindered the fact I've heard everything as clear as if I'd bugged the place.

Not only are the floors creaky, but the walls are thin as tissue. I'm sure we'd all lose sleep if an ant hosted a gala below the floorboards.

Listening to Cole interact with his father and daughter has been more painful than taking a bullet to the gut last week. Red has done nothing but grumble about my presence and Abbott has done nothing but talk about her mum—demanding to know when Tabitha will be home, when Tabitha is moving into their new farmhouse, why Cole brought a strange lady home, and when will Cole and Tabitha give her brothers and sisters.

That's when Cole threatened to cancel Disney Plus right before I could hear his every stomp followed by the front door slamming so hard, it threatened to rattle the house down.

Every ugly word was expressed clear as day, drifting through the closed door like it wasn't even there.

As if it were a set of bars.

Bars to a depressing prison cell, which is apropos, since it's how Cole's bedroom feels.

With my eyes shut tight and my breaths steady, I sense him walking around the bed to the adjoining loo. After long minutes of water turning on and off, the toilet flushing, and some other banging around, the bed dips behind me.

"I know you're awake."

I drag my eyes open and sigh.

"See?" He crawls in and I can tell he's taking care by the way he's moving, as if I'm made of crystal. Cole has never treated me as a breakable piece of china. He knows I can take him down. Or rather, I could before I was recovering from two surgeries. His fingertips drag up the skin of my bare arm like an erotic memory. "You can pretend all you want, sweetness. No one knows how you breathe while you're sleeping but me. I used to lie awake for hours listening to you."

"I'm not sure if that's romantic or creepy."

"Definitely creepy." His fingers continue tormenting me with promises of what I know they can do. I focus on my pain as if it's my life's mission.

"Do you not have a divan or a cot? If I'm going to get out of here anytime soon, I need my rest and it's impossible to sleep while you're knocking around in the loo and taking up my bed space."

He's exasperated—I hear it in his sigh. "I could have ten extra beds and twenty sofas and I still wouldn't allow you to sleep anywhere but next to me."

I pull my arm away. "Then I'll find another place to lay my head."

"Quit being ridiculous and go to sleep. As much as I like having you here, I want you healthy so we can fix your problem."

"I appreciate you digging to the pit of hell, but it still won't keep me here."

He yawns. "We'll see about that. Do you need anything?"

I try not to groan as I roll to my back. "I need a lot of things, Cole. Some clothes would be nice. A phone."

He sits up, grabs an extra pillow, and throws back the covers. "Put this under your knees. It'll take the pressure off your back and abs. And I made a call. You'll have clothes tomorrow."

I exhale and close my eyes because his pillow is like a down-filled miracle. My pain pill is kicking in and my limbs are getting heavy. "I should give you a list of what I need."

Leaning on his elbow, he looks down at me. "I know what you need."

I open my eyes and glare at him through the shadowed room. "If you try to dress me in red lace while I feel like rubbish that's been trampled on and thrown to the wolves, I promise you won't fare well."

He does something he's only done once since I woke up in the hospital when he practically dared me to marry him—he smiles. It's so genuine, it almost feels like old times. "You know how much I like you in red."

I ignore him and my eyelids become heavier. "You're hopeless. Black would be lovely. And I still need a phone."

"You need to rest. And you need to lie low."

"You know I'm not stupid enough to jeopardize my position. Get me something. An encrypted line, a sack full of burner phones—something. I have people to keep up with."

When he doesn't answer, I turn to him. His shadowed features are darker than normal, everything that drew me to him in the first place emanates through the dim room.

"Cole. I know you can get me what I need."

His jaw ticks and he narrows his eyes. I know what that means.

He'll give me what I want.

I close my eyes and sigh. "Thank you."

I feel the bed move again and for the first time since I've known him, he leaves space between us. Not that I expected anything else in my condition, but it still feels odd.

I start to drift into a wonderful abyss where pain pills are floating clouds and my broken body is deliciously heavy—one with Cole's soft bed. So much so, he sounds miles away and it doesn't even make sense when I hear, "Get comfortable, sweetness. I'm keeping you right here."

Cole

"Your asset is a wild card we can't afford to gamble with. Get him in line or we'll cut him loose. No skin off my back."

I pull my hand down my face and turn to look at the house. My phone started silently blowing up an hour ago. And since I'm harboring an ex-MI6 who's on the run, I'm more than a little jumpy. I thought things would smooth over once we got home since I live in BFE, but the way my skin crawled the moment my phone started vibrating, it seems I'm no less calm here with Bella in my bed.

Where she belongs.

When I got sick of texting, I moved outside to get this taken care of. Now it's three in the morning and I'm standing in my driveway so I don't wake the house.

So far, I don't think Bella is on anyone's radar, but that doesn't mean my gut isn't stirring.

One of my assets went dark the week before last. And not *dark* like normal, where I still know what's going on. Dark, as in, *gone*.

Black.

Onyx.

Poof.

Raji disappeared into a cloud of smoke thicker than the Middle Eastern air in which he lives. I know my people. If they have to take a break, I know when and where to expect them to surface. It's planned—the way it should be.

When Raji finally came up for air and let me know his head hadn't been chopped off, it was just as Bella was being rushed in for her second emergency surgery. Since my mind was on her almost bleeding out, I haven't had time to grill him on his whereabouts.

To top it off, Abbott wants no part of any woman who isn't her dead-beat mother. A mother who not only lost all rights, but has a court order to stay the fuck away from my daughter.

Not sure if things could be shittier than they are at the moment.

All sides of my life colliding into something grander than the Big Bang theory has been a shit ton to handle.

"I said I'll take care of it. I know my people and he's back on track. I need one more personal day and I'll be back in the office."

"He's gone off the rails. If you don't take care of this by noon today, I will. I'm not taking the heat on this."

Nick Peterson is my supervisor. Nick Peterson is also a class-A I'd-like-to-smash-my-fist-in-his-face-daily asshole. He's made a government career by sitting at his desk and running his mouth. I have no idea whose ass he's rubbed his nose in to get to where he is, but it wasn't by making cases. He's not only difficult to work for, but he's a miserable person to be around. And since I have to do both on a daily basis, my fist finds itself wanting to make contact with his fucking face on the regular. He's a liar, he takes credit for others' work, and he enjoys messing with people and their careers. I've never known Nick to take the heat for anything. Every shitshow he creates, he pins on someone else, and in the end, he's sitting as pretty as a show dog—and not the working-class kind.

The toy kind.

Lately, I feel like I'm at the top of Nick's *To Fuck With* list and the man is soundly committed to checking shit off quicker than a teenage girl at the mall.

I swallow every word I want to spew at him and keep my cool because, with Bella in my bed, I don't need any more attention than necessary. "I trust him and can take care of it from here. You'll have a detailed report when I get back to the office."

"Make sure it happens."

"I always do," I add, trying to keep my tone genuine and soften the *stick it up your ass* edge of my tongue I'd really like to give him.

He doesn't bid me a goodnight or apologize for waking anyone with shit that could've been handled during daylight hours.

I'm not worried about waking Red or Abbott. My daughter can sleep through anything and Red lies on his good ear. My creaky house usually isn't an issue. I hope Bella's last pain pill still has some kick behind it because she usually sleeps with one eye open. I'm the same way. It comes from years of watching your six day and night.

But it's time Isabella *Carson* rests easy. She did what she had to do because of what the Queen's government pinned on her even though there's no way it's true. No one knows Bella better than me—other than maybe her own family.

Her father was one of the best. Her older brothers are still active. Bella's mom is pure gold and her biggest fan.

Besides me.

I need her family on my side. I was in contact with them right after I pulled Bella out of hot water and helped her get out of the country but had to cut off all communication when the British government started poking around the CIA about me.

It's time to break the silence and reach across the pond. I need to get in touch with the Donnellys.

Until then, I need Red and Abbott to cool their shit. They need to get used to Bella being here because I plan to win our bet so she'll be my wife—and not the fake kind I've already contrived. The legal kind, the before-God kind, and the out-in-the-open kind where she can move freely around the world as she pleases, but with me by her side.

Red and Abbott need to see what I see.

I have so many missions, I feel like a circus clown juggling running chainsaws. And if shit doesn't calm down soon, I'm in danger of dropping one and cutting my head off.

This cannot backfire. I'm no idiot—I know I've got one chance. If I fuck this up, I'll never pin down Isabella Donnelly.

5

RED

Bella

I've lived by myself since I graduated from uni, though, *living* may be a stretch.

While with Secret Intelligence, I was on the go for months at a time. *Living* meant bouncing from one seedy hotel to renting a less-than-modern room for a few weeks. Isn't that what most women dream of?

As much as I loved the work, I actually hated the rest of it.

Growing up in a home with parents who doted on me and brothers who loved me—even if the Donnelly way of showing it might seem odd to some—one would think my choice of career and lifestyle would be more miserable than a piss-poor manicure. But I loved the work so much, I overlooked the dingy motels and shady hostels. Let's be real, despite the lies James Bond films feed the world, we covert agents do not zoom around in private jets and sports cars while wearing haute couture from Harrods.

If only.

Slumming it was my life until I started spending my time off with Cole. Actually living together, no matter how much I've secretly dreamt of it, was never an option. I worked for the British government and he the U.S.

And then there was Abbott.

If all the above made it hard enough to build a lasting relationship, the little girl hopping around like a jumping bean on the floorboards above Cole's bedroom sealed the deal. Even before I was set up as a traitor, I knew Cole and I would never work. My job was not conducive to being a mum, or even a mum figure, to anyone. Hiding out in the Middle East for a year proved it. The last time I saw Cole—he tried to convince me otherwise.

He was unsuccessful.

Then he yelled down the pukka I call home. He was angry and accustomed to getting his way.

I sent him packing and was left with a heartache that still throbs.

Abbott wasn't with him full time then and the child already has a mum who's off her rocker. She needs a woman in her life day-in and day-out—and not the one who birthed her or the one who's hiding from the authorities.

I snuck into the States without Cole knowing because our last visit did not end well. Waking up to him sitting next to me in the hospital was more than a shock to my already-jolted system.

He knows how I feel and he brought me here anyway. Cole hasn't changed. He wants what he wants and he's used to getting it. It makes him the best at what he does, but it also makes him an infuriating man in every other aspect of life.

I look up when the door to his bedroom opens— and not quietly, I might add, the way one would slip into a room when the occupant just survived two surgeries and should be resting.

He stands over his bed I'm currently lying in. "Baby, you need to get up and walk."

I angle my eyes to him right before I nearly roll them out of their sockets. "I have been walking. You weren't here to witness the grand event."

The arsehole has the nerve to cross his arms and glower. "You can leave this room, you know."

I pick up the remote and change the channel to a different station, hoping to catch some world news. "I'm fine here."

He drops his arms and rounds the bed. When he reaches me, he snatches the remote and tosses it out of my reach. "Come on. You hardly ate breakfast, which isn't like you. I'll make you some lunch and we'll sit out back so you can get some fresh air."

"Cole—"

"Sweetness, as much as I want to keep you here, I want you strong and that's not going to happen unless you eat and move your beautiful body."

"Bring me a sandwich."

He shakes his head and the standoff ensues. "No can do. Get up."

I change the subject. "I thought you said you were getting clothes for me."

"They should be here today." He gives my hand a squeeze and hikes a brow. "Even though I'd rather see you swimming in mine any day of the week."

I pull my hand from his and close my eyes. "I feel and look like death and don't have the energy for you."

The mattress dips and I open my eyes to find him sitting next to me, invading my space the way he does. Leering, with hands rested on either side of my pillow, his dark eyes are as intense as his tone. "Tell me what I need to do to get you out of this bed. I'm desperate, Bella. I'm trying to get you better, deal with Abbott, and shut Red down because he's a grown-ass man and needs to act like one. If he weren't my father, his ass would be in the ditch by the main road right now. I've got shit stirring at work and I'm trying to figure out why you were here to begin with since you refuse to tell me."

I roll my eyes again, and in turn, he leans in closer and lowers his voice even more.

"And that right there," he continues, "makes me hard. You know it does. But I refuse to even kiss you until we come to some sort of understanding. There's a middle ground, Bella, we just need to find it. I swear, it's on my list right after I check off all the other shit, the first is nursing you back to the kick-ass woman who ensnared me years ago."

I look up at him, his lips close to mine despite his promise not to kiss me. I'm honestly relieved. My resolve is not weak but my body is. I don't have the strength to punch him in the face. "You're a shitty nurse."

"You're a shittier patient," he boomerangs.

True. I decide to negotiate because the four walls of his bedroom are about to close in on me. I can't remember the last time I've laid in one position for so long. "I'll get up on one condition."

"Name it. I'm desperate."

"A phone. A laptop. A tablet. Something to check my messages and touch base with my people."

He pulls in a deep breath and stands straight, all six feet and four inches of him, holding out his hand again. "Done. But in return, you eat every meal in the kitchen, walk around the house, sit in the family room. I want Abbott to get used to you being here. You can cuss at Red for all I care—he deserves it. But unless you're sleeping, you'll spend time among the living."

Damn. He knows I'll do anything to communicate with the outside world. He has me by my lady balls.

I put my hand in his and bite back my wince as I sit up. "If you're hell-bent on torturing your family with my presence, then you're the craziest bloke I know. Fine. I'll do what you want—I needed a phone last week in the hospital."

He helps me to my feet as I try to ignore the smug look in his dark features. His lips even tip on one side and the pain in my chest it creates has nothing to do with the hell I've been dragged through in the course of the last week. His warm hands land low on my hips where he gives me a light squeeze. "Your phone was delivered two hours ago. I encrypted it. I know you know how to cover your *arse*, even though I'd rather be the one in charge of that. I'm fond of your ass and miss it."

I narrow my eyes and mutter, "Bloody hell."

"You agreed." He gives me one more squeeze before dropping his hands and turning away. "I've got to go back to work tomorrow and I need to know everyone under this roof isn't going to kill one another when I leave." He turns back one more time as he reaches the door. "You're a woman of your word. Now, get out there, fetch your new phone, and take in some fresh air. It might not be the shores of the Mediterranean, but you could use some color."

And he's gone.

Well. If he wants me to run roughshod over his household, he can think again. He's forgotten how skillful I am at blending in. I'll do whatever is necessary to survive my time in the Carson home with the least amount of drama possible.

But first, I need that phone. Then I need a shower.

I move slowly out of my self-imposed prison for the first time in the light of day and get a look at the rest of Cole's home.

It's not fancy, but I didn't suspect it would be. Besides dressing for an undercover role, Cole might be the least fancy man I know, and that's saying something since I pretty much only know men.

I move toward the voices wafting from the back of the home that looks out to trees so thick, Cole's home might as well be a castle surrounded by a wall of foliage.

Trees, trees, and more trees.

I almost make it to my target—my new, encrypted cell and the rest of Cole's family, the likes of whom I'd rather avoid like a modern-day plague—when an off-key chime rings through the space.

Abbott tears around the corner and almost runs me over followed by Red, who glares at me. "I was gonna feed you leftover weenies but the boy is making you lunch. Don't expect that kind of service when he goes back to work."

He doesn't give me a moment to answer and shuffles off in his coveralls after Abbott. When I turn the corner, I find Cole standing in front of the stove in a large farmhouse kitchen—almost as expansive as the family room.

I'm about to ask him where my phone is when I hear voices.

Feminine voices, to be exact, mixed with that of a child—an enthusiastic one.

Cole's gaze twists to me. Then he takes me in from head to toe as female voices come from the front door. "Good to see you up, sweetness. I opened a can of soup and I'll make sure to give you your payment for getting up, but first, you've got some visitors."

"Visitors?" I shift to see who could possibly be here for me.

Two women, both petite and beautiful in their own right, are parading toward me carrying bags for days. On their heels is a small child about the size of Abbott —blond and tiny with too much energy. The child runs past us but the ladies' eyes are on me when they greet the man standing at my back.

It's the strawberry blonde who speaks first. "Cole, you didn't tell me how thin she was. We could've gone down a size in everything."

His hand lands heavy on my hip. "She's lost weight. I'll make sure she gains it back."

"Isabella." The tiny brunette with bright blue eyes addresses me carefully. "You don't remember me, do you?"

"Baby." Cole's lips brush my hair but nothing close to the kiss he promised to withhold until he *figures my shit* out. "This is Grace Cain. She was with you after you were shot until the medics got to you. She kept you from bleeding out."

"Ah, Grace." I exhale and try to smile.

I'm not a woman who's afraid of anything. But that night ... I've done all I can to not think back on it. However, this woman's young face and dramatic eyes bring it all back. Her image was the last I saw before I lost consciousness. I don't even recall being transported to the hospital.

I clear my throat. "I understand I have you to thank for not dying on the banks of the Chesapeake—"

She shakes her head and those bright blues cloud just shy of a spring shower. "Call me Gracie. And don't thank me. I would've handed over my own blood had I been able to. Noah is walking and talking and planning our future because of you. Keeping you alive so I could thank you properly was the least I could do. I wanted to visit you in the hospital but—" her eyes dart over my shoulder before she shrugs, "—well, that didn't happen." She lifts her hands which are gripping approximately five hundred shopping bags. "But I am able to thank you this way. Keelie and I shopped 'til we dropped. Noah's credit card got quite the workout."

Cole motions to the older, but no less beautiful one, who looks like she's been held hostage in an American mall by the sheer number of her own parcels. "Baby, this is Keelie Hollingsworth. I work with her husband. And the little one, who shot through here, is their daughter Saylor. We're trying to get her and Abbott together—they'll be in the same class together in the fall."

I look over my shoulder and see the girls in Cole's family room. Specifically, Abbott doing all she can to get away from this Saylor child who isn't respecting her personal space. I can't count fast enough, but I'm pretty sure Abbott is only getting in three words to every ninety of Saylor's. The poor girl doesn't know what hit her.

"Saylor is our..." I look back to the lovely Keelie who's wearing a wince on her fair face as she apologizes for her daughter, "extrovert."

"Abbott needs to break out of her shell." Cole is quick to forgive the pint-sized tornado a little too quickly for my taste. If Abbott doesn't want this child in her face, she should bloody-well speak up about it. "She'll be fine."

"Where can we unpack these?" Gracie changes the subject, for which I'm grateful. "I have to admit, we went crazy—and before you insist on paying him back, Cole, you can stop right there. Noah said this was on him. It's the least we can do for Isabella. I know what it's like to all of a sudden be without everything. Trust me, you're set." She looks back at me. "And you need to get off your feet. I'm a nurse—I insist."

Keelie and Gracie parade to the sofa as poor Abbott is being pulled out the back door by Saylor, who's blathering on about a donkey, of all things.

I turn and find Cole gazing down at me. "She's right, you need to sit. I'll bring you a bowl of soup."

Bags rustle and tissue paper crinkles as Keelie announces, "I hope you like everything. Cole told us you love red. You could fight bulls for days with as much as we bought."

My jaw goes hard, and through a deathly whisper that I hope holds the promise of his demise, I grit, "You didn't."

He tucks a chunk of my unruly hair behind my ear before brushing his thumb over my bottom lip. "I did."

"I hate red," I seethe the fact he knows all too well.

His voice lowers to match mine as a satisfied smirk settles on his lips. "You know what it does to me when you wear red."

"You're unbelievable."

"Everything you do taunts me, but you in red? You better believe I'm going to keep coming at you."

"You'll never get what you want."

"Wave your matador cape, sweetness. We'll see about that."

I reach out and touch him for the first time on my own accord since I woke in the hospital with him by my side. It's not the kind of touch he wants, I can tell from the narrowing of his eyes. I squeeze the pressure point at the inside of his elbow to remind him I can take him down in a hot second should he need the reminder. "You'll never win."

"Do you like?" I look to the family room where Keelie is holding up a maxi dress the color of dusk in the desert. "It'll be nice and loose while you're recovering."

"I love it and can't thank you enough," I call.

Familiar lips brush my ear and his words aren't just a promise, they're so steadfast, they come as a warning. "I'm the bull in this scenario and I'm fucking relentless. You'll eventually let your guard down and I plan to take every advantage."

I turn and he's so close, his dark eyes are burning into mine, red hot—the way he likes it.

I hold my ground. "Are you laying a challenge at my feet?"

"There's no challenge. You know you're mine. I'm righting wrongs which should've been taken care of a long time ago."

I want to argue but we both know I'm standing on shaky ground as it is. Unfortunately for me, that meaning isn't only figurative, it's literal too. I've been standing in one place for far too long and the pain is starting to creep in like sheers, carving me from the inside.

My new phone will have to wait. My mum would lecture me into next month if I were to bury myself in messages or tell these lovely ladies that I, in fact, hate red and prefer colors that reflect my dark, hardened heart.

I tip my head and give Cole my brightest and fakest smile to hide the pain eating away at my gut. "My darling, self-righteous, forsaken man. If a fight is what you want, the years have only sharpened my sword—it's deadlier than ever. The bull is going down."

"You know that turns me on more," he challenges.

He's right.

"There was no way to color-match you, so we decided to go with a tinted moisturizer. I'm sure you could use a little TLC after your stay in the hospital," Gracie says.

I drop my hand from Cole and turn to my new friends. "You don't know how true that is. A stiff drink would do the trick but a good facial cream comes in a close second."

The sooner I get this over with, the sooner I can get my hands on the phone I bartered my freedom for.

6

UNLESS YOU PISS ME OFF

Cole

"I'm going back to work tomorrow. I expect you to be on your best behavior. You pulling this shit isn't helping me any."

"Don't know what you're talkin' 'bout, boy."

"Like hell. You know exactly what you're doing."

He *humphs* without a glance as he toys around the shed, pretending to fix a lawnmower that's already lived eight lives. Red Carson can mend what others consider garbage—rebuild any engine and reincarnate scrap metal into something a million times better than it was before—basically work general magic in overalls and a dirty T-shirt. It might not be a pretty process, there are usually left-over pieces when he's done, and most of the time he's shed blood, but it's him. It's what he does, what he's always done, and what makes him happy.

That and Abbott.

I'm an only child and Red never minced words

when I was younger—he wanted a daughter. Hell, even my mom never complained about only having a boy. My dad loves his granddaughter. So much so, I'm not sure I've ever seen anyone so happy to hear the news that a mother walked out of their child's life. When I became a full-time parent with no help, it was his idea to move in with us. He said Abbott had experienced more shit in her short life than any one person deserved. My mom died a year earlier and he'd since retired from his job as a maintenance worker for Union Pacific. He sold the only house he and my mom ever owned—the home I grew up in and the one he loved—to move in with me and help with Abbott.

It's why I sold my townhouse and bought this old farmstead. It sits on enough land that I can't see my neighbors, there's no street for Abbott to dodge traffic, and it has a barn for all of Red's junk. But it's falling apart around me and there isn't a day that goes by that I don't miss the city.

Living with Red again isn't what I'd call the perfect life. Hell, some days it's the perfect storm. He's a gruff, grumpy old man who misses my mom. She was a saint, especially to put up with his ass. But nothing puts a smile on his sun-aged face like his granddaughter.

He's less lonely. I don't have to pay for childcare. Abbott gets to grow up with her grandfather. Even surrounded by old pipes, creaky floors, and a roof that needed to be replaced ten years ago, it's a win-win-win.

Red tosses a wrench into his messy, rusted toolbox and turns to me. "Months ago, my son came home and damn near poisoned his liver because the Queen of England broke him. Now she's here and you expect me to wait on her hand and foot?"

I cross my arms. "You've been watching too much daytime TV."

"Lifetime Network has nothin' to do with it. I keep that old tube on for background noise while I work out here."

"Maybe you should turn on a ballgame instead of the shit you watch that's causing you to see life as a soap opera. No one's broken and quit calling her the Queen. She doesn't like it and it pisses me off."

"I can call her whatever I wanna call her. What're you gonna do, kick me out?"

"For fuck's sake," I mutter and drag a hand down my face. "I don't need you acting like a child, I already have one and you're doing nothing to help with the situation. I need Abbott to warm up to the idea of Bella being here."

"You said she doesn't want to be here. I'm not gonna be part of some dog-and-pony show to romance a woman who doesn't deserve my son."

"You must be smoking crack out here in the barn at night. Mom would lock you out if she saw you acting this way."

That stirs a reaction because he takes a step, his beer gut closing the distance between us, and I get a grease-covered finger jammed in my chest. "Your mother only locked me out four times in our marriage and I always got her to let me back in before the sun rose."

"Right," I agree. "For being a hard-headed idiot like you're being now. You know for a fact she'd kick your ass out for what you're doing to me."

He crosses his arms and I can tell he knows I'm right. I might not have grown up with a lot but my parents made sure our family was happy and it wasn't done by throwing money and stuff at me. They couldn't have afforded it if they wanted to.

I lower my voice. "This is the last time I'm going to ask. I need a fucking break and I'm certainly not getting one from anyone else, so it's going to come from you. She almost died. But she's here now and I'm not going to let anything get in my way—especially my own father. Get your head out of your ass and act like an adult."

He's pushing sixty-five and has lived a hard life while working a labor-intensive job. He also loves beer and fried chicken, and it shows. His dark hair is mostly gray and he's worked in the sun his entire life, all while wearing fifty pounds too many. There's no question we share DNA, but I've somehow learned how to wrangle the control he can't.

He narrows his dark eyes. "Abbott doesn't need another woman walkin' outta her life."

"You think Bella doesn't know that? Abbott is the only reason she walked away from me to begin with."

"What's changed?" he demands.

I pull in a big breath because he has me there. What has changed?

Nothing.

Fucking nothing.

But then again, everything.

This might be my one and only chance. Calling it a chance is like comparing a hangnail to a heart attack. To say everything is on the line is an understatement.

Because the woman who's danced around my heart for years suddenly shows up in Maryland with a gunshot wound. You bet your ass I'm going to take this chance.

"Everything has changed. I've got my neck on the line, Red. I know you care about me so it's time to shut your shit down and step up. I'm going to work tomorrow and I need to know you aren't going to run her off while I can't keep an eye on her. She damn well better be here when I get home."

"You could really be in some hot water over this, huh?"

"That's putting it mildly."

He stuffs his hands in his overalls and shakes his head. "She better be worth it."

"I'm your son," I shoot back. "You think I'd do something that wasn't worth it?"

"Don't act like you're cut from my cloth. I married your mama when she was eighteen 'cause I was afraid if I didn't, she'd wise up and find someone better. You're thirty-five—you've played every field on five continents, attracted a crazy-ass baby-mama who might've given me a beautiful granddaughter, but let's be real, son, that woman's got shit for brains. And when you finally do find a lady worth fightin' for, she's got an international target on her back and you could go to prison for hiding her here." His arms swing out before flopping to his side. Damn, he really is picking up a dramatic flair from all the daytime TV. "And now I'm gonna be an accessory."

"Red—"

"Shut your mouth. You know I'll do what you need me to. I'll also be here when she leaves and you inhale another bottle of whiskey."

I'd like to shake him for being such a pain in my ass but the girls come running around the side of the house. More like Abbott is running and Saylor is chasing her.

My daughter looks as frustrated as her grandfather.

She runs right to my side and whispers, "When are they gonna leave?"

I put my hand on top of her head and brush back her wild hair Red and I are still trying to figure out how to tame. "Baby, don't be rude."

"Why don't you have any pets?" Saylor asks, skipping in circles. "I have goats. And a donkey. And my new sister has a dog. And we have cats but they live outside and aren't friendly like the goats. You should get a cat because I saw a mouse when we were playing hide and seek and I never see a mouse at our house."

Abbott keeps talking to me like Saylor isn't standing right in front of us. "She sounds like Dr. Seuss."

"I love Dr. Seuss!" Saylor exclaims. "Asa—I mean my new dad—reads it to me all the time."

"Saylor?!" We all turn toward the back of the house where Keelie is standing at the door. "It's time to go. We need to get out of their hair."

I feel Abbott's body relax against my leg where she's attached like a spider monkey.

"Gotta go." Saylor doesn't even glance at us and hops to Keelie, who must have the patience of a saint. I've known Asa for years but from the looks of him at his wedding, he's happy and loves his new blended family. We have no trouble hearing every word Saylor bosses when she reaches her mother. "Next time, you can come to my house and we'll play with the goats!"

Keelie smiles at her daughter before waving to us. "I'll have Asa call and we'll get together when Bella feels up to it. If you need anything else, don't hesitate to call."

"I appreciate it." I wave back at the same time Abbott whispers, "I'll stay with Grandpa."

"Don't blame you, peanut. That's not a party I'd leave the house for, either," Red agrees.

"Can we get a cat?" I look down at Abbott who's wearing a different kind of frown that has more to do with panic than irritation. "I don't wanna see that mouse."

I question my parenting skills on a daily basis, but before I can say no because I don't need to add an animal to my list of things to fuck up, Red reaches down to snatch Abbott up, pulling her into a grizzly hug. "I'll take you to the pound and you can pick one out."

All of a sudden, Abbott is happier than I've seen her in a week and I don't think the timing of Bella crashing back into my life is a coincidence.

Speaking of the woman who almost died twice in the back of an ambulance, I head for the house. "Stay out here with your grandpa."

"I'm gonna get a cat!" she squeals and I shoot my father a glare as I open the back door.

All I can say is, thank God for small miracles—my father has my old air conditioner running smoother than a fine, aged bourbon and colder than Bella, who's swimming in a sea of red right now. I slam the door behind me and stop to take it all in.

Gracie wasn't kidding. They did some damage to Jarvis's card.

"You're as irritating as always, Cole Carson." Bella is sitting in the middle of an explosion of clothes, bottles, and tubes of crap that women like, and more shoes than she'll need while she's here since I don't plan on her stepping foot off my property. Her fingers are flying over the screen of the phone I had delivered this morning and she doesn't spare me a glance as she multitasks. "I'd rather wear Red's dirty overalls than make you happy by wearing the color of the devil himself."

I can't help but smile and make my way to the old recliner my father refuses to part with. "I don't think Red's into sharing clothes."

She jabs at the screen a few more times before tossing the phone into the mountainous wardrobe. "Your father hates me, and from the looks of it, your daughter isn't far behind."

"Abbott doesn't hate you. She's six and has mommy issues—I'm working on it. She doesn't know she has a shit mom and I don't feel like telling her because that reflects on me. I walk that line with my daughter every single day. It doesn't matter if you're here, I'd be doing it anyway. And Red doesn't hate you, he loves me. All he saw was that I came home from the Middle East pissed and empty-handed. He blames you."

Her eyes fall shut and she leans back into the sofa. "I didn't bend to your wishes. I can completely see how it's my fault and I now own an entire wardrobe of your favorite color. It makes perfect sense."

I try to keep the smile out of my tone. "It wasn't always my favorite color."

Her eyes open but she doesn't move a muscle. "Don't take me for an idiot."

"You don't get it and you never have."

"Enlighten me."

I lean forward and pick up the first thing I see. It's soft and smooth, and when I let it slide through my fingers, I see it's a silk robe. "The first assignment we had together. You were young and **as green** as George on the one-dollar bill." I fist the red **as tight** as I want to hold on to her. As tight as I've tried in the past and it's never worked. In fact, the tighter I've gripped, the more she's slipped and melted away from me. "I had a job to do and you were my decoy."

I see it in her eyes. She remembers the day as clearly as I do. She hated me—I could see it and feel it. I didn't think much of her at the time, either.

But the moment we walked into that mansion, there was nothing green about her. She not only did her job, she fucking killed it. And it had nothing to do with the red dress she wore to make sure she was the center of attention.

But that red dress hugging every curve of her body as it was pressed against mine on the dance floor did have an effect on my dick, which at the time annoyed the fuck out of me. I never mixed business with pleasure.

Ever.

And I had no desire to shake things up for a fresh-out-of-college MI6 who probably landed the job because of her last name and beautiful face.

She knows where I'm going with this and says nothing so I keep on. "You annoyed the hell out of me that night."

"Because I proved you wrong and not only did my job, but bloody aced it? You planted the bugs while I romanced our target with small talk. Your operation had been trying to infiltrate that mansion for weeks. But when I was added to the case, it was done in a matter of ninety-four minutes—if I remember correctly."

"You were a natural, but that's not what annoyed me. I'd worked for years to get where I was. I was the best—"

She interrupts me. "I see you still struggle with poor self-esteem."

I ignore that. "—and always focused on my assignment completely. I never had to work at concentrating until that night. Until you waltzed your fine ass out of the shitty motel bathroom in a dress that annihilated the brain cells of every man within a one-mile radius."

"How dare you insinuate my worth is based on my dress size—"

"And then you worked the room like a seasoned operative. You had the touch, the cool, the collected, the instincts. You know I'd never imply anything else at this point. You quickly won me over and you know it. So you, sweetness, in red, takes me back to a time I'll never forget."

Her eyes close. I'm sick of seeing her exhausted. Not when I'm used to her full of life, giving me a run for my money at every turn.

"Can we please not rehash the past?" Her head falls to the sofa cushion. "I'm not used to making new friends —I'm exhausted."

"You'll be fine."

It looks like it takes all her energy to lift her lids and gaze at me. "I know. I now have both Keelie and Gracie's numbers. They said they're going to check in on me and to ring them if I need anything. And do you know what's even more shocking?"

I toss the red robe on top of the mountain of clothes. "What?"

"I think they meant it. I'm not accustomed to nice women."

I get up and head to the kitchen. "It's amazing what can happen when they aren't intimidated by you."

"I'm not intimidating unless you piss me off," she calls after me.

That's the truth.

7

WHERE DREAMS AND FEARS COLLIDE

Twenty-two years ago
London
Age five

Bella

"**I**t's fuckin' not. And if they think it's the way it'll happen, they can kiss my arse."

My hand flies to my mouth to muffle my giggle because Daddy said the bad words Mummy would chew him for if she heard. I take a chance and open the door a bit so I can see. He's where he always is, in his leather chair that's wrinkled from him shifting to and fro. He's told me how he loves that chair because it was my grandpop's before it was his and all he ever wanted to do was to be like him. I love that chair too. When Daddy's away for work, I spin until my head gets wobbly.

He stands and goes to the closet in his den. It's always

locked—whether he's home or away. He takes the phone with him and unlocks the three deadbolts, all with different keys that clank as he moves.

"I can be there by morning and we'll set this straight. Don't warn them. At this point, I'll do it myself."

When he comes out of the closet, the phone is pressed between his ear and shoulder because his hands are full. He has a gun in one hand and a stack of pounds in the other. I've never seen Daddy with a gun before. The only time I've ever seen a shooter was on those shows Archer and Devon watch.

"Catch you when I land. I'll call the States—fill them in."

"Bella."

I jump at Mummy's whispered voice and turn to her as she pulls the door to the den shut with a click, closing me out from Daddy. She narrows her eyes but her pretty pink lips tip up on the side.

She picks me up and puts me on her hip, giving my bum a squeeze. It's a warning but I'm not worried. Her warnings pack no punch. Neither do Daddy's. Even so, she leans in close. "Why are you out of bed, sneaking around like a sleuth? It's late and you should be sleeping."

My insides twist, but not because I got caught peeping. "Daddy's leaving?"

Her smile deflates. "Yes, love. But he'll be back in time for your recital. He promised."

I frown. "I hate ballet. I want to quit."

She turns toward the stairs on her way to my bedroom that's the color of a canary. I hate yellow too. "But all your friends take dance."

"Miss Mary hates me," I complain as Mummy tucks me back into my soft bed and snuggles next to me. "She calls me hard-headed and difficult."

When I'm tucked up against her, she runs her fingers

through my messy hair and smiles. "Well, Miss Mary is crazy. You're beautiful-headed and spirited. She doesn't understand you."

I yawn. "Why do you make me go?"

"Because you're a little lady and **ballet** will teach you to be graceful."

"I don't want to be graceful. I want to take zu zitsu with the boys. It's not fair."

"Jiu jitsu," she corrects gently like she always does when I flub a word. "You love your big brothers, don't you?"

I nod because she's right. Archer and Devon aren't like my friends' brothers. They don't pick on me—they include me. Sometimes I think it's only because Daddy would raise his voice if they didn't, but I don't care. "I want to be like them. I don't want to learn stupid ballet."

"I agree, it's not fair. You can do **anything** you put your mind to and if you want to kick the snot out of a bag like your brothers, then you will. I'll enroll you for the next session, my little firecracker. But you'll also keep up with ballet. You'll thank me someday."

"Love you, Mummy." My eyelids get heavy. "I want to say 'bye to Daddy."

"Don't fret. He'll come in and kiss you. He'd never leave without loves from his beautiful Bella."

"I'll stay awake," I promise, rubbing my face before I look at Mummy and lean in to kiss her nose. Daddy says she looks like a fairy.

She smiles and returns my nose kiss with one of her own. "Yes, you stay awake, little bug."

It's the last thing she says before she starts to hum the way she always does—a song I've never heard from anyone but her.

MY EYES FLY open and my body jerks. The pain in my gut is a reminder of where I am, how I got here, and why I'm stuck in Virginia.

"You okay?"

Cole is next to me in bed, yet still so far away. It's my second night in his bed, in his house, and co-existing with his daughter and father.

I'm barely surviving in an odd purgatory, some-where between utopia and the deepest pits of reality where dreams and fears collide, rivaling an eruption not seen in modern-day warfare.

I say this and I'm not an overly-dramatic woman. I mean, I have found ways to flourish while hiding out in Pakistan, amassing information on some of the most brazen terrorists in the world.

Ever since I regained consciousness in the hospital, dreams of home infiltrate my sleep more often than not. If they were nightmares, I could see how it would be problematic. But these aren't anywhere close to night terrors. These are good dreams of good times—better ones than I've had in years. But even so, every time I wake with these memories, there is a weight bearing down on my chest heavier than anything I've endured—I miss my family and secretly crave stability.

"Baby. You okay?" The roughness of his voice punc-tures through the dark as he reaches to squeeze my hip under our covers.

I take a deep breath and do my best to ignore him. It's not the first time he's reached out to me since I arrived here but Cole Carson has kept his promise—he hasn't touched me. Not really. Not the way I'm used to— the way I came to beg him to when *we* were an *us*.

"Bella—"

"I'm fine," I lie. "Trying to get comfortable."

Through the moonlight peeking between his old blinds, he looks down from where he's propped himself up on a forearm. "It's not time for your meds. What do you need? Another pillow?"

I blink slowly and tell him the truth. "This sweet side of you is honestly freaking me out. If you don't watch it, you're going to be forced to turn in your arsehole card."

That doesn't win me a smile, but rather a hike of his thick, arched brow, which is more like the Cole I fell for a lifetime ago. "Don't worry, the asshole will be back when you can roll over in bed without wincing from pain. Tell me what you need."

I close my eyes and do my best to roll away from him. "I know you think you're the answer to everything, but I'm capable of getting comfortable on my own."

That's a lie too. I've never known physical pain like I've experienced since I woke up after surgery.

"I might be an asshole but you're still the biggest pain in the ass I've ever met."

I'm about to argue, but before I get a word out, his muscled chest is flush with my back, his pelvis cradling my bum, his quads glued to my hammies.

"What are you doing?"

His hand hits my hip and pulls my body to his. "Give me your weight."

"I said I was good."

"And I know you sleep better on your side but that's

got to hurt like a motherfucker right now. This will help."

His warmth seeps into me and I tell him the least of my worries. "I'll get hot."

He flips the covers off both of us and his scruff pulls at my hair. I'm not sure he's shaved since I've been in the States. "There. Now, be quiet and go back to sleep. Unlike you, I've gotten used to six hours in a row. Don't make me irritable tomorrow."

Cole's hand is locked on my hip, holding me to him where we've become one in his bed.

He runs his hand down the outside of my thigh and isn't gentle when he gives me another squeeze. "Not trying to fuck you, sweetness. Just trying to get some sleep. Relax."

I sigh but do it rolling my eyes. He knows how I feel about him demanding me to relax.

But allowing some of my tension to dissolve into him does feel a bit better.

"See?" he gloats as our bodies meld. "You'll be begging me to fuck you soon enough."

I pull my pillow into my chest because being cocooned is the first thing that's taken the edge off in days. Being able to rest on my side while feeling weightless might be orgasmic in and of itself. "Don't be so full of yourself. And you'd better go to sleep. The elderly need their rest."

A rumble from his chest vibrates through me and he shakes his head. "It's what drew you to me. Practically had to beat you off with a stick."

I close my eyes. "I see dementia is setting in."

"I agree." He pushes in tighter, demanding not only

my weight, but everything else I don't want to think about at the moment. His cock, that I will only admit to myself how much I miss, has sprung to life proving his virility and youth. "I've got to be crazy to be taking you on."

Finally.

Something we agree on.

"I'm going back to work tomorrow."

My eyes fly open.

He keeps talking. "You'll be fine. Told Red to be on his best behavior and I'll make sure he feeds you a decent meal."

"I don't need your father to cook for me. I can keep well enough on my own."

He rubs a hand down my thigh. "I know he doesn't need to but he's going to—not for you but for me. Give him some time and everything he'll do will be for you. He's got an odd way of showing it, but he's got the biggest heart of anyone you'll meet."

Cole doesn't know my mum and dad well, so I doubt it.

And I plan to be gone before I get the chance to know anyone's heart.

It's my turn to boss him. "Go to sleep, Cole. I doubt the chaps at Langley will be pleased if you nap on the job tomorrow because you're too busy harboring an AWOL MI6. Americans are weird like that."

"I think it's safe to say it's not just Americans."

No truer words have been spoken in the dead of the night.

"You're giving me a case of blue balls. If you don't shut your sweet mouth and go to sleep, I might have to get up and take care of myself."

That brings back memories I do not need to think about right now.

Or ever.

His voice dips. "You remember."

I'll never forget—not until I expel my last breath. "Vaguely."

"You remember," he repeats and his lips brush my ear through my tousled hair. "It was unforgettable. I had to do it to take the edge off. If I didn't, there was no way I could make your first encounter what it was."

I hug my pillow tighter.

He won't stop. "Pretty sure your words at the time were *fucking brilliant*."

"I take back what I said," I snap. "You won't lose your arsehole card anytime soon."

"You wouldn't want me any other way."

"I'll never sleep if you keep droning on about yourself."

"I'm only droning on about you," he argues. "But you're right. Go to sleep."

"For the love of all that's holy, stop talking."

His cock grinds into my ass. "You stop talking."

I let my lids fall and try to pretend I'm not where I am and tomorrow will be different than reality will offer up. As much as I need a mental break from the man who's literally supporting my weight right now, I'm not looking forward to a day alone with Abbott and Red Carson.

Either the pain pill I took over an hour ago finally kicks in or it's the six-foot-four beast of a man I just can't shake.

When I finally give in to exhaustion, it proves to be the best sleep I've had in a very long time.

8

TOU-FUCKIN'-CHÉ

Cole

"Ya sure ya want to be nosin' around there again?"

I fall back into my chair, tired from being up half the night and dragging my ass out of bed two hours before dawn for the first time in over a week. "Trying another angle. I need to find her brothers and you're the only one who can help me."

"I haven't seen Donnelly in over a year, mate. Ya need to drop it. She knows her arse will burn at the proverbial stake if she surfaces. Her beauty of a mug is on everyone's shit list north of the Mediterranean."

"I know," I grit. "I'm not trying to find her this time —but I do need to find Archer or Devon."

"Those fellas aren't gonna tell ya where she's hidin'. I've seen the suits drag every single living Donnelly into Vauxhall—even her sweet mum. I'm sure they know where she is but not a one of 'em is gonna give her up. Not even to ya—maybe *especially* to ya. It's time to mend your wounds and find yourself a nice little American chickee. Maybe one who likes to drink out of those red plastic cups while sportin' cut-off jeans that go up to her arse cheeks, showing off legs that stretch as far as the horizon in a pair of cowgirl boots."

"Fuck me. You and your obsession with country music," I mutter. If he only knew where Bella really was. He's nosy and always has been, but right now, I need him to test those skills for me. He's my only contact in all of Great Britain I trust right now. He owes me his life. I saved his ass over a decade ago when we were both greener than two guppies lost in a puddle of rainwater. "Look, Oliver. I appreciate your concern—"

"Or maybe a cheerleader. Ya should move to Texas, they've got good ones down there from what I've seen watchin' your American football."

"Oliver—"

"Or that beauty with the knockers like puffy little pillows who cooks on the satellite. She's Italian but she's also American. The two of yas would make a handsome couple. What's her name..."

"Dammit, Oliver—"

"Giada!"

"Oliver!"

"I'm just sayin', you're a strappin' lad. Ya need to pull your head out of your arse and check yourself back into the game, as they say. Dive in head first. Put your dry spell out of its ever-loving misery. Dip your willie between some pompoms—I betcha cheerleaders like that."

I close my eyes and rub my temples, not believing it's come to this—me relying on him. It doesn't say a lot about my options when he's my best bet. "Are you done?"

"Look, my favorite American. I'm gonna tell it to ya as plain as I can make it. I feel comfortable enough in my manhood when I say, I love ya—"

"You've got to be shitting me."

"—and you deserve more than a fine-feelin' woman."

"Again with the country songs."

"You, my American counterpart, deserve a chick-adee who isn't on the run. Ya know what else?"

I give up. "No, Ollie. But I bet you're going to tell me."

"That Donnelly woman fed your need for adventure. She might as well have needled herself straight into your veins and pumped ya full of adrenaline. She gave ya a high and now you're jonesin' for it. It's why you won't settle down for a spicy little cook or a perky cheerleader."

He is not wrong. "Thank you, Dr. Phil. That was enlightening."

"Who's Dr. Phil?"

"Look him up. You'll become obsessed."

I hear him pecking away at a keyboard. "Lookin' now."

"Call me when you have a line on one of the Donnelly brothers. Either is fine, but I need to talk to one of them and it needs to be discreet and off the record."

"Everything you do is off the record."

"Right back at you, Ollie."

A deep laugh booms over the pond and about blows my eardrum out. "Touché, my beautiful American man. Tou-fuckin'-ché."

"Make it happen, Oliver. I don't have time to be dicking around with this."

"Well, kiss my arse. Now I have a pudgie at the thought of you dicking around."

"You've got forty-eight hours, tops. I'd prefer to hear from you tomorrow," I demand.

"Don't make it a full-on woody by goin' all alpha male on me, Carson. I'm at my desk."

"Talk to you tomorrow."

I hear a smile. "I love ya, mate."

And I hang up.

Oliver Abram might be odd but he's always come through for me. I know it'll be the same this time. He might look like he's continually fucking around, but in a weird way, it makes him stealth in what he does. No one takes him seriously but they should—he's a sneaky fuck.

I can't take a chance on contacting Bella's parents. I know for a fact their lines are tapped and the Brits are watching them like hawks. I'd bet everything I own that Thorne Donnelly knows this too. He was MI6 himself and one of the best who's ever strode through the doors of Vauxhall. He retired before everything went to hell with Bella. From what I heard, Annie is heartbroken for her daughter, and Thorne, who was once as loyal as a golden retriever to his country and agency, is done with both. He saw what the rest of us saw—shoddy investigating, finger pointing, and a shit show fit for crap TV.

I'm about to press send on an email to my boss with my report on Raji when my burner phone rings. It's an unknown number.

I pick it up on the second ring. "Carson."

"Boss. I only have a short time."

Speak of the asset of the hour. He's out of breath and on the move, causing me to step back from the send button and brace. "Raji. What's wrong?"

Raji and I go back seven or eight years. Before Abbott, before Bella, and before I had to give up a career as an operative. There's a grapevine in that part of the world and he's so entangled, I'm sure his head spins from having to watch his back from every angle. I've kept in touch with him and pad his bank account nicely for information he feeds me.

"Your target's first-hand man is on the move. And I don't mean in the back of a shitty SUV. I followed his small caravan to an airstrip." His words are labored and I hear his boots grinding into the sand at a flat-out run. "He boarded a plane—small, prop engine."

I reach up and hit the delete key on the email I was about to send because I have a feeling everything has changed. "You get a tail number? Where's he going?"

"No tail number and I don't know. It's pitch dark here in the early morning hours. I've got a friend who works at the main airport. I'll pick his brain tomorrow. Until then, I know nothing."

I squeeze my eyes shut and shake my head. "You didn't know he was taking a trip?"

We suspected a small up-and-coming terrorist cell was behind an attack on a commuter train last month in Germany. I've had Raji on them ever since and it hasn't been an easy go. Especially for the whole damn week when he didn't check in with me.

His car door slams and an engine sputters to life. "No. I followed the convoy as far as I could before moving in on foot. I saw him board the plane with two lower-level soldiers. They were carrying small bags but that's it."

"I want to know where they're going. In a plane that size, it can't go far without refueling. Names, Raji. I need names."

"Don't treat me like a fool, Carson. I know what you need."

"Listen." I lean forward and lower my voice. "My boss is up in my ass about you. I know you're doing your best and you know I'll cover for you because you're good. I was working from home last week and somehow he found out you weren't answering my calls."

"I explained. You think I'm gonna call you if it isn't safe?"

"That's what I told him. He sees you as a piece of his budget—and a big one. I'm the one justifying your paycheck. Keep feeding me information, Raji. You about gave me a heart attack last week—thought our whiskey-drinking days were over."

His old engine revs to match the laugh I'm more than familiar with. "You know I'm always up for whiskey. Make it Irish, even better."

"You give me a name, tell me where this guy turns up, and what the hell he's doing there, I'll send you a case and find a way for Uncle Sam to foot the bill."

"Deal."

"Don't lose your head."

"Don't worry. I like my head where it sits."

The line goes dead.

I open the document I spent the last hour drafting. I need to get this shit done so I can get home and make sure Red was on his best behavior during his first day alone with Bella.

Bella

"COLE HAS BEEN FINE, all on his own."

I nod to the woods in front of me and pick up my glass of water. I'm grateful my strength isn't up to par or I might crush it with rage-filled adrenaline alone.

"He's got Abbott and he's got me to help with Abbott. From what I can tell, he should be up for a promotion soon."

After taking a sip of my too warm water, I don't look at him when I finally respond, "I have no doubt Cole is flourishing in his life here, Red."

I escaped the cool house over an hour ago to move my body. I was a pile of rubbish after only fifteen minutes—flat-out exhausted. Escaping my current state of hell isn't going to be on the docket anytime soon if I can't do more than hobble through the woods like a maimed animal.

I'm used to the heat and humidity so sitting outside in the summer is nothing. At least it wasn't until Red decided to join me. He planted his arse on the opposite side of the front stoop from yours truly. Ever since, Cole's father has been informing me of all the ways his beloved son is handling life on his own—meaning, without me.

"Flourishing? Nope, that's what my tomato plants are doin'. Cole is fuckin' killing it."

For the first time since he joined me, I look over at him and force myself to smile. "I've no doubt."

The phone Cole gave me yesterday vibrates where it's sitting on my thigh.

Cole – How're you doing, sweetness?

No sooner than I put my fingers to the screen, Red demands, "Who's that? Cole told me to keep an eye on you."

"I'm sure he did," I mutter.

Me – Fine.

Cole – Why do you not sound fine?

Me – No, really. I'm good. I managed some exercise. I'm up to a 5k.

Cole – The fuck you are. You couldn't even sleep on your side last night without me.

Like I need to be reminded.

"You still working over there on the other side of the world?"

I look at Red. "Yes. It's harder not actually being there, but I'm trying to keep up."

Cole – I hope my dad isn't giving you hell.

"Good. The sooner you get back there, we'll all get back to normal. Abbott wants her daddy to herself. Cole's job is stressful enough—he doesn't need you here addin' to it."

"It was never my intention to intrude in your lives. I plan to leave as soon as I possibly can."

Me – Red has been lovely. He fixed me one of your all-American hot dogs for lunch. A Carson specialty, for sure.

It's the truth. I heard a bang on Cole's bedroom door where I was hiding out when he announced it was *tea time.* When I opened the door, a plate was sitting on the floor waiting for me with a naked hot dog lying limp on a piece of bread.

Cole – Shit. I'm sorry. I'll make you something before I go to work tomorrow.

Me – I don't need anyone to wait on me. I'm perfectly capable of feeding myself.

"Grandpa?"

I look up from my phone and Abbott is standing in the open doorway. I've heard every move she's made through the paper-thin walls today but this is the first I've seen of her since Cole went back to work this morning. I've been doing my best to not be seen myself. Her long, dark hair is flowing down her back in beautiful curls. It doesn't look like it's been brushed but that's okay. Red doesn't seem like the hair-brushing kind of caretaker.

My phone vibrates again.

Cole – Maybe, but I want you to rest. Preferably on me, like last night. You needing me is a new development and I don't hate it.

I cringe as his words seep through my brain because I think I've needed Cole Carson since the moment he laid a hand on me when we went undercover the first time.

Red's entire demeanor flips its switch from an angry, defensive father to that of a loving grandfather. "Yeah, darlin'?"

"I'm done reading."

My smile settles into something from my soul and for the first time I try to make conversation with Cole's child. "What are you reading?"

She fidgets around on bare feet and mumbles, "*Secret Garden.*"

My eyes widen. "Impressive for a girl your age. It was a favorite of mine but I wasn't quite as young as you when I read it for the first time."

Abbott looks at the rug she's standing on and shrugs.

"My grandbaby is as smart as a whip. She's gonna leave the rest of the first graders in the dust this fall at her new school, aren't you, Abbs?" Red stands and moves to his granddaughter. "Your daddy said you could have the iPad after you read."

The child has no desire to continue our conversation and turns to skip away from me as fast as her little legs will take her.

Cole – I'll stop at the store on the way home. You know my shitty skills in the kitchen but I'll do my best. What do you want?

I ignore Cole because Red pauses where he stands at the front door. So much for leaving me be and putting me out of my misery. "Gotta admit. You're not at all what I expected."

I'm not sure I want to know but lean back in my chair and ask anyway. "How's that?"

"Thought you were gonna come in here and try to stake your claim to my boy. Cause drama in the life he's tryin' to build for Abbott. Worm your way in then escape back to your job that's so important to you. You do that, Cole'll never recover. He finally settled down and neither him nor Abbs need a woman flyin' in and outta their lives like a drive by."

I shake my head and swallow over the lump in my throat that feels more like the bullet I caught. "I know my place, Red. Trust me, I've been trying to stay in it for years now."

"My son is nothin' if not persistent."

I know that better than anyone. "Yes, he is."

"You care about Cole?"

Cole – Baby, what sounds good?

My eyes shift to the old man whose expression shows me he's as serious as a terrorist threat and I tell him the truth. "A great deal."

"Then do him and Abbott a favor—don't let him win. Take your show on the road and keep it there. I know why you're here, why you're a secret, and why you've been creepin' around that part of the world. He thinks he can save you, but we don't need your drama, not when life for my granddaughter has been turned on its fuckin' head. We're workin' to get her back to happy, so she can forget her good-for-nothin' mama. But you bein' here does nothin' but dredge all that up."

I shake my head and look back to the woods—alive with birds, bugs, and who knows what else. My palms bead with sweat that has nothing to do with the heat and humidity heavy in the air. If I could, I'd damn myself to hell for my own weakness. Dress me up as a cocktail waitress and throw me into a room full of terrorists—I will find their leader and have him tipping me in the process. But anything to do with Cole Carson and my nerves are a shoddy mess.

I focus on the forest as I keep speaking the truth to the man who just put me in my place. "You won't have to worry about me. I plan to leave as soon as I can. You have my word."

"Good," he belts and smacks the chipped siding next to the front door. But he adds one last zinger before allowing the rickety screen door to smack him in the arse, finally ending the berating he's so soundly handed me. "If only my son would fall in line, we could forget this ever happened."

My phone vibrates again.

Cole – Bella, don't go silent on me.

I'm exhausted from the heat, the pain pills, and I swear, I still have an anesthesia hangover. It also seems nothing can take it out of me like Red Carson. All I want to do is go back to bed and pray I wake up in the humble home I've created in Pakistan.

Instead, I pull myself to my feet, determined to make one more lap around Cole's property. I need my strength and I'm not going to build it wasting away in bed.

But, first, unlike the truths I told his father, I lie to the man who will probably haunt my heart for the rest of my days.

Me – I'm good. Going to catch a quick nap. I'm knackered.

I step down onto the forest floor and put my hand to my belly over my nasty scar. It doesn't hold a candle to another one that's proving to get uglier and deeper by the day.

Cole

I pull the covers up and tuck her in. "Night, baby."

Abbott grabs my T-shirt and her words come out in a rush. "Don't leave."

"It's late and Grandpa said you got up early this morning."

I've been home from work for two hours and she's been glued to my side the whole time. Not that she isn't usually when I'm home. It was worse in the beginning when Tabitha was newly out of the picture. I did everything I could to make sure my daughter knew I'd never leave her—that she'd always have one parent who cared about her more than anything else because she never got it from her mother.

"Sleep with me." Her little hand grips tighter. Like I usually do when she wants something, I give it to her. It's easy. Abbott only ever wants my time and attention. I'm sure it will change someday when she's a teenager and she'll want all the shit I know nothing about but, for now, when she wants me, I'll be here. She deserves it.

"I'll stay 'til you fall asleep."

"No, don't leave, even after I go to sleep."

I settle in beside her as she wiggles out of the covers and practically crawls under my skin. I put my lips to the top of her head where her hair is still drying from her bath. "You know I have to go to work before the sun comes up."

"Will you come with Grandpa and me tomorrow to get my cat?"

I shake my head. "I'll try to be home early but work is busy right now."

"I don't want you to go to work. I want you to help pick out my cat."

"Baby, you know I have to go to work. Someone's got to pay the bills. And, apparently, buy cat food."

She looks up and I see the purest smile I've seen on her face in days. "And cat toys!"

I smirk. "You think the cat will need some toys? I thought it was going to catch mice."

Her little face scrunches up. "Ew. I decided I don't want my cat to catch mice. I want it to be inside with me."

I tap her nose with the end of my finger. "So basically this cat isn't going to be pulling his weight around here. I get it now."

"I want a girl. There are enough boys here."

I sigh and pull her into my chest to drag my hand through her hair the way that makes her fall asleep in no time. As much as I want to bring up the subject of the other female currently residing under my roof, I'm not cracking that can right now. Abbott avoids Bella like the plague.

She won't look at her.

She barely responds if Bella speaks to her.

The only time she recognizes the fact Bella is here is when she asks when Bella is leaving.

I knew it wasn't going to be easy but I'm not sure it could be worse.

I have no idea what the Carson household was like while I was at work today, but from the moment I got home, Bella hasn't left my bedroom. In any other cosmos, I'd be fucking jolly about my Brit never leaving my bed, but not now. Now, I need Abbott to like Bella and Bella to want to stay. I want to rip the band aid off and I don't care how painful it'll be.

But quick is not on the agenda. Hell, we're not even taking a step in the right direction. As the days click on, we're one step deeper into this awkward hell.

"We could use some more girls around here," I agree.

My daughter is as smart as a whip, which I take complete credit for because she sure as shit didn't get it from her mother. "Just a cat. That's enough girls."

I put my fingers to her chin and lift her face from my chest where she's resting. "I know what that means and I don't like it."

She pulls her face away and burrows back into my T-shirt. This time she stays silent.

"Abbs, I need you to try. Bella is important to me and once you get to know her, you'll like her."

"Grandpa doesn't like her."

"Your grandpa doesn't like a lot of people. He can be a crotchety old man."

"He loves me."

"More than anything. But Grandpa also doesn't see the world for what it is sometimes. I don't want you to be like that, and Bella has a good heart. Your Grandpa will come around, like you need to."

She yawns and her little body sinks into my chest. There, she mumbles, "Doesn't matter. She's leaving soon. She said so when Grandpa told her to today."

What the fuck?

My hand freezes on her head for a quick second but I force my muscles to relax. I need to pull all the information out of her I can without her knowing she's selling out her best friend. "Grandpa's ornery."

I feel her smile against my chest. "I know."

"What'd he say?"

Through a yawn, the words are jumbled yet still clear as day. "He told her to get her *show on the road* like he says to me when I'm a slow-poke. And some other stuff. She said she'd leave. That's when Grandpa gave me my iPad."

Shit. There's nothing else to get out of Abbott because when she's staring at a screen, the rest of the world might as well melt away. I can barely get her to acknowledge me, let alone get her to comprehend. I want to stomp on the damn thing some days and it's not even connected to the internet. "Not too much time on the iPad, okay, baby?"

She yawns again. "I know."

"Go to sleep and dream about cat names."

She doesn't answer this time.

"Love you, Abbs."

"Love you, Daddy."

It doesn't take but another few minutes for her

breaths to deepen and her body to become heavy on mine. But I don't get up. If I do, I know for a fact a bomb will detonate and my father might not survive. I don't need a wedge between him and me, but hell if I need another force pushing Bella away. There are too many as it is.

I warned Red. And to have my own father stab me in the back...

Bella

I'M NOT sure the days here in Virginia could drag any longer or be more utterly miserable, but here I lie. The day will not end, no matter how much I will it to.

At least I'm exhausted. I didn't nap today.

After I walked Cole's property three times at a pace slower than a slug—which was more than frustrating—I managed a shower and found myself some dinner. That was before Cole came home. Luckily Red and Abbott were in the backyard nosing around the vegetable garden.

I'm a wizard at hiding, which makes escaping to Cole's bedroom the easiest thing in the world. Keelie texted to check in. I know it's what women do—even if not many have extended that gesture to me—and I appreciate her kindness.

Gracie, however, more than checked in. She can jabber on, that one. Even to my surprise, I found myself smiling during the marathon text thread we amassed. When she finally brought our conversation to an end because Jarvis had arrived home, I knew more about

Gracie Cain than I ever expected to know, but not before she demanded I contact her should I find myself needing clothes, makeup, accessories, or pretty much anything else under the sun.

Then I had other things to keep me busy. I have contacts to keep up with. Leads I cannot allow to cool. And, most importantly, a certain senator to spy on. He is the reason I'm here, after all.

I've also decided I'm done with pain pills. I need my brain sharp and alert.

But I planned to be dead asleep at this point.

When Cole came home from work and interrogated me about my day, what I ate, what I did, if I was still hungry, and what I needed for tomorrow, it was surreal. Like so many times in the past, he changed clothes right in front of me as if this is what we do every day. Then he demanded I join him and his family for the evening.

Well. I've had about enough family time for one day. Of course, I didn't tell him that.

I lied, said I wasn't well, and needed to rest.

Once I assured him my stomach was plenty full and quiet time would be the only thing to heal me, he frowned and stormed out of his room.

That was hours ago.

Now, the bed dips behind me but doesn't stop there.

Like a rerun of my favorite show, he plasters himself to my back and a hand grips my hip, pulling my weight to him. It's not terribly late and Cole Carson does not need a full eight hours to be at the tip-top of his game. He's never been an early to bed type unless there were sexual aerobics going down in the bedroom—or anywhere else we felt the urge.

I allow the heat from his body to creep into mine like the ghost of us that continues to haunt me.

I sigh.

He buries his face in my messy hair and inhales.

Neither of us utters a word.

There is no yin and yang when it comes to me and my American. We're not opposite nor do we complement the other. We're cut from the same cloth, and during our time together when we were at our best, we probably argued more than we didn't. Cole is all alpha —headstrong and takes no prisoners in anything he does. And I'm no fool. I know my assets are feminine, but I also know how to use them in a man's world, and as a bonus, can kick their arses if needed. As an operative, I've definitely had to. In the end, Cole respected that and he respected me.

Together, we were a force.

The best.

Even butting heads. I think that fire made everything else all the better.

But I knew we would never be more. From the beginning, I tripped over myself for him, knowing he had Abbott and she was his first priority. As Abbott grew older, he made the correct decision to return to Langley, to be a constant in her life.

He knew I wasn't ready to hang up my hat. Then life went to shit and I had no choice but to go dark.

As he tortures me by running his hand up and down my thigh, like we're something we're not, I finally decide to break the silence because I need Cole's help.

"I need something."

His hand on me squeezes. "Look, if this is about today, I promise—"

I shake my head where I'm lying on his pillow and interrupt because there's only one thing I want to talk about right now. "I need a ticket to a fundraiser. I'll foot the bill, of course."

The room goes so stale, the locusts singing outside seep through the thin walls. "Excuse me?"

"You hardly have a polite bone in your body, Cole. That *excuse me* did not come from the heart."

"Okay, then. What the fuck?"

I sigh. "That's more like it."

"Fundraiser? To actually attend? In person?"

"Yes."

"Well, blow my mind, Bella. Tell me why."

"Because I care about ... *things*. I want to attend."

He presses into my back and the sudden energy zinging through his muscles is palpable. "Tell me about these *things* you care about so much you're willing to risk everything for."

I shrug, and in the process, try to push him back. "The Everglades."

He allows me no room and repeats through gritted enamel. "The Everglades."

"Yes. Catch up, Cole. I'm tired."

"Why do you give two fucks about the Everglades?"

"I'm empathetic to nature. The Everglades are an important part of our ecosystem. I'd like to purchase a chair, maybe donate a bit more once I get there. It will be something to do while I'm in the States. And I've never seen the Kennedy Center—Camelot ... all that jazz."

"The Kennedy Center is a building and has nothing to do with Camelot."

"Well, thank you for ruining it for me."

He knows I'm blowing smoke **up his** arse. "Who's gonna be there?"

"I assume other Everglade-loving humans, such as myself."

"Quit fucking with me, Bella."

"Seats are one thousand of your precious American dollars. I'm sure I'd like to give more at the event and we both know I can't simply write a check with my name on it."

"When is this shindig?" he growls.

"The week after next. I'm sure I'll be ready for a night out by then. I'll arrange for a car. I don't want to be caught without a driver's license."

"Yeah, it would be bad if you were stopped without a DL since you're wanted all over eastern Europe and North America. An Uber is the way to go."

"You know me. I'm nothing if not thorough."

"Dammit. Tell me what's going on." His tone is as tense as his arm wrapped around me.

"The event is sold out but I know if anyone can score a ticket, you can. I'll only need one, please."

His forearm angles up—above my stitches, between my breasts—and I have to work to keep my breaths even. His lips brush my ear when he whispers, "I'll look into it. But I have one condition."

I tell him something he damn well knows. "I don't like conditions."

"I know. And you know I don't give a shit."

I close my eyes. "Go ahead."

"Tell me what happened today with Red."

I open my eyes and look across his shadowed room. "I told you. He made me another hotdog. It was no pork pie but it was thoughtful."

"That's not what I mean and you know it. Something happened. Abbott mentioned it and I want to know what the hell my father did."

Shaking my head, I tell him the truth. "Nothing happened that I didn't expect from you forcing me into your home. Red loves you, as he should."

Still supporting my weight, he leans on a forearm and turns my face to his. "Red doesn't understand. I want to know what he said."

I shake my head. "I've seen you extract information from scarier subjects than your father, ask him. If you expect me to cooperate because I'm sleeping up against you, you're sorely mistaken."

"He told you to leave, didn't he?"

"Red didn't say anything I don't agree with. Only now that I have a gala I'd like to attend for my favorite charity, I'm afraid he's going to have to deal with me for a bit longer."

"Bella—"

"The ticket, Cole." I rip my chin from his grasp and settle back into my pillow. And because it does take the pressure off the niggling pain in my gut, I freely give him my weight.

He settles behind me as his frustrated sigh brushes my hair. "Sweetness, you haven't changed. You're as frustrating as ever which makes me hard as a rock. The only thing I know for certain right now is I'm fucked in the head for agreeing to any of this."

"If you'd prefer I call Crew, I'm sure—"

"You know I'll do it."

I hug the pillow that smells of his body wash. "I've already wired the money to your account."

"That doesn't surprise me, either," he mutters and

presses his groin into my ass, proving my determination does, in fact, turn him on.

You'd think, after all this time, it wouldn't please me so.

Yet, it does.

10

COMPLICATED

Cole

I swing the door to my office open with my phone to my ear as I listen to Hollingsworth push back on the favor I need. "I have a lot of contacts around the District, but politicians? I don't touch them with a ten-foot pole."

"I can't be the one nosing around about this guy. I can pull a lot of files but not on a senator. That'll throw up red flags and get me called into my supervisor's supervisor's office. A simple Google search leads me to believe Charles Randolph is knee-deep into ninety percent of the dark shit going on in Congress. Somehow he keeps coming out smelling like roses instead of the outhouse he plays in. He's the keynote at an event the week after next—the one she wants a ticket to. I don't need to pull his file to remember him shouting from the damn rooftops after the explosion in Barcelona." I don't say it out loud but we both know he's why she's here.

I toss my bag on the floor next to my desk and listen to silence.

"Asa?" I bite.

"Bella is going to waltz her ass into the Kennedy Center where Randolph is the big attraction?"

"That's her plan. And you know she's gonna do it whether I help or not. The only way for me to manage this is to be there as her backup."

He laughs.

The bastard actually laughs at me.

"Only you," his words shake with fucking amusement at my expense. "Would harbor the most-wanted former British Intelligence asset in modern history in your fixer-upper farmhouse and then help her get close to the man who heads up the Anti-Terrorism Committee in the Senate. Not only that, he's the one who called for her head in connection to a bomb that killed a bus load of people."

I drag a hand down my face. "Had she known about that, she would have stopped it. You know it."

"I never thought she did know about it. Crew wouldn't work with her if he thought she did, either."

"Then why are we going through this again?"

"Because it's ironic."

"Nothing ironic about it. Now I know why she came to the States but I still don't know Randolph's connection."

I almost hear him roll his eyes. "Maybe you should ask her."

I fall to my chair. "It's complicated. That's not how we operate. Look, I've had your back over the years— helped you and your boys with all kinds of shit that I probably shouldn't have. I need you to do this for me."

"He's a politician which **means** he's a scumbag. What else do you want to know?"

"I don't know what I need to **know,** which means I need to know everything."

He sighs. "I'll see what I can do."

"I appreciate it. I also need two **tickets** to that event, if you run into any while you're **asking** around, buy them and I'll pay you back." I take **a gulp** of my coffee. "And bring Saylor over to the **house again** soon. Red's taking Abbott to the Humane **Society** to get a cat today."

"Saylor would love that. How's **Abbott**?"

"Quiet. Shy. Doesn't want to **leave** the house, not interested in making new friends, **and** she's got *mommy issues*." I sit back in my chair and **turn** to look out the window. "Nothing has changed. And I don't know what to do about any of it."

"You've got a full plate."

"I do. I've got calls to make. Let **me** know what you find out."

"Talk soon."

I hang up and pick up my oth**er phone**, pushing go on the number that had better pick **up the** other end.

A groan creeps over the line. "I **was asleep**."

"The deposit wired into your **bank** account in the last hour is proof enough I don't c**are if** you're dreaming of sugarplum fairies, Raji. I need **an update** and you didn't call last night like you said **you would**, so here I am—fishing for the information **you've** been paid for. Again."

I hear rustling in the backgro**und.** "Since when did you become such a micro-manager?"

I pull his file out of my bag. "**Since** you don't check

in when you say you will and my boss is all over my ass about you earning your paycheck."

"Fair enough. I had a late night and crashed."

"Your late night better have had something to do with our target."

"Who do you think you're working with?"

"Raji, unlike you, I do have other cases. Can you get to it today?"

"Fine. I picked up the trail of that plane. It made three stops before finally landing at a small airstrip in Yemen. All I know is it's heading back my way. I assume our friends are not on it."

"I need names of the lower-level, Raji. Pictures would be better. Who got on the plane?"

"I'm not a hundred percent, but I've narrowed it down to who I think they could be by who I haven't seen. My guys here helped. Arif Nahas, Harb—I don't have a first name, and a Tom Crowley."

I pause as I scribble in the file. "An American?"

"Unless he renamed himself ... your guess is as good as mine."

"I'll run these and see what I come up with. You don't know where they're headed from Yemen?"

"I don't but I have a call in to someone in Oman. I'll see what I can find."

"This is a good start."

He yawns. "Will do. Next time, if you could call during the day, I'd appreciate it."

"No promises. Talk soon."

I type the password into my computer to run those names when my boss, Nick Peterson, appears at my threshold. Before he has a chance to say anything, I hold my hand up. "I've got names. I'm running them now. Raji is back on track like I knew he'd be."

"Finally. But that's not why I stopped by."

I hike a brow and wonder what other hell he could slap me across the face with.

"We've got a new assignment. Backgrounds have already been done and vetted so we can skip that part of the process—it's become our number one priority. You'll be getting an email in the next hour. Move it to the top of the list. I need your best on it."

I bite my tongue because informing him I don't contract with anyone but the best will only prolong his flyby. Seeing as my list of things to do is more complicated than the Mayan calendar, I don't need him here any longer than necessary. But I know for a fact not one of my people will take a contract if I tell them our usual vetting process is being skipped. Nor should they.

If I don't do it myself, they will. It's a risk no one with a brain the size of a dime would take.

It's amazing what management seems to forget once they acclimate to fluorescent lights and fake plants.

But with the goal of getting him out of my face, I don't elaborate. "I'll take care of it."

"This is sensitive and needs to be carried out as soon as possible. Don't put anyone green on this," he stresses.

Like I've ever done that. This time I need a vise to keep my true thoughts of him to myself. "Of course."

He slaps the door jamb, and with a curt nod, finally leaves me to my less-than-peaceful day.

When my computer dings with the email, curiosity gets the best of me. Setting aside the names I need to run, I maneuver my way through three levels of security before opening the encrypted document containing the information of our latest target who my supervisor wants wiped from this earth in the quickest way possible.

I scan the first three pages before going back to the beginning.

This can't be right.

I read every single word and then read them again.

No fucking way.

I look to my open doorway where my supervisor stood and gave me an order. A kill order which has already been so-called *vetted* by higher-ups...

This is like nothing I've seen before.

The background noise of secrets and intel and covert operations drift through the building—operatives and case workers doing what they do best—but I hear none of it.

I look back to my screen and read the description of the so-called target that has apparently been moved to the top of our list.

"This cannot be real," I mutter to no one.

Then I pick up the phone and dial Hollingsworth.

And I make plans that do not include orders from my boss. This target will be vetted deeper and more comprehensively than any I've ever done in the past.

Someone is playing a fucked-up game and we just got to level ten. All guns have been loaded and the stakes couldn't be higher.

Bella

"I CAN'T BELIEVE Cole arranged for you to do this. I could've cut them out myself."

"What else do I have to do?" Gracie doesn't look up as we have a chat while she works on the stitches I refuse to focus on because of the ugly scar I'll be left with for eternity. "I hope you're taking it easy and giving your body a chance to heal. You'll create scar tissue if you overdo it. That will create complications later."

Gracie showed up at Cole's house right before lunchtime. If I were a dramatic woman, I would have fallen to my knees in gratitude. Not only did she arrive with a mammoth vineyard gift basket full of wine and nibbles, but she had a pork pie.

It was divine and instantly reminded me of home. What was even better, she slaved over it herself since I mentioned a pork pie to Noah while I was in the hospital.

I must have been snockered on pain killers because I have no memory of the conversation.

I've decided Gracie might as well be my American fairy godmother. Her version of meat pie was so delicious, I had two helpings with two glasses of wine. It's the most I've eaten since I was shot and definitely the first drink.

Red proved I am the only person on earth he's salty about because he fawned over Gracie and the pie in the same fashion he grandfathers Abbott. And since I need information to operate in everything I do, this was a good bit for me to file away. Red is only irritable with me.

Good to know.

Little Abbott ate half of her lunch and then dropped her fork when Gracie explained she made it because it's a popular English dish and she heard it was a favorite of mine. That's when she announced she was full and ready to get her cat.

Lord have mercy. That child hates me.

Gracie, with her wide, beautiful blue eyes, simply poured me another glass of Meritage and instructed me to drink up.

That was an hour ago. Red and Abbott left me to my bloated stomach, relaxed head, and new friend.

I'm lying on Cole's bed with my shirt tucked under my breasts as Gracie snips away. "I know my body. I'm not doing anything it can't handle."

I feel her stop and open my eyes to find hers on me. "I have a feeling that means you're overdoing it."

I shake my head as my lids fall again so I can enjoy my relaxed buzz. "I'm doing exactly what I need to do to get the hell out of your country as soon as I can."

Snip.

"You don't like Virginia?"

Tug.

One more stitch is a bad memory. "You're with Jarvis and you're Grady's sister, which means you know Crew. I assume you know all there is to know."

Snip.

"I do."

Tug.

"And you've been sent here, to work on me privately, as opposed to my returning to the doctor for a follow-up visit."

Her touch on my belly is gentle and methodical. I had no idea she was a surgical nurse until she announced that fact during lunch. She was sent here to check me over and remove my stitches if she deemed they were ready to bite the dust. I was planning to rip them out myself in the next day or so but how could I argue after she made me pork pie and wined me up? This might be the loveliest thing anyone has done for me since my Pakistani neighbor boy brought me a stack of warm chapati fresh from the skillet.

Who am I kidding? Sleeping up against Cole Carson is mighty lovely, as well. Even if it takes a lot of wine to admit it.

But it doesn't count right now since he's basically holding me hostage in the middle of a forest with his family who hates me.

"Yeah, Jarvis explained how you don't need a trip back into the public right now. It's all good. I'm here for whatever you need, but do me a favor and don't get shot again. I don't exactly have the tools back at the cottage for that."

"Bloody hell. If I go through that again, let me die."

Snip.

"I don't even want to think about that. You didn't answer my question and you seem hellbent to get out of Dodge. Why don't you like it here?"

Tug.

"I can't be here while the intelligence world is looking for me. Even if I wasn't living this nightmare, I'm not ready to give up my work. Cole and I are complicated and became something I never planned. He's lived his exciting career and I still want to live mine."

"How old is Cole?"

"Thirty-five."

She stops and sits up. "And how old are you?"

I open my eyes and focus on her. "Twenty-seven."

She goes back to work on my many stitches.

Snip.

"And you and Cole stayed a thing all that time?" She stops before yanking out another stitch and looks up to me. "Noah filled me in on everything he knows. I hope it's okay to ask you all this. I have three sisters—I'm chatty and nosy by nature. Sorry if I'm crossing the line."

"I have brothers. They're not chatty or nosy. It's fine, Gracie."

She goes back to work on me.

Tug.

"Okay, then. I want to know it all. Start from the beginning and spill, my new British friend." She stops and sits up straight. "Wait. I should get you another glass of wine."

I don't correct her that I'm English. "Only if you'll join me."

She holds up a pair of precision medical scissors in one hand and tweezers in the other. "No can do. I'm working and driving. Plus it's your gift basket from Addy, and after everything you've been through, you deserve every drop of it. Next time."

I put my hand on her arm and give it a squeeze. "Thank you. I grew up with brothers, work in a man's world, and have lived in a country where other women don't know what to think of me. Besides my mum, I've never gotten on with females well. I'm not used to women being kind without wanting anything in return or gossiping about me behind my back."

Her smile is small and I'm afraid it's not a happy one, but rather one that says she pities me. "I'm moving to Virginia. It's all set. Noah and I went to Columbus and cleaned out my apartment."

"I'm happy for you, Gracie."

Her smile turns mischievous. "I'm just saying, I could be your first friend here in the U.S. There's no bullshit when it comes to you. I like that."

"No, I definitely don't bullshit anyone."

Her focus returns to my fresh scar. "And I like to listen to you talk. You sound fancy and there's nothing fancy about me."

"Hmm, if you saw how I live, you'd rethink that."

"Noah told me you tried to kick his ass."

"No, I *would have* kicked his arse had he not been Crew's man. I went easy on him."

She laughs.

"I'm serious, Gracie."

"If you say so. Now, I want to know everything about you and Cole. And why you want to leave."

I look down at her. "I'm afraid I need another favor."

At first I thought she was going to demand I tell her everything in exchange. But instead, without even thinking, she agrees without knowing what she's agreeing to. "Sure. Anything."

"I need a dress."

She looks up again. "A dress?"

"Yes," I confirm and then add, "a formal one—classy, but flashy. I need to be *seen*, Gracie. Shoes, jewelry, and a thin handbag—not smaller than twenty-one centimeters in length and bejeweled like a firecracker. And a wig. The darker the better. I need to look like I've been dipped in money."

Her eyes widen and she doesn't say anything for a few ticks. Finally, her brow puckers and she bites her bottom lip. "Your new best friend only works in inches. I'm going to have to look up what twenty-one centimeters is. I can't remember that from elementary school."

"I'll pay you back," I promise.

She gives her head a tiny shake and finds my hand for a squeeze. "Noah would never allow it. When do you need this getup?"

"By the end of next week. Can you help me?"

She rolls her eyes. "Easy. I can have it by the end of tomorrow."

I exhale, feeling lighter than I have in days, and it has nothing to do with the wine. One less thing to think about. "Thank you."

"Girl, I've got your back."

"Aren't you going to ask what it's for?"

"No, even though I'm nosy as fuck. I'll be your shopper, your nurse, and your wine delivery girl. You had Noah's back and I've got yours—*forever*. No questions asked, no matter how much I want to know."

She goes back to my stitches.

Snip.

Tug.

And she doesn't ask me another thing.

Silence settles over us so heavy, the snip of the scissors scream as they fill the space.

I'm not sure if it's the wine or Gracie Cain or lying in Cole's bed where he's fused himself to me every night yet still hasn't kissed me once. Whatever it is, I'm moved to do something I've never done before.

I share a bit of me.

"Cole was my first."

Gracie stops mid-tug.

"And he's still my only," I add.

She sits up. "Wow."

I nod. "As I said, we're complicated."

"I'll say."

"He has Abbott and she needs a mother-figure. I'm not ready to stop working and I don't do anything I can't give myself to one-hundred percent."

I get a sympathetic smile. "That's understandable. And honorable."

I tell her the truth. "Abbott is smart and beautiful and favors Cole. After meeting her, I'm questioning everything. Now that I'm here, it doesn't feel honorable —it feels selfish."

She sighs and tucks a foot under her where she's perched next to me on the bed. "I don't know everything so I can't offer any advice. But I can say from my own personal experience, there's more than one way to be happy. It took me a long time to learn. Search every road, Bella. And never, ever slam a door. You never know what your future might hold."

"Easier said than done. You're not wanted in over fifteen first-world countries."

Her lips press into a thin line and I think she actually winces. "Ah, yeah. I've got nothing to follow that." *Snip.* "So, tell me. How flashy does this dress need to be?"

"I'm not up for sporting my new scar but the rest of my skin is fair game."

"This is so exciting." She grins and tugs. "There. You're a stitch-free woman. Promise you'll take it easy."

I look down at the ugly pink, puckered keepsake I'll always have.

Complicated doesn't do our situation justice.

"Come on." Gracie takes my hand and helps me up. "Let's get you more wine so you'll tell me the rest of your secrets."

11

CHECKMATE

Cole

"Come on," I demand, pulling her up. Never in my life would I think I'd want to work so hard to get Bella out of my bed once I finally got her in it. "Tonight you're joining the living. I can't take you lying there any longer unless I'm next to you."

"I drank a lot of wine today and I'm exhausted. I've not had a lick of the bottle in months," she complains.

When I got home, Gracie was on her way out. She'd been here most of the day. There was an empty bottle of wine sitting next to a basket big enough to hold basketballs for a bitty ball team. I'm pretty sure a cocktail party had exploded all over my kitchen.

When I get her vertical, I swing her around and sit so she's standing in front of me. "Why do you get to sit? I'm the one recovering from surgery and a bottle of wine."

I reach for the hem of her shirt but she grabs my hand.

"What do you think you're doing?"

I look up. "Gracie cut out your stitches. I want to see your wound since we can't risk taking you for a follow up."

"I'm fine. It itches but all healing wounds do."

"I want to see for myself."

"Gracie said I'm textbook perfection and could start doing whatever I want. She's the medical professional, not you."

I grab her hips and pull her between my legs. "I know for a fact that's a lie since she told me on her way out to make sure you don't overdo it because she had a feeling you already were."

She narrows her eyes. Eyes that are buzzed and sexy as fuck right now. "I know my body and what it can do, Cole."

I run my hands down the sides of her thighs and lower my voice. "Sweetness, I was the one who sat next to you in ICU waiting to see if you were going to live or die. You were doped up but it seems you need a reminder that I was the one talking to the doctors, managing your identity, and making sure no one knew you were here. And as far as your body goes, I'll bet your fat, off-shore bank account I know it better than you."

Her full lips that I've yet to taste again press into a thin line.

"Yeah," I stress. "It was mine first and I'm claiming this body again. You know I'd wrestle you to the floor— I've done it more than once—but that's not in the cards right now. I'm not asking you to spread your legs for me, I want to see your incision."

"Oh, for the love." She rolls her eyes to the ceiling and leaves them there while yanking her shirt up to her tits. "There. Happy?"

When I lower my eyes, her scar is glaring at me—pink, puckered, and angry as an aggravated snake. I saw it when it was fresh and new, before she was alert enough to be annoyed by my presence in the hospital. The swelling is down and her sweatpants hang low on her hips. She's always had lean, cut muscles but this is different. She's too thin and too weak—not the force I crashed and burned for years ago.

And I fucking hate it.

When I brush my thumb over the irate wound that has disfigured the one person in this world I can't shake, her tone hits me hard. "Scarred, marred, and ugly, I know."

When I look up, her blues are as sharp and cold as deep-frozen crystals, cutting through the short distance to mine.

"Scarred and marred, yes," I agree and can't stop my fingers from biting into her boney hips. "But never ugly."

She throws her hand toward me before motioning to the topic at hand. "Opinion versus fact, *Carson*."

Sliding my hand up her midsection between her tits, I press my touch into her chest over her heart. Splaying my fingers, it beats into my palm. "This isn't ugly. This is beautiful. It means you're alive and here with me, where you belong."

Her glare follows as I stand and my hand moves farther north, my thumb landing on her jugular. She doesn't flinch, she's as controlled and tempered as ever on the outside, but her pulse races like it's on the home stretch of a marathon.

She's tall but I still tower over her as she stands barefoot in front of me. Pulling our bodies flush, her cutting eyes narrow when I drop my hand to her ass. My dick betrays me—the bastard—twitching as his only magnet in this world wakes him.

I press into her neck and tip her face to mine. "Don't be critical about your body, *Donnelly*. Not to me. You know how I feel about it and you."

She shakes her head and pushes my hand away but I hold her close because my dick might kick my ass if I let her go. "I'm not the naïve woman I once was—overtaken by your charmless self. Our attraction was purely fueled by adrenaline and our jobs. It's time to get over yourself."

I shake my head and *tsk* her. "Lies. You can spew them to everyone else on the planet but not to me."

"I only speak the truth." Her tone is cutting.

I hitch a shoulder and my smile has nothing to do with pleasure of any sort, no matter how much I'd kill for some pleasure right now, especially the kind only Isabella Donnelly can give.

No.

My smile is as cutting as her tone and has *checkmate* written all over it. "I've had a day, baby. But I got you into the fucking Everglades bullshit."

Her tone softens, ironically hardening my dick further. "You did?"

I might do it lightly because of her wound, but I press my cock into her lower stomach. "You're questioning my skills?"

She brings her hands up to my chest and tries to

push, but my dick is more determined than the both of us and refuses to be torn away from its one true obsession. "Of course not. But that was fast."

"Not only did I come through but I scored two tickets. You've got yourself a date."

Back to cutting she goes. "No."

"Yes. And I'm holding your fucking ticket hostage. I'll give it to you but you have to meet certain guidelines."

Her fingers fist my shirt in a way I bet she wishes it were my flesh. "Why must everything be a negotiation? This is important to me and yet you insist on acting like a rotten arse."

"As poignant a picture as that paints, it's not me being the smelly ass, it's my father. I took him to the shed for a talk as soon as I got home tonight and that talk was a one-way street. In fact, it was more of a tongue lashing for how he's treated you. He knows where I stand and how far I'm willing to fight him on this, which is to the fucking edge of the earth, baby. Which is also why—since I hold your very literal golden ticket—there will be rules in this house or else the damn Everglades will have to struggle on without any love from you."

Bella doesn't blush. Blushing is for skittish school girls. But when she's not undercover and it's just her and me, her anger shows like a branding iron.

Case in point, her fair skin reddening to flames right before my eyes. "Spit out your fucking rules, Cole. When you're finished, I'll kick rubbish on your grave right after I stick a pitchfork in it with a sign attached, reading *Here Lies a Selfish Cock.*"

My smile splits my face. "Baby, you give new

meaning to bitchy-proper speak. *Selfish Cock* isn't even one of your British-isms."

"I'm livid," she bites. "You know you have me squeezed. I've no options and, yet, you take advantage. Spit out these rules before I bust open my fresh wound whilst kneeing you in the balls."

I pause and wet my lips. "You know that turns me on."

"You know I don't give an English fuck. Not even an Uncle Sam fuck. Nor a flying one over the pond between the two."

"Damn." I pull her to me tighter. "You're making my boys blue."

She tips her head. "I hope they turn celestial and fall off."

"It's going to be a long month but you'll come around," I mutter.

"Never. Now spill these so-called rules so my life can be even more miserable than it already is."

"Fine." I nod and think. I hadn't planned on putting parameters on taking her to the damn fundraiser, which is a cover for her to get close to the senator from hell. "One—no more lying in bed and no more holing yourself away in my room."

She shakes her head. "I know where I'm welcome and where I'm not. I'm used to hiding."

"You're not in the Middle East and my room is not a cave. Consider yourself done hiding out. You're here and that means you're going to be present. We're gonna be one big, happy fucking family if it kills me."

She rolls her eyes. "It'll kill someone, that's for certain."

I ignore her because I'm over **anyone** dying right now. "Two—I want you to spend **time** with Abbs every morning to teach her French. Consider it earning your keep."

This time her eyes widen and **all the** fire leaves her face. "Abbott wants nothing to do **with** me. I will not force time with her."

I dip my face to hers. "She won't throw a fit if I tell her it's happening. Despite the **dumbass** who gave birth to her, she's smart, Bella. *Gifted.* Her **brain** is hungry and it doesn't matter what I introduce **her to,** she eats it up like I haven't fed her in days."

"Then why don't you teach her?"

"As you can see, my time at home **is** limited."

"I can attest to the fact if a **child** is not open to learning something new, it can be **detrim**ental to shove it down their teeny, tiny throats. I **was that** child, Cole."

I nod. "I'm not surprised but if I tell her this is happening, she'll do it because she **doesn't** like to disappoint me. And it's a way for you two **to get** to know each other with a purpose."

"And what will happen in a **few** weeks when I'm gone? I highly doubt Red will be **able to** carry on with French lessons."

"I refuse to talk about you leaving. I have three-and-a-half weeks to convince you to stay."

She sighs. "Anything else?"

"Yeah. Two more things. Quit **rolling** away from me at night. My dick and I have missed **you.**"

"Still, you talk about your **penis** as a separate being?"

"As you can tell," I press into her **again,** "it is."

She shakes her head.

"Admit it," I demand. "You miss him as much as he's missed you."

"Cole—"

"He misses everything about you—your mouth, the curve of your ass, your tits—"

"—would you stop—"

"—and especially your pussy, which is really mine and always will be."

"As crude as ever."

"Crude as fuck," I amend. "Admit it, you liked it before and secretly still do."

"Please, when you're done thinking with your cock, do me the honor of telling me the final rule so I can focus on clearing my name to live freely again."

I let her go and she steps away immediately. I rearrange the cock she secretly loves so my hard on is less painful than had she really kneed me in the nuts. "Three—I reserve the right to add more rules. I have full faith you'll come around eventually, but right now you're a pain in my ass. And not in a good way."

I grab her hand to physically remove her from my bedroom. She tries to pull away—but I'm determined.

I look back one more time and give her a nod. "Trust me, Red is nothing compared to the terrorists I've seen you take down. I'll explain to Abbott about the French lessons. Everyone will get used to everyone soon enough. Consider this me ripping off the duct tape."

We cross the threshold of her prior sanctuary to jump into the proverbial fire of the Carson clan. "It's always duct tape with you, Cole. To any other man, it would just be a measly bandage."

I don't look back as I give her the God's-honest truth. "Any other man wouldn't be able to handle you."

Hell, who am I kidding?

I don't have a handle on her yet.

12

I LOOK FUCKING GOOD IN A TUX

Cole

"I thought I told you it was a priority," Nick Peterson growls through the phone. "Do I need to explain to you what that means? Why are plans not put into motion already, or better yet, carried out?"

It's been a week since my boss marched his ass into my office and demanded I set up a kill order.

On an American.

A fucking American.

Not only that, the target is a military vet. He's also a businessman based out of Geneva and works with multiple countries fulfilling military contracts for armored gear and weapons. Over the past seven days, I've learned everything I need to know about retired Marine Sergeant Penn Simmons, down to the fact he has three cats named after Shakespearean villains: Claudius, Lady Macbeth, and Edmund.

I have no room to judge. I'm now the proud owner of

my own feline named Daisy. It also seems I'm the only human in the house who Daisy doesn't like, given the fact she hisses at me every time I get near her.

From what I can tell, Penn Simmons' cats are the only villainous thing about the man. After landing a high-paying gig in Switzerland, he appears to be a family man living out the dream of working in the worldwide center for diplomacy. He has contacts throughout the United Nations and donated a big chunk to the Red Cross last year. He spends his winters skiing the Alps and summers sailing the waters of Lake Geneva.

Besides his sailboat named The Tillie, after his wife, he's downright as boring as a two-by-four. His wife, who works as an instructor teaching English to French-speaking students, is equally as mind numbing.

Penn is not exactly the kind of person we usually target—as in never-fucking-ever. And especially not since I've been put in charge of managing covert assets —people we pay to do our dirty work, like Vega and those he trains.

"Turn."

I look down from where I'm standing on the short pedestal and face the mirror. The tailor at my feet pins the hem of the tux trousers I plan on wearing while supporting the damn Everglades.

He looks up at me and raises his brows in question. I inspect the break in my pants before giving him a nod and return to my call. "Nick, the plan has been put into motion."

That's a lie. I might've put a plan in motion, but it's mine—not his. One thing is for sure, no one is on their way to Switzerland to put a bullet through Penn

Simmons' head. On the contrary, Asa has tapped my bosses line. The last few days have been interesting.

Nick is on the move, at a quick clip, going who knows where and doing who knows what, huffing and puffing all the way. I take that back—Asa probably knows since he's tracking his cell, so there's no reason for me to ask. It's not as if I can judge, it's the middle of a work day and I snuck out to be fitted for a tux I'm oddly anxious to wear.

"Then explain to me why the target attended a meeting this morning with his contact from the British Armed Forces? Usually when shit is carried out and business is taken care of in a timely manner, those people tend to miss meetings—for the rest of eternity."

I fasten the single button of my jacket and turn to the side to inspect myself as I listen to him become more and more frantic, which is the most interesting thing that's happened today.

Also fascinating is the fact my boss's tension only makes me calmer. "Nick, you and I have been at this for some time now. Without elaborating since I'm not alone, you know these things don't happen overnight."

"It's been a week," he bites.

"And you said to make it a priority, which I have. You didn't give me a deadline."

"You should have assumed the deadline was as-soon-as-fucking-possible when I told you to make it a priority. Now I've got people breathing down my neck while you're trying to get your shit together."

The tailor at my feet stands and takes a step back. "How does it look, sir? You chose wisely—simple, traditional, timeless. This will carry you through for years."

I take one more look in the mirror and remember

the last time I wore a tux. It didn't make it back to the States. But I don't see the six-foot-four CIA officer whose shoulders and chest fit surprisingly well into this custom fit.

I see the man who broke in a certain MI6 in more ways than he had a right to.

If I had to do it all over again, I would.

And I plan to, even though my final conquest of Isabella Donnelly will no doubt be my hardest. Training her and making her mine feels like a walk in the park compared to getting her to stay.

Making good on our deal and marrying me—sealing her fate to mine.

Forever.

One thing I've got going for me, I look fucking good in a tux. I'll look even better with Bella by my side.

I take my cell, hold it flat against my chest, and look at the tailor through the mirror. "It's perfect. Can you have it ready by Friday?"

He nods and moves behind me to slip the pin-filled jacket down my arms. "You paid the rushed fee. It'll be ready."

"Perfect." I put the phone back to my ear as I step into the dressing room. "Nick, I have my shit together but from the sound of it, you may not. We both know the work I coordinate cannot be rushed. And as far as having someone breathing down your neck? Well, I've learned how to work through it. So can you. From my experience, I suggest you smile, choke down that pride of yours, and move on. There are some things in life that are out of our control."

"Damn you, Carson. If you can't get this done, I'll do it myself."

"You know you couldn't get it done even if you wanted to." I unbutton my trousers. "I've spent years gaining the trust of my contractors and they are not going to rush a job for any deadline. They have more money than most people have sense and could stop working yesterday to live fat, dumb, and happy. Be patient."

"I'll write you up for insubordination faster than you can blink," he threatens.

He has no leg to stand on and he knows it. What, is he going to put a letter in my file stating I'm dragging my feet on carrying out an order to kill an American veteran? "Do it and we'll see what happens."

"Don't push me, Carson."

"I'm not pushing anyone. I'm doing my job, Nick, and I'm killing it as far as I can see. No pun intended."

"Dammit." His exhale hisses through the phone with sounds of honking and traffic acting as his backup band. "I'll hold them off as long as I can. There had better be progress in the next two days."

"Do what you've got to do. See you when you get back from wherever you are." I hang up, exit the dressing room, take the paperwork from the tailor, and head out.

The big event is Saturday night, which is also the two-week mark of Bella living under my roof. Not going to lie, when I threw down the one-month gauntlet with Bella, I thought I'd be farther along by now. Good news is, things have gotten to the point where she, Red, and Abbott coexist with little angst while I'm at work.

I know she's still recovering, but hell, we haven't done any more than sleep pressed against each other at night. I told her I'm not kissing her until she wants it and she's holding out on me—white-knuckling her convictions like a devout nun would her vow.

My other phone rings and I answer it immediately. "Asa. What's up?"

He laughs. "You sure can wind up your boss."

"You enjoyed that, huh? He's a tool. What else do you have for me? Who's pressuring him?"

"I've listened in on every call since we got his personal cell tapped. What do you know about his direct-line supervisor?"

I walk to the end of the block and wait for the light to change. "Not a lot, she came from the field. Her name is Wendy Sisson and she was promoted a while ago. She doesn't mingle with case officers. I'm too busy to keep tabs on one more person right now."

"Since I usually rely on you to pull files for me, I had to get creative. I did some digging, found a copy of her application to the Agency two decades ago. She was hired right out of college as an analyst and pretty boring until recently. I had to dig even deeper."

I throw on my aviators as I cross the street to my car. "I don't want to know who you're getting your information from. Please keep me out of it so if this goes to shit I can answer honestly on a polygraph."

"I wouldn't give up my source anyway, but you've got it. About four years ago she started attending a new ... shit, I don't even know what to call it. On the outside it looks like a church but once I learned more, it's fucked up."

I beep my locks and climb in my truck. "Fucked up how?"

"Fucked up, as in it's no church, fucked up."

"No shit?" I turn the key and flip the AC to high. The humidity is a bitch today.

"Yes shit. And this *church* does not operate on its own. This, I'm still looking into. Grady's helping me. We think their funding is coming from a bigger source. They operate on about fifty acres west of our camp. Ozzy has taken the lead on this—he's also a licensed drone pilot. We're trying to get an aerial view."

"This is not what I expected."

"Us either. Sisson is so far up Peterson's ass about this assignment, she's got him shaking in his loafers. We're working on the connection between Sisson and the veteran they want dead. But Peterson is having no problem throwing you under the bus because it hasn't happened yet."

"Why am I not surprised?" I mutter.

"You shouldn't be, you work for the asshole. But Crew isn't going to take an assignment on an American, much less one he can't prove is doing anything wrong. He's pissed and wants to get to the bottom of it now that we're all investigators. Let me tell you, this is time consuming as hell."

"I appreciate it since I can only do so much without anyone noticing. And there's the fact I'm already buried."

"Crew would've done anything for Bella before she stepped in and saved the day with Jarvis. Now there are no boundaries he won't cross."

I sigh. "Then he needs to do me a solid and quit contracting with her. I'm doing everything I can to keep her here. She doesn't need to be in the middle of a fucking warzone to do what she does best."

"Talk to Crew."

I back out of my spot and head to Langley. "I have. And I will again. I need him to have my back on this."

"Crew has Bella's back. He won't go against what she wants. She's too good and integral to his work. He respects her and my guess is you will not be a part of that conversation."

"Right," I seethe into the phone. "I appreciate you digging."

"I'm all for pushing boundaries. Talk soon."

I hang up and veer onto the highway. I've never thought twice about Wendy Sisson. I don't know what she's up to but she doesn't know me. I do not fulfill kill orders that aren't vetted and I don't take blind directives from my superiors. I'd rather ask for forgiveness later than live with something on my conscience that can't be undone.

My phone lights up again. Fuck me, I feel like a Super Bowl champion quarterback, I'm so popular today.

I answer on Bluetooth. "Ollie, my main man. Tell me you found the Donnelly brothers. I need some good news."

"Carson!" he belts over background noise. "I miss the sound of your voice, my luscious fella. Why don't we talk every day?"

"Because I have a life."

"Huh?!" His voice booms through the cab of my truck. "I can't hear ya."

I yell back. "Yes. We should talk daily."

"That's what I'm talkin' about. Ya do love me!"

"Ollie. What do you have for me?"

"I'm at the pub so I can't say much. But you'll be

getting a call from a certain brother sooner than later. How much do ya love me now?"

I take a big breath because it's finally time the ball falls in my court. I need something to go right for a change. "I love you, Ollie."

"Pinch me in the knickers, I knew it!" He angles the phone away but I can still hear every word. "Hey, love, I need another pint. Bless ya. Okay, I'm back. Listen, I've been watchin' Dr. Phil. If you need my help or advice or simply a good rubdown to release some tension, I'm here for ya. I'm afraid ya could end up with some family drama made only for the telly."

"I appreciate the offer, but I'm good." I keep yelling into my cab. "And I appreciate you getting me in touch. I owe you."

For a second, I only hear the party in the background. Then Ollie finally comes to life. "Carson owes Ollie? Fuck! I need to figure out how I want you to pay this debt. I could use a good American handjob right about now. Why do we have an entire bloody ocean between us? I feel like the universe is plotting against us, Carson."

"It definitely is." I silently thank the continental drift for the ocean between Ollie and me. "Like I said, I owe you. Have a good time, man."

"Love ya right back! I wish I could kiss ya!"

I hang up. If Bella weren't at my house right now with my father and daughter, I'd turn the damn phone off. A few moments of silence would be a gift but I don't want to tempt the gods.

Shoes will start dropping eventually and I need to be able to juggle those suckers. Not one of them will touch the ground if I have anything to do with it.

When I open the door, the murmur of voices hit me in the chest. It comes out of nowhere, like a falling anvil in a bad cartoon.

I don't slam the door like I do every night when I return home from work, announcing my presence for all those who want to welcome me home to my crumbling castle. Easy on my steps because a mouse could make my floorboards creak, I make my way down the hall but don't round the corner.

I need to see this with my own eyes.

An English accent mingles with a child's, both counting in unison.

In French.

I peek around the corner and Abbott is sitting with her back to me, looking up at Bella who is laser focused on my daughter.

Bella smiles when she gets to ninety-nine and points to Abbott to let her finish.

Nothing.

And then, finally, Abbott remembers. "*Cent*."

"Very good!" Bella beams. She fucking beams at my daughter. "I'm so proud, Abbott!"

I can't see her face but it doesn't surprise me my daughter doesn't share in her celebration. Instead, Abbott's little shoulder rises once.

I exhale.

Abbott isn't exactly throwing herself at Bella, but I'll take it.

"Let's go over the months and days of the week. When your father gets home, you can show off your new skills!"

"Okay, those are easy."

"Well, then. You're a pro, aren't you? How would you like to move on to food? I can teach you how to ask your grandpa to make you bangers in French."

"What're bangers?"

"Hot dogs or sausages. It's what we call them in England."

I suck in a breath when Abbott's tone changes— lighter than it's been in days. "That's so weird."

Bella's blue eyes go big when she grins. "No, it's weird that you Americans name them after poor, little pooches. Hot dogs? What is that? A puppy on fire?"

Abbott giggles. It's short lived, but I hang on to it like a desperate man.

And then a grunt.

My eyes shift across the family room. Red is hiding out, like me, watching his granddaughter and the woman I've been trying to tie down for years. Arms crossed over his gut, his dark eyes are intense as he takes in the same sight I am. He sees what I do.

And he lifts his chin once before turning to disappear into the laundry room.

Baby steps. Everyone in this house is fucking killing me, but we'll get there.

13

RULES

Bella

R ules.

So bloody many of them.

Time under his roof has clicked by at a slow, painful pace reserved only for waterboarding or torture chambers during medieval times.

I have spent hours with Cole's standoffish, yet equally brilliant, child. The girl is like the desert-cracked earth during a rare rainy day—it doesn't matter how much I present to her, she soaks it up and turns around for more.

I know what Cole is trying to do, forcing time together on me and his daughter. It's what he's wanted for years—to integrate me into his private life outside of spies, liars, secrets, and hidden agendas. This life, the one here in Virginia, where Cole Carson is a father and so protective of his child, he's not willing for anyone to care for her other than her grandfather.

If I had allowed Cole's family to infiltrate my heart

the way I would a terrorist cell, my defenses would shatter. It's why I refused so many times. Why I said *no* to every request, every plea, and every proposal.

Because Abbott Carson is about as perfect as miniature humans come. I assume, anyway. Not that I've had the privilege of knowing many beyond smiling at them and offering an afghani here and there, in hopes of bringing a light to their little lives.

Okay, so she's perfect aside from not wanting me in her home. But who can blame the girl?

Not me. I feel as sorry for her as I do for myself. Cole is holding us both hostage in his picture-perfect American dream, more determined than ever to make it a syrupy-sweet reality.

It's clear Abbott wants none of it or me—even if she can count to one hundred in French and has moved beyond basic words to colors and foods. The way she can separate her indignation for me while learning a new language is proof enough she has Cole's blood running through her veins. Her father was always able to separate his desires, frustrations, or displeasures from any assignment he was given.

Speak of the devilish man himself, his voice booms at me through the thin walls. "Get a move on, sweetness. It's gonna take us over an hour to get to the Kennedy Center in Saturday traffic."

I smooth the inky locks framing my face before sliding my hands down my breasts to adjust the dress. I've lost weight and that has unfortunately affected my cleavage, even though I never had much to begin with.

Gracie worked her personal-shopper magic and did what I needed her to do. I might not prefer red normally, but in this case, it's perfect. Unlike the last few years where I've had to hide and **blend** into the rocky landscape to keep from being **burned** at the stake, tonight I need to stand out. I **want the** attention of everyone in that room if that's what it takes.

My neckline plunges deeply and a slit spikes up my leg, both to dangerously sexy levels. I said I wanted to show some skin, and this gown shows a lot while still hiding my scar. The halter clasps **behind** my neck and I'm bare to the small of my back.

From the black wig that kisses **my** shoulder blades to the fire of my dress, they're **both a** stark contrast against my fair skin. I finish painting **my** lips ruby and take a look at myself in the mirror.

My gut twists a tinge and has **nothing** to do with my itchy, healing scar or insides which **surely** aren't up to snuff yet.

My mind wanders and I'm **brought** back to another time and another world. When I **was new** and nervous —but only inwardly so. I never all**owed any**one to know that about me. Not even when I **was th**rown into the caldron with the arsehole American **by** my side who had no desire to indoctrinate me **on how** to cross the street, let alone to the ways of work**ing under**cover.

Cole Carson owns so many of **my firsts**. Sometimes I love it, and others, moments such **as this** one, it may as well be a slash through my heart. **Everyth**ing important to me will always be tied to him.

Knotted and tangled.

Tight.

Like a noose.

"Baby, did you hear me?"

I look up from the stranger **I'm staring** at in the mirror who doesn't even have my **eyes**, thanks to the dark brown contacts I asked Gracie to get me at the last minute. When my imposter browns meet his authentic ones through the mirror, the air in the room grows thick.

I should have known when Cole insisted on butting his way into my plans he would play his role perfectly. As *extra* as I am right now, he's utterly simple—if a man as beautiful as him could ever be referred to as basic. His raven tux is classic with straight lines, fitting his strapping frame like a second skin. His crisp white shirt has yet to be buttoned at the neck, and the black tie I know for a fact he can whip into a bow with his eyes closed, hangs loose and uneven around his neck.

"Feels like I've been thrown back in time." He snaps the silence in two, like a cracker on Boxing Day. His eyes drop to my arse before popping back up to mine in the mirror. "But I don't remember your ass hanging out during our first operation."

My red lips thin and I snatch the silk clutch sitting in front of me and spin on my Louboutin heel, because Gracie does not fuck around when it comes to shopping. "I'm ready."

Now he gets a look at the deep V, taped to my shrunken breasts and below so it won't budge. "You really think now is the time to attract the attention of the western hemisphere?"

"I know whose attention I need. From my research, he's a womanizing, misogynistic pile of cow shit." I lift my naked shoulder and tip my wigged head. "I'll be hand feeding him poisonous grapes in no time."

He stands rigid and his body goes wired. "You told me you wanted to get close to him, not shimmy up to him to make half his dreams come true."

I round the foot of his bed. "Darling, you sound jealous, and quite frankly, you look horrendous in green." When we're toe to toe, I slide my hand down his lapel and tip my head back an inch since my heels bring us close, just like our days on the job. "I do like you in black, though. It matches my soul."

He lifts a hand and it lands hot and heavy on the bare skin above my ass. He presses in before it slides south, where he cups my cheek and squeezes. "Don't fuck around tonight. I mean it. I'm working another angle to clear your name and am making headway. This is not the time to dance close to the flames."

"I've never been burned and you know it."

"Then explain to me why you're hiding out in my rundown farmhouse in the middle of the forest. You've been burned so bad, I'm surprised you don't leave a trail of ashes with every step you take."

I narrow my eyes. "My being framed doesn't count. And why didn't you tell me you're working another angle? Don't you think that could've been a topic of conversation at your tense dinner table?"

He shakes his head. "You're working this alone. I'm working mine alone."

"I'm hardly working alone, hence you standing here in a tux with your hand down my dress, cupping my bum."

He squeezes me tighter and his eyes crinkle. "Despite the fact you're in my bed, you haven't told me shit about tonight. I'm here to make sure you stay in my bed. Consider me your chaperone."

"I'm not a baby. I don't need a daddy figure watching over me."

His smile spreads from his eyes to his lush lips. "I could get into some **Daddy** kink."

I roll my eyes. "**We're** late, Cole. You said so yourself. I need to get there early enough to socialize and dump enough money to get noticed."

He slides his hand out of my dress and tips his head. "Long live the Everglades."

I push away from his hold and stalk past him on spiked heels. "Indeed."

When I turn out of the bedroom, I hear male voices —many of them—discussing what sounds to be American sport. I come to a stop when I see Jarvis and Crew standing in the middle of Cole's family room with Red.

"What happened to your hair?"

I look to my left where Abbott is sitting on a barstool eating cheesy noodles with her little face twisted into a frown. Had I not just inspected myself in the mirror, I'd be worried I looked like the scariest clown who strolled the earth only to terrorize small children.

"It's a wig," I explain without offering any reason for it. "What color is my hair in French?"

Her face blanks and I'm all of a sudden grateful Cole doesn't have a teenager. She turns back to her noodles but answers correctly. "Noir."

"Bravo!" I turn to our guests. "Jarvis, Crew. Good to see you. What are you doing here?"

All three men take me in from top to toe before Crew steps forward with a shit-eating grin on his face. "I hope you feel as good as you look because you certainly look better than the last time I saw you lying on the banks of the Chesapeake."

I shrug and reach up to twist my fake hair around

my manicured finger. "Thank you. I am feeling so much better. How are the baby and Addy?"

His face lights up, and if dark eyes could twinkle, his might. "Perfect. Amieé will be a month next week. Hard to believe. And nothing agrees more with Addison than motherhood. We need to get you over to Whitetail soon. It's closed on Mondays—you can have a private tasting. Addison will set it up."

Warmth settles on the bare skin of my back and Cole's words brush my temple. "Thanks. Now that she's feeling better, I want to get Bella out. If we can do it privately until we get this sorted, even better."

"Gracie would be up for that," Jarvis pipes in. "She and I are living on the vineyard right now and she's really taken to you."

I flip my hand, motioning to myself. "I adore Gracie. When she's not busy keeping me from bleeding out, she's playing my personal shopper. Not sure what I'd do without her while being held hostage."

My lower hip is suddenly in a vise and Cole grits, "You're hardly being held hostage."

I hike a brow and glare at him over my shoulder. "Says the man who dragged me here against my will."

"I can see things are going great," Crew states. "Here. I have what you asked for."

I reach for the small velvet bag he's holding out and frown. "I didn't ask for anything."

"I did." Cole reaches around me, snatches the bag, and turns me to him. "I might be your eyes, but if you think I'm going to let you waltz in there on your own without ears, you lost brain cells along with all that blood."

He yanks the bag open and produces a handful of gold.

Jarvis steps forward. "Not only ears but this will record everything. You get the shady Senator to talk, we'll have record of it."

I look down as Cole clasps a gold cuff around my wrist followed by a choker with a gemstone set in the middle that matches my wig. "I couldn't exactly set you up with equipment from work without anyone asking me a million questions. Sucks to not be in the field anymore so Crew took care of it."

"We tested it before we got here—you're good to go." Jarvis tosses a set of keys to Cole. "Here. You want to look like you're exhaling money, you need to act the part. No offense to your truck."

"None taken." Cole swings the keys around his finger and looks at me. His eyes are sharp and his stare cuts through me like the blade I have tucked in the lining of my clutch.

Abbott hops down from her barstool and runs to her father. "Daddy, when will you be back?"

Cole tosses her up into his arms and kisses her cheek. "It'll be late and you'll be asleep. But tomorrow is Sunday and you know what that means."

Abbott's face lights up. "Donuts!"

"Have fun with your grandpa. Love you."

She wraps her little arms around Cole's neck, making him seem larger than life. "Love you, too, Daddy."

He puts her down and I might as well not be here because she doesn't spare me a glance.

But Cole does.

He extends his hand for me, not unlike an olive branch. "Like old times. Let's do this."

And that, right there, shouldn't excite me. It shouldn't settle low in my belly or make my lacy, hardly-there thong wet. And it definitely shouldn't make my nipples so hard, I'm suddenly overly grateful Gracie thought of everything and added petal stickers so I didn't nip out.

Working alongside Cole Carson again ... well, it does all that.

And that scares me.

It also excites me.

And *that* scares me more than anything.

14

EXONERATION

Bella

"I hope there's room in your big head to remember I've managed plenty long without you. An arsehole Senator is nothing compared to the roads I've navigated."

"I know," he states coolly. He might as well be a commercial for the most expensive cologne, or maybe bourbon, as he speeds Jarvis's shiny black Porsche across the bridge over the Potomac, the Washington Monument coming into view as the sun sets. "You didn't get yourself into a pinch until you stepped foot onto American soil. No one knows better than me that you're more than capable of handling any situation on your own."

"Then why have you insisted on squeezing your way into my overtly simple and straightforward op?"

His big paw lands high on my thigh bared through the slit of my dress causing it to inch higher. "How many reasons do you want?"

I place my hand on his to keep it out of the danger-ous-to-my-insides territory. My focus needs to be sharp and I don't need to worry about what Cole's touch is doing to me. "I don't know, I'd ask for your top-ten countdown but we're almost there. I'll settle for three."

He throws me a glance before exiting the highway. "I know you're better but you're not up to taking down armies on your own yet and you know it. I watched you outside yesterday and saw you trying to jog. I know you're still hurting and I can't let you go in there by yourself when you're not one hundred percent."

I let out a breath and shift to watch the cars zip by as he waits to turn left. I had no idea he saw. Had I known, I would have pushed through, no matter the pain—and hell, the pain was bad.

He doesn't stop talking. "I've also looked into Randolph and I get why we're here. I had to dig, but I found the connection you're chasing."

My eyes widen and turn back to him. "You did?"

He lets off the brake when he gets an arrow to turn. "I did. I've got to admit, you're swinging for the fences on this one, but if you're right—"

"I'm right," I interrupt.

"Like I said, *if* you're right, then this is going to turn into the biggest spectacle our country has seen in years. The Iran-Contra affair is going to look like an Easter egg hunt in comparison."

"I agree. This is only the tip of the iceberg, Cole. I'm nowhere close to finding out who framed me, but this is the trail. It's hot—I can feel it."

His fingers press into my skin. "Baby, you talking about the *tip* and *hot* and *feeling it* while you're dressed for the hottest sex of the decade is going to do me in."

"Cole."

He pulls up to the Kennedy Center. Cars are lined—some dripping in luxury and others stretching around the block—dropping off socialites and movers and shakers of DC, no matter how sleezy or backstabbing they might be.

Coming to a stop, he moves his hand from my thigh to entwine his fingers through mine. Bringing my hand to his mouth, he does what he said he wouldn't do until I begged for it—press his lips to the top of my fingers.

A kiss.

Not the one I've put off or the one I've secretly dreamed of, but a kiss all the same. He's taken my hand plenty since this entire nightmare began, but not like this. He's kept to his word and has held out on me.

My breath catches. Like I always am when it's just us, I'm too transparent for my liking and his name tastes much differently on my tongue this time. "*Cole.*"

"Missed this," he murmurs before catching my gaze in his killer trap. "Missed you. I miss the job, the excitement, but most of all, I miss it *with* you. When it was you and me ... I was at my best. I'd like to think you were too."

I swallow over the lump in my throat. "You taught me well."

He takes my hand and I have to lean on the console to steady myself. He presses it against his cock—hard and long in his trousers—as he brushes the tip of his nose alongside mine. "I'd like to think I taught you a lot of things."

Damn him for turning me on right here and right now. "If you're considering laying a finger on me before I have to search out Randolph, you'd better think twice,

Cole Carson. I do not need to be recovering from an orgasm before I walk in there."

His hand finds my thigh again and slides danger-ously close to Ground Zero. His smile says it all before the words fall from his lips. "We've done it before. I think it made you oddly more focused than your normal razor-sharp alertness."

I give his erection a good squeeze in warning as I stop his hand from hitting its target—no matter how much my body fights my brain. It's been so long since I've touched him. The feel of him and the thought of us whip into a weird little tango through my chest. "Don't you dare."

He tips his head in challenge. Or maybe it was because of my grip.

So, I might have squeezed his balls a bit harder than necessary. What can I say? This moment is extraordinary.

He leans in and nips at my earlobe. "I see you haven't forgotten a thing. Been a long time, sweetness, don't think I won't call this whole thing off and drive you to a back alley to fuck your brains out right here in the driver's seat. I promised not to kiss you 'til you begged for it. Fucking you is a whole different beast and something I can't wait to do."

He presses into my hand before I rip it away and do the same to his, plastered to the inside of my thigh. "Not happening."

"Baby, it's not a matter of *if*, it's a matter of *when*. And you in that dress all night? The when is going to happen a lot sooner than it would've otherwise. My Bella Clock is a ticking time bomb."

A horn blares from behind us and we shift away

from each other. The line of luxury vehicles cleared while we were stuck in our own sex-charged world and it seems others aren't in the mood for patience. Cole puts it in drive and pulls up to the curb where we agreed he would drop me before parking Jarvis's car.

I reach for the door handle but he grabs my arm first. When I turn to him, an erotic smile sits on his face. "I know it'll be hard since all you're thinking about is my face buried between your legs, but be careful and stay focused."

The man is exasperating. "That's not what I was thinking about."

He gives me a lazy shrug. "Right. But you are now, so focus."

"Unbelievable."

"I'll be minutes behind you. You'll have my eyes all night."

I know I will. Cole has never let me down.

With my heavily-jeweled clutch in my hand, I climb out of the sports car with my fake ID and single ticket to the gala.

As I slam the door shut, I realize I haven't felt this alive in years.

I'm not sure if it's recovering from a deadly gunshot wound, working my own case again, or having Cole at my back.

There's no time to contemplate. I have a Senator to hit on.

Cole

As I jog up the stairs to the Kennedy Center, my phone vibrates. I frown and pull it out of my pocket because she's only been out of my eyesight for minutes.

It's been a long time since we've worked together and I didn't lie—I know she can handle her shit. She's more capable than most operatives I've worked with, but seeing her on the brink of death has brought out a side of me I didn't know I had. Not with her anyway. Not with anyone really, other than maybe Abbott, but that's different.

I never thought about being a father. Hell, I never thought about settling down before I realized living a life without Bella was downright painful. I'm not proud to admit this, but Abbott was never in my plan.

It would take a much bigger asshole than myself to look down at the six-pound, seven-ounce pink bundle and not have your world shift on its axis in a way you'll never find your equilibrium again. Even before the paternity test came back, I knew she was mine. Not only does she have my eyes and coloring, there was something about her. I knew it from the first moment she was born.

And I never question my gut instincts. Ever.

I'm beyond protective of my daughter and that includes keeping her far away from Tabitha. Just because I made mistakes doesn't mean I'm going to subject Abbott to a lifetime of drama at the hands of her poor excuse of a mother.

With Bella, it's the same but different. Protective isn't the right word. Sure, everyone can use someone at their six, even if they are as capable as her.

But from the first time I laid a heavy hand so low on her back it was practically her ass, it started and never stopped. As much as we fought, butted heads, or disagreed on how to get from A to D, the pull only became stronger.

I exhale when I unlock my phone and find a text.

Jarvis – I don't give a shit how long you two have been apart or how bad you need to get your rocks off. This is a warning—if you have sex in my Porsche, I will sniper your ass so fast, you won't know what hit you.

I ignore him because something catches my eye. Something in red.

She's been stopped at security.

Fuck.

My phone keeps vibrating but I don't take my eyes off her. She's been moved to the side and feigning confusion. The female guard pulls out a wand and swipes it up and down, front and back, left to right.

Nothing.

She opens her purse and I hold my breath.

Bella pulls out a compact, lipstick, credit card, a stack of bills, and her cell.

Finally, the guard nods and Bella smiles, motioning to her long skinny purse with more fake jewels glued to it than on a hooker standing on the scariest corner of the District.

I let out a stale breath.

Of course, even with me at her back, she wouldn't go in unarmed. She didn't tell me, which pisses me off, but I'd bet my old farmhouse she's not packing a gun.

Damn you, Bella.

I unlock my phone.

Jarvis – On second thought, forget the bullet. I'll tie you up and torture you for days if there are any bodily fluids spilled in my car.

Asa – Your woman has been stopped by security.

Jarvis – Is Bella packing?

Jarvis – Can't lie. Her changing her accent to a plain-Jane American is equally impressive and freaks me out at the same time. I'm not used to this shit.

Asa – She talked her way out of it. You're good to go.

Jarvis – What's it like to sleep with someone who's such a skilled liar?

Jarvis – BUT NOT IN MY CAR.

When I get in line for security, I respond to our group text but ignore the *getting my rocks off in a Porsche* comments.

Me – I know this isn't your thing but you cannot text me all night. I'll let you know if I get separated from her.

Asa – Roger.

Jarvis – Just saying, if you two get separated, my car is safe.

"Sir, empty your pockets into the basket and step through the scanner."

Unlike my partner, hidden weapons are beyond my boundaries and I slide through security smoother than lube.

I'm thirty feet behind Bella and move to a separate check-in table with my ticket. Once I collect my seat assignment for dinner, I stay far enough back for her to take the lead into the main ballroom.

Now it gets interesting.

It's been years, and the thrill—not only the job but working with Bella again—hits me in waves. This is the adrenaline shot I can't get any other way, a concoction that only comes from working with her.

When she walks to the bar to order a drink where

Randolph is talking to another man, I know it'll be a dirty martini.

———

Bella

"Dirty martini, please."

"Coming right up."

I turn to the side and open my clutch to pull out a twenty. Charles Randolph is an arm's length away—how I'd like to reach out and choke the bastard. I would if he weren't the only human I know who could lead me to my path of freedom.

Exoneration is so close, I can taste it.

"You know I can't do that, Jack. I need to keep my constituents happy. Florida is a swing state and I have too many retirees to support the bill."

Jack is not happy. "We need you on this issue. The party needs you."

Why do they not sound like they're talking about the manatees who are now on the endangered list in the Everglades? Yes, I did my homework before attending tonight.

"I get where you're coming from but I can't bend. I'm up for re-election this year—"

"You mean you're going to make a move for Majority Leader," Jack corrects him.

"Ma'am, your martini."

I turn to the bartender and hand him my Andrew Jackson. "Thank you. And keep the rest."

He winks at me right before his eyes lower to my never-ending neckline. "Let me know when you need a refill. From the looks of it, you'll need it to get through this downer."

I raise my martini glass. "Don't I know it."

Randolph chuckles and I've never heard anything more bogus in my life. "If the party needs me, I'll step up."

"Dammit, Charles. We need your vote so others will follow suit."

"Good luck, Jack. I'm not sure I'll be in town the day of your vote. You know how things go during a campaign. I need to get down to Florida to spend time with my people."

And just like that, Randolph has efficiently dismissed the poor bloke.

The Senator starts to turn to the bar but his eyes land on me. Without looking away, he brusquely orders a vodka tonic without a please or a thank you.

An arse with no manners to boot.

"I'm not sure we've met and I know a lot of people here." He extends his hand and I take it, at the same time my insides roil for what I know he's done to me. "Charles Randolph, Senator from Florida. And you are?"

"Kim Cartwright. The pleasure is mine. I've never met a Senator before."

"Kim. And I disagree—the pleasure is in my court." He gives my hand a squeeze before releasing me and stepping in closer. "What brings you here tonight? Nature conservationist or just a love for sea turtles?"

Charles Randolph is a handsome man—as much hatred that flows through my veins for him, even I can't deny it. I knew this from studying him. But actually meeting him in person? He's all JFK plus ten years.

Tall-ish. Salting at the temples enough to add fake character and false wisdom. A tan that tells me he often travels home to the Sunshine State. I can see how someone like him, who carries the power and prestige in combination with his all-American-man aura, would win over the ladies he's rumored to leave in his wake.

I know this because the all-American-man look definitely gets my British blood pumping.

However, I'm smart enough to look deeper. And deeper on the senior Senator from Florida is not good.

His wandering eyes give credence to the rumors his wife of twenty-two years does, in fact, have the right to live her separate life in their second home in Nassau.

The poor woman. I hope she's busy spending all his money while shagging the pool boy. She deserves it for putting up with this wanker.

I pick up my martini and pretend to take a sip. "My boss purchased a seat but something came up at the last minute. He begged me to change my plans and fill in."

Nodding, he bows his head like some regal gentleman from a romance novel. Idiotic and full of himself. "Well, I am the keynote tonight. I hope I don't disappoint you."

I run the tip of my finger around the rim of my glass. "My hopes are high, Senator."

"Vodka tonic, sir."

Again, no manners from the lying, cheating American, so I turn to the young bartender. "Thank you."

Randolph picks up the highball but doesn't take his eyes off me. "No need for formalities. It's Charles—I insist."

I smile before pulling my bottom lip between the

tips of my teeth, pausing. His response is to lean into the bar and run a fingertip down my forearm.

Lord have mercy, anyone who falls for this must have rocks banging around their skulls.

"Charles, it is," I agree.

"Who do you work for? I might know your boss."

Before I have a chance to think up a quick answer, I hear a familiar gruff voice behind me. "Hey, man. I'll take a whiskey. Neat. Whatever you've got will do."

What in the hell?

This is not having eyes on me from across the ballroom.

The friendly bartender reaches for a bottle. "Bad day?"

I can't see him but I can feel him—heat radiating off his classic tux. He proceeds to slap his hand on the bar, with a bill, no doubt. "It's been an interesting couple of weeks, that's for sure."

I ignore my American who has a lack of understanding for boundaries in any way, shape, or form, because I've lost the senator's attention. He's zeroed in on something over my shoulder.

"Charles—"

He takes an aggressive gulp of his cocktail and his demeanor changes when his eyes land back on me. "Kim, I'd love to hear about your job, but unfortunately, I see someone I need to speak with. Trust me, if it weren't urgent, I'd never leave. Please find me after my speech. I want to get your contact information so we can continue our conversation very soon."

"Of course." I smile and do my best to allow my assets to speak for themselves because I need his attention to have any chance at getting close to him. "Break a leg. Or is that only said in Hollywood?"

His expression relaxes a bit and he leans so his lips brush my wig next to my ear. "You can say whatever you want, honey."

I giggle because it seems to be what females with marbles for brains would do when a married man calls them *honey*. "All of a sudden, I'm very interested in sea turtles. I'll see you at the end of the evening, *Charles*."

He touches me again, this time across my midriff, right below the plunge of my neckline. Then he disappears into the room of black tuxes and smart cocktail dresses that are nothing like the gown I'm donning.

"Make it a double," Cole demands from behind me where it's getting hotter by the nanosecond.

I turn to the bartender. "*Please*. I swear, men have no manners." I turn to Cole for the first time since I've walked into the ballroom. His dark eyes have turned the color of smoldering coal about ready to burst into a pile of flames. "Tip him well—he deserves it for having to put up with demanding, thirsty imbeciles."

With my martini in one hand and my loaded clutch in the other, I leave my tail where he belongs so I can do my job. I need to know what was so important that Randolph ignored his carnal desires and walked away from me.

15

RAGE

Cole

This is harder than I remember.

But it's how Bella works. She could charm the rust off my dad's garage sale lawn mower and is gorgeous enough to draw attention from three counties over. I knew how tonight was going to go, but damn. They say time makes the heart grow fonder but it's not the case with me. Right now, I'm not feeling fond what-so-fucking-ever.

Rage.

It's jackhammering in my chest and might be what does me in. Who knew years of working covert cases in the most militant areas of the world would be nothing compared to watching Bella work a room after all this time?

I'm obviously no romantic because time has only created a wrath inside me that's itching to claw its way out, strangle a Senator, and throw a certain Brit over my shoulder to run away and fuck her brains out until she remembers nothing but me.

I'll keep her there for the rest of time. If it's against her will, so be it.

Pretty sure these are the things only madmen dream up and follow through on. The ones who get caught with their pants down end up in jail with docudramas made about them years later. If they're lucky, they might get a whole Netflix series and FBI agents will spend careers psychoanalyzing them.

They might not be famous but they sure are infamous.

I don't want to be either, so I need to get a handle on it. Watching a target barely lay a finger on Isabella Donnelly while she's working shouldn't send me into a murderous, angry-fuck mood.

But fighting a hard-on while she sashays her sweet ass away from me in that red dress, I'm thinking an angry fuck is just what the psycho ordered.

Whatever. If I'm the unbalanced one in this scenario, at least I know how to not get caught.

I pick up my double and follow my prey.

She glances at her ticket to find her seat before moving to a table at the north end of the room. It's next to the exit and this is not a coincidence. I'm sitting straight across from her at the same table of eight. If we need to get out fast, we can.

She takes out her phone and pretends to scroll but I follow her eyes and she's focused on the fuckwad who just dug his own grave by daring to touch her. He's standing off to the side in the shadows, now arguing with a petite blonde. I squint because she looks familiar but I can't place her.

They're mostly hidden by fake trees set to the side of the stage but their tension is tangible, even from here.

The woman might be small but she's mighty—when she pokes a finger into his chest, he takes a step back. They're halfway across the ballroom but I can still see he's surprised.

Shaken.

Different than the smug ass who was trying to figure out how to MacGyver his way into Bella's barely-there dress with only a chocolate bar and a paperclip.

What the hell?

He runs a hand down his face and checks his watch before manhandling her by the shoulders. His lips are running a million miles a minute, spewing shit I'd really like to know.

I knew I should have learned how to read lips, dammit.

The woman shrugs him off and whips around, but he fists her bicep with a fierceness I sense from across the room. He looks around to make sure no one is watching and my eyes shoot to Bella, who's now chatting on her cell as her gaze wanders. My guess—she's talking to Asa and Jarvis, but through her bracelet. Not sure who else she'd call other than Gracie Cain to give her another shopping list and she'd never do that at a moment like this.

The blonde tears out of his grasp and marches away in her skintight dress. She caught a break because Randolph is approached by another man with a clipboard and earpiece. Before I know it, elevator music—boring enough to shoot me into a coma—fills the room and the three enormous screens spring to life with sweeping videos of the Florida Everglades. Waiters march in rows, balancing enormous trays, reminding me of the musicals Abbott forces me to watch on the Disney channel.

But the most interesting thing going on in the room is the petite blonde heading straight for Bella.

Shit.

Thank fuck I arranged to sit at the same table. This should be interesting. I throw back the rest of my whiskey and make a beeline for my one-thousand-dollar meal.

When I get to my dinner companions for the evening, my bedmate is across from my seat with an older couple separating us. The blonde is even grumpier up close and I'm itching to know how I know her. Three other men are settling in, and by the sound of it, they've been here awhile—halfway to drunk and all the way to annoying.

I pull out my chair. "Ladies, gentleman. Honored to be eating this overpriced meal with you."

The older couple frowns. One of the single guys says, "Our company bought our chairs. Sucks if you had to shell out your own dough for this."

Bella rolls her eyes and takes another sip of her full martini she's been pretending to drink. When she sets her glass down—even as salads start appearing in front of us—she wastes no time and shifts to the blonde, switching up her personality for her new target. "You look so familiar. Do we know each other?"

Nice line, sweetness. I'm wondering the same thing.

"I know you—" the elderly woman next to Bella pipes in.

The blonde doesn't allow her to finish and whips her napkin off the table to make room for her slightly wilted salad and isn't impressed that everyone seems to know her. "I don't know you, but you probably know me." She picks up her fork and stabs a soggy crouton with such force, I wonder if she's picturing Randolph's eye. "Marie Kasey, Channel Five News."

Ah. That's it.

"I knew I recognized you!" Bella exclaims, talking faster than a cheerleader. "Wowza. You're, like, a celebrity! What's it like to read the news in Washington, DC?"

I stuff my face with a forkful of lettuce to hide my smile because Bella offended Ms. Kasey.

"I don't *read* the news. I'm an investigative reporter. I work on the Hill."

"Ah. Sorry." Bella pops a cucumber between her teeth and, uncharacteristically, continues to talk around it. "An investigative reporter. Impressive. I bet you meet *so* many important people."

Ms. Kasey is in a mood. "Yes, I do."

"Are you working tonight? I mean, this is only a fundraiser, right?"

The elderly man leans in and mutters, "Pass the salt."

I reach for the shaker and get a good look at Kasey for the first time as she turns to Bella. "I never stop working. It's events like these where the real deals go down, not in Congress or on the Senate floor. Who are you?"

"Don't you dare pass him the salt!" the elderly woman snaps her fingers at me. "Bert is on a low-sodium diet."

"I paid two thousand dollars for this crappy meal because you had to keep up with those hags in your bridge group who walk around with sticks up their asses. I'm gonna salt the hell out of my dinner and you can't stop me."

I ignore the woman and pass the man his salt. He has a valid argument. And I don't blame him—I'm not happy to have paid for this meal either.

Bella wipes her mouth and shoves her hand into the journalists personal space. "Kim Cartwright. I *love* meeting new people."

Kasey, not hiding the fact she does not enjoy meeting new people, dismisses Bella's hand and pushes her salad plate away.

"So did you have to buy your ticket to this or do you get in free because of your job? I bet there are *sooo* many perks to being on TV. You can probably badge your way into every event in this city."

Marie doesn't answer.

Grateful I'm sandwiched between three business men droning on about the Wizards shitty season and the couple fighting over salt, I pretend to scroll on my phone so everyone will continue ignoring me.

Bella keeps jabbering to her new BFF. "Well, I'm only here as a favor to my parents. My dad is an executive at Disney and was pressured to buy a ticket. He *hates* DC and I live in Maryland now. I took a job in PR for the crab industry. Anyway, I'm here as a favor for *dear old dad*," Bella sing-songs. "I mean, he does pay for my condo. Starting out in PR pays squat."

Kasey throws Bella a frown. "The crab industry?"

"Mm-hmm. I love crabs. You know, like Sebastian? I run their Instagram account. I also love sea turtles. Crush is my favorite Disney character *ev-er*." Bella rips off a hunk of bread. "I bet you make the big bucks, being on the news and all."

For such an expensive meal, they sure are hurtling through the courses at the speed of light. Plates are switched out and now we're all looking at a dry hunk of salmon, limp asparagus, and a pile of watery mashed potatoes.

Bert is making it his life's mission to shake the hell out of his salt.

"Have you *seen* the keynote speaker for tonight?" Bella asks, leaning into Kasey. "He's hot. I mean, if you're into old men, which I'm not."

My water glass hits the table like a ton of bricks and Kasey looks like she wants to strangle my bedmate.

Bella keeps talking about *old men*. "But, you know, some women are. I don't need a sugar daddy. I've got my own daddy, *obviously*." Bella rolls her eyes. "And I get a Disney Fast Pass that never expires!"

Just when I think Kasey is going to stuff a roll into Bella's trap, the lights dim and Morgan Freeman's voice replaces the elevator music as a new video plays on the big screens.

Bella claps her hands faster than our dinner was served. "Oh, yay. It's starting!"

Bella

WORKING UNDERCOVER IS tedious and tricky. Sometimes you need to disappear in a crowd and, others, you demand the spotlight so you can dance in it. Playing the room, understanding your role, and most importantly, keeping your eye on the target is the key to any successful operation.

Then, there are other times when the universe looks down and bestows you with a sprinkle of luck.

The latter is what happened tonight when Marie Kasey—investigative reporter and now my number one person of interest—plopped her grumpy arse down beside me. Though, I have to say, she's shit at her job and has no business calling herself an investigator of any sorts since she's dismissed my attentions all evening.

But I'm not one to look a gift horse in the mouth. I'll take my luck and have it with a side of biscuits.

I've taken my spotlight and have done what's needed of me. Cole, on the other hand, has sat and gobbled up our mass-produced and over-priced meal as if it were his last without uttering a word. Tonight, his job is to be invisible. Like always, he's brilliant at it.

I jabbered into Marie's ear relentlessly and she continued to ignore me throughout Randolph's entire speech where he went on and on and *ON* about his own efforts toward conservation in his home state, but really just about himself. Tonight screamed red, white, and blue politics. If Marie is one of his side pieces, I do wonder how she manages living through his self-righteousness while remaining conscious.

I clap when he finishes and the lights come up. "That was *so* interesting! I wish someone would do this for the crabs."

Marie doesn't try to hide the somersaults in her eyes as she scoots her chair out. Surely it's a lie when she states, "It's been fun."

"Oh!" I reach for her forearm to stop her. "Let me get your number. We can meet for drinks."

"I'm busy."

"Of course you are. Your job has to be so demanding. But if you're ever in Orlando, I can get you free passes to Disney!"

She pulls her arm from my grasp. "I'm not into amusement parks."

"Really?" I frown. "But there's something for everyone at the Magic Kingdom."

Her eyes shift to the stage before she shoots me a cheeky smile that might as well be death lasers. "Like I said, it was fun, but there's someone I need to speak with."

"Right. Always working. Find me before you skedaddle!"

Her smile is tighter than my dress and she turns, escaping my glittery charms.

Randolph is also on the move, shaking hands and politicking his way through the masses. I stand so I can be seen and collect my clutch, knowing Cole will be close behind. Probably too close—we'll have a chat about that later.

I start for Randolph but slow when he changes course and storms toward the exit. I've worked too hard to be here tonight and cannot allow him to get away. As quick as I can in my fancy new shoes, I follow.

He's out the door and I have to double time it to keep up. I ignore the twinge of pain zinging through my midsection and silently curse the fact I'm not up to par. I miss my healthy body and took it for granted.

Randolph takes a right and slides behind the coat

check counter closed for the season, and disappears behind a door. I peek in before following and find rows upon rows of tall mahogany garment racks. I move quickly over the worn carpet to the right, behind a set of lockers—their keys dangling from the locks. The place is a ghost town since it's currently hotter than hades in Virginia.

Randolph paces and mutters profanities. Peeking around the corner, I see him put his cell to his ear. "We need to talk before you leave. I won't put up with this shit. I'm in the coat check room."

I silently open my clutch and pull back the lining I tucked away perfectly. I'd bet all the pounds I've earned with blood and sweat during my time in Pakistan that he called my new friend, the reporter. Normally, I wouldn't need to arm myself with the likes of the two of them, but since I'm not up to snuff, I slide out the narrow switchblade I found in the back of Cole's dresser drawer. I doubt he even knew it was there. His things are *that* untidy.

As I witness Randolph fray at the seams into a pile of tangled knots, I flinch but don't make a sound when a big hand wraps around my mouth.

I grip my knife and ignore the pain, whipping around only to come nose to nose with the man who's supposed to stay far, far away but can't seem to stick with the plan. He isn't careful or gentle when his other arm wraps around me like a band of steel, pressing his front into mine, gluing me to the end cap of the lockers. We're out of sight but definitely not out of earshot. If he blows this for me, I might stab him with his own knife.

His hand slides off my mouth and his index finger presses against my blood red lips. Shaking his head, he tips it toward the entrance of the coat room as he slides his thick thigh between mine.

I put my arms on his biceps and push but he's having none of it. Instead he does something he's yet to do since I arrived in the States.

He touches me.

He *really* touches me, like we haven't had a half a world separating us, or our careers, or his loyalty and love for Abbott, or Red, or even my fucked-up situation all keeping us apart.

This is not like his touch while I was in the hospital or in his bed, supporting my weight so I'm comfortable to rest.

No.

He *touches* me.

The way he did back when we were an *us* and we couldn't get enough of the other.

Even with Randolph on the other side of the lockers, pacing more holes into the mossy carpet, Cole slides his hand down, hot on my skin, and over my gold necklace. He rips at the garment tape and pushes the material to the side, exposing my breast.

Palming me—or pawing at me—I can't tell what mood he's in right now besides completely and irritatingly exasperating.

My eyes widen and I mouth, "*What are you doing?*"

And do you know what the arse does?

He smiles.

He bloody smiles as he pinches my nipple.

I have to clamp my jaw shut to not scream in his face or moan from the electric current shooting between my legs.

"I don't appreciate you summoning me, Charles. If

you want to reconsider my offer so badly, come to me next time."

I freeze but Cole does not.

He's so close I can taste his breath when I wet my lips, exhaling when his hand slides down my body leaving my breast exposed.

"I don't have time for you or your bullshit, Marie. We're done and we've been done for months."

"This is not about us and you know it. I told you what I want."

Cole tips his head and hikes a brow as if we're taking in a film, and a mildly interesting twist was thrown into the mediocre plot. But instead of asking me to pass the popcorn, he reaches between us and yanks my dress up by the slit.

I shake my head. We cannot do this, especially not here. Cole Carson is incorrigible, even while on assignment. He always was and it seems nothing has changed.

With the weight of his wide chest pressing me to the lockers, I bite my lip when he fully cups me between my legs.

My adrenaline skyrockets and my skin zings at his touch.

Marie goes on. "You have two choices and I suggest you pick the smart one—I want twenty-five percent of your cut."

Cole's hand tightens on my sex and his eyes widen at the current development happening on the other side of the room.

That is, right before he dips a finger into the gusset of my thong, swiping a finger through me.

Bloody, Cole.

"If you don't pay up, guess who'll be the lead story on every news network from here to the South Pole?"

I squeeze my eyes when he slides a finger inside me, followed by another. Damn, I've missed him.

"You have no proof," Randolph argues.

"Try me," Marie dares. From the sound of her voice, I wouldn't take her up on that. "I figured it all out. So either I get rich off your little side hustle or I get a slew of job offers from national networks. Either way, I win. The choice is yours—go to jail or give up a quarter of your kickbacks."

Blackmail. But it's not enough. I need to know *why* he's getting kickbacks.

I exhale silently and Cole tips his forehead to mine, yanking my panties to the side. I try to squeeze my legs together but his thick thigh is giving him all the access he wants.

And he takes it.

I shudder when his eyes bore into mine at the same moment his finger swipes my clit. Instead of allowing him to press me into the wall of lockers, I can't help myself, and lean into him. My breasts to his chest. My face to his neck. My pussy to his hand.

Because ... *holy hell.*

"There are no kickbacks, Marie. You have no clue what you're talking about. Tell me what you think you know and I'll explain."

"Right." Marie laughs evilly as Cole circles my clit harder. "I have copies of the wire transfers. What percentage did you weasel out of them, huh? Defense-Jet's bids are always the highest, yet you continually make sure they get awarded every contract by the Department of Defense."

Cole leans back far enough to make eye contact with my hooded ones after that ditty of information. But he doesn't stop and I'm not sure I'd want him to if I were in a position to ask. Barely able to stand on my own two Louboutins, I'm halfway to an orgasm that feels so strong, I'm actually afraid of it.

And I'm not afraid of anything.

"You stupid bitch," Randolph bites. "I will take you down and ruin your reputation. You won't be able to get a job reading the traffic report in the middle-of-fucking-nowhere Wyoming. I've done it before and I'll do it again. Who knows? You might not even make it across the country to your new shit job."

Cole's phone vibrates against me through his tux but nothing stops him. Not the blackmail, not the death threat, and definitely not a phone call. He starts to fuck me with two fingers as he grinds the palm of his hand into my now swollen and desperate clit. My poor, lonely clit has been in solitary for so long. At this point, if Randolph rounds the corner to find us, I might not care. Obviously, I would, eventually, but only after Cole finished what he started.

"Try me, Charles. Fucking try me. This is not my first rodeo in this town. I have copies of the wire trans-fers in so many places, it'll make your big, fat head spin. Especially if something happens to me—but do you know what? I'll do you the favor and send you a copy. Watch for it in your email. I'll even send it to your offi-cial government account so there will be record of it—for-fucking-ever. I'm considerate like that."

Cole's eyes drag down my body and he brings his other hand up to maul my bare breast. I press into his hands, both of them, and my ears begin to tunnel.

Cole's damn phone vibrates again.

"Okay, let's talk about this." Randolph's tone turns desperate. "Let's meet on Tuesday. I promise, we'll work this out. I'm leaving tomorrow, I have a meeting down south, but I swear, I'll make this right. Give me forty-eight hours."

"You're going to St. John, aren't you? Who are you taking this time?"

My eyes fly open but not because of Randolph's travel news. I am a woman, I can do two things at once. Cole's hand between my legs freezes. He looks down at me where I'm slumped against him and his lips pucker to shush me.

The arse is toying with me as I gulp for air.

And just like that, Randolph sounds like he has the upper hand. "Jealousy doesn't become you, darling. It never did."

Marie's tone turns to granite. "I'm not jealous, jackass. I'm impatient. And for the record, you're a lazy fuck and I faked every orgasm you thought you gave me."

Cole bites back a smirk.

Someone's moving. I try to reach for what little neckline my gown has but Cole stops me and shakes his head.

"Tuesday, Charles," Marie raises her voice. "Or be ready for a shitstorm that'll rival cigars in the Oval Office!"

Cole is still holding me hostage, cupping me. With no choice, I grip the lapels of his tuxedo jacket and hold my breath. I'm pretty sure one of them is still here. I turn my head to the side and would love to peek around the corner if my dress weren't askew to hell and back.

I'm about to push him away—for real this time—

when the tones of a cell break through the stale room like fireworks.

I look up to Cole and widen my eyes.

Marie speaks with enough malice to take down a small city. "Yeah, it's me. I'm positive he's leaving for his place on St. John tomorrow."

And dammit, Cole's phone might vibrate through his new tux jacket.

For the love. There's only so much multitasking a woman can manage.

16

LIKE OLD TIMES

Cole

My brain is filing everything away while my cock is rock hard with the rage I've been fighting all night.

Hell, I've been fighting it for a long time, trying to get Bella out of her mess and into my bed. Since she's finally under my roof and sleeping next to me every night, I'm halfway there but still have a long way to go.

I have a plan. Granted, this was not part of it. But I'm adaptable and took advantage of the fact Bella could not rip me a new one or tackle me to the ratty-ass floor, because I would have let her. I'll sanction any activity if it means physical contact, even if I end up with bruises in the end.

But she's so wet and even more ready. I'm patting myself on the back for jerking off in the shower while getting ready for tonight, otherwise I might come in my pants like a teenager.

"I need to be careful. He threatened me and we all

know how things ended with his staffer three years ago during a *hunting* accident. I do not need to be hit in the head with a stray bullet from the next field over."

Bella's grip on my jacket tightens and her eyes grow big. I don't want her to come yet but I'm fighting the need to see her fall apart in my arms. I push into her pussy and clit enough to keep her teetering on the edge.

"Do it," Kasey demands and it sounds like she's on the move. "Put a copy in your safety deposit box and mail another to my PO address. I'll call you tomorrow with the rest of the details."

Bella and I freeze for a second as Kasey mumbles to herself about the asshole she's currently blackmailing. We wait. Ten seconds turn to twenty, and those into thirty, all the while, I stay connected to Bella in every way I want to from here to fucking eternity.

I exhale and say the first words either of us have uttered since I found her in here. "Kiss me."

She shakes her head.

I pump my fingers and circle my palm on her clit. "Kiss me. It's time. Give it up, sweetness."

She pulls on my jacket and stuffs her face into my neck. "I can't."

She starts to move, grinding herself onto my hand. My fucking phone won't give it a rest and if it didn't require taking my hands off her, I'd throw it across the room. "I'm going to make you come either way. What I really want to do is rip your dress off and fuck you against these lockers until we both forget the rest of the world, but we don't have the time. But the kiss ... it's in your court."

"Cole," she murmurs into my neck and her tit rises and falls under my touch as her breaths labor.

"Gave yourself to me once, baby. Do it again."

She doesn't have the chance to answer. Her pussy pulsates on my fingers. Her arms become a desperate clench around my neck and her fingers dive into my hair.

It's been too long. Since the goodbye sex when she tried to make me promise to leave her be. I've never gone this long without Isabella Donnelly since our hostile first encounter when we met.

She gasps and I have to hold her to keep her on her feet but I don't let up. Rubbing, finger fucking ... her moans shooting straight to my dick, which is cursing me. I push her back into the bank of lockers to help support her weight and her grip on me doesn't let up.

I can't help but think back to when I first had her like this. We were in Italy. Our first assignment together went so well, our agencies whisked us off to a new case, a bigger one. There has never been anything but sparks between Bella and me—big and bright and hot. The first time I put my mouth on her, we had just infiltrated a group for the first time and things got dicey for about two minutes. I thought we might actually have to call for backup to get our asses out of there alive.

My blood was racing, and though I didn't know it until later because she looked as cool as a frozen cocktail on a hot summer day, hers was too. Together, we turned it around and won their trust. But after...

After.

When we got back to our hotel, we barely made it to the elevator. I didn't just kiss her, I devoured her. She practically climbed me. After two months of working together with sexual tension tighter than a hammy after sprinting a marathon, we both succumbed to what we'd been silently pushing away.

I thought that was it, that we'd finally give in and fuck each other's brains out, working off the high we both got off on from the job.

And we about did. For the first time since I'd met her, her tone turned hesitant even though I knew for a fact she didn't have one uncertain bone in her beautiful body. It was the moment she muttered the words I'll never forget...

I've never.

A five-gallon bucket of Gatorade at the end of an MLB game is nothing compared to what I experienced. My young Brit never failed to surprise me.

She was a virgin.

We didn't fuck each other's brains out that night but I also didn't leave her. I slowed things down to a snail's pace and gave her two orgasms. Then I found out I was the only man who ever touched her that way and that was it—there was no walking away. Not that I wanted to before.

Nail my coffin shut, I was a goner for Isabella Donnelly.

I slept with her that night while sporting the most severe case of blue balls in my life. I actually slept, with her in my arms, all night long—and I'd never done that with anyone. It was the night we began all our firsts.

I sure didn't think it would happen so soon, but two days later, she became mine. When she handed over her virginity, I took it like a man on the brink of death and she was my only lifeline.

"Kiss me." My demand is desperate. I'm not proud of it but I also can't help it. I'm two weeks into our deal and having her half-naked with my hand between her legs could really backfire on me. I didn't plan on this when I followed her in here but, I'm not sorry.

At least, I'm not sorry yet. And even if I might be sorry later, it won't be by much.

"Cole." She shakes her head into my neck, catching her breath and coming back down to earth from the ride I just gave her. "No. This is too complicated as it is. We can't throw *us* back into the mix."

"But this is you and me. This is what the high does to us. You melted under my touch and the only reason I'm not buried balls deep inside you right now is because when I have you again, it's not going to be like this." My grip on her tightens. "And there's the fact you haven't kissed me. But our bet stands."

She drags her eyes open. "Clearing my name is the only thing I can focus on right now."

"We're close," I argue. "We haven't figured it out yet but what we learned tonight is huge. We can have both."

My damn phone vibrates again and we continue to ignore it. Her eyes are calculating and she might not look exactly like my Bella, but having her here in my arms, she is through and through.

"I'm going to St. John," she says.

I nod and pull my hand out from under her dress not bothering to fix her panties. "You bet your ass you are. And I'm coming with you."

She shakes her head and pushes me back. This time I allow it and she starts to fix her dress. "Absolutely not—"

I hold one hand up and pull my damn phone out of my pocket with the other because it seems Crockett and Tubbs can't follow directions and leave me the fuck alone for an evening. It's not like they couldn't hear everything that went down, and I don't give two shits about it. "You're not going down there alone. And there's no way I can drum up a passport by tomorrow anyway. Crew should be able to arrange a flight—I can get you in and out of the country easier."

"Yes, I guess there's that," she mutters and I see her fight slowly return as her post-orgasmic mood evaporates. She motions between the two of us as she picks up her purse and my knife off the floor. "We'll talk about this later—what just happened—Cole. You and your shenanigans while on surveillance, I swear."

I motion back to her purse. "I can't believe you stole my knife and didn't tell me you were armed."

"I can hardly defend myself when I can't manage a sit up. Did you really think I was going to waltz in here defenseless?"

I wave my phone around before unlocking it to check the encyclopedia of messages and missed calls. "What do you think I'm here for?"

She tugs at her panties. "We need to get out of here."

Three missed calls from Crew.

Crew – Call me asap. I'm hearing chatter and it has nothing to do with Bella.

What the hell? Crew hardly ever calls me.

Jarvis – Better in the Kennedy Center than my car.

Asa – Not sure I'm going to be able to look you in the face again if I have to sit here and listen to you two hit it in the coat room.

Jarvis – How long has it been since her surgery? Damn, she's tough.

Asa –I'm going to have to see you at elementary school concerts and shit. I hate you, Carson.

Crew – Time is of the essence. Answer the damn phone.

I don't bother listening to the slew of voicemails. "Hang on. I've got to call Vega and we need the crowds to clear before we leave."

She adjusts her wig and pulls out a compact to check her once perfectly-applied lipstick, which is now ruined and probably smeared all over my new dress shirt. I sound like an adolescent teen, but I may never wash it.

I press callback and put my cell to my ear. Crew answers. "Where are you?"

My eyes dart to Bella and she snaps her mirror shut when I answer. "Kennedy Center. Why?"

"Bella with you?"

"Yeah. She's right here."

"How fast can you get to your car?" Crew bites.

"What's wrong?" Bella asks.

I look at the woman who had surgery only weeks ago. The car is parked a couple blocks away and we could normally make it fast when she was operating at peak performance. But she's not and she's also dealing with that damn dress and those shoes I really want to fuck her in. "We're a couple blocks away from the car."

"Your boss knows where you are but not because of Bella. Her name wasn't mentioned. Nick Peterson and Wendy Sisson started digging and found out you never put the order on Simmons. Peterson tried to reach out directly to me two hours ago. I covered for you, told him we're on it. But over the last thirty minutes, they somehow found out we're not. Carson, they're tracking your work cell. They know you're at the Kennedy Center and are sending someone to you and not to talk.

I have no idea who that someone is and none of this shit sounds official."

I pull out my other cell, the one issued to me by none other than the Central fucking Intelligence Agency.

I stare at the piece of technology they're now using against me.

Bella breaks into my thoughts. "Cole?"

"Get the hell out of there," Crew demands.

I end my call in one hand and fist my work cell in the other.

"Answer me," Bella demands.

I turn and toss what my employer is now using as a tracking device into the first locker I see. Slamming the door shut, I twist the key and yank it out before turning on my heel. I look down at the woman I just gave an earth-shattering orgasm to and hope it didn't suck all of her energy. "I'm sorry, baby, but we're going to have to test your post-op endurance. You'd better lose the shoes because we need to move fast. I'll explain on the way."

Bella

"You okay?" He doesn't look down at me nor is he winded, as I am.

My bloody body.

I'm barefoot, fisting my very expensive shoes with my purse tucked to my chest. Cole's hand is strangling my other and I dare the beast who tries to separate us— that's how tightly he's holding onto me.

He hasn't said much, but what he has explained is

downright fucked. I'm not sure what this means for him or his job. What I do know is, the Cole Carson I have worked with does not get riled.

Like him, I'm scanning the city streets as we move through the dark and now I'm cursing the fact I wanted to be seen this evening. This getup is definitely doing its job and we're gaining the attention of every pedestrian and driver we pass.

I try not to let on that the pins and needles are pecking away at my midsection as he pulls me along. "I'm fine."

"Half a block," he grits, picking up the pace.

I'm going to feel this tomorrow.

"Cole?" My breaths are shallow. "If they traced your phone, they're going to know where you've been and where you parked."

His dark eyes roam the landscape in front of us. "I know, sweetness. Almost there. I'm going to get you in the car first and then we'll get the hell out of here."

"I'm more than capable of getting in the car. We can get out faster."

"Not the time to argue, Bella," he mutters.

Jarvis's Porsche comes into view in a parking lot dotted with cars. I don't see anyone as its lights flash and beeps sound when Cole unlocks the doors. I try to twist my hand out of his but he's having none of it. When he reaches for my passenger door, both of us almost twirl in unison when we hear a car door slam across the lot.

Cole steps in front of me and stuffs the key fob into my open palm as voices fill the night from six spaces over. I'm about to reach for the switchblade in my clutch until those voices turn to laughter through the dark.

Loud, drunk, annoying laughter.

"Get in," he demands, and I can't pretend any longer —my midsection is aching. As much as I've complained about being in Virginia, I'm ready to get back to Cole's bed.

He gets in and is pulling out of the parking lot as I'm still hooking my safety belt.

"Explain why the CIA would track your phone and come looking for you on a Saturday night."

He exhales a huge breath. "It's complicated."

I grip the console as he speeds through DC streets as if he has diplomatic immunity, which he absolutely does not, otherwise his employer wouldn't be chasing him. "Ah, yes. Well, that's interesting and thank you for not elaborating since I already know everything you do for a living. It's not as if you've ever respected the boundaries of your employment. Case in point, the coatroom twenty minutes ago."

His eyes are sharp on the road but he doesn't hesitate at my words. "You liked it."

Beyond the point. "Tell me why your boss is after you."

"Fuck," he mutters when the light ahead of us turns red and he can't run it like he has the previous two because of perpendicular traffic. He slams on the brakes and I press my hand onto my midriff from the pain as the sports car screeches to a stop.

I look into the passenger side mirror and see the open road behind us. "I'm sure we're fine but if you could tell me what's going on, I'd appreciate it. If we get into a scuffle, it would be nice to know why."

He reaches for the only cell he has left on him and stares at the black screen. Wheels turn under his thick head of hair when he mutters to himself, "Would they ping me illegally?"

"You think? I mean, Crew does it, but he's not held by any sort of oath."

He looks at me. "Who the fuck knows. I'm in the capitol of my own fucking country, I work for the CIA, and apparently my boss is after me because I won't put a hit on an American veteran who, from my digging, has done nothing wrong."

I gasp. "That's what this is about?"

He nods. "I told them I ordered the hit, but I didn't. Crew is looking into him and so am I. We have no clue why they want him dead."

"Bloody hell," I mutter and sit back in my seat.

"*Bloody hell*, is right," he shoots back.

I shift to him and am about to open my mouth to lambast the CIA and British Intelligence for what they've done to both of us, when I see it...

I can honestly admit, not many moments as a spy have surprised me. Preparation, training, and research before an operation is key, not only to be successful, but coming out on the other end alive and in one piece. Have I had to adapt to surprising situations? Clearly. But adapting and reacting are two very different beasts to deal with on the fly.

That's why when I see it, my words echo around us in an eerie shrill.

"Go, dammit!"

I grip his forearm at the same time Cole shifts his eyes to his window. One moment we're alone at the intersection and, the next, we're face to face with a masked passenger in the car next to us.

And staring down the barrel of a long gun.

Cole hits the gas at the same time his other hand grips the back of my head, folding me at the waist. This, coupled with hoofing it blocks at a half-jog post-surgery, would probably do me in at any other moment, but glass shattering has a way of spiking one's adrenaline.

"Fuck!" Cole growls as loud as the tires screech on the pavement below us. The safety belt is no help when the car is pulled to the left, my body thrown the opposite way into the door.

I twist and find the small window behind the driver's seat gone. When I turn farther, I find a black sedan on our bumper. The passenger has switched weapons and now a handgun is pointed at us.

We speed through city streets, swerving this way and that. Cole takes his eyes off the rear-view mirror long enough to reach under his seat and shoves a Glock into my hands. "Get them off my tail."

I flip off my safety belt and hike up my dress to kneel in the seat and find bullets ricocheting off the pavement in our dust. I press the button to lower the window and silently curse the fact I wasn't born left-handed. Cole gets rid of his second cell, tossing it out my open window as I demand, "Faster, Cole."

"Hang on." His arm cages me to the seat as he takes the corner on what feels like two wheels. "Shit. One way and we're going the opposite."

I don't dare take my eyes off my target and can only imagine what's happening in front of us from the honking.

"You're taking your sweet time over there, baby."

His arm across my back tightens and he yanks the steering wheel to the left. The sedan veers to avoid a minivan and I cringe. "I'm not shooting with innocent people near."

The engine revs and we gain some space. "Soon, Bella. I can't get on the highway into gridlock with this guy on my ass. Hang on—turning."

I grip the back of the seat but after he turns, we slow and the sedan closes in. "What are you doing?"

"Fucking construction," he growls as we speed past orange barrels.

Bullets ping and chip at the Porsche while Cole weaves in and out of traffic. There's no way to get a clean shot with my left hand.

"Shit! Hang on."

I peek over my shoulder. Cole has run out of room to pass and plows into a sea of orange. Barrels, cones, and signs light up the dark night.

We're never going to get rid of them like this.

"Watch out." I lean over and press the button to his window before twisting my arse and planting it in his lap with my back to his door. His arms cage me in where his hands are gripping the steering wheel. "If you can avoid the debris, I can get a shot. I only need a moment."

"Taking a left. Hang tight, you should be clear."

I grab onto him and brace.

As Cole turns, I lean out the window. A hand with a gun attached to it appears from the sunroof of the sedan but I don't hesitate. I shoot three times—the passenger, the front left tire, and straight through the driver's head.

A lovely trifecta, if I do say so myself.

The sedan spins, the driver's side slamming into what's left of the construction mess, crashing into a pit a half-meter deep. Smoke billows and a flame licks the night from under the hood. I pull my arm back in the car and Cole glances at the rearview mirror with a bloody, arrogant smirk playing on the strong lines of his face. "You left a mess, baby."

As we race away, I hear sirens in the distance. "They're not after us any longer. You're welcome."

He releases the steering wheel with one hand and plants it on my ass, tucking me tight to his groin. Without taking his eyes off the road, he holds me snug to his chest. "Seems both our agencies are after us. As bad as that is, this feels like old times, sweetness."

I bite my lip because the last thing I need is to give him the satisfaction of agreeing. We left a pile of rubble in our wake and, to top off the night, trashed Jarvis's fancy car. *Like old times* is absolutely not an understatement.

And it seems tomorrow we'll be on our way to St. John.

Not exactly the Mediterranean, but I'll take it.

.

Cole

Crew Vega runs a camp straight west of DC. It sits on almost three-hundred acres. I used to think it was in the middle of nowhere, but that was when I lived in Alexandria and could walk out of my condo to hit restaurants and bars—you know, civilization. I moved to the country for Red and Abbott but, I admit, I do love the privacy of BFE. I grew up here and it felt weird to be back after traveling the world.

But after tonight?

I've never needed privacy more. I took back roads out of the District and it's taken an age to get back to nowhere land where cows outnumber humans and horse farms are the norm. After what went down tonight, there's no way we can go back home right now.

Since my cell is in bits littering the construction-filled streets of the District, I've been on Bella's—coordinating and planning. Before I had a chance to return Vega's call from the coat room, he'd already sent his man Grady Cain to my house. He packed up Red, Abbott, and the new cat who hates me. Vega assured me they're safe at his house where he and his family live on his wife's vineyard. Abbott is back to sleep but Red is reported to be more irritable than ever about the turn of events.

I don't have the luxury of worrying about him right now.

"How're you doing, baby?"

After she got rid of whoever was after us, Bella climbed off my lap and reclined her seat. I could see she was hurting. Her body isn't ready for what she just put it through.

"Lovely, though I could really use a bottle of whiskey to numb everything from my neck down." Her words seep through a groan and she hasn't taken her hand off her midsection.

"I can make that happen."

She winces as I pull into Crew's camp, which might be the most secure piece of property in all of Virginia outside of the beltway. I can't lie, this will be awkward returning the Porsche even though Jarvis is the least of my problems right now. The fine piece of machinery was already creaking from what we put it through, but the gravel road makes it feel more like a tractor. The narrow drive through the trees finally clears and an old farmhouse appears, the one Crew uses as his headquarters for recruiting and training mercenaries. The house and drive are lit up and standing off to the side are Crew and Grady.

Jarvis stands front and center with Bella's new personal shopper and BFF, Gracie, glued to his side. She's gripping his forearm and her other hand is wrapped around his bicep. If I didn't know better, and she wasn't a slip of a woman, I'd think she might have some super power, holding back the Hulk in the latest installment of *The Avengers*.

I come to a stop in front of Jarvis—I'm sure it's salt in the wound since I can hear him groan through the shot-out window. I kill the engine—hoping it will eventually start again—and climb out, ignoring the death glare the owner is surely sending my way as I walk around what was a pristine sports car a little over an hour ago. Bella's door complains and it takes a little muscle to pry it open, metal on metal, like nails on a chalkboard. Bella moves slow and I'm worried she did damage to her not-yet-healed wounds.

"I'm fine," she argues but doesn't push me away when I help her stand and reach in the car to collect her jeweled purse, phone, wig, and the gun Crew supplied me with earlier when none of this was on our radar.

I help her carefully walk barefoot across the gravel and we come to a stop in front of Jarvis. I put my arm around Bella and hold her to me, hopefully to remind him he's standing here today because of her, so a fucked-up luxury car should be no big deal. Especially with the money he makes off the CIA and other countries under the table.

No one has said a word and Jarvis doesn't take his eyes off the pile of rubble parked behind us. I reach into my pocket and his eyes snap to me in a toxic stare when I toss him the fob.

He stays silent. I decide to break the ice. "No sex was had in your car."

Grady doesn't even try to hide it, his white teeth blind us with a wolfish grin.

Jarvis does not find the situation humorous. "Are you fucking kidding me?"

"It's no big deal," Gracie pipes in. Jarvis throws her an *I love you, but what the fuck* look. She ignores it and rubs his arm, trying to soothe her beast. "I'm sure we can get it fixed."

Jarvis shakes his head and looks back to the Porsche and does not lie. "It'll never be the same."

"I'll buy you a new one," Bella announces from beside me and I'm about to argue, but she keeps talking. "Let me know how much and I'll wire you the money. But I'm knackered and need to be up when the sun cracks."

"We've got to dump it somewhere and Jarvis needs to report it stolen. We raced through every city street of DC. I'm sure someone caught the tag number. I'm surprised you haven't gotten a call already," I add.

Jarvis drags a hand down his face. "I'll deal with the car and make the call."

Crew tips his head to the farmhouse that makes mine look like the Taj Mahal. "You guys are staying here. Red and Abbott took our last two bedrooms at Whitetail. It used to seem like a big house when it was the two of us but now it's full."

I sigh and don't want to think about what this means, how it's not safe for my family to sleep in my own damn house. How the CIA not only traced my government phone but tapped my personal one too. There's no way they could've found us otherwise.

"Are you okay?" Gracie probes, eyeing Bella.

She sighs and gives me more of her weight. "Exhausted. I hate to complain, but I need to call it a night." She looks to the men standing in front of us. "Is everything set for tomorrow?"

Grady nods. "Our most trusted pilot is scheduled. You take off at seven. I have transcripts of Randolph's conversations for you to read. We're working on Kasey's line to see who she called tonight. Asa is still manning the wires. Between your boss, his boss, Randolph, and the reporter, it was a busy night."

"Come on." Gracie breaks away from Jarvis and reaches for Bella's shoes, purse, and wig. "Let's get you settled. I went to Cole's house with Grady and packed you a small bag. Girl, all I have to say is I'm sorry you're not ready for a trip to the islands. I never thought you'd need a bikini. You can get one when you get there."

I give Bella a squeeze. "Get settled. I'm going to check on Abbott and talk to Red since we're leaving. I'll meet you in bed."

Bella winces and makes her way over the rocks to the front porch. Before she gets in the door, she pinches her contacts out and turns around to look at me once more. And just like that, she's back. My Bella—blond hair in a mess of waves and bright eyes piercing me through the dark.

I lift my chin to tell her to go and find myself left with Crew, Grady, and the overly-irritated Jarvis.

I hand Crew his gun. "It came in handy. I assume you all heard everything?"

"Everything," Jarvis bites.

I shake that off because I don't care. I wouldn't change a thing about tonight.

Okay, maybe the car chase.

And the shooting.

And trashing Jarvis's car.

And paying a fucking mint for a crap dinner.

But other than that, not one thing.

"Was Nick Peterson chatty after our incident?"

"Not really," Crew answers. "No one to be chatty with. He's tried to call his men more than his boss called him, which is a damn lot. They're not happy you might be living and breathing right now and there was more chatter about Penn Simmons. They want him dead and you wouldn't do it, so now they want you dead too."

I pull in a big breath. "Going to work next week will be awkward."

"That's one way to put it," Grady drawls.

Jarvis turns away from his car for the first time. "We still know nothing about Simmons that would explain why Peterson and his boss want him out of the way. We've also been watching the *church* Wendy Sisson attends. There hasn't been much activity. Certainly no pot lucks or bible studies."

"You're disappearing for the next few days. Even though this isn't our lane—" Crew hikes a brow and glares at me, "—we'll stay on top of it while you two are chasing Randolph. Our priority is Bella. The rest of what we're doing for you is also for her. I am not excited about illegally tapping anyone from the CIA."

Crew Vega and I had a run in a few years ago. He worked his ass off to get out of the game and retire but wouldn't do it until he could bring Grady with him. Grady wasn't ready. I didn't know Grady Cain coming back would be a bad thing and gave him a job.

It didn't go well.

Vega has held it against me ever since.

"I'm glad she's your first priority because she's mine too. She and Abbott. I appreciate you getting to her and

Red tonight. I need to figure out what to do with them until I get home."

"They're welcome to stay here. We've got the room and Vivi will like having someone around who does more than eat and sleep."

"We've got room too," Grady adds. "But Asa has no room. We'll do everything we can to wrangle your dad and make sure they're safe."

"Put Red to work," I say. "He doesn't sit on his hands well."

"My wife owns a vineyard and a farmhouse old enough for George Washington to have stopped over for the night. I have plenty of shit that needs to get done," Crew adds and this time it doesn't look like he wants to smash my head into a vat of grapes. Progress.

"I'm going to check on Abbott."

"Through the trees. Follow me." Crew turns into the dark.

I start to follow but pause next to Jarvis. We both stare at what was once an orgasmic automobile. I slap his shoulder. "I am sorry. It was a great car."

Jarvis's eyes shoot to me. He frowns but doesn't say a word.

It's too soon. He needs time.

I leave him to mourn and walk off into the dark forest in my tux.

At least everyone likes Bella. I plan to ride her coat-tails with this group as long as it takes. I have no other choice.

Bella

THE BED DIPS as it always does when he comes to me. Except this time, it creaks too.

He pulls a blanket over both of us that smells of fresh lavender and is as heavy as the silence that has settled over the room. In what has become a habit, he presses his front to my back. I don't argue because I'm tired and settling my mind after tonight seems impossible.

I waited for him to come to me. After receiving another lecture from Gracie about scar tissue and doing too much too soon after such major surgery, I choked down a couple pills and washed the makeup away.

Cole pulls my weight into him and I hate that I like it. Hate that he's wearing me down. He doesn't say a word, which is oddly stirring the tension in my gut and my gut has been through quite enough.

I feel every tense muscle in his body so I break the silence. "Is Abbott okay?"

His fingers wrap around my hip. "Yeah. Woke her and explained I have to go out of town for a few days. But dealing with Red was another story. He didn't believe the shit that happened tonight was on me and not you. I set him straight."

Red is an interesting gent, one like I've never dealt with before. That's saying a great deal since I work in a world of penises. His attitude toward me, for the most part, has improved—enough that we've coexisted under the same roof while Cole is at work and I'm giving French lessons to his beloved granddaughter. He clearly puts up with me for the sake of his son.

I sigh. "You should listen to your father, Cole."

He buries his face in my hair and inhales. "I plan on winning our bet. You belong right here next to me. We'll find a way for you to do what you do best. You're too good to give up your career—you proved it tonight. Not that I need you shooting up the streets of DC, but you can work in other ways. I promise."

I lean into him farther. "That's a tall order, Officer Carson."

"I can make it happen." His lips hit my ear. "Tonight gives me even more reason to fix everything. Abbott needs me and I need you. I'm done being shot at and that goes for you too. After the last few weeks, I don't want you anywhere near a bullet for the rest of your life."

I close my eyes because this is not a conversation I'm anxious to have. "The alarm will ring early, Cole."

"You sure you're feeling okay?"

"I'll be fine. I already took a tongue lashing from Gracie—I don't need one from you, as well."

His voice changes, dripping like honey. "Then maybe we should talk about what happened in the coat closet."

I grab his hand that begins to creep up my side. Unlike earlier, I can't allow him to put me in such a vulnerable spot if my plan is to keep him at bay. "I need sleep."

My hair flutters as he sighs. "Soon, baby."

It's a promise. I hear it in his tone.

One I wish he wouldn't make.

18

MONEY

Cole

We step off the ferry from St. Thomas. The smell of ocean water and revenge hangs thick in the tropical climate of St. John. Thanks to Vega and his frequent-flier mileage with a private charter service, we made it here three hours before Charles Randolph. A first-class seat doesn't make a commercial flight any faster.

The senator seems to like the sand. In addition to his place on South Beach and Nassau, he also has a condo here. From the travel records Asa supplied, he's here at least once a month, which seems like a lot for someone who should be busy working for his constituents since they're the ones paying his salary with their tax dollars.

But if the shade of his tan is any indicator, he's got his ass in the sand more often than serving the good people of Florida.

"It's been a long time since I've been to the beach."

I turn and give Bella my hand as she follows me down the steps to the tarmac. Shrugging our bags over my shoulder, I lead her to the small office where keys to our car should be waiting. "That was an amazing weekend."

She doesn't let go of my hand this time and I feel like Team Cole just won the pennant. Tipping her head back, I can't see her bright blue eyes for the huge black shades she's sporting, but her pink lips creep up on one side. She remembers what has been etched into my brain and what I've been hanging my hat on ever since.

"It was," she agrees. "It was also a time when things weren't complicated."

I shake my head and let her hand go long enough to swing the door open. "It's only as complicated as we make it, sweetness."

"Yes, you keep saying that. Yet after last night, I'm not sure how much more problematic life could be. Now we're both on the run."

I try to bite back my smile. "Don't give me any ideas. All I need is Abbott and I'd be happy living on the run with you." The rusty bell sitting on the desk looks as pathetic as it sounds when I whack it. "Maybe we should take this opportunity to try our hand at island life. No bullets. No bosses. No informants. Sounds like a wet dream."

An old lady who can't be taller than five-foot-nothing with more wrinkles than a pug, shuffles out of the back room. She greets us and I don't even have to show her my fake ID to get her to hand over the keys. She disappears faster than she arrived and we're left to guess which Toyota is ours for the time we're here.

An old Camry honks and lights up in the far corner of the lot. Before we climb in, we both go to the trunk to see what we've got to work with.

"I hate not relying on my own resources," Bella mutters and bends to dig through the bags Crew arranged for us. "You think this stuff washed up from the ocean?"

"We didn't give them much notice and this is an island. I doubt there's a Home Depot on every corner. I should be able to make it work." Tossing our duffels on top of the pile of tools that look like they might've been used to build planes in World War II, I slam the trunk and pop the locks. At least we brought our own surveillance equipment. We probably would've ended up with bugs used in Watergate.

When I crank the engine and flip on the AC, I shift to Bella and am dead serious when I state, "Before we leave this island, you're going to kiss me."

She pulls her hair up into a pile on top of her head. "Your optimism is both inspiring and sad, Cole. We're not on vacation."

"Every day with you is a vacation."

Flipping off her shades, her eyes roll before landing on me and I'm positive she doesn't appreciate my humor. "We have less than three hours, and that's if no one is in the condo. There's literally no time for this."

"Quit talking dirty to me. You know this shit turns me on. And we still haven't talked about your orgasm in the coat room."

"Do I need to wrestle you out of that seat and drive myself?"

"I'll wrestle with you any day and you know it. Back to your orgasm—you liked it." She opens her mouth to argue, but I don't allow it. "No, you fucking loved it, especially when I had you half-undressed with my hands on you during an operation. I know it turned you on. I had to keep you from coming until Randolph and the reporter left."

"Cole—"

"You're wet right now thinking about it, aren't you?"

She says nothing, but her head falls back against the cracked pleather headrest.

"I have a plan," I state.

Her head rolls toward me and exhaustion is etched into her frustration.

"You're going to kiss me before we leave this island," I repeat because it's true. I'm determined and pretty damn proud of what I've got up my sleeve.

"Stop," she whispers.

I shake my head. "Never. You want to know why?"

"I give up." Her tone is as drained as her expression. "Why?"

"Because I love you."

Her jaw goes slack and her piercing eyes widen.

"You're fucking frustrating as hell, but I love you. I think I have from the day you steeled your spine and stood up to me when you had no clue what you were doing. You're who I want to teach Abbott to be a strong woman. I want more babies but I only want them with you. You might not be ready and that's okay. I'm willing to wait. We're going to clear your name, figure out why my boss is trying to kill me, and then we'll find a way for you to do the job you love until you're ready for me to knock you up—at least twice. I'm up for discussions if you want more."

I stop because this was actually *not* a part of my

plan. That shit spilled from my mouth but I can't say I regret it. Yet. It actually feels pretty damn good to get it off my chest.

I'm not sure I've ever shocked her to silence and she still hasn't moved.

"Bella," I demand. "Do you have anything to say?"

"Bloody hell," she murmurs.

"Exactly my thoughts." I throw the Camry into reverse and pull out of the parking lot. "But I do plan to practice knocking you up. And it's going to happen right after you break down and kiss me."

Bella

CREW VEGA HAS CONTRACTED my services since my name was dragged through the sludge by my former employer. He worked with my father for only a year or two before Dad retired and I ran across him through my cases in the beginning of my career. When I was forced to leave behind my life or be burned at the stake for something I *did not do*, I was desperate and needed security. And we all know nothing provides security better than money.

It was risky, but I reached out to him. He worked in the part of the world where I was hiding and I knew he could use my services. It took a couple encrypted phone calls and I was in. I've worked with Crew and a few others like him. He pays well, he shoots straight, and he believes in me. I provide him information and sometimes equipment, should his men need it locally. Until I met Jarvis, I've never worked directly with his people. I usually make the drop and they find it. It's how I prefer to operate.

So, until I arrived in Virginia and ended up with a point-blank gunshot wound, I had never met Asa or Grady in person. They've proven to be advantageous men to know. Asa somehow booked us in the condo next to Randolph's through Airbnb, despite the fact it was already booked. I didn't question this but I did thank my lucky stars he's on my side.

Grady shot me a sly smile on the way to the airport this morning, informing me they can make most things happen when they need to. If the old adage *money talks* is true, these gents seem to make it scream, even on the island of St. John. They're now investigating the notorious reporter who seems to have all the goods to completely ruin Senator Randolph. I need to figure out his connection to my drama before she's done with him. If he goes away too soon, I may not find the pot at the end of my gloomy rainbow.

"Done," Cole announces as he tosses the ancient electric drill that barely did the job onto the chair next to us. "With thirty minutes to spare."

It took him less than an hour to plant three listening devices—one behind the refrigerator in the wet bar, another above the baseboard in the bedroom, and the last in the main hall. They're sensitive enough to cover the entire place. It's huge compared to my living arrangements in Pakistan, yet modest for American standards.

I turn to the wall of windows overlooking the deep balcony and, beyond that, to blues and turquoises dancing in the endless Caribbean. I need to focus on Randolph, not the fact that Cole *loves me*, wants me to *be in Abbott's life,* or how he wants to *knock me up multiple times.* And that's all after he plans to practice. Cole Carson doesn't do anything halfass. By the time he *perfects* the act, I'm sure I'll be eating for two.

"You've been quiet."

I nod and continue my silence.

"I'm running out of time, sweetness. I'm not scared of anything, but the deadline is making my skin crawl."

His heat hits my back, followed by his hands low on my hips, caging me in ... and I don't hate it. Cole was always the worst type of addiction. It took all I had to cut myself off from him. He has no business being tied down to the likes of me since I'm not in a position to live a real life.

My hair moves away from my neck, pulling through the shadow of his whiskers since he didn't take the time to shave this morning before our early flight. His lips hit the sensitive skin of my ear and I brace, worried what he'll say next, but I'm saved by the literal bell. Or tone from the app on my phone, alerting us of activity in the next unit.

I whip my head around to the cell sitting on the table and Cole is back to business. He stuffs a wireless earbud in his ear and tosses the other to me. I press record on the app and sit on the edge of the bed, praying we'll learn something—anything. Even if it's another crumb in the long trail where my freedom sits at the end.

Minutes click by. Long ones. Ten turn into thirty, then forty into sixty.

Cole and I are sprawled on the king-size bed and my eyes are closed. Patience is something I've always had in abundance until the day my freedom was ripped from its root. His fingers methodically drag across my scalp through to the ends of my hair as we listen to Randolph bang around his kitchen, the shower, and, to prove how good Crew's equipment is, a lonesome ice cube rattling against glass.

Rattle.

Rattle.

Bloody, fucking *rattle.*

I've always loved Cole's touch on me—his heavy hand is like a weighted blanket. I sleep better, deeper, and even though I've never been a worrier, I'm lighter, sharper, and my focus is beyond superior with him.

He breaks through the silence for the first time since Randolph walked through the door to his condo. "I'm going to tell you something and the only reason I'm saying it is because your body isn't what it used to be."

I grab his hand and turn to glare. "What do you mean my body *isn't what it used to be*?"

His damn smile lights up the room and he looks pleased with himself. "Not like that. You could be a pile of mush and I'd be obsessed with you."

I look at the ceiling and sigh. "Then what are you talking about?"

"I'm talking about the fact you're not strong enough to try to hogtie me. Not that you could at your peak, but it was always fun when you tried."

I listen to glass clinking on glass followed by a slosh of liquid. I hope the old bloke is getting sauced and will eventually spill every secret in his big, fat head. "Please get to the point and quit wasting words."

His hand returns to my head and this time there's nothing methodical or hypnotical about it. His touch presses in, bossing one lonely word. "Relax."

For the second time in a matter of moments, I grab his hand but this time throw it across the bed at him. "You know how I feel about being told to *relax*."

He starts to laugh but a knock breaks through our conversation. And since Cole and I were the only ones talking, we shut it down because the three strong raps on wood did not come from our door.

I look at Cole and he loses his cocky and demented sense of humor.

The crystal and ice we've been listening to for far too long hits a hard surface right before the latch to his condo turns.

"You're late." Not the friendliest of greetings. I assume it's not a lover he's intending to woo.

"Ah, Chuck. We've got time." Hmm. A man. An American he could have met in the States?

The door slams. "I'm busy and don't have time to wait around on you."

"You're in paradise. You can't be busy."

It doesn't take much for Randolph's fire to burn as hot as the tropical sun. "I have no desire to be near you —this is the only safe place we can meet to discuss business. And we have a lot to discuss."

More ice cubes and glass clinking followed by a dramatic sigh. "Go on then, Chuckie. Get to it."

A pause settles over the wires before Randolph spills. "I'm raising my rate. From now on, if you want your contracts, I need twenty-five percent."

If I were a jumpy person, I might jerk out of my skin. But instead, I look at Cole and cock a brow when the gent howls with laughter at Randolph's pathetic excuse at negotiations. Once he finally gets control of his hilarity, I can barely make out his next words. "You made me leave the country, change planes three times so I wouldn't be followed, and fucking sweat my ass off to ask me *that?* I told you how I feel about the fucking heat."

"I'm not asking," Randolph bites. "This is non-negotiable. My prices are going up. It's called inflation. It's the American way."

"Bribery." His associate drawls. He might as well be speaking to a small child, and not one as bright as Abbott. "*Bri-ber-y* tends to raise prices more than inflation. So many people want a cut, don't they?"

"Prices have spiked," Randolph bites. "I can't help what's going on with the Euro. Manufacturing costs have increased, so have other services."

Glass hits glass angrier this time—followed by an even louder bang, and now I'm worried for his decanter. "I'm in the business, Randolph. I know what military-grade weapons cost. You shouldn't've brought me here to feed me shit about an industry I know inside and out. You get fifteen percent to make sure we get awarded the contracts. It won't change. I won't allow it. Whatever extra expenses you have are on you and you alone."

"Dammit, Ambrose. Listen to reason. We need each other for this cycle to keep going."

Ambrose. My eyes shift to Cole but his are on a laptop he's tapping away on.

"Wrong. I don't need you. Without you, I'll have to make my bids competitive. You seem to forget, your kickback is what we're gouging from the government. I'm not making any extra, just a guaranteed contract."

"Raise your bids." Randolph's desperation leaks through the wires. I might not be in the same room but his anxiety is easy to feel in his tone. "No one will take a hit—not you and not me. You know my take is small. I might get fifteen percent, but I send most of it to Europe to keep this shit moving. We need to make sure the defense committee continues to buy at the rate they do."

The man lowers his voice, yet it eerily becomes louder as he's gotten closer to the bug. "You might've started this cyclone, Randolph, but do not fucking tell me how to run my business. You gave me an opportunity years ago, I took it. What you do with the government's money I feed you under the table is on you. You're the one who turns your kickbacks into fucking blood money—not me. I keep my employees in jobs, make sure they have health insurance, and offer them a safe place to make a competitive wage. You create havoc on the other side of the world so our military stays engaged. You'll take that to the grave—not me."

I sit up straight and ignore the stabbing pain in my abs. When I twist to look at Cole, his expression mirrors my surprise.

Randolph keeps arguing his point. "You're in as deep as me. The cost is low but the payout high."

"The cost, you assured me, would be destruction not death. That hasn't been the case. And yet, you demand more money you won't have an issue dipping into a vat of blood."

Another pause and Cole threads his fingers through mine.

"Don't stop talking," I whisper, begging them through the wall to feed me more.

"A busload of people here or there isn't much. It's not like we had another nine-eleven. I'm making sure the demand is there so our troops will stay busy. It's basic macroeconomics. Are you familiar with the simple bell curve?"

"You killed those Americans in Spain. You might as well have detonated that bomb with your own middle finger as a *fuck you* to your own country," the man clips and all the oxygen leaks out of my body. Cole squeezes my hand but I barely feel it.

It was Randolph. I knew he was linked but I had no idea it would be him.

Randolph keeps spilling. "We needed to make a statement. How was I to know there would be a fucking bus full of tourists from Idaho there?"

The man's tone takes another dive into a deeper and more dangerous zone. "Consider this your only warning, if more humans die—from any-fucking-where in the world—I'm out. Find yourself another manufacturer to do your dirty work."

I can barely breathe as there's movement in the neighboring condo. No, don't leave. Not yet.

Randolph mirrors my thoughts. "Wait. I'm sure we can come to some sort of agreement."

"Nice try. Already disgusted with myself that I ended up in bed with you. I don't want to be in any deeper. You disgust me. I have no idea how you sleep at night."

No, no. Don't leave!

Cole lets go of my hand and grabs my cell—the only one left between the two of us after the last couple days. After pressing a button, he speaks into the phone. "Asa. You heard? Yeah. I need someone to tap into the CCV of this building. Ambrose—I want an ID and bio. If you can't do it, I'll log into my CIA profile to do it myself. I need a picture for facial recognition."

Cole pauses and I can't find the words in my brain ...

not even one to express the piercing pain in my heart. But I can find others because I know exactly what needs to be done next.

"Money," I mutter and look at Cole. "We need to follow the money."

He holds a finger up and continues speaking to Asa. "Yeah. I want to know every single move he makes electronically. He's storing funds somewhere and we need to find out where they're going."

A slew of tones come across the wires and I smack Cole in the arm to get his attention. "He's making a call."

"Asa, hang on." Cole pops his earbud back in just in time because it's not a long conversation, but holy hell, what he says next drops my jaw.

"Yeah, it's me," Randolph bites. "I tried, but couldn't negotiate for more. Marie Kasey needs to disappear. For good. And I need to know who else she's talked to. Make it happen in the next twenty-four hours. I want it done before I land in DC tomorrow night."

19

DO YOU TRUST ME?

Four Years Ago

Cole

"Never?"

She doesn't answer, but just like my Bella, she doesn't cower and doesn't back down. She definitely holds her own. Even after she informed me she has never.

As in, she's a virgin at the age of twenty-three.

I try not to move a muscle but it's really fucking difficult seeing as though I'm hard as a rock and my blood is pumping so fast I might as well have just finished a triathlon.

She bites her lip and exhales, her small tits heave inside the bra I was about to rip off. "I'm sorry."

I don't move from where I'm lying on top of her, trying to control my lungs and will my blood to leave my cock the fuck *alone since he's pressed against her pussy which has never seen any action. We're only separated by her panties and my boxers.*

I try to wrap my mind around this. This is not what I expected from Isabella Donnelly. We've worked together for two months, and I can honestly say, if I ever thought I experienced sexual tension in the past, I was wrong. No woman has ever consumed my thoughts, had an effect on my decisions, or driven me to such a state of frustration I've wanted to put my fist through a wall on a daily basis.

"You're apologizing for being a virgin?"

Okay, probably not appropriate for this exact moment, but to be real—I did not land in bed with Bella stripped down to almost nothing by saying the right things. Not sure I can count on one hand the times I've said the right things in life.

Her fingers—along with her nails, dammit—press into my biceps and her face turns hard. "No, Cole. I'm apologizing because I allowed it to go this far. I should have told you sooner. I've just never gotten to this point with anyone."

I know I'm not improving my averages when it comes to perfect words, but I can't help it and I damn sure can't keep the self-satisfying grin off my face. Despite what she admitted, I press my cock—that is now even hungrier—into her uncharted territory. "You mean, no one's ever done this?"

Her panties were soaked when I slipped her jeans off fifteen minutes ago. By the look in her eyes, I know she feels it in her clit.

But she doesn't answer.

I lean down to take her mouth—her lips might be as swollen as her clit is when I'm done. The need to taste every inch of her just shot through the roof.

I let her mouth go but our breaths are still entangled in a way that might leave a scar on my soul. "Why me?"

Her chest heaves below mine where I have her pressed into the hotel bed. She shakes her head. "I don't know. You piss me off on a daily basis, Cole. Trust me, I've asked myself that same question."

I slide my hand under her back and roll, pulling her on top of me. But my cock has no desire to lose contact, especially now, so I grab her behind the knees and pull them up my sides. "I'll tell you why *me."*

"For the love, you are a cocky arse. Yes, Cole Carson, please enlighten me as to why I'm here, close to naked, and have just admitted how I've never been like this before—with any*one—yet, for some reason you are the chosen one. Tell me. I cannot wait to hear."*

I slide my hands up her thighs and cup her ass, easily palming each beautiful globe as I file away all the wicked plans I had for them. They're going to have to wait.

It can all *wait.*

"Because I challenge you. Because I respect you. Because you know I know how good you are at your job. I've even stood up for you over the last two months with assholes who have dismissed you because you're young, beautiful, and they think you got where you are because of your name. And also because I'm hot and you turn into a knot of sexual frustration waiting to be untangled every time I brush a finger across your fair skin."

Her golden hair curtains us and I've seen every emotion pass through the bright eyes I've tried my hardest not to get lost in over the last two achingly-long months.

She doesn't argue, so I run a hand up her spine and press in, her tits molding to my chest. "For a little while there, I thought maybe you were into older men, but now I know that's not the case. You're only into me."

"Cole—"

I shake my head and lift my hips, watching her breath catch. It might be the most fascinating thing I've ever experienced—to have complete control over something as complicated and spectacular as Isabella Donnelly. How I can control the oxygen that feeds her body and gives her life by what I do between her legs. And I plan to spend a lot of time there in the foreseeable future.

Who knows, maybe my unforeseeable future too.

I pop her bra clasp with a flick of my fingers and I'm well aware my actions do not mimic my words. "I'm going to slow things down, sweetness."

I lose her eyes and she buries her face into my neck as her bra hangs slack. I drag my hands up her sides, brushing the small swell of her tits that are still pressed into me. Not sure I could be more obsessed with her body. She's tall, lean, and strong, yet so very fucking female.

"No sex," I announce and feel a smile spread across my skin. I dip my hand into the back of her panties and easily reach between her legs where she's spread wide—open and ready—only for me. And like I knew from earlier, she's wet. "But I am going to make you come."

Keeping her tits pressed to me, she leans up on a forearm to gaze down. I see it in her eyes. She wants it.

"Then I'm going to come," I add and her eyes widen. "And you're going to watch. I want you to see what you've done to me for months."

I flip her to her back and her bra hits the floor before I have a chance to settle between her legs. We never bothered to turn off the lamp when we stumbled into her room—lips locked and pawing heavier than a couple of lions mating on National Geographic.

She doesn't try to hide herself but it could be because she can't take her eyes off my boxers sliding down my thighs. When my cock bounces free, I silently promise him some action to make him feel better—just a different kind than we thought tonight was going to bring.

When the only piece of clothing left on the bed are the panties still snug on her ass, I don't take my eyes off hers as I fist myself followed by one tight pump. Bella's tongue sneaks out and I'm forced to wipe the vision of her swallowing me balls deep. After what I learned, that's not going to happen for a while and I'm surprised at how okay I am with it.

"Do you trust me?" I ask, slowly pulling my fist up and down.

She drags her feet up to her ass and presses her thighs together. "With what?"

"With everything."

Those long, smooth thighs overlap and I lose her eyes.

"Bella," I call for her.

She lifts her lids and swallows hard before giving me the nod.

"Say it," I demand. "After what you just told me, I need to hear it."

Very English and all Bella, her words wrap me in a vise with no key. It's at this moment I realize I'm fucked—in every way I never expected. "I trust you, Cole."

I let go of my needy dick and reach for her hips. By the time her panties pass her toes, she tucks her feet back to her ass with her legs glued together. I'm knees to the bed, looming over her.

There's no push or pull when I slip a finger between her knees. Her long legs part willingly and I find myself in a place I only imagined while in the shower or late at night in the room next to hers, hating the wall that kept her from me.

Now, there's nothing between us, nothing tangible, anyway. Had I only known there would be something else much bigger than I ever imagined.

Huge.

Her innocence.

I've never been with a virgin.

I cut the gaze between us, dropping my eyes to her spread before me. Open. Trusting. Untouched.

All fucking mine.

I spread my knees, sitting back on my calves, and drag a finger down her inner thigh. Only when I touch her pussy for the first time do I look up at her. "What about this?"

Her tits rise and fall quicker now with each breath. "What about what?"

"You never," I look down at my index finger circling the topic at hand, "but has anyone done this? Touched you?" I spread her farther and find I was right. Her clit is as needy as my cock. I circle her swollen little organ, promising it great things in the future. "Played with you?"

She closes her eyes and her exhale comes sharper than a razor. "Would you care for my sexual CV, Carson?"

"Carson." I barely dip a finger inside her, enough to spread her want everywhere, clit to ass. Getting to know her as she gets to know my touch. "Thought you dropped Carson a long time ago. I'm not Cole to many people, baby, but it's who I want to be to you."

"No, dammit," she clips and opens her eyes. "No one has done what you're doing besides me. Are you happy?"

"Yeah." I confirm the feeling coursing through my veins. "I'm actually really happy. Not going to lie—tonight is not turning out like I thought it was going to. Never

could've thought this up but it's actually a hell of a lot better."

I feel like I know her well by now. Working two months straight with someone while traveling gives you the benefit of learning a whole lot more about your coworker than you would sitting at a desk.

"Love being the first to do this, baby. The first to touch you."

Her eyelids fall and she white-knuckles the sheets below her. "Oh my God."

"I know. I'm pretty fucking amazing," I agree.

"Cole," she calls for me, her beautiful tits rise and fall with her quickened breaths.

"Breathe deep. It'll last longer. I could do this for hours."

She tries to pull in a bigger breath as I grab her shin and lift her foot from the bed. She moans and, finally, I dip a finger into her pussy. It's tight but my finger goes in smooth, so I add another, and my cock almost explodes with jealousy.

I can't wait to bury my face between these legs, but next time. Right now, I don't want to miss a second of this. I want to watch and burn it on my brain for the rest of my days.

Her legs start to tremble as she tries to bring them together. I don't allow it. Putting more pressure on her clit with my thumb, I watch her pussy start to spasm around my fingers as I fuck her with my hand, and think my future is looking pretty damn bright right now.

Gasping for air, moaning for me and God—in that order, fuck you very much—her body is even more beautiful when controlled by me. Shaking and convulsing and arching, she presses her pussy onto my hand, and I'm forced to let go of her leg. I grab my cock and have never fisted it so hard. With her juices spread over me, I lean over her, hand by her head on my extended arm as I cage her in, and jack myself off. She

*opens her eyes and they move down my body, watching
what she does to me—what she's been doing to me for
months.*

*Her hands aren't timid when they land on my abs and
move south. I can't take my eyes off her face as her thin
fingers trail over my fist, moving up and down my shaft. I'm
holding off my orgasm as long as I can manage.*

"Touch me," I demand.

*I need to take my own advice and breathe deep, because
as her thumb brushes the head of my cock, I almost lose it.
Even though I'm about to come, I unhand myself so hers can
find me. It doesn't take long—maybe I should be embarrassed—but after all the teasing, thinking tonight was going
to be the night, learning her secret, and then making her
come, I have little fight left in me.*

*I engulf her hand in mine and together we jack off my
beloved cock harder than I ever have, all over her stomach
and up to her tits. Making the best fucking mess I've ever
made. And that's saying a lot since I've been a literal mess my
entire life.*

*She looks down at her chest as I spread it over her tits
before lowering myself to her, my now semi-hard cock
dangerously close to her no-man's land.*

"Kiss me," I demand.

*She doesn't hesitate. Bringing her sticky hands to my
face, she pulls me to her mouth.*

THERE ARE moments you never want to lose, ones you
replay over and over and over in your head. The ones
that are so big and epic in your otherwise mundane life,

you might give your left nut to erase time, go back, and live them all over again.

Every single first with Bella is like that.

Not that the ones following aren't earth shattering. I am me and she's the shit. Everything we've done together is fucking spectacular. We're the grand finale on the Fourth of July, lighting up every inch of the horizon.

Until the real world went and fucked it all up for us.

Today was big. Outside of my parents, I've only told one other person on earth I love them and that's Abbott. I've said it to Bella one other time, months ago when I begged her to come home with me. I was desperate, but it was the truth.

Desperation seems to be a taste I find on my tongue often lately.

After I made arrangements with Asa to have a twenty-four-seven tail put on Marie Kasey so she doesn't end up six feet under, I about lost my lunch when we had to listen as Randolph fucked some woman he barely said a handful of words to when she showed up at his door. After a short time—as in really, really short —he kicked her out with her five-hundred-dollar fee and drank himself to oblivion. As much as I wanted to know more, there was only silence from the Senator.

The entire time, Bella didn't say a word. She stared at the damn ocean for hours, her face blank and her eyes lifeless. The sun set hours ago and I was about to pull my hair out from the silence. I set the devices to record and grabbed her hand.

The beaches are quiet now, only a few stragglers. If the tourists aren't asleep, they're at the bars tying one on. I tucked her under my arm, fisted our shoes in my other hand, and we walked. It's been a long day and she's got to be exhausted after last night.

We finally stop, she plants her ass in the sand, staring out at the waves that kiss her toes. It's a new moon and cloudless sky—the stars light up the clear, black night.

"You know, you're going to have to talk to me sooner or later." Like I've done since the moment she woke in the hospital, I don't allow her any personal space. I'm behind her, caging her in, with my feet in the sand and knees angled to the stars. It's taken her a bit, but she's finally relaxed into my chest.

Her English hits me flat and lifeless. I hate it. "I'm tired."

"You've had a long day. You're still getting your strength back after surgery—"

"No, Cole," she bites. "I mean, I'm *tired*. I've been doing this ... running, hiding..." She sighs. "I knew Randolph had something to do with it. I feel like I'm close, yet so far. And I'm tired of being tired."

I wrap my arm around her chest. "I know. But we're *close*, baby. I know it."

"I shouldn't complain. It hasn't been that long but —"

"It's been a long fucking time," I interrupt. "Time you could've been progressing in your career. Time I lost with you. Time I wanted you in my life and time you could've had to get to know Abbott when she was younger. I know what you've said in the past but it doesn't have to be either-or. You can have both. Hell, you can have it *all*."

Her chest rises and falls under my hold as the waves pick up momentum. All of a sudden, our asses are wet. I don't move and neither does she. I could sit here for hours.

"We're going to make it out of this," I go on. "There's no other option. I won't allow it."

"The thought that anyone thinks I was behind the attack in Barcelona and did nothing to report it or stop it ..." She shakes her head. "And everyone believes it, Cole. It makes me physically ill. All those innocent lives ... I'd have laid down my own to save them had I known."

"I know you would've and we're going to prove to the world it wasn't you. Someone made you their pawn. Someone set you up and when I find out who did it, I'll fucking take them down myself before putting them in front of an international jury."

"I'm sorry. Somedays it feels as if this will never end."

I twist her in my arms and put my hand to her cheek. Her bright blue eyes are brimming which isn't like her. I've only seen Bella cry once—when I went after her in Pakistan and she told me to leave. Didn't think anything could gut me more, but seeing her now? My strong and beautiful Brit, broken and I can't do a thing about it?

Yet.

"It'll end," I promise. "I swear."

I'm about to break my word and take her mouth— there's nothing I want more right now. Kissing her in this moment feels right. Hell, burying myself in her balls deep to make her forget about the rest of the world and all her troubles feels more than right. And I could.

But I know her. Even though I gave her an orgasm last night and have been sleeping next to her, I know she's in her head. I also know no one can control her and I don't want to. She needs me but not in that way.

She shakes her head out of my grip but leans the side of her face on my chest. I wrap my arms around her as the warm Caribbean swallows us up from the waist down. She burrows into me, proving she does need me.

The rest will come.

I'll make sure of it.

20

PLANS

Bella

For the remainder of his stay, Randolph has proven to be more boring than watching paint dry. When he woke this morning after his utterly vomit-inducing romp, he ordered a meal for delivery. It seems his lonesome bender from the previous night kept him from building sand castles because he lounged on his balcony and worked on his man tan for the remainder of the day.

He's sure to wrinkle prematurely or get skin cancer.

I paced our condo for hours in pure frustration, which has seemed to soar higher than the cloudless, tropical blue sky. I'm exasperated with every-bloody-thing at the moment. Randolph's lack of talk, his lack of electronic activity, and his basic lack of cleanliness, if I must be honest. I'm not sure the man has washed his hands since his lady of the night came and went, nor after any of the times the loo has flushed in the last twenty-four hours.

I shook the man's hand at the fundraiser. The thought has me wanting to jump into a pool of bleach and swim laps for hours. The germs on that man right now have to be toxic.

And Cole woke me with his hand on my breast and his erection pressed to my bum. I was equally irritated at myself for wanting him to slide that hand between my legs where he would have found me positively drenched. Last night on the beach, I had a moment of weakness and admitted things aloud that I've only permitted myself to think while alone in the dark of night. As if it wasn't hard enough to steel myself against his graces, I don't need my sensitive nipples or antsy uterus betraying me.

I have shit to fix before I can think of any of that.

And damn, Cole. He's more relaxed than a beach bum—shoulders to the headboard and legs crossed at the ankles while wearing only a pair of tatty gym shorts. Everything is on display from his bare chest down to his large feet, and in between is the bulge in his shorts reminding me of how we wake every single morning.

I know him like a second skin. He's commando under those shorts—I'd bet my life on it. He always was after a shower when it was just us. I'm sure that hasn't changed since nothing else has, either.

He hasn't taken his eyes off me—back and forth, back and forth—wearing a path on the rug in front of the king-size bed where his taunting biceps are bulging as he casually lounges with his arms crossed.

I'm not sure if my starlit confession about my being *tired* lifted the anvil off my chest or what, but in addition to waking frustrated as hell, I also opened my eyes this morning invigorated with energy seeping from my pores. The need to move my body is overwhelming. It's as though my two surgeries are from another lifetime. If it weren't for the burning desire to listen to what Randolph might utter next, I'd definitely be walking on the beach, or maybe a run if I could manage.

My pacing is interrupted by a snap.

Literally Cole snapping his fingers, breaking my nervous energy in two.

I stop in front of the bed by his bare feet. "What?"

He points to the earbud he's listening to. "He called for a taxi."

"Please tell me he washed his hands."

Cole only winces and shakes his head.

"He said nothing else?" I press.

"Nope. But we knew this might be it." Cole looks at his watch. "He has a flight back to Washington in three hours."

My head falls back and I stare at the ceiling fan, spinning and spinning and spinning—racing itself yet going nowhere.

An ugly metaphor for my miserable life.

"We still have his line tapped. Asa will let us know what comes next," he assures me. "And, baby, there will be a next. He put a hit on a journalist's life last night and failed to upgrade the deal he's been doing under the table for years. Life is not grand for the shady Senator from Florida. He's juggling fire right now and the man has no coordination."

"Maybe he'll contract hepatitis from his lack of hygiene," I mutter and pace to the balcony windows where I plant my hands on my hips.

"Maybe." I hear a smile in Cole's tone as the bed creaks.

I turn to find him up, moving to our bags that have exploded all over the floor. He and I were never tidy when we traveled. No point in settling in when we might have to be on the go at a moment's notice.

He produces a pair of clean boxers and before I know it, drops the gym shorts, standing buck naked.

"What are you doing?" I ask.

His lips tip on one side. "Don't look at me like that. You'll make me hard. And even if you begged me for a quick fuck right now, the answer is a hard no. We don't have time."

I don't give him the satisfaction of talking about any kind of fuck—quick or otherwise. "When is our flight back?"

He steps into his boxers and yanks them up, tucking his cock inside. "Tomorrow."

"Tomorrow? But we knew Randolph was scheduled to fly out this afternoon."

"We have plans tonight."

"What plans? There's too much going on. We need to get back."

He pulls on a clean pair of shorts but leaves them unbuttoned as he grabs my hips and pulls me flush to his bulge. "Team Bella has it covered back in Virginia. Get ready. Doesn't matter what you wear but we're getting on a boat."

"A ferry back to St. Thomas?"

"No, a different kind of boat. A charter. Just for the evening."

I shake my head. "No. We need to get back. There's nothing more for us to learn here."

A big hand dips into my hair, gripping the back of my head. His lips come close to mine, and when I think he's going to kiss me, he stops. The tip of his nose brushes mine and it feels like a threat when tangled with his words. "Sweetness, do not argue with me. Tomorrow's Monday and I'm not anxious to walk the halls of the CIA where people are threatening to kill Americans—me being one of them. I can't strut my ass back into work like nothing happened."

"You can and you should," I argue. "I killed both men. They have no proof it was us, and if they did, they can't very well pin it on you when they are the ones who wanted you dead to begin with. The walls of Langley might be the safest place for you right now."

He cocks a thick brow. "Maybe."

"Definitely," I counter.

He shrugs. "I need to consider my options. Either way, we're still getting on a boat tonight."

"Does this boat ride have anything to do with me getting my life back?"

"Not particularly."

"Then I have no desire."

He shakes his head. "Baby. You said you trusted me and I take that for what it means. Now, if there's anything else for you to do to get ready, do it. We're getting on that fucking boat even if I have to tie you up and carry you onboard. We leave in an hour."

He slides a hand to my arse for a quick grope before letting go and disappearing into the bathroom. The man has given me an orgasm, felt me up in my sleep, feels free to palm my ass, but has kept to his word and not kissed me.

One more thing to be hella frustrated about.

Damn him.

Cole

"This is not a boat, Cole. This is a yacht. An enormous one."

"Welcome aboard the *Endless Horizon*." A man in a uniform takes Bella's hand as I board behind her. "I'm First Officer Metivier. This way. Everything has been arranged."

I put a hand to Bella's back to give her a nudge but she stops, turns to me, and lowers her voice. "What is arranged? You know I hate surprises."

"If you'd follow him, it won't be a surprise anymore. You're only torturing yourself by standing here and dragging this shit out."

"You know I'm not enjoying this. Being out here on the water, I feel stranded and out of control."

I lower my voice. "Do you really think after all you've been through I'd put you in any position that wasn't safe? The crew doesn't know our real names. No one on the island knows our real names. Randolph is home. Marie Kasey is still walking around, being annoying-as-hell. And from the last reports, my boss is shaking in his boots since Asa went to my house, logged into my laptop, and sent an email that I was taking a sick day tomorrow for Abbott but will be back Tuesday, ready to rule the world. I'm getting sick of saying this Bella, but you need to trust me."

She doesn't move and crosses her arms.

Hell, she could keep this up all night. I grab her hand and move through the aft open patio of the yacht and into the door where the guy in white disappeared.

Looking left and right, I see him at the end of a hall, waiting for us in front of a closed door. Ignoring the pull on my hand, I surge forward until we reach him.

I turn to her as I grip the handle to the door with my free hand. Dipping my head enough to level my eyes with hers, I'm dead ass serious when I say, "You know I'll do anything for you. This," I tip my head to the closed door, "is just the beginning."

She says nothing, but if the grip on my hand means anything, I know she gets me.

"And sweetness?"

Her eyes fall and she pulls in a breath. "What, Cole?"

"I love you, baby."

I turn the knob and push the door open.

"Love?"

The color drains from Bella's face and I hear a gasp.

Bella

COLE'S ARM wraps around my waist and his lips hit my ear. "Go hug your family."

Mum's hand flies to her mouth and her eyes—the same ones she gave me—pool with unshed tears. Dad is standing next to her, Archer and Devon next to him.

It's been too long. I've only dared contact them once and Dad told me never again, how they were being watched because of me. But he followed by telling me they loved me, believed I was innocent, and knew I would never do what I was accused of.

Cole gives me a push and it's all I need. One

moment, I'm exhausted from life, and the next, Cole gives me this.

My mum's arms wrap around me first, followed by Dad's, holding us both.

And my empty, broken heart beats with new life.

"I can't believe you're here," Mum cries. "It's been too long, love. No one should be kept from their child."

My dad's lips hit the top of my head. "Bloody hell. Missed you, darling. You're a sight for sore eyes."

I grip them tight, never wanting to let go as what little makeup I put on is surely streaking my face.

"Let me look at you." Mum pushes me back and a big smile shines through her own tears. "You're so beautiful you hurt my eyes."

"You're all bones, sis." A hand grasps my bicep and my oldest brother, Archer, pulls me into his arms. "You always were but you could really use a sticky toffee pudding right now."

I wipe my face and punch him in the arm. "Always an arse. Nothing has changed."

His toothy grin feels like home.

Devon draws me in next. "Being on the run hasn't been too hard on you, Bells. You still look like a pile of gold."

"How?" I ask, reaching for my mum again, realizing how much it's hurt not to see or talk to my family. "How did you get here?"

"Carson." Dad motions to the man behind me. I look back and he's standing like the god he's proving to be with arms crossed, watching the Donnelly show play out in front of him. "He's been in touch with Archer for over a week. We've been trying to plan a meet. We got a call the day before yesterday about your trip here and knew this would be the time. We're officially on *holiday*. We knew it would be too hard for us to go to the States without raising a shit ton of red flags."

Cole lifts his chin.

I sniff and don't care if I'm wiping my nose on the back of my hand. I'm too damn happy. I look into the dark eyes I love, eyes I've missed, and eyes I've gotten pretty bloody used to seeing on a daily basis. And that sets my already frayed nerves on end. "It couldn't have been easy. Nothing with my family ever is."

"Your dad sprang for the boat. This is out of my budget but it gives you the privacy you need," Cole adds and looks at his watch. "You've got three hours, sweetness. I wish you had a week, but no one here wants to risk exposing you."

Mum squeezes me and I turn to her—my smile is genuine and straight from my heart. "I want to know everything I've missed."

And I settle in to enjoy the sweetest gift I've ever received.

21

THE BELLA LOTTERY

Cole

"We're close. Bella has a lot of people at her back. I want her free to live her life as much as you do, Thorne."

Bella's father made such a name for himself with British Intelligence during the course of his career, he's known worldwide among people like me. He retired sooner than needed but he had book deals and took advantage of the opportunities he created from busting his balls. I don't blame him. He was at a point where he didn't want to sit in management for years, instead choosing to spend the time with his wife.

Thorne Donnelly pulled her brothers and me aside for a brief as Bella sits with her mom, doing what I brought her here for, catching up and soaking in what little time I could manage to give her with her family. The second I realized we were following Randolph here, I knew it was the perfect place to meet. I arranged it with Archer. The Donnellys were booked on the first charter to the islands from London.

"Fucking kills me. In my gut, I always thought what happened to her was some demented attempt to get back at me. I'm not blind to the fact I've made enemies through the years. Did my job the way it needed to be done and pissed people off along the way. Never thought it would come to this, though, and not to my Bella."

"Not your fault, Dad," Devon insists. "We'll get the cocksuckers. No one messes with a Donnelly."

Thorne runs a hand through his salted hair. "I've got a shitty feeling about this, Dev. Real bad. Doesn't help my conscience that my baby girl has been on the run and taking risks to clear her own name."

I'm not surprised he feels this way. I would too if it were Abbott. "Doesn't matter, Thorne. She snuck into the U.S. and paid the price with a bullet. But we're back on track. I swear I'll keep her safe until we can clear her name."

"You tell me what you need, Carson. I'm still on a case in Greece for the next month but I'm on leave for the next few days. I can nose around on my way back," Archer offers.

"Wish like hell I could do something," Thorne muses. "Outside of the walls of this boat, not sure who I can trust. Those I thought I could trust within the walls of Vauxhall are the ones trying to burn her at the stake. I know my Bella. She's as tough as nails—got that from me—but she has her mum's heart, pure gold. She'd go to any length to stop an attack like the one they've pinned on her. She damn sure wouldn't help carry it out or keep it a secret."

"Thorne," Annie calls for her husband from where she's parked on the sofa next to her daughter. "Quit talking shop and come sit with Bella."

Archer and Devon obey and I'm about to follow when Thorne grabs me by the bicep. I turn back and he lowers his voice for only me to hear. "You need anything —call me. Money, resources … anything. I know for a fact our lines are still tapped—both Annie's and mine. I don't want to draw attention to ourselves and haven't let on we know where she is. But Ollie knows how to get hold of Devon so you've got a direct line to me."

"I'm good, Thorne. The people helping me work with Bella. They know she's innocent and they don't have to do anything by the book. Unfortunately, I do so it's good they're on our side."

Thorne doesn't look relieved. But he wouldn't be since the establishment he used to be part of is the one he can no longer trust. Hell, even in my agency, I'm not sure who I can look in the eye and know they're not dealing under the table to pull off some shady shit. Exhibit A—wanting Penn Simmons wiped from the face of the earth.

"The boys heard about you." Thorne studies me. "The American their sister apparently tied herself to before all this went down."

I give him a shrug. Winning over the Donnellys wasn't at the top of my to-do list but it sure wouldn't hurt my case with Bella. "I'm here and that's not going to change. Bella knows what I want and what I'm willing to wait on, which is everything."

He looks to his family and back to me. "She mentioned you have a daughter."

"I do."

His head bobs once methodically. "Then you know. Whoever your friends are who don't have to play by the same rules you do, tell them to hurry their shit up. I want my family back. My wife and I want our daughter back. There's nothing I won't do for my family, but when I'm being tapped..." He shakes his head. "Feels like my bloody hands are tied. I'm counting on you."

I look over at Bella and she's smiling like I haven't seen in a long time. "Don't worry. I'm counting on me too."

"Thorne." Annie demands her husband's attention again. "Please. We only have a short time."

Thorne slaps me on the shoulder. "Don't worry, love. I have a feeling we'll have our girl back sooner than later."

When Bella's gaze shifts to me, gone is the carefree expression she had moments ago. This one is hesitant, hopeful, and maybe even a little scared. Or who knows, maybe scared to hope.

I pick up my beer and move to the group, listening to Annie grill her daughter about their time apart, what she's been doing for work, and if she's safe.

———

ALL TOO QUICKLY, time passes and Bella and I are standing on the pier watching her family disappear into the night on the boat back to St. Thomas. It was a hard goodbye to watch, even for me, and I've never met her family before. Seeing tears on Bella's face for the second time since we've been here might **as well** be a turning knife in my gut.

The salty wind whips her long **hair** around her face but she doesn't take her eyes off **the black** horizon until the lights disintegrate into the night.

I reach over and take her hand. "**Let's** get back to the condo. It's late and we leave early."

She doesn't utter a word on **the walk** back to the street.

The silence continues in the taxi.

She doesn't afford me a glance, **even though** her grip on my hand is as intense as her mood.

I toss the driver a handful of **twenties** because we barely roll to a stop before Bella **is out** of the car and rushing to the building, as if a fire **were** blazing on her heels. The elevator doors almost **shut me** off from her by the time I catch up.

"What the hell?" I growl. "What **did I** do now?"

It's late and the building might **as well** be giving me the same silent treatment as Bella. **Feels** like we're on an expressway to heaven as we shoot **to our** floor without stopping. I lose her blue eyes when **they** fall shut and she drags both hands through her **wind**blown hair like she wants to rip it from its roots.

My irritation is escalating as **quick** as this damn elevator. She shakes her head, and **when** her lips part, she looks like she's about to throw **me** another curveball, but the tone of the elevator **breaks** her off. She makes a move for the door but I s**hift in** front of her and hold it, caging her in the small box.

"No, dammit. Tell me what the **fuck's** going on?"

Her face falls. "Move. I need off **this** lift. I need—"

"No. You need to tell me wh**at I did**. Why you're

pissed at me when you looked the happiest I've ever seen you with your family only an hour ago. Tonight was not easy to arrange."

She puts a hand to my abs and pushes. "Cole, let me out."

I don't budge. "Not a chance. You turning into the ice queen is pissing me off. It's not you. It's not the woman I met years ago and it sure as hell isn't the woman I fell in love with. Spar, fight—hell, fucking scream at me. Do your worst. You're not the silent treatment type of woman, Bella. I fell in love with you as much as for what you are as for what you aren't. You're one of a kind and made for *me*. Come at me and give me your worst, I can handle it."

I'm selfish and I know it. I'd bet my life on the fact I want her more than she wants her career. I'm willing to make any concession needed, as long as she's mine in the end.

And I'm ready to reach the end, dammit.

Her hand on my abs tightens into a grip on my tee so tight, my already stiff frown deepens. But then she uses the grip to pull herself up.

And I finally get what I want. What I've wanted for weeks—no, what I've wanted since before I begged her to come home with me, even if it meant her hiding out in the States forever.

She closes the space separating us and her mouth lands on mine.

A kiss.

Something I refused to give her until she was ready.

I open my mouth—greedy and hungry—taking what only she can give me. I hold the elevator door with one hand but my other dips into her hair, plastering her mouth to mine. Now that I have her, there's no damn way I'm letting her go or allowing any regrets to fuck up my plans.

Or my life. I've fucked it up well enough on my own and I'm doing all I can to unfuck it now. And it starts with Isabella Donnelly in my bed.

Forever.

But I feel no regret in this kiss. I press my tongue in her mouth and she doesn't argue. She sucks it, pressing her body to mine, here on the threshold to the elevator.

And she kisses the frown right off my face—something only she has ever been able to do.

I step back and pull her with me, moving down the hall to the unit we've shared in paradise for the last two days. Our teeth clash but our connection doesn't break until I'm forced to dig the fucking key card out of my wallet.

"Cole." She's breathless and I'm pissed I had to give her the chance to fill her lungs. "Tonight has been—"

"Shut up," I clip and throw the door open, tossing the key card followed by my wallet into the room. I push her in and have her pressed to the wall as my mouth finds hers before the door clicks behind us. I'm not afraid of much but I am afraid of losing any traction I've gained. "Don't. Don't think. Don't talk. And don't fucking go back, baby."

She nods—not letting our connection break, not pushing me away, and not kneeing me in the nuts, catapulting me into next week.

I did it.

I finally won The Bella Lottery.

Let the celebrations commence.

22

LOST TIME

Bella

Whant Cole did for me tonight was the most precious gift. One I had no idea how badly I craved.

My parents, Archer, Devon...

The Donnellys.

Together again.

Some families fight and argue and complain about the ones they're tied to by blood, but not us. We've always been close—we'd love one another if it were a choice instead of purely being stuck with the ones we were born to.

I've missed my parents and brothers—so much. But until I saw them standing before me tonight, I didn't know how deeply it ran. The hole in my heart from not seeing or communicating with my family was a pain my subconscious had built a wall around.

Cole knew what I needed, he always has. He not

only gave it to me, he delivered it on a silver platter and filled that void with flowers so beautiful they'll surely bloom for a long, long time.

I'm overcome. I have been for weeks but when the door opened and I saw the gift he arranged, I was filled with happiness and gutted by guilt for pushing him away.

It was all I could do to get back to the condo without claiming what I should have long ago. Greedily grasp the gift that was dangling in front of me and stop being a tunnel-visioned imbecile.

I'm not proud of myself and plan on doing everything I can to fix what I've mucked up.

"Baby." Cole's lips on my neck tease my sensitive skin as he yanks my cami over my head. It whispers to the floor next to us with promises of what's to come and I'm left standing braless in a pair of wide-legged linen trousers.

I pull at his T-shirt and he helps, reaching between his shoulder blades. Then, from my bare breasts to my fresh scar, I'm skin to skin with the only man I've ever been with, the only man I've ever loved.

"Thank you. For tonight." I look into his dark eyes, to the lust and need settled in them. "I'm sorry I've been too deep in my own problems to see ... *everything.*"

He runs a hand up my side, his thumb spanning my midsection and dragging over the mark I'll always have to remind me of what brought me to him. "We'll talk later. All I can think of right now is how to fuck you without hurting you."

I shake my head as he takes a step back and unbuttons my slacks, dropping them to the floor. "Sometimes

I worry about my own sanity because that shouldn't turn me on, but it does."

He says nothing as his lips hit mine again, devouring me. I swallow his moan, feeling it low in my belly and then, farther down, between my legs when he paws my arse with both hands in a firm squeeze.

This reminds me of times long ago when we were new. We had worked together for months and couldn't fight it any longer. Every time we were together it was about me—him teaching me, leading me to new places which would only make me blush before driving me wild, and making me forget all the reasons why I blushed in the first place.

But as much as it was about me, it was also about him. Cole didn't hold back and made sure I knew my naïveté and lack of all experience did things to him he couldn't put into words. He might not have been able to explain them, but he showed me all the ways me being me drove him wild.

"The last time we were like this, you were giving me goodbye sex," he murmurs against my temple as he fondles my nipples into pebbled peaks. "If you try that shit again, Bella, I'll tie you up and keep you in my dingy basement. I don't give a shit how weird it makes me."

My thong lands on the floor and Cole drops to a knee next to them.

He presses his lips to my scar before tracing it lightly with his tongue. I look down my bare body, watching him give all his attention to the worst of me and remember what he said not long ago about seeing the beauty in my healing wound rather than the nasty mark I'll always carry. "I haven't seen your dingy basement. It can't be worse than some of the places I've called home while hiding out."

His hands slide down my abs and pelvis. When his thumbs settle on either side of my clit where I'm more than wet, he easily spreads me, making my breath catch. "Baby, don't make me think of lost time, it'll piss me off. Not when I'm here." He looks to his hands and my most private parts he's re-familiarizing himself with. His thumbs massage my lips but nothing else.

Electricity zings through me—every square inch of my bare skin acutely aware and sensitive to his touch. Gone are the warm and humid island temps. All the heat I'm feeling now is purely and utterly Cole Carson.

He flicks my clit with the tip of his nose right before his tongue teases me. My head hits the wall with a thud and I press my hips forward as his name drips off my lips, as desperate as I feel. "Cole."

"Sweetness." His tongue explores, his fingers continue to torment, but he doesn't come close to my clit again. "Missed this. Missed losing myself the way only you can make me do."

I shift my legs apart in hopes he'll take everything I'm greedy to give. "I've missed you so much, I think I blocked it from my bloody brain. Please, Cole. Do your worst later, but don't torment me now. I won't be able to handle it."

"Oh, I'm going to torment you." His tongue circles my clit as he slides a finger deep inside me. I press onto his hand, finally allowing myself to want so much more. "I think you deserve a little payback for pushing me away."

My body slumps into the wall and I have to fight for balance. "If this is your idea of payback, then I'll take it."

I don't see it since my eyes have rolled to the back of my head, but I feel it—his smile as he adds a second finger. Then, he gets down to business and sucks.

"I might collapse."

His free arm rounds me to support my weight and it happens—the tunnel only he can shove me down. I start to tumble, my hearing and vision and every other sense begins to fade, I only feel our connection. When it starts to swallow me up, he hooks a finger inside and draws my clit between his teeth. And I thank the stars the unit next door is empty.

Because this is different than it was in the coat room. As good as that was—and with Cole, it's always good—we both had to maintain some type of control. We weren't alone.

Now, there's no control.

Cole is hungry.

I'm *desperate*.

I fall apart under his touch, his lips, and the overwhelming power he's always had over me. And that power hasn't faded. If anything, it's intensified—exploding into a sea of color, bright behind my eyelids, artistically created for only me by Cole Carson.

Fighting for my breath, he milks my orgasm for all it's worth, draining me until I lose his touch as his hands grip my hamstrings. "Hold on."

I do, wrapping my limp arms around his neck and my legs that barely hang on to his narrow hips. With my face buried in his thick, dark hair, I realize I'm moving.

My back hits linen bed covers the color of the sand when it disappears into the sea. I lose his touch and I draw my feet up, folding into myself, and pry my eyes open. He's digging around in his overnight kit that has exploded on the nightstand.

The lamp pops on, its low glow like a warm hug, reaching only us. Cole rips at the button on his pants with one hand and lifts a condom to his teeth with the other to rip it open. "Annoyed after all these years you're still not on birth control."

The fact he's annoyed with me about anything right now makes me smile. "I suppose you're always annoyed with me about something or other."

"Yes. Only I would fall for the most infuriating woman on the planet. Hell, I had to travel around the world to find you."

"You love my annoyances." I bite my lip as my eyes drop to his hand that's now wrapped around his cock. Swollen, hard, and all bloody mine.

What few female friends I had growing up complained about American men and their circumcised heads but I've never known anything other than the beautiful one standing erect and greedy in front of me. I wouldn't want him any other way. Cole fists himself, pumping once as he grips my knee. I give him what he wants and my legs splay. His eyes are as greedy as his cock leering over me, trying to decide what he wants first.

Dragging a finger down the inside of my thigh, he hits my very wet sex and starts to play with me again. "This is it, Bella." His eyes shift to mine and I'm not sure I've ever seen him so serious. "We'll figure out your work and my family, but you're mine. I'm not fucking around anymore. When I sink into you tonight, there's no going back."

My insides flip and scrunch and tense.

"Love you, baby," he adds, his tone low and solemn. "Not interested in living life without you any longer."

My skin prickles with nerves as his words wash over me. I force myself to punch away every wall I've built around my heart while I've had to live without him.

"Bella." My name falls sharp and demanding from his lips.

"Yes." My throat tries to strangle me but I push past it for him. I reach for his hand and pull it up to my chest, pressing it flat to my heart. "I'm frightened, Cole. So scared about what's to come. But, yes. I promise … no going back. Unless I get thrown into prison or burned at the stake."

He lets go of his cock and bends at the waist. His forearm hits the bed beside me first and then his mouth takes mine—rough and possessive and, yes, even victoriously arrogant.

My breath catches as his cock slides easily inside me because, for the first time, we're connected, skin to skin, nothing between us. I moan into his mouth and my fingers dig into his shoulders. He's never taken me bare. Ever. I know he loves Abbott with all his heart but he's made it clear he won't ever take a chance again. Cole Carson does not like surprises in any area of his life.

"Just for a second. Fuck, baby." His words are jagged, and if I didn't know better, I'd think he might be in pain. "Feels like I'm taking you for the first time all over again."

My thighs tighten and I lift my hips for more. Every muscle in his bulky frame is taut and still, as if he's afraid to move.

It's something I understand. Having him again after all this time with nothing between us is too much. We're poking a sleeping dragon and I'm afraid of what we'll both do—or not do—if he moves another millimeter.

But Cole tempts us both. He slides out to the tip before taking me again with even more force. He groans and this time I'm sure he's in pain. "I need to wrap up."

"Yes," I agree but hold him tighter. "Now is no time to be careless."

"I don't know," he growls and starts to move. "You're the only person I want to be careless with."

He shows me how strongly he feels about throwing caution to the wind. Circling an arm around my lower back, he lifts my hips from the bed, his thrusts reaching deeper. Cole is proving exactly what he said, that I'm his.

I always have been and always will be.

"Baby." His lips press against my temple and he starts to move faster.

I know his body when we're like this ... he's close. "Cole—"

"Shh. I know."

"But—"

"Fuck," he hisses into my hair and pulls out.

He presses his hips into me, the underside of his shaft rubs up and down on my still-sensitive clit. I gasp for a second time and he lets go, his body tensing when he comes. When he rolls me to my side so he doesn't give me his weight, he holds me close, gluing our bodies together in a sticky, wonderful mess.

"That was—"

His lips stop my words and he takes my mouth. When he finally breaks for air, he finishes my thought. "That was fucking magnificent and you're getting on birth control as soon as possible. Do you know how hard it's going to be for me to wrap **up** after having you like that?"

I press my lips to his jaw because **he's** right.

"Love you, sweetness." He doesn't **let** me go. I'm so worn out from Cole's surprise and **now** this, I'm sated and exhausted. I have no desire to **move** away from him.

"Cole—" I can't seem to put two **words** together and am interrupted by the ringing of **the** only cell phone we have left between the two of us.

He reaches over me without **breaking** our connection. "This better be a four-alarm fire, Hollingsworth."

I press into him and drag my **hand** down to his ass and squeeze. His gaze shifts to mine **and** his cocky smile he shoots me too often starts to form.

Then, it freezes.

He frowns.

"What is it?" I whisper.

"How the fuck did that happen?" **he** bites.

"Cole," I demand.

He looks at me and shakes his **head.** "Shit. Okay. Keep me updated." He pauses. "**Yeah. We** take off first thing in the morning. I'll meet you **at** Vega's."

He disconnects his call and tosses **the** cell to the bed behind me.

"Dammit, Cole. Tell me."

"Marie Kasey."

My brows pinch. "The irritable **reporter.** What about her?"

"She was shot tonight."

23

WELCOME TO CREW'S FUCKED-UP FAMILY

Bella

What's the saying?

Two steps forward...

Three *million* steps back.

Fine. That's not the saying. But I've gone from treading water in the middle of the deepest oceans to drowning in a hurricane.

Despite Crew's men putting a tail on Kasey, someone got to her when she was in a crowded bar in Georgetown. The result is not the one Randolph wanted, but that doesn't mean it's good, either.

Cole and I are in the backseat of Grady's enormous SUV after he picked us up at the small airport in Virginia. I haven't bothered with pleasantries, demanding updates on every damn storm swirling over our heads at the moment. "Any word on Marie Kasey?"

Grady glances back as he changes lanes. "ICU and it doesn't look good."

"Shit."

"Shit is right," he echoes. "Ozzy's beating himself up over it. He was following as close as he could, she slipped into a crowded bar in Georgetown when he lost her. The next thing you know, screams came from the back near the restrooms. She was found on the floor bleeding out—GSW to the chest. Whoever Randolph hired is a piss-poor shot because it's not hard to kill someone at that range and she's still alive."

That hits a little too close to home and a chill runs down my spine. Cole reaches over and grabs my hand, gritting, "Yeah, we know all too well."

Grady's eyes shoot to the rearview mirror, wincing. "Damn. Sorry, Bella."

I shake my head. "No worries. Thank goodness for piss-poor-shooting bad guys, right?"

"We need to decide what to do with the recordings of Randolph ordering the hit. It's not exactly like it was a judge-approved wiretap but it also wasn't on U.S. soil, either. Everyone is ready to meet and discuss when we get back. This is not our usual MO. We don't play by your rules, Carson. I'm not gonna lie, Crew is on edge about this—especially with you being involved."

Cole shakes his head. "I'm the one coordinating your work. If Crew thinks I have an issue with any of this, he's wrong. I have two goals in life right now—to clear Bella's name and figure out why my boss wants me dead. There aren't many boundaries I won't cross on a normal day and I'll fucking bulldoze through the rest of them to meet those two goals. I should be the least of his worries."

"I'll take care of Crew," I add.

Cole's eyes narrow on me. "It's my working relation-ship, sweetness. I can handle it."

I hike a brow and hope he can translate my glare for what it means. Just because *we* look different upon returning to the States than we did before we left, does not mean he can strong-arm me as if we're operating in the wild west.

I turn to him fully. "Whatever means you're using to *handle it* with Crew Vega hasn't worked in years. I need two minutes with him and I promise whatever alpha rodeo you two have going on will be brushed under the rug once and for all."

A frown sets into his handsome olive-skinned face. "No."

In contrast, my expression is smug. "A wager?"

He shakes his head and turns toward the front. "No."

"Oh, but you like wagers, right, love?" I ask, reminding him of the one he threw down, the dare of a lifetime, while I was still weak in the hospital. I reach up and poke Grady on the shoulder. "Are you a gambling man? Who would you put your money on when it comes to your boss? Cole or my charming self?"

I can't see his entire face through the mirror, but his blue eyes crinkle. "My money is on you, Bella."

"Fucking-A," Cole mutters and squeezes my hand.

"Indeed." I smile for the first time since we were in the presence of my family last night. Well, I take that back—I did smile in the shower this morning when Cole cursed the invention of condoms right before he slid one on and fucked me in the shower. I do need to get some birth control sorted quickly. I hope Gracie can help me out with that as well. I pull my hand from his and put my fingers to his chin. When he turns to me, I brush the pad of my thumb over his bottom lip, wishing we were alone again—I've missed every part of him. "Don't be a sore loser, darling."

The next thing I know, my thumb is caught between his teeth and a smirk plays on those lips I've enjoyed for the last twelve hours.

"Fuck me," Grady sighs. "Now I know how Jarvis feels. I take my kids to preschool in this car. When all this is said and done, you two need a long vacation where no one has to see you or listen to you on surveillance so you can work this shit out of your systems."

I smile bigger when he kisses my thumb he just bit. "Will I ever work you out of my system, baby?"

"I'm counting on it never happening."

Cole

A THICK FOLDER lands with a thud on the table.

Crew's dining room in his shitty farmhouse head-quarters has been transformed since we left two days ago. Three enormous screens have been hung over the faded wallpaper that looks older than Red. Each screen displays a live surveillance feed. One of the land we're standing on, another is a building in the woods I don't recognize, and the third is my house and property.

Didn't know they were doing this but seeing as my boss and his boss want me dead, can't say I'm not grateful.

Crew, Asa, Grady, Jarvis, and Ozzy—who I just met —are a group of men trained and more than willing to carry out the shit the rest of us can't because that shit is against the law. They get paid handsomely for it because they're on their own. Should they get caught, no one will claim them or help them out of a situation besides one another.

A group of risk takers—measured risk takers—who get paid a shit ton for taking out the dark underbelly of the world.

Crew flips open the folder. "We need to get to it. Our list of shit to discuss is long—"

"Excuse me," Bella butts in.

All their attention turns to her.

"Bella, don't do this," I warn.

She ignores me and levels her eyes on the leader of this secret group. "Do you trust me?"

He shows no emotion whatsoever. Not a tick, a frown, or even a damn shrug to appease her. Definitely not a smile. "What kind of question is that?"

"A fair one," she insists, crossing her arms. "Have I ever once given you reason to question my work or my judgement?"

Crew doesn't take his eyes off her. "You're not."

"What you're doing for me, I'll never be able to repay the debt. You're working to give me my life back and I'll be forever grateful. Should I not end up dead or in prison—"

"Don't talk that way," I warn.

She continues to ignore me and I wonder if she remembers I'm the one delivering all her orgasms.

"Whatever this is," she motions between me and him, "is done. I trust you and Cole equally and I need your respect for each other to mirror that."

Now I'm definitely going to need to remind her of

the fact she trusts me more than anyone, because I love her.

And, orgasms.

Crew Vega's eyes shift to me and he pauses before lifting his chin. "Done."

I accept his one-word apology and nod because, one: I'll do anything for Bella, and two: I didn't fucking do anything wrong to begin with.

Bella turns to me. "See? Less than a minute."

Grady barks a laugh and Crew clears his throat. "Let's get started. The last couple days have been busy and we're all doing shit we don't normally do. Ozzy's background includes military imaging and surveillance. This shit is impressive," he waves to the screens on the wall behind him, "and an investment."

Ozzy is one of Crew's newer recruits but hasn't been sent out on assignment yet. He has been busy, like everyone else, with Bella's shit.

And now, mine.

He points to the first screen. "This is camp. It's a good idea to have another eye on things besides the ground cameras."

"Where are the feeds coming from?" I ask. The CIA can do this shit any day of the week, but not everyone can.

Ozzy keeps talking. "Satellite. Crew's not kidding, this is an investment. He's the proud new owner of Reskill, a satellite company with over one hundred and forty satellites around the world."

"You bought an entire satellite company while we were in the Caribbean?" Bella asks, mirroring my thoughts.

Crew shrugs. "I've been contemplating it for

months. I can follow my men while they're on assignment and keep a better eye on my property and Whitetail. It was in motion and this pushed it along."

"It's not only video surveillance. We can now communicate with camp safely over our own private network—no more going dark. We can also capture electromagnetic wavelengths to sense radar and hyperspectral images. Fuck clouds and buildings—we can sense figures through them and measure something down to a millimeter. This," Ozzy juts a thumb over his shoulder, "is the shit."

I cross my arms. "Impressive. I bet you can do almost anything we can do."

"That's my plan," Crew says and nods back to Ozzy. "And he knows how to work this shit because the rest of us have no clue yet."

I point to the middle screen. "I see you're spying on my house, but what's on the other one?"

"The church." Asa moves to the head of the table. "But it's no church. And Wendy Sisson made her first visit we witnessed. There was a meeting in the backroom of the building where every human on the property congregated. It lasted fourteen minutes then she was out of there like a streak of shit. We're working on getting facial IDs on the others."

I sigh because this is a lot, but it's also nothing. Not one new piece of information we can do anything with.

"Your boss is a prick," Jarvis adds.

"Tell me something I don't know," I mutter.

"Your house has been quiet other than a couple of deliveries. It seems you living and breathing stresses Peterson out. We heard it on the wires. He's got his tighty-whities in a bunch over you returning to work tomorrow."

I pull a hand down my face. "Yeah. I can't wait."

Jarvis pulls something out of his back pocket and flings it across the room to me. When I catch it, I see it's my government issued cell phone my boss was using to track me. "I went to the Kennedy Center. Had to BS my way through security and tell them my cell was locked up in the coat room. That was almost as enjoyable as dealing with my insurance company over my *stolen and fucked-up* Porsche. You're a fun guy to have around."

Bella and I would be D-E-A-D if I gave a shit about his car, so I ignore that and wave my phone at him. "Appreciate it. You saved me a shit-ton of paperwork over a lost cell."

"Don't turn that on until you hit the highway tomorrow," Crew warns.

"You know, we don't usually work together in this capacity, but I'm not an idiot," I bite.

"This is all fascinating," Bella interjects. "But can we please move on to Randolph and Marie Kasey?"

Crew holds up a hand. "Hang on. We're getting to that because this shit is a puzzle we're still piecing together."

Grady steps up to the table. "Here's the most interesting thing about the last twenty-four hours. As soon as Randolph touched down in Virginia, he texted Sisson."

I feel my own expression fall. "What the fuck?"

Grady flips open the phone book of a file and hands me the top piece of paper. "Here's the transcript. They're arranging funds to be wired overseas. We're still trying to figure out who the recipient is and what's being done with the money. But your gal," Grady points to me, "and your guy," he points to Bella who reaches out to grab my hand, "are in cahoots." He continues to look at Bella. "Told you I'm a betting man, but I wouldn't've taken that wager."

I take the paper and Bella leans in to scan it too.

It's true. And we're talking a lot of fucking money— more than any senator should have at any given time if he's serving his country, as he should be. This is where his kickbacks are going. But what is he supporting and what the fuck does Sisson have to do with it?

"Right," Jarvis agrees and I look up. He's standing there with his arms crossed. "This is enough to make my head spin. It's so much easier putting a bullet through someone's head."

"This is all fun and games when it's a mystery on the back of a cereal box we're trying to solve with a sugar-coated magic ring. But this shit is real and not what we do." Grady levels his glare on me. Gone is the fun guy who picked us up from the airport. "You might be the CIA but what we're doing isn't sanctioned by the Agency or anyone else. We didn't sign up for this. We've got families to think about—wives, kids," he throws Jarvis a glance. "Even my sister—who I still can't believe is a part of this life—is now in the mix. What I'm asking is, what do we do when we get to the end of the maze?"

My jaw goes hard. I don't take my eyes off him but I do put my arm around Bella and pull her front to my side.

Ozzy stands silent.

"Fuck," Asa mutters.

Jarvis takes a step forward and his tone comes out with a warning. "Grady—"

"No, Jarvis," Grady stops him and turns to Crew. "What do we do then?"

Crew looks down at the table where his index finger traces the woodgrain, as if it'll lead him to the answer. His chest expands and he nods, as if finding the meaning of life in the complex lines of its history. Leaning forward, hands flat to the wood, he lets his head hang before lifting it and piercing everyone around the room with his dark eyes.

Those eyes finally settle on the woman I plan to marry and make a mother to Abbott and my future children.

You know, in time.

"Bella, you've done a lot for me. Dedicated and always coming through for me when I need you." Crew looks to Grady and then to Jarvis. "She helped get to Gracie and saved your ass. She's one of us. So when we get to the end, we finish it," Crew says. "*That*, we know how to do. I'm not in the business of waiting on the justice system or letting politics or the media fuck things up. We'll do what we always do. I'll sleep better at night—we all will. We'll do it for Bella and Carson and Red and Abbott. It's what we've always done."

"Fuck, yeah we will," Asa agrees and looks to me and Bella. An almost evil smile plays on his lips as he hikes a brow. "Welcome to Crew's fucked-up family."

24

UP YOUR GAME

Bella

"I'm sleep deprived, haven't worn makeup since we brought Aimée home, and am up to my ears in laundry," she says without looking at me as she questions me about everything. "I don't have the energy to be subtle,"

"Please, Addy, let me help with something."

Crew's wife, Addy, turns from where she's standing at her kitchen sink loading the dishwasher. I have asked countless times to help. Food, dishes, change a nappy—though I'd have to figure that one out. She insists she's simply happy I'm here since she hasn't had the chance to dote over me like Gracie and Keelie have. She sits me down at her farmhouse table which is longer than an eight-day week and pours me a glass of wine.

"Are you kidding?" She sways as she talks, patting the baby on its bum where the little one snoozes, wrapped inside something that looks like a kangaroo pouch tied to Addy's chest. "I'm thrilled you came because I want to know all the things. Crew thinks a lot of you and considers you essential to his business. It seems some of the men knew about you and Carson before you were shot but the rest of us didn't. So, tell me," she keeps swaying but picks up her water to take a big drink, "*everything*."

Again, this is the female talk I'm not at all familiar with. I pick up my glass of wine that's smooth and going down much too easily after the last few days. "Are you sure I can't fold a load of laundry? Sort your socks?"

She smiles. "Nice try, my new English friend. Look, I've done my best to get what I could out of Red and Abbott in the last two days. Red grunts and heads back outside to help Morris with whatever Morris will allow him to do. All Abbott has told me is that you talk funny and pulled up a map on her iPad to show me where you're from. But, yesterday, she was teaching Vivi how to count to ten in French—which Crew is thrilled about."

Crew ended our briefing with the big bang of *we'll end this the way we always end this* and that was that, but not before informing everyone dinner was to be at Whitetail and everyone in his *fucked-up family* was expected to attend.

I take a big gulp of my wine because I feel like I'm going to need it since everyone will arrive shortly. "Red doesn't much care for me."

"Really?" Addy stops swaying and her brows pinch. "I didn't sense that. Why?"

I pull in a big breath and look out her window where Cole, Crew, and Jarvis are watching Abbott and Vivi play. "He doesn't like me for his son. I've known this for some time. Cole doesn't keep much from me and has always been honest about how his father feels. I didn't even know Red and Abbott were living with him full time until he brought me home from the hospital. Abbott was cold as ice in the beginning, but she's slowly thawing. I believe the French lessons are helping. Or maybe she's giving up on hating me since Cole hasn't made it a secret he wants me to stay."

She starts swaying again when a squeak comes from the bundle tied to her middle. "Wait. You don't want to stay? I thought once this was all over—and for the record, Crew has no doubt they're going to fix your problem—you'd be around for good."

I give her a small smile. "I'm not sure what I want anymore. I always assumed if I were lucky enough to clear my name, I'd stuff it in the faces of those who wronged me and return to Vauxhall." I shake my head and pick up my glass. It seems a little vino helps when one is learning how to girl-talk. "But honestly, if I go back to work, my cover will be blown. My mug is already plastered internationally for being most wanted. I couldn't work anyhow. But am I ready for this?" I motion around her kitchen and through the back window. "To settle down in one place for the rest of time? Even if it is with Cole."

Addy glances at the clock before moving a chair next to mine, scooting close. I try not to frown when she reaches out to take my hand in hers. We literally just met, but I'm oddly okay with it.

Addy lowers her voice. "You don't know my story but if Crew gives you his trust, that means everything to me. I spent my life running and pretending to be someone I'm not. There was no end in sight. Looking over my shoulder became a way of life. No one should live that way." She squeezes my hand. "Crew made it all go away.

And the rest of these men helped. Trust me when I say, nothing is sweeter than living free—and doing it right here in the middle of nowhere is even better. It's a dream. One I didn't even know to hope for."

I'm about to open my mouth—to say what, I have no clue—but we're interrupted by voices from the front hall of Crew and Addy's enormous home.

She gives me another squeeze before letting go. "Things continue to be exciting around here, Bella. Take it from me, don't discount this life too quickly. You'll be the only loser in the situation."

"Yoo-hoo! I have cookies and cheesy potato casserole and paper plates. And not those thin, flimsy ones you can't pile food on. I sprang for the thick ones because Morris said we were having barbecue and you don't want some messy rib flopping on the floor. Now, where's my baby?"

"See?" Addy laughs. "And this excitement has nothing to do with drive-by shootings, stalkers, or nasty mothers."

I don't hide my surprise but also don't have a chance to ask what in the bloody hell that's all about because an older woman appears at the threshold to the kitchen, weighed down with bags and dishes. "Welp, there she is. I've never had a British friend before!"

"Bella, this is Bev," Addy says as she wrangles the baby out of her pouch. "She's everyone's grandma. Just go with it."

Bev shoots me one of the most genuine smiles I've ever been awarded. "I can't wait to listen to you talk, but first I need to put this stuff down and get my greedy hands on that baby."

More voices echo through the old walls and my very

first all-American barbecue dinner is off to a roaring start.

COLE and the rest of Crew's men consumed their meals at the speed of light and returned to the compound. I tried to join them but Cole insisted I stay behind and *relax*.

Damn him.

The next time he demands I bloody *relax*, I will take him down. I don't care who's there to witness it.

Of course, I was going to ignore him but Maya filled my glass to the brim and sat down next to me since we haven't had a chance to *get to know each other* yet. I happily guzzled the entire thing because girl talk pairs perfectly with a full-bodied, oaky Meritage.

The women who belong to Crew's *fucked-up family* are lovely, kind, generous, open, and nosy as hell. I found it oddly easy to give them every bit of information they wanted. They're just that nice and I'm just that tipsy.

Who knows, maybe I'm actually better at this female bonding thing than I thought. I'm sure it helps these particular women are lovely.

The sun has set and the woods have come to life with the constant song of the cicadas. It's warm and humid but I've lived in the desert for so long, I love being hugged by the forest and its varying shades of green. The ladies have scattered to tend to their children and this is the first quiet moment I've had in days.

I lean my head back onto the lush patio chair and close my eyes.

"You're back."

I take a deep breath and pray for patience before I turn to him. Red has flopped into the chair next to me and I must have been too deep in my wine fog to hear him since Red is not stealth in anything he does. He's a bull in a roomful of English teacups.

I don't hesitate. "I'm sorry I took Cole away from you and Abbott. I know how you feel and tried to convince him I could go on my own. I don't plan on it happening again."

He puts his beer bottle to his lips for a pull before looking out to the rolling vines snaking over the land. "You stayin' or goin'?"

"Pardon?"

His dark eyes are guarded but sharp. It takes me back to when Cole sought me out and begged me to come to the States with him, even if it meant hiding in plain sight. But I couldn't give up working, wasn't ready to hang up my dreams, or claim a new identity. He was hurt and I was still mourning the death of my career. Contracting with people like Crew privately was my only way of not giving up.

Cole wanted one thing—me. And as much as I wanted him, I held back.

I was selfish and stubborn and I knew it. I sent Cole away and started down the path of freeing myself. I knew I would never be able to give myself to him fully if I weren't completely and totally free—mind, heart, soul, and in the eyes of the damned British government and western world.

It doesn't surprise me when Red is impatient for an answer. "Well?"

"I want to stay." I almost don't recognize my own

voice. It's the first time I've allowed myself to believe it might be possible, let alone utter it aloud. "I love him."

Red says nothing. He studies me like I'm a rusty piece of machinery he's trying to decide to keep or throw out with the Tuesday trash.

"I've never loved anyone outside of my family," I go on, laying my heart out for him even before I admit this to Cole. I'm not sure if it's the wine or the last few days or the hope that's been planted deep inside me, but for some reason, nothing feels more right than baring my soul at this moment. "It's always been him. He challenges me, he believes in me, and he unnerves me. But he deserves more than only part of me. I love him too much to allow him to settle for anything less. It doesn't help that I'm greedy, Red. I want my life back so I can live it to my fullest with him and with Abbott."

He stares me down—thinking, pondering. I wish he could fix me and my problems the way he does old mixers or weed whackers. His beer keeps spinning around the bottle like a mini tornado. Not a word. I'm positive if I were a pile of rubble, he'd dump me.

"I'm done apologizing," I tell him the truth. "I can't tell you exactly what the future looks like but I plan to be in Cole's life. I can't imagine it any other way. He's mine and I'm finally claiming him—"

"Loved Cole's mama," he interrupts. "Only woman in the world for me. A father wants a lot of things for his child but nothin' more than that—for him to have what I had."

"I'm sorry you're not happy with me—"

"Didn't say that, Bella."

I frown.

"Do me a favor, love him the way his mama loved

me. Because I already know how he feels about you and that'll guarantee you the best life a woman can have. When you think he's happy, up your game. Then do it again. Never stop trying to love him more. Because he's doing it for you."

Something comes over me, something I'm not accustomed to, but it seems to be happening too often lately. My eyes well and my throat thickens. I nod and reach over to give his forearm a squeeze. It's all I can manage.

"Always wanted a daughter," he mutters and stands, but before he leaves me to my frayed emotions, Red Carson does something sweet I never thought possible. He leans down and presses his lips to the top of my head. It feels reminiscent of my father or even my grandfather, but even more, it's a seal of approval. It happens so quick I wonder if I imagined the whole thing because he clears his throat right before the patio door bangs shut.

I swipe the tear before it rolls off my chin and feel some tension ease.

Red has accepted me. For some reason, all our other problems seem to pale in comparison.

I'll cherish this moment forever.

Cole

"Raji, if you fall off the face of the earth again, I'm gonna come over there and hunt you down myself. Pick up your fucking phone and call me back. I need a location on our world-traveling friends."

I toss the phone on the dining table and rub my temples. I really need a new personal phone. I'm using Bella's and she's going to need it when I go back to work. Tomorrow should be interesting. Ozzy is going to follow me in. Once I get inside Langley, I'll be fine.

I look back up to the monitors covering Crew's dining room and punch a few keys on the laptop, watching my house light up. Crew had the forethought to wire them so we could make it look like someone was home. Aside from eating dinner at Crew and Addy's and then going back to tuck Abbott in and read her a book, I've been here, listening to the wires and watching the monitors. My house is quiet, thank fuck, but the church is not. There's been plenty of activity and my boss's boss returned for another meeting. Most of it happened near the southwest corner of the complex. From the electromagnetic waves and multiple trips made to that area of the building, I'm betting it's a storage room. And my guess, it's not filled with bibles.

Raji hasn't returned my calls since before we went to the Caribbean. Peterson is going to be the least of his problems if he doesn't get his act together. Paid informants cannot be flakey.

At least not that flakey.

It appears my boss is not the only one unhappy their hit wasn't carried out. I caught up on Randolph's wire transcripts tonight. He's downright pissed his former lover and Channel Five News reporter still has a heartbeat, even if it is being supported by medical equipment. He's sweating more bullets than have been shot at us in the last few days.

I sent everyone home two hours ago. Crew's men have been working on this shit day and night for Bella and me. I'm here and can give them a break, plus I wanted Bella to have tonight. She needs to fucking relax. From what I saw when I ran over to put Abbott to bed, she was doing just that. Though, my ulterior motive is for her to get to know this tribe. I need her to like them, maybe work with them, and want to be around the women so she'll have even more reason to want to stay.

I'd like to think I'm enough of one. But I know she loves her work.

Red was not wrong about my state of mind when she wouldn't let me bring her home. I was more than broken. I was un-fucking-done. If she leaves now, after I've had her here, I'm not sure how I'll recover.

Something catches my eye on the screens in the vineyard. A body moving through the vines. I switch over to that feed on the laptop and zoom in.

Speak of my personal devil in red, even if she is dressed in all black. The women must've wrapped it up for the night.

I move to the front door and stand on the dark front porch. It only takes a few minutes—sticks and leaves and brush crack beneath her feet before I see her. When she finally emerges through the trees, her quick clip comes to an abrupt stop.

Silence hangs between us until I finally ask, "You have fun?"

She takes in a deep breath before closing the distance between us.

Clomp, clomp, clomp up the stairs without a word and I start to frown wondering what's wrong until she grabs my hand before walking straight into my arms. She lifts up on her toes and I don't lose her eyes until our mouths collide.

When it comes to Bella, I turn into a feral animal. My every emotion, action, and reaction is red-hot instinct. It hasn't changed since day one. Nothing is more miserable than fighting the natural drive inside me that wants only her.

This moment is no different. My arms cage her and my lips possess hers, moving, taking her with me until my back slams into the front door. I refuse to lose her mouth—I've lived without it far too long—and fumble around until I find the knob and we fall into the house.

She yanks at my tee until her hands find my back,

her nails biting into me, molding us together. I turn her and papers go flying from the dining room table before her back hits the wood.

I rip my lips from hers and don't pretend to catch my breath as I drag my hand down her torso. "Did I hurt you?"

She shakes her head, her tongue sneaking out to taste her lip I was mauling. "Please, Cole."

Her eyes are hooded, maybe from the wine, but I'm going to believe it's because she wants me and my very hungry cock. Bending at the waist, I plant my forearm by her head, brushing the hair from her face, and bump her nose with the tip of mine. "Need a condom to fuck you, sweetness. Let's go upstairs."

She fists my shirt and twists her hand, bringing me close until our mouths are fused again. Her tongue swims in my mouth, like it's lost at sea and can't find its way home. Her other arm snakes around my neck and if her leg weren't wrapped around the back of my thigh in a vise, I might be worried she was trying to punk me by twisting me into a headlock.

It's never actually happened but not by her lack of trying.

I press my needy cock into her pussy, separated only by her denim and my shorts. I drag my lips away long enough to look down at her. "Baby, I'm warning you, if we don't go upstairs soon, there will be no condom and I will not pull out. As much as I like to come all over you, I don't want that tonight."

Her leg around my thigh tenses, daring me to pull away.

My favorite Wizards shirt is in definite danger of being shredded by a Brit possessed by desire.

And I don't think her goal is to flip me into a headlock.

"Last chance, Bella," I warn. "I have no desire to wrestle out of your hold. If you don't let go, it's officially open season for baby-making. I'm happy to marry you first but you also know I have no issue with doing shit out of order. If anyone is going to buck the system, it's me. I don't think it's what you want but nothing would make me happier."

She bites that damn lip.

I pause and tip my head. "Wait. Are you drunk?"

She pulls in a big breath. "No. But who knew there was so much wine in the Commonwealth?"

I slide my hand up the back of her neck and cup her head, my tone low and rough. "Are you fucking with me?"

"I'm not drunk and I'm not fucking with you."

I exhale against her mouth. "What changed?"

She shakes her head. "Nothing has changed."

"No," I grit. "I mean, *this* is different. *You're* different. You know I don't like secrets, especially from you."

"I'm not different." The words fall from her lips with an ease I don't recognize since I've basically had to wring them out of her. "I'm finally being honest—with myself. It's always been you, Cole. I want everything from you. Every bloody thing you'll give me."

My chest tightens and I freeze. I don't dare move— afraid I'm dreaming or she'll finally kick me in the figurative balls and take it back. "Everything?"

She doesn't confirm. Instead, she admits, "It scares me, Cole. And you know I'm not afraid of anything."

I have to force myself not to grip the back of her

head harder than I already am. "Not with me, baby. Nothing to be afraid of with me."

"But—"

I shake my head. "No. You'll never give up a thing to be with me. You still want to work—we'll figure out a way to make it happen. I'll never make your world smaller, Bella. I want you to have everything because you deserve it. We've got a lot of time to make up for and we're going to start on that soon."

Her grip on my shirt loosens and she flattens her hand to my chest. It slides up and around my neck before she pulls me to her. This time her kiss is different. Her desperation and need mixes and mingles with my carnal desire, creating a storm ready to burst. I dip my hand between us and flip the button and zipper on her jeans. Not messing around, I dive in to take what's mine.

So wet.

With our lips still touching, I demand, "Last chance for you to claim a condom, baby."

Her breath catches. "The only thing I'm claiming is you."

Fuck.

I stand and yank off my shirt. Her flip flops land with soft thuds against the old, faded floor followed by her jeans, taking her panties with them. Her tank and bra join them as fast as I can make work of the damn clasp. When I finally have her bared before me in all her beautiful glory, I dip my head and press my lips to her scar.

At first, I hated it. It was a reminder of what I've come to refer to as *hell week*—the time in the hospital when I thought I'd lost her for good. And then it happened all over again after the internal bleeding. But since I brought her home, I've come to love it. I shouldn't be obsessed with a mark that represents how she almost died. But I am.

I run my tongue up the fresh, pink puckered skin and continue to her tit. A shiver vibrates over her when I pull her nipple into my mouth and suck. She lifts her legs and her feet go flat to the table, her knees falling to the sides.

"Cole," she breathes.

"If you were a hundred percent, I'd flip you over and take you from behind. Love seeing your ass on display when I take you." I nip at her tit and her hips lift, needing purchase on something but I don't give it to her. "Not yet, sweetness."

I work my way down her body, pressing on the insides of her thighs. The dining room light over us shines down on her and I take her in before dipping my head.

She moans as I take my first taste.

From her pussy to her clit, I take a hit—feeding my addiction has never been more satisfying than after she's agreed to give me everything. I dip my tongue inside her, followed by two fingers before I find her clit, swollen and ready.

I swirl it with my tongue and she tries to lift off the table but I grab her ass to pull it to the edge. Dipping a finger in her one more time, I slide it down to her puckered hole.

She gasps.

I grip the back of her thigh to lift it high and wide.

I suck on her clit.

And dip my finger into her ass.

"Bloody ... oh, fuck."

I'd agree, if my lips and tongue weren't busy.

Instead, I suck harder and pump my finger.

She smacks the table with an open palm before her body starts to quiver and her neck arches.

When she comes against my mouth, my world balances. And my cock turns painfully hard. He feels like he's been thrown into solitary for bad behavior. I let go of her leg, rip my shorts open, and free him as I milk the last of her orgasm before coming up for air.

I give my cock a pump as I slide my finger out of her and put a hand flat to the table. I enjoy the fruits of my labor as she lays before me like a soggy, British biscuit. Her eyes close and she has to work at catching her breath.

"Bella."

She drags her lids open and her gaze immediately falls to my cock. She watches as I stroke him twice.

Taking in a big breath, she rocks my world. "I love you."

All of a sudden, I forget about my selfish cock. I drop and take her mouth. Her fingers dip into my hair and her legs wrap around my back. All it takes is the underside of my cock to rub against her slick pussy once and I can't wait another second.

I slide inside.

And every problem swirling around us in tornadic fashion evaporates on the spot.

Her pussy hugs my cock like she was made for me.

What the hell am I saying? She *was* made for me—body, mind, and soul.

I slide an arm under her to cushion her still-healing body because I am not going slow or taking it easy. I gave her every chance for a condom and she turned them all down.

"Harder," she pleads and lifts her knees higher up my sides.

"So fucking perfect," I growl into her hair and give her what she wants.

Her fingernails bite into my skin and she presses her face into my neck. Her pussy convulses and every muscle in her body contracts around me.

I groan and pump into her three more times until I plant myself so deep, I'd happily be lost forever. And for the first time, I come inside Bella with nothing between us.

It's fucking amazing and I could stay here forever.

My cock isn't anxious to move from where he's landed, either.

She starts to run her fingers through my hair as our hearts return to a normal rhythm.

"Cole?"

I drag air into my lungs. "Hmm?"

"I had a moment with Red. I think he's accepted me."

I feel my lips tip and I pull away from her enough to look into her eyes. "Yeah?"

She nods.

I kiss her nose. "Told you."

"You're not always right about everything, you know."

I press my cock into her and enjoy the flare of her eyes when she feels it. "The effects of your orgasm wore off fast."

She tries to hide her smile but fails. "And what effect is that?"

"The one where I trick you into believing I'm the end-all-be-all ... that I rule over the kingdom you get to live in and am overly generous with the sex you get to enjoy."

She slaps my bare bicep. "How did I fall for such a cheeky man who's so full of himself?"

I shrug. "All I can say is you're one lucky woman who gets to practice making babies with me."

"Take me to bed, Cole," she demands. "Between the drama, the wine, and the orgasms, I could sleep for a week."

As I pull out, something catches my eye on the new big screens.

"What the fuck?" I growl.

I stand and bring her with me. As naked as the day she was born, she presses herself to me and frowns as she takes in my expression before twisting in my arms and gasps.

Flames billow, lighting up the night sky like a burning star.

My fucking house is on fire.

26

FLIRTING SPERM

Bella

I t's amazing how a four-alarm fire can burn off a
buzz and ruin your postcoital, mellow mood.

Cole grabbed my cell and called Asa right
before nine-one-one. Asa called everyone else. I wanted
to go, however there is still the little tidbit of the intelligence community looking for me and my showing up in
the presence of law enforcement would not be ideal.

Plus, someone has to man the wires and satellite
feeds. Or, in my case, woman the hell out of them.

I don't take my eyes off the feed of Cole's home,
smoking and smoldering. The place he brought me to
against my will. Were the walls thin and the paint chip-
ping? Yes, but it was his—a place that Red kept in
working order and the home in which he planned to
raise Abbott. It's only been a matter of weeks but I've
come to love his old farmhouse. I've been with Cole for
years but we've never had the opportunity to be
domestic together.

And now it's gone.

What's left of it is in shambles. I'm afraid of what it will look like in the light of day. This latest event will most certainly send Red right back to irritable land.

It's after two o'clock in the morning. Red and Abbott are still sleeping as Cole insisted we let them be. I think it was a good decision given the fact Red probably lost most of his tools in his shed.

As I watch Cole and Crew's team sift through rubble as the fire department finishes, my attention is drawn to a different live feed. There is activity at the so-called church Cole's boss's boss attends.

A mid-size crossover—something I realize Americans have a thing for—rumbles up the drive to the building, dust billowing in its wake. I enlarge the frame.

A somewhat official looking woman emerges in a plain business suit. Odd for this time of night when most are snoozing.

Hmm.

Three men meet her at the front door of the building and usher her in as if she were royalty. I look down at the files in front of me and open a plain manilla folder labeled *CIA*. I keep flipping until I find her profile.

The one and only, Wendy Sisson. The woman who is fucking with my future.

I study the feed, seeing only a grouping of heat—bodies congregating in the center of the building and I wonder when X-ray technology will improve so we can see through walls and roofs. I'm about to call Crew, but there's movement outside and I don't dare take my eyes off the screen. Cole will have to wait.

Yes, it's definitely Wendy, the wicked witch of the

CIA. She's stomping to her car with one of the men tight on her heels like an angry predator. She's about to reach for her door when he grabs her by the bicep and swings her around with so much force, even her short, low-maintenance hair flings in her face.

I enlarge the frame to its highest capacity and am impressed with the technology Crew invested in. The picture is quite clear and their expressions tell the tale even though the feed has no sound—they're angry.

Wendy rips her arm from his hold and he motions to the building behind him, then the sky dramatically. Wendy pokes him in the chest and I'd roll my eyes if it didn't mean looking away. Seriously. She's CIA upper brass and poking the bloke in the chest? I'm embarrassed for her and wonder how many arses she's had to kiss to get to her level because it doesn't seem like she did it by ninjaing anyone on her own. No self-respecting woman who works in intelligence would do that unless she were working covertly, and I'm guessing this is not the case.

I bet Wendy is wishing she were more of a badass about now because the man has her back against the car, standing nose-to-nose with her, speaking so fast, I can't read their lips.

She finally pushes him out of her personal space and rips open her purse. A wad of cash is shoved at him.

Arguing ensues.

Another handful of bills is pushed his way with a few fluttering to the ground. This must be enough to appease the man because he steps back and almost gets hit in the head with her hastily-opened car door when he bends to pick up the fallen blood money.

Or, in this case, fire money?

Wendy is off, her cloud of dust bigger and dirtier than when she arrived.

Well, then. That was an interesting turn of events.

I grab Ozzy's cell since Cole has stolen mine and make a mental note to ask Crew for a secure phone attached to his new satellite network.

———

Cole

"NO SHIT?"

I turn and look at the rubble that was my house. It's mostly gone—leveled and still smoking. The firefighters are doing their jobs to make sure it doesn't reignite. I can't believe I'm standing here in the middle of the night thinking I'm lucky, but I am. Firefighters got here soon enough, it didn't spread to the forest or my neighbors.

Bella called me and about blew my mind when she told me Wendy Sisson was at the church property a few minutes ago, paying someone off for something.

The timing sure is eerie since my house just blew up.

"I ran the footage back," Bella adds. "The explosion happened minutes after you flipped the lights on remotely. Cole, someone thought you were home."

"It was an IED."

The line goes dead for two beats. "They confirmed this?"

"No." I watch Asa barking orders into his phone as Crew, Grady, and Jarvis dig through shit at the back of my house, seeing what they can salvage. "I know—I've seen it before. It's classic. And there's the fact the arson investigator got here thirty minutes ago and already found traces of ammonium nitrate. From the angle of the blast, it came from the front porch. There were two packages delivered. That had to be it."

"Cole," she whispers. "Your home. I'm so sorry."

I shake my head. Was it a home? Haven't had a home since my mom died and we sold their place for Red to move in with me. Life has been such a shit show, it sure didn't feel like a home even though I was trying to make it one for Abbott. "No one was hurt. That's all that matters."

"What's the plan?"

"We're waiting for the fire department to finish, then we'll come back to you and regroup. Watch every move at the church—we're going in before sunup, whether anyone is there or not."

"Hmm," she hums. "I assumed so. I haven't taken my eyes off it. As far as I can tell, there are three men still there."

"Three—piece of cake."

"Precisely," she agrees. "Damn, I wish I could go."

I huff a laugh in the midst of my life falling apart around me. "Next time, baby."

I hear her tapping away at the keyboard as she mutters, "Yes. I need to get back to the gym. I'm ready."

"The doc said six weeks—you're hardly ready. I don't have time to discuss this now. You've got eyes on us, you'll know when we'll be on our way."

"Cole," she calls.

"Make it quick, sweetness. I need to help."

"I'm going to reach out to Gracie and Keelie first thing in the morning. Abbott didn't bring much to stay at Crew and Addy's. We need to make her as comfortable as we can after this. If there's anything special you think she'll want replaced right away, we need to make it happen. I don't know her well enough to know of any special trinkets or lovies she may have."

I drop my head to look at the ground under my feet. I have to clear my throat to get the words out. "Thank you."

"Ha," she spouts. "I do believe it's the first time you've ever thanked me for anything, Cole Carson, even after I gave you my virginity. One for the record books."

"Baby, don't piss me off right now. You doing that for Abbott means a lot. You even thinking about it needing done means even more."

Her tone softens. "You're welcome. Now, go finish. You gents have three men to abduct."

"See you soon."

"Cole, wait."

"Baby—"

"If you can find my robe Gracie and Keelie bought me, that would be lovely."

"I'm sure that would be fucking *lovely*." I shake my head and kick a charcoaled toaster that landed in the front yard all the way from the kitchen. "I'll do my best."

I hang up, more annoyed I have to deal with this than it happening in the first place. I head back through my entryway and to the family room. That's when I decide we'll rebuild this fucker bigger and better than I ever imagined I'd have. And since there's a chance my sperm could be flirting with Bella's egg at the moment, we'll need it.

27

WINDMILL

Cole

I t was easy.

Which kind of sucked since I don't work in the field anymore. I was looking forward to traveling back in my operative time machine to kick some asses for a change, instead of ordering everyone else to do the fun shit.

We assumed they weren't holding a bible study in there, so we went in prepared. Helmets, shields, vests ... your basic ballistic wear. Bella used to say firepower and flashbangs were perfect accessories. She was not wrong.

They didn't see it coming.

Now they're blindfolded, hogtied, and lying on the mat in Crew's barn. I must note, this place is the shit. More workout equipment than these men could ever use at one time, enough weights for the Jolly Green Giant and Goliath to spot each other, and a mat—the one Crew uses to kick every new recruit's ass to put him in his place. Jarvis confirmed this since his ass was, in fact, kicked on it.

They haven't seen our mugs and we're going to keep it that way.

"Who gave you the wad of cash and what was it for?" I demand even though I know. I'm actually more curious to know if they know who they're dealing with.

The one on the left has been crying since we pulled him out of the back of Crew's old truck, which for some reason smells like cows. "I don't know! Please let me go. I needed the money. I had no idea we were building a bomb!"

"Shut the fuck up, you spineless prick!"

Okay, now we're getting somewhere. The one on the right is in charge.

"What about you?" Grady's boot connects with the guy in the middle. "Who paid for the fireworks you shit-heads arranged tonight?"

"Fireworks?" the guy on the left asks as his voice cracks.

"You know what we're talking about," Crew steps forward and stoops, elbows to his knees. "What's your name?"

The guy on the right yells, "Shut your fuckin' mouth!"

"Don't listen to him." Crew is calm and cool. "He's tied up tighter than you—can't do a thing to you. But do you know who can?"

The kid in front of Crew breathes, "Who?"

"Me," I interrupt. "The motherfuckers who tied you up like sheep at a rodeo don't have a dog in this race, but I do. The way I see it, you have choices. Tell me who you're working for and there's a chance we'll dump you in the middle of nowhere. You won't die, so this is the path I suggest you choose. Or," I pause and watch them sweat. "You do what your friend over there insists and keep your mouth shut. If you take that road, you're no good to us, which means we're not going to take the time to dump you anywhere—we'll get it done here."

"Oh shit." The kid starts crying again.

"Shut your fucking mouth, Jace."

"Jace." Crew starts in again. "Now we're getting somewhere."

"Please. I only wanted to make some quick money —"

"Tell us who visited you at your camp tonight, Jace."

He shakes his head. "I don't know her name. Gary said we didn't need to know."

"Gary," Jarvis belts and gives the one on the right a kick to the gut with some force behind it. Gary groans. "Gary, Gary, Gary. You've heard your choices. Tell us what you know."

"Tell them, Gary!" Jace begs. "Please, tell them!"

"Fuck you," Gary seethes.

"We should separate them," I announce.

"No!" Jace and Gary yell at the same time.

"You've been quiet." Asa toes the guy in the middle on the tip of his Air Jordan Classics—a throwback, but still a nice choice. He winces and I sense the fear rolling off him in waves. "Don't let your friend scare you. We want information on the person who paid you to do what you did tonight. We don't have time to fuck around —someone needs to speak up."

"If you open your fuckin' mouth—"

The kid in the middle talks. "He made me do it."

Asa tips his head. "How old are you?"

"Sev-seventeen."

"Seventeen?" Asa whistles and the kid shudders. "I bet you wished you were hanging out at the pool with a bunch of girls rather than being tied up and blindfolded right now, huh?"

"Shit," I mutter. I do not need a child's life on my conscience—arsonist or not. I look over at Crew. "Do you have a way to ID them?"

"Dammit!" Gary yells.

Crew stands and crosses his arms, looking to Jarvis. "Get the scanner and print them."

"Oh fuck, they're police," Jace sobs.

"Trust me, kid. You'll wish we were the police," I mutter, losing patience with this shit.

"What's your name?" Asa demands.

Jace's morals must be kicking in. "Leave Ben alone. He didn't know what he was getting into. This isn't his fault."

I see Asa drag a hand down his face. "You still in high school, Ben?"

"He is!" Jace gives Ben up, proving I only need thirty seconds in a room alone with this guy and I'll have all the info I need plus his life story and that of his ancestors. "Let him go. This is my fault—seriously, it is!"

"It's your fault you got involved making a bomb and now could end up in federal prison?" I clip.

"No, that's Gary's fault. It's my fault Ben's here," Jace admits.

"Fuck me," Asa mutters. "Where do you go to high school, Ben?"

When he tells us, we all look at each other and Asa drops his head before he shakes it.

The kid is local.

And I'm pretty sure Keelie works at his school and Asa's kids go there too.

Isn't this the shits.

"You still in high school, Jace?" Asa keeps on.

"No way. I've been out for a year."

Asa looks up at Crew and tips his head to the ringleader.

Crew sighs. "Let's separate them."

"No!" Ben and Jace scream at the same time but we don't move to them.

Jarvis and Grady have Gary up and are dragging him out of the barn. I have no clue where they're taking him and I don't really give a shit because these two are the ones who will talk. If they turn out to be young and stupid like it seems, we'll drop them and they can make their way home and will never know where they've been or who we are.

"Here's how it's going to go," I start when I know Gary is out of earshot. "We found the fuel cans in your building. The arson investigator already traced the ammonium nitrate. That shit put together is lethal."

"I didn't know it was going to be so big," Jace admits. "I thought we were going to blow up a mailbox or something. He didn't tell us what was really going to happen when we filled the box. I mean, shit. It was small."

"How do you know Gary?" Asa demands.

"He's my cousin," Jace says. "What are you going to do to us?"

"Who was the woman who came to your camp tonight?" I demand.

"They didn't introduce us, but Gary called her Wendy when they were fighting. She didn't pay up like she said she would. She found out no one was at the house. I'm glad no one was there. I don't want to hurt anyone. Gary told us this chick only wanted to send a message. Can you at least take this thing off my head?"

"No. And trust me, you do not want to know what happens if you see our faces," Crew says.

Ben whimpers, "Was anyone hurt?"

"No." I roll my eyes. "Ease your conscience, kid. You only blew up a house; you didn't kill anyone."

"I'm so sorry," Jace chants.

Apologies aren't going to replace my Nationals T-shirt collection, which was practically vintage. Thank fuck I have Abbott's pictures stored in the cloud. "I'll think about forgiving you if you start talking. Who else have you seen there who might want to create havoc in people's lives and blow shit up?"

Ben says nothing and I wouldn't be surprised if he pisses himself soon. I'm also not surprised Jace keeps running his mouth. "Some guy, but that was a week or two ago. If they said his name I can't remember. He was older, sort of balding but trying really hard to make it look like he's not. Sort of talked through his nose. It's the only thing I remember because he reminded me of a cartoon character."

If that wasn't Nick Peterson then I'm not a-fucking-mazing. I look to Crew and nod.

"Was he with the woman who was there tonight?" Crew asks.

"Yeah."

A modern-day Bonnie and Clyde, trying to fuck with my already-complicated life.

Those two cannot support that bankroll on their own. "No one else has been there? Did they mention any other names?"

"No one, I swear. I'd tell you because I really want to get out of here," Jace says.

"This is what we're going to do," Asa states. "We're going to drop you two shitheads off somewhere. As you find your way home, do it knowing we have your fingerprints on the ammonium nitrate and the fuel containers. We also have footage of you fucking around at the house you blew to smithereens. On top of that, we've got enough footage for a ten-episode series on Netflix of you two coming and going from that place. If you don't think that's enough to throw each of you into federal prison, you're more stupid than we gave you credit for. And Ben, there's almost a hundred percent chance they'll try you as an adult. And all the shit you hear about prison is real. Given your boy-band look, they'll love you."

Not surprisingly, Ben starts to whimper again. "I promise. I'll never go back."

"What about Gary?" Jace asks.

I shrug. "Not sure. Depends on what he can do for us."

"Oh, shit."

"We don't fuck around, guys. In the last three minutes, we found your addresses, parents' names, know how many dogs you have, and if you skipped class during your sophomore year. This is your only chance so don't fuck it up."

"No." Ben shakes his head. "I won't. I swear. You'll never see or hear from me again."

Asa looks at me. "I'll stay with them. Go see what they're getting from the ringleader."

I turn and head for the door. When I get out in the dark of night, I go to the only other building that's lit up. Unlike how we went easy on young Jace and Ben, Jarvis and Grady have taken a different tactic.

Gary's wrists aren't bound by zip ties anymore. They're wrapped so tight with duct tape, his fingers are now a nice shade of indigo. They remind me of my favorite suit which I'll never get to wear again because this asshole blew up my house.

I have no sympathy for him.

He's hanging three feet off the ground from a meat hook attached to a chain on a pulley system. I'd wonder why Crew needs a device like this if it weren't for a punching bag lying on the floor. Sure, Crew and his men are killers but I don't think they're in the business of torturing people.

Until Bella and I walked into their lives.

Before I have a chance to say shit or punch Gary in the balls, Jarvis looks at me and says one word. "Randolph."

I stop in my tracks and his balls get a reprieve for at least a minute. "What the fuck?"

"Let me down," Gary begs. His tough-guy act is gone and I see blood dripping from his nose and mouth. It seems Jarvis and Grady haven't wasted any time.

"Randolph is funding the party," Grady adds. "This guy," he points to Gary, "has been managing the church. He hasn't seen Randolph since they registered as a religious nonprofit. It took Gary losing a tooth but he finally spilled. We knew they were connected from the text, but this explains more."

I let out a whistle on my exhale.

"Proves circles in the district run tight," Jarvis notes.

I nod and think we won't be able to find the money trail fast enough. "You're on the wrong guy's payroll, Gary."

"What do you want to know?" he pleads. "I'll flip—work for you. I won't even charge you."

I almost laugh. "If you're worried about money right now, you have no idea how serious this situation is. You're hanging from a meat hook, Gary. Only dead shit hangs from meat hooks."

His shoulders give out and his body stretches another few inches. "Please. Don't hurt Jace and Ben. I'll do anything."

"Tell me about Sisson. Why were you blowing up houses tonight?"

"She said someone was in their way and needed to be taken care of sooner rather than later. She does whatever Randolph says 'cause he pays well. I guess Sisson has connections all over the world. She was fuckin' manic cause Randolph was on her ass about planting that bomb. She said my money would dry up if we didn't make it happen. I had no choice—"

"No," I interrupt. "You did. What do you know about Randolph that caused him to resort to murder?"

"I told you what I know. I don't ask questions—I do what they want and take the money. It's too good not to." He arches and groans. "What are you gonna do? This fuckin' hurts."

I'm about to work a little bit of aggression out on this guy's face, thinking about how every possession I own is now ash, thanks to this piece of shit who doesn't want to put any effort into making a buck the honest way, but I'm stopped when Bella's cell vibrates against my ass.

I pull out the phone and find a text from Ozzy.

Ozzy – It's me again. I would not have to text you from Ozzy's phone if you wouldn't steal my cell every other minute of the day.

Ozzy (really Bella) – Are you about done doing the things I'd rather be doing myself?

Bella (but really me) – Can't be without a phone, baby. We're about to finish up.

Ozzy (Bella) – Then hurry your yummy arse back to me.

Bella (but me) – Do you know how weird it is that Ozzy thinks my ass is yummy?

Ozzy (sweetness) – You know how much I love your arse. I haven't seen nearly enough of it since I've been back.

Bella (me) – Who's fault is that?

Bella – You're seriously going to go there?

(me) – Baby, if naked is what you wish, I'll gladly windmill my cock for you twenty-four-seven.

Bella – Mmm. Finish up.

(me) – Okay, but you know I'll do it for you.

Bella – I know you will.

(me) – And since we've pulled the goalie, I can't wait.

Bella – We did not pull the goalie, love.

(me) – Pretty sure it was you I fucked bareback. We pulled the goalie.

Bella – I know my body. I'm nowhere near ovulating. It was not careless. It was calculated.

(me) – Wait. Are you saying you told me to pull the goalie because it was unlikely my sperm would mate with your egg to create superhumans?

Bella – We will make beautiful superhumans someday.

(me) – Damn. You really owe me a blow job.

Bella – I don't owe you a thing. But you know I'll gladly take you in my mouth. It's been a long time.

(me) – Yes, it fucking has. Make sure you're hydrated—I'm on my way.

28

TREASURE FOREVER

Bella

"I've had enough. The whole thing began with Penn Simmons before we knew it was related to Randolph. I'm going to Geneva to get to the bottom of it."

Everyone in the room looks to Cole, but I'm the first to speak. "In the last few days, your boss and his boss have tried to silence you permanently—not once, but twice. Not to mention, Randolph tried to kill a reporter. Do you really think that's the best course of action?"

Cole crosses his arms and his eyes penetrate mine. "I want to look Penn Simmons in the face when I ask him why someone wants him dead. Then I want to see what he does when I inform him they want *me* dead when I wouldn't make *him* dead. You know there's no better tell than body language. I want to witness each twitch on his face and every uncomfortable shift of his feet. I can be out and back in thirty-six hours and the C-I-fucking-A can kiss my ass. They left me out to dry when I refused to be their puppet. If I don't check in for a few more days, they can assume I blew up with my house."

I sigh. I hate that I can't go along. The Caribbean was one thing but stepping foot into Europe again? I can't risk it.

"You're staying here," Cole echoes my thoughts.

I hike a brow before rolling my eyes. "For your information, I don't want to go."

He winks at me. "If that makes you feel better, sweetness."

Damn him.

"You need to go," Crew says to Cole. "We know nothing more about Simmons than we did the first time we ran his name. I'll arrange for a plane to get you over there." Crew looks to Ozzy. "I want eyes on Simmons' house."

Ozzy has quickly become the most popular man in the room since he can spy on anyone we wish. He lifts his chin as if it isn't the big deal it is. "Done."

"Asa and Grady left to drop the kids in BFE. They'll find their way home. They're running so scared there's no way they'll nose around even if they knew where to go. Jarvis is still with Gary. I think we'll hang onto him for another day or so, see if there's anything else he remembers. It'll also make Peterson and Wendy nervous to lose contact with him—shake their cages. We took him off the hook and will get him some food and water soon." Crew shrugs. "He'll be fine."

"Also," Ozzy tosses a report on the table. "Ambrose, the guy who hiked all the way to the Caribbean to meet with Randolph, checks out—I mean, other than giving the Senator kickbacks. But otherwise, his business is on the up and up. Taxes paid on time, hasn't had any

OSHA issues, no EEOC. Besides the money under the table shit, he looks as clean as a whistle."

"I'd have been surprised if you found anything more. He was angry and his hatred for Randolph practically seeped through the walls," I add.

"We'll continue to watch him even though it looks like his road will be a dead end." Cole pulls me to his side. "It's been a night. We need some shuteye since I'm going to have to explain to my daughter and father in the morning how we have no house to go back to."

I lean into him. "I'm so sorry."

"Here." A cell phone flies through the air and Cole reaches out to nab it before it hits him in the face. Ozzy's expression contorts into something between a frown and a wince. "I read your text messages. Thank you for polluting my phone forever. I wiped it clean—technically speaking, though I'm sure it could use some bleach after your conversation. It's yours, I'll buy a new one." He points at me. "You're never borrowing my shit again."

I bite back my smile as Cole hands me Ozzy's phone to keep as my own. "I'm sorry if we burned your young eyes."

Ozzy moves for the front door and shakes his head. "You're younger than me Bella. I just don't want to know about your sex life."

"I don't give a shit what you use the cell for, just keep it close," Crew says as he follows Ozzy out. "I'll call you with your flight information."

And that's it. I shouldn't be surprised they don't wish us a goodnight. The sun will be rising over the Virginia countryside soon. Cole turns me toward the stairs. "Let's go to bed. I'll take a raincheck on the blowjob."

I look back where he's following me up the stairs. "Who said you're getting a raincheck?"

He smacks my ass. "I did. You know you've missed him."

I sway my hips as I move up the stairs in front of him. "You and your cock."

"We both love you. Wish you could come to Geneva. It's a long flight with plenty of time for me to cash in my blowjob voucher."

We turn the corner to the bedroom we're staying in. "For so many reasons, I wish I were able to go, as well."

His dirty shirt lands on the floor next to the bed before he reaches for me. He smells like a campfire but I don't even care as he pulls me into his chest. "As much as I've loved working side-by-side with you again, you don't know what it means to me you'll be here with Abbott and Red. Especially after what happened tonight. I swear this won't be a normal thing. I hardly travel anymore and the last thing I want is to ground you here while I'm gone."

I push my jeans down my legs before I lift up on my toes to press my lips to his. "I know, love."

His arms constrict around me and my peck on his lips is a sorry excuse compared to the one he lays on me. It's more of a promise than a kiss. I'm in desperate need of air when he tips his forehead to mine. "I want you to do whatever you want, baby. But when the op is done, when you come home after a trip, or lay your beautiful head of hair down to sleep at night, I want it to be next to me."

I press into his wide chest. "I won't be anywhere else. I promise."

With the whirlwind swirling around us, I'm not sure if he's used to the idea he won't have to tie me down, how I'm willingly and freely giving myself to him, his family, and his life here in America. Because, when we finally do fall into bed, Cole holds me tighter than he ever has before. Either desperation or disbelief ... he doesn't deserve to let that eat away at him. Whatever it is, I silently vow to do everything I possibly can to wipe that clean.

Cole and I deserve a fresh start.

"WHY CAN'T we go see it?" Abbott asks for the tenth time.

Cole explained what happened as best he could to Abbott first thing this morning. Kudos to him for not using the words *arson, attempted murder,* or every four-letter word that usually spills from his lips. Though, when he pulled his father aside to explain what really happened, he used all those and more.

So Red is grumpier than usual, but at least it's not directed toward me. A light in the darkness, for sure.

Cole left for the airport. As much as I want to run over to Crew's camp and monitor his new spy satellite and illegal wiretaps, Abbott has been unusually ... what is the word?

Present.

I would draw the line at clingy. We're not there yet.

But she wants to be in my company.

"The area around your home isn't secure yet, love. Ashes and rubble are everywhere. It's for our safety. There's more to do here anyway, right? You can play with Vivi before her nap, we'll work on your French studies, and maybe visit the cows."

Her arms cross tight around her front and she worries her lip. "Where'd Grandpa go?"

"You know your grandpa." I take her hand to lead her to Addy's home office. "I think he went outside to putter around the barn. When you have a home the size of this one, there are always things that need tweaking, no?"

"I thought we were going to wait 'til later for my French lesson."

"We are." I pull out the chair and set her on my lap at the desk in front of the monitor as Daisy curls up on my foot. "Right now, we're going to do something else. Do you know what the only good thing is that comes from something as horrid as a house fire?"

She looks up at me and frowns. "No."

"Shopping. I haven't shopped much lately so I figure this is my time to shine. Would you like to start with clothes, toys, or books?"

"You mean, I get to pick what I want?"

"Of course, darling. Who else would choose your things for you?"

She shrugged. "My mommy didn't let me choose much."

Of course she didn't. This might be more fun than I thought. "Today is your day. I assume you'll need a brand-new copy of *The Secret Garden* and some school clothes. Beyond that, I'm going to need your help."

Nervousness leaks through her innocent face. "Um … I don't like to wear dresses."

"Well then, no dresses for you. How can you swing

and run and play in a dress? I don't blame you one bit. Tell me, where should we start?"

She chews on a piece of skin around her fingernail and shrugs. "Books?"

I click on the browser to pull up the bookstore. "I thought as much."

After I add a copy of *The Secret Garden* to the basket, we continue our search. I can't say it's as much fun as shopping with my mum when I was little, and if I were able to actually live my life in public, I would have bought her a cup of hot chocolate to sip while strolling the aisles and aisles of children's fiction.

Someday.

But for today, this will do. Abbott doesn't hate me for being here instead of her mum or for loving her father. She might not be close to trusting me with her secrets, but this is a step in the right direction. Even this morning, Red didn't once look as if he were going to blame me for his son's home being blown to bits.

The road in front of me might be long and I'm not sure where it will lead, but, for now, I'll take this and tuck it away in my healing heart. As opposed to the physical scar which now decorates my body, I don't want the one on my heart to disappear. It's a reminder of this—Abbott trusting me, Red accepting me, and Cole doing everything in his power to hand me the world.

That's one scar I'll happily treasure forever.

29

MACPUSSY

Cole

Nothing has fucked over the intelligence community more than the franchise of James Bond. The idiots who won't let that sucker die have no idea how off-base they are.

If we get into a shootout, we've fucked up.

If we get into a car chase, we've done something wrong. My most recent incident with Jarvis's precious Porsche notwithstanding ... that shit was not my fault.

I've never been on a high-speed boat while working. Well, there was that one time when we had to *borrow* a single-engine outboard. We weren't able to return it due to the fact it sunk but I did track down the fisherman and sent him a check from Uncle Sam.

And if we had the kickass technology Tony Stark uses to support the Avengers, intelligence jobs would be downright obsolete.

In reality, our best-practice techniques are basic human psychology and understanding what motivates people. Networking. Analyzing. Studying. Then taking that data and deducing what might happen next.

It doesn't hurt to know your way around a security system or how to pick a lock the old-fashioned way, either.

Which is what I did three hours ago. Since then, I'm back to being patient. Before I left, Ozzy tracked Penn's wife and kids to the States where it looks like they're visiting family over the summer. Penn stayed behind to work so I had no one but a gang of villainous Shakespearean pussies to worry about. They do not live up to their names, weaving their way in and out of my ankles, not giving a shit I broke into their house. This makes me wonder why Abbott's cat hates me so much. I'm not that bad and I'm the one paying for catnip. There are so many reasons why I should be her fucking favorite.

I helped myself to a whiskey neat but kept it to two fingers. I am working after all, even if it's off the record.

I've sat here for hours—waiting, sipping, stroking pussies—but finally it happens. What I traveled across the pond for. When I hear him, I only move my hand to lift my Glock.

The door opens but doesn't close.

I wait.

He was a Marine, not an operative. I'm impressed by the fact I can hardly hear his steps.

Penn Simmons appears, moving around the corner from the kitchen to the family room, but he enters second, behind the pistol pointed at me.

Well, fuck you very much, Penn Simmons. Mine is drawn and aimed right back at him.

He's steady but his tone is even more stable. "Who are you?"

I don't answer nor do I lower **my** weapon as Lady Macbeth's tail swipes my face from **where** she's curled around my neck. "You have good taste in whiskey."

"Who are you?" he repeats with a force behind it that would make most people cower.

"No, I think the better question is, *who are you*, Penn Simmons?"

"You know my name and are sitting in my favorite chair so I'm not answering that. The only reason you're not dead right now is because I don't want blood all over my recliner and I like that cat. I can't put a bullet through your head without killing her and she's the only one I've ever been able to teach to fetch, so quit fucking around—who are you and why the fuck are you in my house?"

I scratch Lady Macpussy on her hind leg since I need her to stay where she is and shake my head. "I might have my gun trained on you, but I only came to talk. Trust me, if it weren't for me, you'd be deader than Romeo and Juliet, only your story might be more tragic. Can we put down the guns so no one gets an itchy finger?"

"You first."

Besides his frown setting deeper into his face, Penn doesn't move a muscle.

I narrow my eyes.

Macpussy meows.

He lowers his voice. "I'm not talking 'til you put your gun down."

"If you shoot me, you'll ruin your chances of seeing tomorrow because I promise they'll find you."

He nods. "You've got two minutes to explain yourself."

I slowly lower my gun until it's sitting on the arm of his favorite chair. I see why he likes it so much—it's damn comfortable and I might need one since all my shit is a charred mess. I show him my bare palm. "Your turn."

Not so slowly, he twirls his handgun around a finger and points it at the ceiling but doesn't put it down.

"On the counter, Penn."

"On the coffee table, asshole."

I lean forward enough to put my gun out of reach and he does the same.

"Who the hell are you?" he demands.

I don't answer. "Some pretty important people want you dead. Do you have any idea why that might be?"

The muscle in his cheek jumps. It's small but it's a tell—he isn't surprised. "No."

I tip my head. "Really? Somehow, I don't believe you."

"Not my problem what you believe."

"You see, this is where you're wrong. I think you and I have something in common. I can't justify why anyone would want you dead. I've also read up on you—pretty sure you and I play for the same team."

"Did my time and did it honorably." He tells me something I know. "I'm not on anyone's team anymore but my own. I'm trying to work and live somewhere my kids can see the world and enjoy a larger life before we move back to the States."

I gaze at him a second before nodding slowly. He won't take his eyes off me and he won't relax.

I tell him something else I know. "You handle military contracts for armored gear and weapons."

"I can't tell whether you're trying to rile me by

showing me how much you know or accuse me of something, but your two minutes are ticking by. I suggest you get to it or else I will pick up my gun."

"Yours is an interesting job," I note, not worried about the shock clock he's put me on.

"It's really not."

I take my hand off the cat's ass and rub my chin. "But it is. So many new people I've met in the last two weeks dabble in government contracts for the Department of Defense. And some of those companies I've come across are winning all the bids despite being the highest bidder. They're not playing fair and they're also not the ones with contracts on their heads. So I'm trying to figure out why people want you D-E-A-D despite the fact you seem to be playing fair. And before you say anything, I know pretty much everything there is to know about your company—it's clean."

His gaze on me darkens when he whispers, "Who the fuck are you?"

"I'm the guy who's kept you alive the last few weeks. If you want to stay that way, I'm going to need some help."

He says nothing.

"Look, Penn. I could've killed you the moment you opened your door. I don't kill people unless it's in self-defense, but the people who work for me do it for the bounty. I have the power to keep them on your good side. And by the looks of it, I'd say you could use a friend at your back right now. I also need to know everything there is to know about one of your competitors, DefenseJet."

His response is immediate. "How do you know about them?"

"Now we're getting somewhere." I smile but I don't think he likes it because his spine stiffens. "They're your competitor and I know about the kickbacks."

"Fuck," he spits.

He takes a step forward and moves to the sofa across from my new favorite chair. He sits but leans forward and swipes a hand down his face. We sit this way for a few quiet moments. Sometimes you just know when people need a second to regroup, and since I'm a nice guy, I give it to him.

Finally, he looks at me. "I need to know who you are. I need some kind of assurance this isn't going to backfire on me. I can't have that happen because I was curious."

"I like curious," I note. "I'll be straight with you. I'm CIA and I have people who want me dead because I wouldn't carry out the order to put a hit on you."

His eyes widen.

"Yeah," I agree. "This is more than stroking someone's back to make it greener."

"Yeah, it is."

"Tell me what you know. Then I'll tell you what I know. I bet by the time we're done talking, we'll both feel a little safer because, if you're anything like me, you'll agree knowledge is power and power is leverage. I could use a little bit of that right now and so could you."

He sits back in his seat. "I worked all over Europe when I was active and saw a lot of shit. Twenty years of duty will create instincts you can't easily turn off when you retire. The last few years, terrorist attacks are on the rise."

I nod. "Like I said, we play for the same team, Penn. Already know this."

He leans forward, elbows to his knees, and lowers his voice. "But these attacks are different."

"How so?"

"They claim to be Al-Qaeda but they don't act like Al-Qaeda. Then Al-Qaeda comes out, denies responsibility, and I hear the same from other sources I trust. If Al-Qaeda wants to stir shit up, they claim it."

"Get to the point."

He leans back. "These so-called terrorist attacks? Most are lame in comparison. Terrorists don't blow up malls at midnight, they do that shit at lunchtime on a Saturday. They don't plant IEDs on a commuter train before the first run in the morning, they do it right before dinner when everyone is going home. Until—"

"Until Spain," I interrupt.

He points at me. "Bingo."

My insides tighten. The realistic part of me knows this won't be the last piece of our puzzle—that would be too easy. But the other part? The romantic chump I've become prays this is it and I can finally announce to the world Isabella Donnelly is an innocent woman right after she tells me my sperm are superheroes. Then I'll throw my boss and his boss in jail and we'll all live like the picture on a Christmas card from now until forever.

Admitting this right now would ruin my CIA cred, so I keep my mouth shut.

"The bomb in Spain was not what it looked like. They pinned it on an MI6 and didn't look back."

I think I have a man crush on Penn Simmons. "You and I *are* playing on the same team."

"Spain was not terrorism. Spain was an accident."

"How do you know?"

"Told you I still have contacts everywhere. I know

for a fact all the bomb materials matched. But that's not what came out in the news. All the fucking media did was report on wide-spread terrorism. No one wants that on U.S. soil, so what does our military do? We offer more troops, more guns, more armored vehicles. The Senate Armed Services Committee is more generous than they've been in the history of our constitution and we're not in the middle of an official conflict. This has been a trend for too long."

"You're confirming what I suspected, Penn. But what you're not telling me is why someone wants you dead."

His fingers thrum his knee and Macbeth proves how much she likes her master by ditching me. She's up and in his lap in no time but Penn doesn't pet her, he's too focused on me.

"I might live in Switzerland, but I'm a patriot—" he throws his hand out to me "—whatever your name is. I don't like anyone fucking with my country and I really don't like it when innocent people are killed. I might've been playing superspy because I'm nosy, but it all changed when an American reporter paid me a visit."

"Let me guess—Marie Kasey?"

He hikes a brow. "We do run in the same circles."

"She's on life support," I inform him. "Shot in the chest."

"No shit?"

"She was trying to blackmail a Senator."

"A Senator from Florida who happens to chair the Senate Committee on Armed Services?"

"That would be the one," I confirm. "Are you happy you didn't shoot me now?"

He doesn't smile, but his eyes relax a bit. "Yeah."

"Why was Marie Kasey interested in you?"

"She said she was looking into DefenseJet and found the public records showing my company lost contracts repeatedly to them. Every damn time, we'd lose the bid. I got so sick of it, I started to lowball them. I was practically bidding at cost—no one in their right mind would turn it down. We never even got a second look. She discovered that and came to me to see what I thought about it."

"And?"

"And I let on I knew more than I did, made a couple guesses, and then had her talking. Either Marie Kasey is more passionate about her job than anyone I've ever seen, or she had an ax to grind. I have a feeling it was the ax. Once I told her what I thought I knew, she gave me enough dots and the rest were easy to connect. But she must've run her mouth because, since then, I've had more close calls than I did in my entire career with the Marines."

I narrow my eyes. "Someone important knows you know. If I were you, I'd get a cat sitter and take a vacation. My people won't touch you, but had I blindly taken the order my boss gave me, those would not have been close calls. My people are that good."

He pulls in a big breath. "Now what?"

"I probably have enough to get some people arrested but I'm not close to the end goal yet. I need to know who planted the bomb in Spain and who paid them to do it. I need money to change hands. You tell me about these dots you connected, I'll tell you what I know, and then we'll communicate on a secure line only. From here on out, you've got yourself an ally."

"I need to know my wife and kids are safe."

"We know they're in Phoenix and have eyes on

them. We'll do what we can, but they might want to stay put for a while."

He scrubs his hands down his face. "This is fucked up."

He doesn't know the half of it but I don't say a word about Bella. I trust this guy but I don't trust anyone that much.

"What do I call you?" he asks.

I shrug. "Cole. You don't need to know more than that."

"Okay, Cole. Where do we start?"

30

YOU WERE AN ARSEHOLE

Bella

"You really don't need to do this."

I throw a smile over my shoulder where Addy is sitting with a cooing Aimée in her arms. "You've recently had a baby, and we've not only taken over your lives, but your home. Cooking and doing some laundry is the least I can do to help."

Addy has a garden big enough to start her own farmers market and Abbott was excited to explore. When she took my hand this afternoon and pulled me through the rows of vegetables in their crowning late-summer glory, we harvested more than enough for an Italian spread.

"It smells amazing. Bev and Morris have manned the garden this year since I could barely bend when it was time to plant. Of course it's flourishing under their care. I've never gotten it to grow the way they have. Pretty sure Bev talks pretty to the plants as she weeds."

"Abbott asked me a million questions and I had no

answers. We had to find Red. He loves that child so much. They garden together—it was the only thing not touched in the fire."

"Maya told me Grady has been handling his insurance. For your sake, I hope the reconstruction gets started soon, but you're welcome to stay here as long as you need. There's nothing I love more than this house full and noisy."

"But does Crew feel that way? I've only worked with him from afar. He seems to like his privacy."

She shifts her bundle of joy to her shoulder and Aimée snuggles into her neck. "I was an only child—it was only my mom and me. I want my people around me. Before I met Crew, my staff knew they could walk into my house anytime. Sure, Crew likes his privacy but he understands what I need too." Her smile turns content. "He'll do anything for me."

I move away from the chicken to stir the fresh marinara before turning to her. "It's strange for me to see the people I work with on the other side like this. I like how they have it all. They deserve it."

"You do, too, Bella."

I shrug. "I never said I didn't."

"No, but you should know, with Crew, you have nothing more to prove than anyone else. Not because of what you've been accused of and certainly not because you're a woman. I probably shouldn't be telling you this because it's not my lane and all, but when this is finished, he wants you to keep working for him."

Hmm.

I turn back to my chicken and crack eggs into a bowl.

"Bella," she calls for me.

"Hmm?" I answer aloud this **time as** I dredge the slices through flour, then egg, and **followed** by seasoned breadcrumbs.

"I suppose you'll have options. **From** everything I've learned, your last name should **carry you** far, and your government would be crazy not to **reinstate** your job."

"I'm not sure. And I'm not sure I **can** simply allow the water to flow under the proverbial **bridge.** I'd like to think I'm a bigger person." I turn **and hold** my hands up since they're covered in sticky muck. "**But** I'm also bitter and angry and there's nothing more **I'd** like to do than stick it to the arseholes who tried to **bury** me."

"I don't blame you one bit."

"But that's *if* I can clear my **name.** There are times when it feels like we're on the ver**ge and** others when I want to say *screw them all* and allow **Cole** to create an entirely new identity for me so I **can run** away to live in the mountains. But I know I'd be **bored out** of my mind. I don't have it in me to quit."

Addy pats the baby's bum. "**You're** like the rest of them. Crew is supposed to be retired. **Same** with Grady and Asa. My husband doesn't have **it in** him to sit even though he could. Bella, for the last **few** weeks Crew has been planning. And girl, however **this** ends, you have options."

I don't get a chance to ask what **those** options might include. What these men do, they're important and their actions are needed when it **comes** to the whole good versus evil. Their jobs serve **a purp**ose and have a place in the process. But that does **not mean** I want to travel the world and do what **governm**ents can't do legally.

But I don't tell Addy this and it's **not** only because

Crew strides into the kitchen with his eyes on his wife and newest daughter. "Smells good."

Addy looks up to her husband. "I told her she didn't need to cook but she wouldn't listen to me."

He leans down to kiss her right before he snatches Aimée away from her mother and rests the baby in the crook of his arm. "If it tastes half as good as it smells, she can do whatever she wants."

Addy smiles at her husband. "I was telling Bella how you're planning."

Crew returns her smile with a frown, but he's not packing much power behind it. "Are you stealing my thunder?"

Addy's smile spreads into a grin. "Yes."

Crew gives her the side-eye before setting his gaze on me. I've learned something about Crew during my time in Virginia. He's different around his family. The word *normal* comes to mind, even though I don't care for that word. *Normal* only stuffs a person into some boring box, leaving the rest as outcasts. I know this all too well since I was *not normal* growing up.

But when it's time for business, Crew's entire aura transforms. He's sharp and cunning and someone you don't want fucking with you. I'm happy this man is on my side.

"I'm making plans. When the time is right, we'll sit down and talk. Know I'm doing everything I can to make sure you have a place here to do what you do best."

"That means the world to me."

"Also, I just came from camp. Cole left Simmons' house and it sounds like it went well. I'm sure he'll be calling you soon."

"Thank you. I wanted to get over there but it was lovely to spend the day with Abbott, especially after what happened last night. Dinner should be ready in about forty-five minutes and there's enough for a small army."

"Good, since it's what Crew is trying to build," Addy adds.

Crew smirks but doesn't disagree. "Aimée and I are going to walk the vines since it seems we're running each other's businesses now. Let me know if you make an official offer to Bella."

Addy laughs and I'm pretty sure she's the only person on earth who can roll like that when it comes to Crew Vega. I love it for her but, more so, I love it for him. He needs balance. My mum gave it to my dad. In the past week, I've felt the craving for it deep in my soul.

"Bella," Addy calls for me after Crew walks out the back door with the little one.

"Hmm?"

"Telling you to be patient seems cruel after what you've been through. But I promise, it's worth it."

"I'm seeing that."

She stands and fixes the pile of long dark hair on top of her head. "The cook needs wine. I'll be back."

Yes, I do think the cook needs a glass. I could get used to living on a vineyard until Cole can rebuild.

COLE HASN'T CALLED me but he did text. He said everything went well—better than we'd hoped. He was managing another case for something completely unrelated, and despite his current status with the Agency, he did not want that case to go cold.

I understand even though I'm anxious to know everything and to have control over my own destiny. If it were anyone other than Cole, I would be in a fit of fury.

But it's Cole. I find myself more relaxed than I've been in years. It could be the wine or being able to cook a full meal for the first time in a long while or sharing that meal with a fine group of people with whom I enjoy spending time.

Or it could be the fact Abbott asked me to read her a book before bed. I expected to like Cole's child. How could I not? But I did not expect for her to pull at my heartstrings the way she has.

"You're getting used to the country."

I find myself on Crew and Addy's patio once again. I didn't feel like making the trek to the old farmhouse yet so I settled here for a few quiet moments, waiting for Cole to call. The view of the vineyard under starlight is a sight.

I look over and smile because Red has settled himself next to me again. "I've never lived in the country. I've vacationed or visited many spots in Europe, but never slowed down long enough to allow it to pull me in the way it has here."

"You and my boy." He shakes his head and *tsks* me. "You both need to slow down. You're in the best years of your life. If it weren't for Abbott, he'd still be chasing that high and I have a feeling you're in the same boat."

I lean my head against the cushion. "I was definitely in that boat, Red. I think I jumped ship and sailed the angry dinghy all by myself. It's nights like this I realize

I'm tired, yet I still want to work." I take a big breath and close my eyes. "Am I crazy?"

"I'm not like you, Queenie, and I'm not like Cole. I wanted a life with his mama and a family. I did what I could do to support them but that was it. Besides them, I didn't have a passion. I fix shit out of necessity because I can't afford to replace it. You and Cole have no balance. He's got me to help with Abbs and he swears up and down a broomstick you're not going nowhere. But if you two don't learn how to stabilize your teeter-totter life, you'll waste the good years."

My answer comes swift and honest. "I'm done wasting years."

"Then you and Cole need to do what you do best and figure this shit out. I won't have my grandbaby living in a house being targeted by a bunch of murderers. Just when you think the world is going to shit in a dirty toilet, life pitches you a curveball and your boss at the CIA wants to off you." He shakes his head. "I worry about Cole. He's always pushed the envelope, ever since he was a baby. I'd draw a line in the dirt with a warning and he'd see how quick he could cross it behind my back. I'd die if anything happened to him."

"Red." I reach for his hand and give it a squeeze, waiting for him to give me his eyes. "Cole does push the envelope, but I've always trusted him. Not only as a partner but with my life. Why do you think I'm okay with him traveling the world trying to solve my problem without me?"

He nods and pats my hand. It's a lovely moment with Cole's father, one I'll never forget. It's why, when he opens his mouth again, I'm simply flabbergasted. "You and him had better give me more granddaughters. Cole did me in. I can't handle more boys like him."

My eyes grow big. "Well, when we get to that point, I'll have a chat with Cole. I'll do my best for you, Red."

A smirk appears. "Sorry I was an asshole."

As opposed to his smirk, my smile is wide. "I've already forgiven you."

He frowns. "You're supposed to tell me I wasn't an asshole."

I give him another squeeze before letting go and looking out to the vines. "But you were an arsehole, Red."

"I can see why Cole likes you."

"Why?"

"You keep him on his toes."

"He certainly keeps me on mine."

"If you two can get people to quit trying to kill you, you might live a happy life." He stands and tonight he doesn't plant a paternal kiss on my head. Instead, he yanks my messy ponytail. "Night, Queenie."

"Goodnight, Red. I'll be back tomorrow bright and early. I have a French date with your granddaughter."

And the door slams shut after him.

Cole

"Are you fucking serious? And you didn't know until now?"

"I just found out who he was and where they're going. My contacts have been asking around for me. We put it together. They hopped on a container ship headed to Quebec. That's when I snuck up to their camp again to see if I could hear anything." Raji is on foot, breathing as hard as his feet hit the ground, trying to get the fuck out of BFE where he's been digging for information.

"Do you know where they're planning to cross?"

"Vermont. They said it was easy."

Dammit. For a bunch of idiot terrorists, they're well studied. That part of the border is loose.

"Send me a report. I don't have time to fuck around with the order of things. I need to make phone calls and I won't be on the ground for," I look at my watch, "dammit. Another three hours."

The glass rattles in his old car when the door slams. "The way they were talking, they're going to cross tonight."

"The report, Raji. Like my ass isn't in enough trouble these days. I need to at least look like I'm sticking to protocol."

"Done—as soon as I get back to my apartment." By the tone of his voice, I bet he'll do it before taking a nap this time.

I stand and stick my head in the cockpit. "I need to reroute."

The pilot glances at the fuel gauge. "How far off?"

"Vermont. As close to the Canadian border as you can get me."

He rubs his chin. "Let me radio in and see what I can do. We should have enough fuel. I need a new flight plan and a clear airstrip."

"I know you're used to working for Crew. I don't have control over shit he does. This is time sensitive and a matter of national security."

He reaches for the control panel and flips what looks to be too many switches, but what do I know? I usually fly commercial. "I'm on it."

"Let me know when it's confirmed and where I'm landing. I need to arrange for a car when I get there."

He starts rattling off enough letters and numbers to confuse a calculus teacher.

I turn back to my phone. So many calls but one is the most important and I don't have the number.

Fuck me, I really need to download my contacts from the cloud.

I thank God for wifi on private jets. I google Homeland Security in Boston.

Bella

My head is about to hit the pillow when Ozzy's phone finally vibrates.

Cole – Can't talk, sweetness, and won't be home when I thought. Fucking kills me to be away from you another night. I'll call when I can. Love you.

I read the message again.

And then again.

Love you.

Kills me to be away from you.

I put my thumbs to the screen after I pull his pillow into my chest.

Me – Come home to me safely, Officer Carson. And I love you too.

I see bubbles and then nothing.

I know if he could talk, he would. And he knows I know.

Even so...

Being away from him was miserable. But now that I've admitted my feelings to him and to myself ... being apart is excruciating.

I wonder how I managed.

STAMPEDE

Cole

The pilot worked his magic and got me to Burlington where I arranged a rental. I had no idea there was a car class below compact. It has so little kick in the pants I'm pretty sure I could've raced to the border faster on Red's twenty-year-old self-propelled mower. Don't even get me started on the leg room.

After a slew of phone calls, I finally got through to my buddy in Homeland Security. An hour later, Raji sent me his report—Nahas, Harb, and Crawley have made quite the trip around the world. From boats to barges to puddle jumpers. I guess you can travel with no paper trail. They must have paid a pretty penny because someone got them across Africa and through Europe, but Raji lost them in Ireland. That's where his contact sniffed them out, but only after the barge had docked in Quebec City.

Now they're headed straight for the Vermont border.

And I doubt it's to sample the maple syrup or cool off with a pint of Ben and Jerry's.

My phone barely rings once before I have it to my ear. "Carson."

"Dude, I've never driven across a state so fast in my life. Where are you?"

I met Jesse Sheen when I first got to Langley. Our cases overlapped and we became fast friends.

"I'm right where you told me to be, though it took me too fucking long to get here in this Flintstones car. You contacted our neighbor to the north?"

"They've got National Defense on it. I work with them all the time. They're monitoring thermal imaging cameras, and I've got drones in the air. I should be close, you can hop in with me."

In my next breath, the road behind me brightens when Jesse winks his headlights. I turn off my clown car and climb out, groaning as I stretch my tight muscles. It's after four in the morning. If this shit doesn't go down soon, we'll lose the cover of darkness.

He greets me after I slam the passenger door. "You look like shit."

"Fuck you very much. I just made a roundtrip to Switzerland in under thirty-six hours. All I've eaten are peanut butter crackers and trail mix. I fucking hate raisins but I choked those suckers down anyway. I'm starving and I could really use a shower. I did brush my teeth on the plane though—you're welcome."

"Thanks, but I don't plan on kissing you."

"What's the plan?"

"Border Patrol is on notice and Canada is surveying every move on their side." He backs out from our meeting place, about two blocks from the border. When he flips a U-turn, he looks at me. "If this doesn't play out per your intel, I'm gonna have a lot of people to answer to. Now that we're here, tell me why am I pretending you're not part of this op."

"It's complicated."

He throws the car in park. "Looks like we've got time."

I look around the darkened space. "Where are we?"

Jesse points out the front window. "See the dead-end street and trees beyond? That's the line. There's another on their side. This is one of the most barren pieces of land in the state. People talk ... word gets around." He points to the top of an old electrical pole. "Cameras and heat sensors for both countries. We work together."

Chatter comes over his portable radio and he turns it down a touch.

"Now we wait," I mutter.

"And now you have time to explain why you woke me out of a deep sleep to tell me about your unofficial-official case."

I like Jesse but no way am I sharing. I do not need my shit or Bella's to leak any farther into the world. "My boss isn't crazy about my informant. Raji is flakey sometimes but still good. When it comes to shit like this, he's always spot on. It'll make it easier if I removed myself from the chain on this one."

He's about to say something else when someone speaks over the radio. "How many agents do you have out there, boss?"

Jesse picks up the radio and pushes the button. "Ten on my side. Why?"

"I'm showing a whole lot more red dots on the thermal cameras."

Jesse looks at me and frowns, but speaks into the radio. "How many more?"

"Double at least, maybe three times. When I scan out, I keep counting."

"What the fuck?" I ask.

"Are they moving?" Jesse asks.

"Negative. Could be a forestry party of bears and moose, but I doubt it. I think we've got company on our side."

"Shit," Jesse mutters, picking up the radio to call his Border agents. "We've got company interspersed in the woods on our side. I have no idea who they are."

"National Defense to Homeland," the radio scratches. "We've got three bodies moving through the woods heading southeast."

Jesse speaks into the radio. "How far out and can you tell where they're headed? Give me their coordinates."

The Canadian rattles off a slew of numbers and Jesse enters them into his phone. "If they stay the course, we're not far off."

"*Not far* seems far when we have company." I holster my Glock. "This isn't good—couldn't be any more opposite than working off an op plan."

"Welcome to enforcement, Mr. Intelligence," Jesse quips as he inserts an earpiece and climbs out of the car.

"You have one of those for me? Or some night vision goggles?" I ask.

He shakes his head. "Sorry. I don't exactly have a tech room at home and you gave me no time to run by the office."

I guess I'm going in blind. I hate not being in charge. I follow as Jesse coordinates with his Border agents. We move to the edge of the tree line, only a wire fence separating the two countries, with Canada a few yards away. I know the agents are at our backs but so are a bunch of strangers.

Jesse presses his finger to his ear and motions to me. I unholster my gun and we move south through the forest, trudging over ground cover, brush, and weeds, which I am not dressed for.

"What the fuck?" Jesse mutters under his breath and his eyes dart to me. "How many?"

"What?" I mouth.

Jesse presses a button on his earpiece and responds, "Please tell me they know we're here." He waits for an answer and motions to the woods behind us. "DEA. Looks like your case collided with theirs. But at least they're on our side, as long as we don't get caught in the middle. They know we're here."

The next few seconds happen too fast. Jesse and I are chests to the earth when it happens.

One moment there are only sounds of the forest— bugs, a few birds who want to catch the first worm, leaves rustling in the night breeze.

Then, like a bulldozer, feet hit the earth, branches crack and break, and low voices mutter through the humid, pre-dawn air.

Feet hitting the earth is an understatement. The sounds turn into a stampede. The Royal Mounted Police have appeared out of nowhere on the other side of the wire fence.

Voices in two languages bellow through the air. Shouts come from behind us, announcing the presence of the Drug Enforcement Administration and Border Patrol.

About ten feet to our right, two men appear from the darkness and do what they can to get through the fence. The barbed wire catches their clothes and skin but they keep pushing through with the galloping beasts approaching.

One guy doesn't take on the barbed wire. He stops and juts his arms in the air, yelling in English to stop, he's giving up, and begging for his life. This only adds to the commotion of the two tearing through the fence, the DEA, the mounted police, patrol agents, and Jesse and me.

A mounted officer arrives and takes down the one on the Canadian side while the other two are yelling in another language—I think Persian, one of the few Middle Eastern languages I'm not fluent in.

"Get down!" I yell, reaching to grab one by the collar, dragging him through the rest of the barbed wire. He twists and contorts, reaching for his pockets. I put a knee to his back, wrestling with one of his arms, still fisting my Glock in my other. I hear Jesse grappling behind me.

A black boot comes down on his loose arm, trapping it to the ground as another pair of hands reaches down with a set of cuffs. I'm surrounded by agents, outfitted in full-on black tactical gear with helmets and rifles.

"Who the hell are you?" one of the agents grits, as a sea of black descends on the guy who's yanked out from under me to restrain and pat him down.

"Dammit!" Jesse yells. "Carson!"

I turn and Jesse is on the ground, struggling for a gun.

Shit.

I throw my weight toward them, closing the distance

between us, bringing my other knee down on the guy's forearm.

He yells but his hold on the pistol is iron tight.

Jesse curses.

And that's when the gun discharges.

Bella

"You said Daddy would be back this morning."

I look down into the eyes Cole gave to his daughter. Only hers aren't sharp or cunning or worldly. Abbott's deep browns are innocent and worried.

"I did," I confirm. "But he texted me last night to let us know he had something come up on one of his cases. He's been a bit delayed, but I'm sure he'll be home as soon as he can."

She picks at the ends of her long, curly strands hanging far past her shoulders. I've done what I could to distract her inquisitive brain since Cole left. She wants her father, she wants to see for herself what happened to her home, and she wants to know what's next.

I wish I had answers. She does not deserve what's been brought down on her little shoulders.

"Did you help your grandpa in the barn?"

Her shoulder lifts and her feet fidget. "He's fixing Crew's tractor."

I wonder if Crew's tractor actually needs fixing. "Have you eaten anything? How would you like some eggs?"

"I'm not hungry. Grandpa and I had cookies and milk before you got here."

My smile might as well crack my face in two. "Do you and grandpa often have cookies and milk for breakfast?"

She nods unapologetically. "Unless we're out of cookies, then we have cereal."

"It's obviously brain food since you're as smart as a whip. Maybe I need to switch up my brekky routine."

This wins me a sweet nose crinkle. "You talk so funny."

I slide my phone into my back pocket so I don't miss a call. I'm accustomed to being in the middle of the action, not left back at home wondering what the hell's going on. I had a restless night waiting for Cole to check in but I know how good he is at his job. If he hasn't called it's because he can't.

Addy and Crew took their girls to town. Aimée had a check-up at the pediatrician and Addy said she was going to take the opportunity to drag Crew furniture shopping. I cannot imagine Crew Vega in any store—more power to her. Abbott and I need a distraction, so I hold out my hand. "I need to move. Let's find the cows and feed them treats. Then we'll dig back into your French lessons. *Oui*?"

Abbott sighs. "*S'il vous plait.*"

I smirk. "Such lovely manners. Please try not to be

too excited. Daisy's new toys should be here tomorrow. You can spend the day spoiling her."

We're almost to the small shed where Addy keeps the treats for the cows and I'm quizzing Abbott on her numbers and colors in French. I never really thought much of it when Cole said Abbott was gifted. Most parents think their children are exceptional but Abbott does love to learn. She's lucky Cole recognizes it in her at such a young age.

I give her hand a squeeze. "I'll get the molasses. You run and find your grandpa to tell him where we'll be. I don't want him wondering where you are."

"Okay," she sing-songs and skips off.

The day is one of the hottest we've had since I've been here but I don't sit idle well. My pastimes have been doing laundry for the Vegas and chasing cows around a vineyard, all while doing what I can to have Abbott accept me. If she simply doesn't hate me, I'll take that as a win. Later, we can work on her liking me, or who knows, if I'm lucky, something more.

My pockets are stuffed with enough molasses to attract a small herd when a scream—shrill and high— cuts through the heavy summer air.

Ignoring the pain in my gut since I have yet to start jogging, I run to the barn where I sent Abbott mere moments ago. If something happens to her on my watch, I'll never forgive myself.

Another scream, this one even more pained, mixed with desperation.

"Abbott!" I yell for them. "Where are you?"

"Bella!"

I follow her voice to the back of the barn where Crew keeps his old truck and tools. I stop in my tracks when I come around the hood and find Abbott on the ground next to Red.

"No," I breathe and rush to them.

Red has collapsed. He's lying face-down on the barn floor and Abbott is shaking his large frame, calling for him with tears streaming down her face.

"Grandpa!"

"Move away, love." I have to physically drag her away so I can roll him to his back. I press my fingers at his neck. "No, no, no, Red."

I pull my phone out of my pocket and dial nine-one-one, putting it on speaker and start chest compressions. I'm no medical professional but I couldn't find a blip of a pulse.

When a dispatcher answers, I can barely hear for Abbott's cries. I manage to explain where we are and what little I know about Red. She offers to stay on the line with me until EMS arrives but it's hard to pay attention to her.

Abbott is clutching Red's bicep, her beautiful eyes that were so innocent only minutes ago are now anything but. Replaced with terror and fear as one of the only humans she's ever been able to count on during her short time on this earth is lying before her lifeless.

Pump.

Pump.

Pump.

I continue with compressions, looking between Cole's father and his child. The redder her face gets, the grayer his turns.

And Cole—I can't bear to think of him at this moment.

DOG YEARS

Cole

It's been a fucking day.

No, it's been a fucking *month,* even though I haven't reached the end of my thirty-day bet with Bella. It feels like a year.

Dog years.

When shit started going down in the forest, it went fast. Sometimes my cases overlap with another agency, but this one ended with the biggest bang.

It's also not the first time I've been shot or caught a knife or had my bell rung. But today has been the most annoying of them all.

"Where is my stuff?" I demand.

I'm at some community hospital in the middle of a maple syrup forest in Vermont. I had to empty my pockets in the back of the rig since they cut my damn jeans off to work on me. The asshole didn't catch an artery or bone, but my calf will now have a bite out of it for the rest of my days.

It doesn't matter as long as I can walk out of here and go home to Bella, Abbott, and Red. I'll do it with one more scar. Bella and I will be quite the pair.

"My phone and wallet?" I ask again. I cannot lose my credentials.

"Your friend went out to the ambulance to look for them," the nurse says. "You're almost done. I think I found a pair of scrubs long enough for those legs of yours. You can't walk out of here in those boxers, as much as I do like plaid."

I look back from where I'm lying on my stomach on the gurney so they can stitch me up. "Are you almost done?"

The doc doesn't look up at me and mumbles, "Almost. You can't hurry perfection."

A curtain barely offers any privacy, so there's no stopping three DEA agents from stalking into my bay while I'm in my underwear.

The one in the middle lifts his chin, and like the frown set on his face, his words are not flowery at all. "Glad you're not dead."

I frown back at Mr. Congeniality. "Thanks. Me too."

He can barely cross his arms over his vest. "Cruz. Brax Cruz, DEA out of New York City. Who knew, yeah?"

"Yeah, *who knew*," I agree, assuming he's talking about our run-in. And he still hasn't introduced his friends.

"No big deal, it happens," he keeps going, as if I'm worried about stepping on anyone's toes, which I'm fucking not. "But it's never happened with the CIA. First time for everything."

I feel a tug on my calf and look back over my own ass at the doctor who's wincing as he mutters, "Sorry."

I roll my eyes and turn back to the tactical army in black standing over me. "My informant has been tracking them for weeks. They're tied to a big..." I glance back at our company who I can't say much in front of. "Let's just say something big. I need to question them."

"They're not going anywhere anytime fast." Cruz has no issue speaking in front of anyone about the details of *our* targets. "My case is airtight. The asshole taken down by the Mounties is a mule tied to the cartels. Your targets are paying them to be smuggled into our country. I thought we were following a load, but it turned out to be people."

Another tug on my leg and I whip my head around and bite, "Are you cross stitching me a damn love note down there? It was only a graze."

The doctor's eyes flit between my new DEA friends —as taciturn as they may be—and me. "Sorry. About done. We don't get many gunshot wounds in here. In fact, this is my first."

"Don't add me to your collection of war stories to impress your dinner party companions—this is no GSW," I assure him, thinking of the scar Bella will always carry. That is a fucking gunshot wound. "It's a *graze*."

The nameless DEA agent on the right laughs. "Dude, that's no gunshot wound."

"That's what I said." I'm fucking tired of this and look back to Cruz. "I'd give you my card, but it's in my wallet which is in the rig."

Jesse waltzes in. "Got it."

"Great ... someone else. I feel like an animal on

display at the zoo." I take my phone, keys, and open my wallet to pull out a business card. "Here. Shit has been busy lately but call me when you get back in the office. I can arrange someone to follow up if I can't get there myself."

Who am I kidding? There's no way I'm going to be able to get there myself. I'm not even officially *here*.

"Also," I add, pointing to Jesse, "put his name on the report, not mine."

Cruz narrows his eyes. "I'll call—we'll figure it out. Anyone who can trace these jackasses around the world has my respect."

Well, at least there's that.

"You're done."

The doctor stands, looking proud of his work on his first *GSW* victim.

I climb to my feet, not giving a shit I'm the only one in the room in my underwear. The nurse hands me the scrubs and I toss my things on the gurney so I can pull them on. "Look, it's a long story but give me a call so we can compare notes. I've got the information you'll need to tie the cases together."

"Got it." He snaps my card between his fingers before stuffing it into one of his many pockets that are surely full of ammo. "Good luck recovering from that gunshot wound."

I roll my eyes and unlock my phone.

"Later," Cruz calls, but I don't pay any attention. I have way too many messages from Bella.

And Crew.

And Asa.

And Jarvis.

"Shoes." Jesse shoves my boots **my** way. I ignore him too.

Fuck.

No.

"Carson?" Jesse calls.

"Sir, are you okay?" the doctor **asks.**

I lean, ass to the gurney, finding **it painful** to search for my next breath.

I haven't felt like this since...

Since I got the call about Bella.

"Carson," Jesse bites.

I look up.

"I've got to get home."

CATCH MY BREATH

Cole

I was an asshole when I was seventeen.

And sixteen.

And eighteen.

A regular jackass douchecanoe who thought his shit smelled like daisies on a warm spring day. At least that's what I was told by a few.

Don't get me wrong, I *was* the shit. Star baseball player, homecoming king, and I barely had to lift a finger to melt the panties off the entire cheerleading squad. I was a jock who could also use my brain to its fullest potential—check out the records for every debate in the thirty-mile radius of my high school. I could argue the ears off Dumbo and make him cry.

See? Asshole.

The God's honest truth is I probably still am two days a week, on average. But becoming a dad has a way of humbling a man. I certainly don't want Abbott to end up with anyone like the seventeen-year-old me, but I do want her to exercise every corner of the brain I gave her.

Since an athlete with brains isn't the most common of cocktails, the scholarship offers started to roll in, making my head swell even bigger. If I could've taken them all, I would have. I wanted to go—get away from life on a tiny, shit farm that was too small to be classified as a farm. I wanted to travel the world, live in the biggest cities, dress like I was someone, and eat food that wasn't fried in the same skillet, day in and day out.

I wanted the opposite life of my dad.

When my mom asked why I wanted to go all the way to the west coast, I did not bite my tongue or mince words—because that's what douchecanoes do.

Despite my wanting a different life, I knew my parents were the best. They had to be to see past my assholeness and love me for the jackwagon I am.

I remember my mom looking up to me, since I was a foot taller than she was, laying a gentle hand on my stubbled cheek. "Go live your life, Cole. I hope you find what you're looking for. But mark my words, someday this will come full circle. Until then, learn, enjoy your experiences, and see the world. You'll be back and you'll realize happiness is right here in the simple things. You're so much like your father, it's frightening. You see this life as settling, whereas we see it as what dreams are made of. Your dad's been trying to tell you this for years. I love you, but I hope those dreams smack you in the face someday, because you deserve it."

She was right.

Red was right.

If my dreams haven't smacked me in the face lately, then I don't want to know what I'm going through. I was too late to get more time with my mom. She was dead before I came home to be a dad to Abbott. But I did do everything I could to rectify my relationship with Red.

I can't say it's been an easy few years, but I wouldn't trade them for the biggest and most covert cases around the world.

But I never knew that until this moment.

Jesse whipped up a small Homeland Security surveillance plane and I was back in BFE Virginia, a place I detested so much as a seventeen-year-old asshole.

I ignore the ache in my calf since my adrenaline burned through the local anesthetic in record time. I think the doctor prescribed me something for the pain but I have no idea where the script is, not that I would've taken the time to get it filled. Not after learning Red collapsed and was being rushed into surgery by the time I got the damn messages.

I'm barely off the plane and through the small building when I see Asa at the curb waiting on me.

I climb in and don't bother greeting him. "What's his status?"

Asa hits the gas the second my door slams. He shakes his head and I brace. "I don't know. We're not family. They wouldn't give us an update after taking him to the OR."

Five blockages—three of them at one hundred percent. Red likes his food fried and his beer cold. Doesn't matter how hard I've tried to get him to eat some damn chicken without the skin on it, he won't listen.

"Where are Bella and Abbott?"

He throws me a glance before merging onto the highway, heading west. "At the hospital."

I drag my hand down my face. "Shit."

"I know. I left Grady and Jarvis with them. Crew is on his way. None of us wanted her there but Abbott did not want to be separated from Red and Bella was determined to do whatever Abbott wanted. We couldn't talk her into staying at Whitetail."

"She's hardheaded."

"I got there before the paramedics. She was giving him CPR. Abbott saw the whole thing." I have no clue how fast he's going but we're speeding past cars left and right. "Bella was doing everything she could."

The image burns on my brain, the three people who matter most to me in the world. I would've been there had I only given Jesse the lead and let him run with it. I've gotten a taste of my old life as an operative in the last few weeks. That hit was like a jolt to my junkie soul. I didn't think one stop in Vermont would be a big deal.

"How's your leg?"

"It was only a graze. And how did you know?"

"I know everything."

"I'm not in the mood, Hollingsworth."

Asa shrugs. "I traced your phone though Bella's and found you at the hospital. I called them to find you when you finally answered Bella's messages. They told me you were the GSW victim."

"Fuck HIPAA laws, I guess."

Asa exits the highway. "We're here."

"Damn, couldn't they get him to a real hospital?"

His truck stops at the entrance. "Carson, I was there. There was no time to get him anywhere else. Go. I'll park."

Time isn't something I have to waste. I'm out and through the doors before I hear him pull away from the curb. I get directions for the OR waiting room but the place isn't exactly Mount Sinai. It takes me less than a minute to find them.

Shit.

Jarvis and Grady are sitting guard on either side of Bella who has my daughter curled in her lap.

Bella's usually light blues are red, bloodshot, pained. She's been mine since she was a twenty-three-year-old rookie operative. I thought I'd seen every side of her—happy, livid, and turned on. But during our time together, I've never seen her like this.

Anguished ... for me.

"Love." She presses her lips to the top of Abbott's head and strokes her hair where my daughter is clutching Bella's shirt. "Your daddy is here."

Abbott jerks and her eyes dart around the room. And my feet come unstuck.

I've got her in my arms by the time I've closed half the distance between us. Abbott wraps herself around me like she'll never let go.

"Baby."

I feel her tears against my skin. "Is he gonna die like Gramma did?"

Bella has her arms wrapped around her middle and shakes her head.

I rub Abbott's back and move to Bella. "I don't know, Abbs."

When I get my arm around Bella and tuck her to my side, the world seems a little less out of whack.

But only slightly.

I press my lips to Bella's forehead. "You shouldn't be here."

She wraps her arm around me and holds on tight. "I wouldn't be anywhere else."

I look down at her. "Thank you."

She shakes her head and turns her eyes to Abbott. "Are you hungry?"

She shrugs and lays her head on my shoulder.

Jarvis and Grady join our huddle and Grady smiles at Abbott. "Hey, peanut. I'm starving. Why don't we go find a vending machine? You can get whatever you want and I'll bring you right back."

Abbott doesn't look like she wants to go anywhere but I need an update on Red and I'd rather she not be here. "It's okay. You go with Grady —I work with him. I'm going to see what I can find out about Grandpa while you're gone. At least get a snack."

Abbott twists her fingers. "I don't know..."

Grady smirks. "I'm a sucker for a vending machine. I hope we find a good one but if you don't come with me, I won't know what you want. I'll have to get you some broccoli or something."

Abbott's face screws up and it seems the thought of broccoli from a vending machine pushes her over the top. "Okay."

Grady takes her hand. "You could not pick a better guy to take you for junk food. We might empty the thing."

Great.

The minute they turn down the hall, Bella plants her face in my chest and a shiver runs through her body. "I'm sorry, Cole. So sorry."

I lift Bella's face and tip my forehead to hers. "Thank you. And thank you for being here for Abbott."

She drags a hand through her messy hair. "She's scared, Cole. I don't know what to say to her. She understands what could—"

"I know she does. There's nothing we can do until we know more. Let me see if I can track down someone to check on him."

I kiss her one more time before letting her go, but the moment I do, a man in blue scrubs appears. He and I are wearing matching pants.

He surveys the room as he swipes off his scrubs hat that, for some reason, has fishing lures printed all over it. The oranges and yellows and blues pop off the black background and I can't take my eyes off them. I'm not sure if it's my lack of sleep or lack of food or lack of sanity, because the colors mesmerize me.

"Isaac Carson?"

"Red," I correct as Bella's hand finds mine but I don't look away from the damn lures on his hat. "Everyone calls him Red."

The man stuffs the hat into his scrubs pocket and I'm forced to look at his face, something I didn't want to do, because I knew if I did, I'd know.

I can read anyone's expression and his might be the easiest one I've ever interpreted.

"You're family?" he asks.

I pull Bella into me tighter. "I'm his son."

The man nods and starts telling me shit I already know. "Your father had three complete blockages and two partials. The echo upon arrival showed his heart suffered damage from—"

I hold my free hand out to shut him up. "Stop."

I need a second.

Just one fucking moment to catch my damn breath.

"Sir," the doctor starts. So much fucking talking. Is one second too much to ask for? "We'd just finished one bypass when he arrested on the table—"

"Fuck," I grit and look at the ceiling.

"Cole," Bella whispers. The tone of her voice might as well seep through my skin and wind its way through my veins. I'm grateful for it. It's how cemented she is within me. Right now she's giving me life.

Life.

I level my eyes on the doctor. "He's dead."

His expression continues to tell the same story it has since he walked in the room. The details of it don't matter.

"I'm very sorry. We did all we could."

A SECOND

Cole

I had to claw my way back when I almost lost Bella. The days when she was touch-and-go, I was so fucking afraid. I was afraid to hope and afraid to plan and afraid to think about a future without her in it, and that's saying something, because I'm not afraid of any damn thing. Even when she sent me away, I knew she was still on this earth, living and breathing. And as long as that was the case, there was hope.

I haven't slept in over twenty-four hours. Abbott needed me. I had to deal with the hospital, a mortuary, phone calls—so many fucking phone calls—and then there's work.

The Central-fucking-Intelligence Agency can kiss my ass right now. Nick Peterson has left me more messages than a scorned teenager after a public break-up at prom. I'm also currently popular with Security Special Investigations for going MIA.

Fuck them. I don't have time for the police who

police the police. I wouldn't have been out of the country had my superiors not put a hit on an innocent man.

After I dealt with the hospital, I couldn't get Bella and Abbott out of there fast enough. Bella can't be in public right now and the last thing I wanted was for Abbott to be lingering around the building where her grandfather died.

We're back on the secure grounds of Whitetail and I've never been more grateful. Abbott seemed to relax once we got back to her cat, Vivi, and the cows. She starts first grade soon. I have no roof. Bella is still hiding from every-fucking-one.

And I'm exhausted.

While Abbott was glued to me, Bella went to Crew's camp and brought what few things we own in the world that aren't burned to a crisp back to Crew and Addy's. We're taking over Red's room to be close to Abbott. I'm not sure what happened to the day, it seemed to crawl; yet, in a blink, it was over.

Our first day without Red.

Done.

It was a fight, but I got Abbott to bed. Once I did, it didn't take her long to pass out—she was emotionally tapped, trying to get used to the idea her best friend won't be home to feed her dessert for breakfast.

The moment her door clicks shut on the second floor of the enormous farmhouse, Bella is waiting. She takes my hand and pulls me into our new bedroom and then to the bathroom that connects to Abbott's.

The door shuts behind us and I hear the turn of the antique lock. She flips on the shower and through the mirror, I lose her face when she pulls her shirt over her head.

"What are you doing, sweetness?"

She doesn't take her eyes off mine as she pushes her jeans to the floor and pops her bra. Before I know it, with her back to me, she's standing the way I love her most.

Naked and present.

I turn her because looking at her secondhand through the mirror is too much separation. She doesn't say a word as her fingers work the buttons of my shirt before pushing it over my shoulders and down my arms.

She runs her hands up my abs and pecs but I grab her chin and tilt her face to mine. "Bella."

She pauses, which is a strange act for her. Bella and hesitation don't play—or live—in the same realm.

Instead of answering, she pulls her chin from my fingers and presses her lips over my heart. I feel the drawstring on my scrubs go slack, and for the second time today, I'm standing in my boxers.

My greedy hands find her hips and travel up her body. That's when she looks up. "I want to take away your pain—I want to take away your day. Even if it's only for a short time. I'm giving you what you need, Cole. I'm giving you *a second*."

Fuck. Today has made me question who I am. But right now, all I can do is hope I have enough time left on this earth to show her how completely fucking obsessed I am with every part of her—inside and out.

Every bone in my body aches from how much I love her.

I put my hands to her jaw and pull her mouth to mine. Her bare tits press against my chest and I can't get out of my boxers fast enough. My cock is alert and aching for her before we can manage to stumble under the hot water.

Always her.

Ever since she pissed me off on the first day I met her.

"Cole," she breathes against my lips with barely enough room for the water to run between us. "I'm sorry. Today has been horrid."

I drag my greedy lips away from hers and I swear she's crying. Her tears mix with the running water.

She shakes her head. "I wish I could have done more ... for you and for Abbott. For Red."

I put my hands under her arms and lift, her long legs circle me as I press her to the shower wall. I reach under and find *my* pussy—spread and wet and ready. Sliding two fingers in, I take what's mine and my cock jumps with jealousy. "Didn't think I could, but after today, love you even more."

She presses down on my hand and I circle her clit with my thumb. "Take what you need, Cole. Let me help you forget, even if it is for only a second."

She has no idea how much I need her.

Bella

COLE HASN'T EVEN WON his bet yet and I'm ready to give him everything. As much as his plans frightened me in the beginning, I'd live through everything all over again.

Other than today.

I thought I knew what it was like for my heart to

break last year when I sent Cole away, but it was nothing compared to feeling Red's life slip away under my own touch and not be able to do a thing to save him. Seeing the pain on Abbott's sweet, beautiful face was too much, and to know Cole was going to lose his father —it killed.

Waiting on him to return from Vermont was harder than telling him Red had a heart attack. I knew it was going to take a miracle to save his father. Unfortunately, there were none of those being handed down from heaven today.

And after it all happened, I needed to be with him.

My head falls back and hits the tile where Cole has me pinned to the wall.

"I'm taking you bare," he warns before stretching me impossibly wide and thrusting inside.

Yes.

It's selfish, I know. To want this—no, to crave this— after what he's lost and been through. I find the longer I'm here with him, the greedier I am. And this time, being together with nothing between us is a gamble. I know my body like I know the current exchange rate. If I'm not currently ovulating, I'm not English with a splash of Welsh.

Greedy.

So much so, if he tried to slide a condom between us right now, I might cry ... again. And I'm no crier.

I lift my knees to sink further. Cole's groan vibrates inside me and I love it. I love what I do to him.

His big hands grip each cheek of my bum, his fingers biting into my skin and muscles and I know I'll wear his handprints for days. He pulls his head back far enough to look into my eyes. "Don't leave me. Don't ever leave me."

My eyes fall shut as he takes me hard. Thrusting over and over and over, every time connecting with my clit in a brutally delicious way.

My hands work themselves up his thick arms, shoulders, and into his hair where I hold on because I feel it coming. After losing Red, spinning myself into a tizzy trying to be what Abbott needed, and worrying sick for Cole, I'm spent. This orgasm might wreck me.

"Love," I breathe and grip onto him tighter. I'm on the edge and he's got me where I have no purchase to move. "Please."

"I'll never get enough of you," he growls and slams into me two more times, not only pushing me over the edge, but picking me up and throwing me over, where I tumble and tumble and tumble.

His grip on my bum is cruel.

My fingers yank at the roots of his hair.

And we both come.

With nothing between us.

Anxiety and tension and pure, raw emotions are washed away, literally and figuratively down the drain, leaving nothing in its wake besides exhaustion.

Still, Cole doesn't put me down and he doesn't pull out.

"If it weren't for Abbott coming to look for us, I wouldn't move an inch. Right here, me fucking you into next week, with no one else messing with our shit, so we can settle and live."

When I exhale, my body slumps and he shifts me, but he must be serious about fucking me into next week because he doesn't pull out.

I put my lips to his stubbled jaw. "There are

moments of hope—flickers of light at the end of the tunnel. Then the universe kicks our legs out from under us and we have to start from scratch."

"There's going to be a light. I swear. It's so fucking dark right now but we've come too far." He squeezes my abused bum and leans back, leveling his beautiful dark eyes on mine. "We deserve a perfect life, dammit. I'm going to give it to you and to Abbott and the rest of the superhumans who grace us with their presence."

I swipe the water from his face and lean in to press my lips to his, letting my kiss linger as the water starts to run cold. "As long as I'm with you, Officer Carson, life will be perfect."

Cole

I'M accustomed to waking in strange places. Hell, I made a career out of traveling the world. It wasn't unusual to see the sun rise in a different city every day. You get used to it.

Though I can say the times I opened my eyes with Bella in my bed, I didn't give a shit where I was or what was on the agenda. Those are the days shit felt right.

Today, I think I woke up in the damn Twilight Zone —in a strange place where my past mingles with my miserable present. I support Bella's weight, something that has become a habit for us since I brought her home from the hospital. It's ironic since she's one of the strongest humans I know and needs no help to survive on a daily basis. I'm lucky she gets off on my cocky and winning personality, because she certainly doesn't need my talents. She's that fucking good.

But I sure as hell need her.

My gut sinks as everything from yesterday slams into my recollection and my brain clears from a dead sleep.

Red is gone.

My Abbott ... her heart is broken.

Bella wants to soothe everyone's pain.

And I'm still fucking exhausted after six hours of dead-ass sleep.

I reach over and grab the culprit that kept me from a full seven hours. I read the message and have to tamp down my anticipation.

Because I've been kicked in the ass enough times in the last few weeks—carrots dangled in front of me, and then ripped away, leading me to wait for more.

Jarvis – Sorry for the early text but I'm manning the control room. Our favorite Floridian has been busy. Finally, a money transfer.

Shit.

I slide away from Bella but don't dare kiss her. If I can sneak out of bed without her waking, it'll be a miracle.

Maybe ... just maybe, the gods are on my side for the first time in a long time. I'm dressed and out of the bedroom without her rolling. I walk through the house of the man who used to hate me, out his front door, and through a vineyard.

Cole

"Someone will access the account soon. It's too much cash to leave there for long. Especially when we know this isn't fun money. *This*," Jarvis nods to the open laptop in front of him, referring to the really big fucking balance that was transferred from an account linked straight from Randolph's phone, "is too big to sit in a simple savings account which sees a lot of movement."

I take a sip of coffee. It was the first thing I smelled when I walked in the door of Crew's farmhouse head-quarters. I feel the need to brace for whatever the world wants to throw at us next and I need to be alert. It's no shot of espresso but it'll do.

"Where is the bank registered?" I ask.

Jarvis flips through a couple screens and scrolls miles before he lands on an address. "There—Amsterdam."

"What do you want to bet it's not an actual place of business?"

"There's only one way to find out." He switches over to the satellite surveillance system and types in the location that was buried on their website. When the screen focuses, we both lean in to get a closer look. Jarvis taps the screen with his finger. "There's your answer."

It's in an alleyway and not one any legitimate or self-respecting bank would operate out of. There isn't even a sign on the door.

Jarvis picks up his cell and starts to type. "I'll get Ozzy on it. He's eerily good at this shit. We've flagged this account. When there's a withdrawal, we'll know."

I gulp down the last of my coffee and contemplate a direct IV. I'm going to need it to get through the day ahead of me. "I'd stay and man the surveillance but I have a meeting with the mortuary this morning. Bella can take over after I get back. I don't want to take Abbott with me. I think one of us needs to be with her for the next few days. Thank goodness she's finally taken to Bella."

"Do what you need to do. I don't mind." He reclines in his chair and looks at me. "None of us do. I don't have a trip for another week. Then I'm taking Gracie back to Uganda for her birthday. Hopefully this shit will be settled by then. I've been around for a few years now. It's what we do."

I pull in a breath. "I know Crew has issues with me—"

He shakes his head and stops me. "Crew is cool with you ... now. I'm telling you, he trusts Bella and he doesn't trust easily. I haven't always been in his good graces either, but once you earn his respect, you've got it for life." Jarvis shrugs with a smirk. "You might be in because of your woman, but you're in. That means he and everyone else in this place will work themselves to the bone for you."

I nod because there's nothing more to say. I need people at my back right now more than ever.

My phone vibrates against my ass.

Bella – You went to work without me?

I can't help but smile.

Me – You were asleep. I'm next door checking on things. You know I wouldn't actually strut my fine ass into work right now.

Bella – You can strut your fine bum right back here because Abbott is asking for you. A big box of cat toys arrived and she's anxious to open it, but wants you to be here. She thinks if you give the toys to the cat, it will like you more.

Me – Tell her I'll be there in five. Oh, and sweetness?

Bella – Yes?

Me – Randolph moved a lot of fucking cash into an account in Amsterdam. We're watching it.

Bella – Finally.

Me – We're getting close.

Bella – At this point, I don't care what's at the end of the tunnel, as long as we get there as quickly as possible. Hurry back.

I look to Jarvis. "I've got to go. Thanks again for this and let me know if a nickel of that money moves."

He picks up his coffee and props his feet up on the desk. "Got it under control."

I walk out of the old farmhouse, for once not worried about the details. And it feels really damn good to have people to trust.

IT DOES NOT FEEL good to retrace your footsteps at a mortuary. I did this only a few years ago for my mom. That time I was comforting Red. Today, I'm flying solo. I know I'm a selfish fucker at times, but I never cared that I was an only child.

Until today. As I sat there and picked out flowers and an urn and music, I decided Bella and I are going to make a shit ton of superhumans. Abbott will not be an only child. Who knows, we might've already started. But even flying solo and having everything fall on my shoulders, I think I did okay. Red would slap me on the ass and tell me good job if he were here because, even though we'll be in a church, I went with Charlie Daniels, just for him.

As I walk out of the mortuary, my spine steels and I stop in my tracks.

He's got some fucking nerve.

"Carson. I hear condolences are in order. I was sorry to hear about your loss."

I slide my hand in my pocket and casually palm my subcompact. Did I expect this? No, because to approach me on the street after everything I've been through would be an idiotic move of grand proportions. But then again, this is Nick Peterson. I should never have given him that much credit.

But there's also no way I'd leave the protection of Crew's compound unarmed.

I look around casually to make sure I'm not going to be ambushed before I settle my eyes on him. "Planning someone's funeral, Nick? Not really surprised to see you here with as many people as you've tried to kill in the last couple weeks. I guess if you keep shooting at the moon, you'll eventually hit something."

He didn't expect that.

"Wow, I actually made you blush," I say into his silence. Okay, so it's a blush of fury. He's about the color of Red's tomatoes. Which reminds me, the blast didn't take out the garden. I need to get over there and water it. Abbott would be heartbroken if it dried up.

I rest my finger on the trigger when his jaw goes hard and he says, "You've gone AWOL."

I shrug. "Maybe. But most people would when their superiors are out to kill them. It's called self-preservation—a natural instinct in intelligent human life. But I get why you wouldn't understand."

"You were given orders," he growls.

"Unlike you," I lift my chin to him, "I'm no one's puppet."

His eyes narrow.

"What do you want, Nick?" I throw my free arm between us. "You want to have it out here, in the middle of a parking lot where they can drag one of our dead corpses inside to get a jump on things? Because I'm game."

His eyes drop to my hand in my pocket and his jaw clenches. I bet he's not carrying. Not sure he could be more stupid.

"We can march it off right here, ten paces, like the old west where the law was interpreted by crazy lawmen and the bad guys always died in the end. I promise you, my ass will not be the one dragged in there. I plan on going home to my daughter, the one you had no fucking problem putting in harm's way when you ordered an IED to be delivered to my front door. I can overlook a lot of idiocy, but not that. Never when it comes to my family."

He finally adds something productive to the conversation, even if it is a lie. "I had nothing to do with that."

"Did your boss tell you to say that?"

He looks both ways before taking a step closer. "You don't know what you're doing or who you're dealing with."

I click my tongue and shake my head once. "That's where you're wrong. And Nick?"

"What?" he grits.

"I'd bet my future children I know more than you do. I'll give you a hint of what your outlook holds— you're fucked."

"I came to warn you to stand down."

"You're serious? You think you can come to me and tell me to do jack shit after everything that's happened?"

"If you cooperate, I can assure—"

"That I'll be as big of a dipshit as you? Yeah, not interested."

"You know too much. People want you dead."

I take five quick strides to close the distance. He takes two back. "I've been running from bullets and blasts. I know people want me dead. You can give them a message—tell them to watch their backs. I know all the angles and who's in with who. It's not me who should be running scared, Nick. So don't piss me off. I've had a bad fucking month."

His chest rises and falls with labored breaths as he searches my eyes, maybe trying to read me the way CIA officers are trained to.

"Tell your boss to go fuck herself. And I'll be back in the office after I bury my father and make sure my family is safe." I start to turn for my car but pause. "You know what? Go ahead and fuck yourself while you're at it."

He shakes his head and lifts a finger to my chest. "I warned you."

"I don't need a warning. I know exactly how big the stakes are."

He stares at me two beats before turning on his very basic walking shoe. It's not until after he slams the door of his g-ride that my finger relaxes off the trigger in my pocket.

I move to my truck and pull out of the parking lot, making sure no one is following me.

38

BRILLIANT BABIES

Bella

Two days.

Two excruciatingly painful days have passed.

The money has not been touched.

Randolph has been mindlessly boring.

Marie Kasey is still unconscious and there's no word on her prognosis other than she's critical.

Cole and Penn Simmons are becoming fast friends. Crew supplied Penn a cell connected to the new secure satellite system and Penn's family is extending their summer holiday here in the States. Penn has proven to have contacts far and wide across Europe—an impressive list even by my standards, which are sky high.

But it seems we've come to a standstill once again in the never-ending saga that has become our lives.

Because of that saga and Cole's run-in with his boss, we have not left the refuge of Whitetail or Crew's headquarters. Even though I'm accustomed to hiding out,

Pakistan allowed me the camouflage to move around and still work. Under any other circumstances, being confined to two properties would suffocate me. I'm utterly flabbergasted I'm not drowning.

I don't dislike children. I've simply never spent a great deal of time with them. I also wonder if it's because she's Cole's and I would literally rip my own heart out for him, but I find his daughter exceptional on the scale of my tolerance of tiny humans in general. Spending time with her has been an honor rather than a sacrifice.

Which makes it even more devastating to see Abbott withdraw into herself, struggling to understand why people in her life, who are supposed to be a constant, suddenly leave her. Yes, she's as sharp as a tack, but she is only six. Despite her mother being an imbecile, Abbott loves her. She might have taken to me recently, however I know for a fact she'd prefer her mother in a heartbeat. I've become a bit attached so, I can't lie, that stings.

Now to have Red ripped from her life...

It's distressing, especially for Cole, who wants to fix everything for everyone. It's what he does—he solves and he fixes.

Then there's the issue of condoms. What are they anyway? It seems neither Cole nor I can comprehend those pesky little buggers since I gave into his ideals of living happily ever after and all that jazz.

The man I cut off and wouldn't allow to help me with anything—let alone the biggest thing—has consumed all of me. I deserve far less than his whole heart he's given so freely. He might be the cockiest man I've ever met, but he's mine. I suppose one can be arrogant when they always deliver in the end. I'm lucky he's as persistent as he is bigheaded, otherwise I wouldn't be here today wondering how I've become the woman who spends every waking minute wondering if she's pregnant.

And I'm unexpectedly okay with it.

Shocking. Damn Cole Carson. He and his cocky-talking ways, making me believe I can have it all.

Since our time in the shower when my sole desire was to be a balm to Cole's pain, there's been plenty of sex with no mention of birth control. We spend our nights in the bedroom next to Abbott's silencing ourselves for the sake of everyone else in the monstrous house. The dark circles under my eyes are proof enough I'm spending far more time wrapped up in Cole than I am sleeping. Thanks to Gracie and the miraculous concealer she bought me, I'm okay with this too.

"What would you like to wear tomorrow, love?"

Abbott and I are snuggled in with one of her new books, taking turns reading, to get her mind off our depressing reality. Addy and Crew are off somewhere in the big house, spending time as a family.

Her dark eyes find mine. "Do I have to wear a dress?"

"I shouldn't speak for your father but I know him well enough that he only wants you to be comfortable and happy. Your grandpa would want the same. And speaking from one woman to another, never allow anyone to tell you how to look. You wear what you want and what you feel good in."

"What about that one thing we bought with the big legs?"

"The romper? That would be a lovely choice and you'll look as beautiful as ever."

Tomorrow is Red's funeral. It was pushed back a day to accommodate for security. Cole and I conferred with Crew and his men after Cole arrived home after his surprise *meeting* with his boss. Red's service, which has not been announced publicly, will be private and small, and held at the tiny chapel where Cole's mother was celebrated. We're doing everything we can to avoid bombs, bullets, and bosses. It took an extra day to make those arrangements. I feel very comfortable with the security in place and Abbott is none the wiser.

"It's getting late," I note the time. Addy put Vivi down over an hour ago. "It's about time for bed."

She shakes her head. "I want to wait 'til Daddy gets home."

Cole went next door to what is now referred to as the *control room*. He needed to speak to Penn and didn't want to do it here. "I'll text him and see how much longer he'll be."

I get an immediate response.

Cole – On my way back. Got word of a miracle—Marie Kasey woke up.

My reaction is not cool or collected because Abbott asks, "What? Is he not coming back?"

I brush her hair away from her face. "No, darling, he's on his way. Run up and brush your teeth, okay? He'll be up to tuck you in."

I'm about to text Cole something with a million exclamation marks behind it, but I'm stopped by little arms circling my neck.

A hug.

My first hug from Abbott Carson.

If I thought I was stunned by the news of Marie Kasey waking from a close call with the dark side, this show of affection gives me emotional whiplash I may never recover from.

"I'm sorry I wanted you to leave when you got here," she whispers into my neck.

I wrap her up tight. "Darling. It's okay."

"I like you and I like your funny voice."

She lets go of my neck and I find it difficult to blink quickly enough to keep my eyes dry. "I like you, as well, Abbott."

"I don't want you to leave."

"I might have to leave for work from time to time, but I will always return. Virginia is growing on me." I tap her nose with the tip of my finger. "As are you."

She hops down and scurries off to the three-story grand staircase that is the central hub of this home. She has a lighter pep to her step than she's had in days.

I'm about to text Cole about Marie, the hug of the century that almost drove me to tears, and that I'll be spending the next few hours in the control room to catch up on the transcripts from the wiretaps. I don't get to do any of this because the front door opens and he comes striding through.

I jump up from my chair and meet him in the foyer. I don't stop, raise up on my toes to press my lips to his, and speak first. "Abbott hugged me."

He slides a hand down to my ass—typical—and smiles. "She did?"

I nod. "And it was genuine and sweet and she said she doesn't want me to leave."

He squeezes. "That's good since you're not going anywhere."

I roll my eyes. "I explained how I might have to leave for work now and again, but I planned to stay."

His smile grows bigger. "I told you."

"Yes, yes, you're omniscient and know all about everything. Now tell me about Marie. I'm not going to be selfish and ask when we can get someone in there to interrogate her. So first, tell me how she is—her health, you know, all that stuff."

He frowns. "Sweetness, I assume she's as grumpy and pissed as you were when you woke up in the hospital. Asa's contact did not report on anything besides the fact she's awake, alert, *and* communicating."

I tip my head. "Communicating? With whom?"

He leans down to kiss me before letting my bum go and strides through the house to the kitchen. "You're the only person who could turn me on by using the word *whom* in casual conversation. Our babies are going to be *fucking-bloody-brilliant*, as you Brits say."

I have to pick up the pace to follow him. "First of all, don't mock me by using *bloody* or *brilliant* like that. And second, tell me whom Marie is speaking with. And do we know what she's saying?"

He gets to the kitchen and grabs a banana out of the overflowing fruit bowl before disappearing into the pantry. When he returns, he's holding a monster jar of Nutella. "She's talking to DC police. She's a GSW victim, shot in a crowded area where there are not usually many bullets flying. Asa said they were anxious to know what she remembers."

My insides turn and I feel as if I might be sick. "If she gives up Randolph, this entire operation will come to a grinding halt, Cole."

He nods and talks around the hunk of banana and

chocolate spread he stuffed in his **mouth.** "So far, she hasn't. And Randolph must have **his own** contacts and know what we know. He's all of a **sudden** talkative on the wire. And by talkative, I mean **pissed and** yelling."

"Would you quit eating that **damn** banana for two seconds so I don't have to wring in**formation** out of you? With whom?"

He licks a bit of chocolate off **his lip.** "There you go again, making me hard."

"*Cole*," I demand.

He takes three steps and inva**des my** space, but he doesn't answer. He lays a big, w**et, chocolate-covered** banana kiss on me. It's deep and **intense.** Only Cole Carson could kiss me like this an**d make** me wet, and I'm pretty sure my nipples are hard **too.**

He seals his deep kiss with a s**mack.** "Wendy Sisson. Do you know how good it feels to **stack up** evidence on my boss and his boss? I cannot f**ucking** wait to waltz into the DOJ with this shit and get **their** asses thrown in prison. I just need to find the evi**dence** to support what I know because the illegal wiretaps **will not** fly."

That is a bit of an issue. "What **did they** say?"

"That *it* is happening next wee**k and** payment for *it* has been deposited and if *it* turned **to shit** like the hit on Marie did, someone was going to **pay.** Oh, and if *someone* comes to the States who he **doesn't want** here, that *someone* is going to get cut. And I **don't think** they meant kicked out of the nice-guy club."

I shake my head. "What in the **bloody** hell?"

"Exactly. What in the *bloody* **hell.**"

My fingers press into his lats. "**Why are** you in such a chipper mood?"

He reaches down to my bum **and picks** me up to sit

me on the island before stepping between my legs. "Because for the last two days it's been quieter than crickets and now shit is happening. All we need to do is be ready. And you not only confirmed to me, but also to Abbott, that you're staying. And Abbs hugged you and she doesn't warm up to many people. I have no choice but to focus on how full the glass is among all the bad shit."

I wrap my legs around his muscled arse. "Speaking of, Abbott is waiting for you to tuck her in."

"That's why I came home. Tomorrow is going to suck—a black day during a time I was counting on Red getting to know you and you, him. We need to get past tomorrow so we can start a new chapter—the three of us—and figure out what the good life looks like."

I sink into his chest and wrap my arms around his neck. "Go spend some time with Abbott before she goes to sleep. I'm going next door to catch up and study the transcripts."

With his hands on my bum, he yanks me to him, his cock long and firm in his jeans, pressed tight to my still-wet sex. "I like seeing you work again. Love your brain, baby."

"You're just saying that when you really want to fuck me."

He shrugs. "Yeah, but I still love your brain."

"Daddy!" Abbott yells from the top of the staircase.

"Coming!" Cole yells and leans in to kiss me. "Go be awesome, sweetness."

And like him, I smile despite the impending funeral and everything else we're still waiting to solve.

39

SIMPLE MAN

Seventeen years ago

Cole

"**N**ot sure you coulda gotten farther away from home unless you went to Alaska or Hawaii."

I look over at my dad who's staring out at the Pacific Northwest. He's right. I might as well be a million miles from home right now.

"It's only four years."

And it's free. I don't add that out loud because my parents would've bent over backwards to pay for school had I not gotten a scholarship.

I didn't want them to make sacrifices. Did I want to get away from Virginia? Fuck, yes. I started dreaming about it my sophomore year when I put on some muscle and made all-state in baseball as a pitcher. By my senior year, I was top ten overall and heavily recruited.

I worked hard in the gym and on the field. I studied harder. But I had to work the hardest at not getting caught fucking around, doing pretty much everything I shouldn't've been doing. If anyone should give me a scholarship in anything, it's being covert at getting into shit I should not be getting into. I could skip college and go straight to the pros in the first-round draft.

Instead, I took a baseball and academic scholarship and moved into the dorm. Mom decided I needed about two million more hangers and made a run to Walmart. When Dad turns to me, it's like looking in the mirror. Same eyes, same hair, same coloring ... but everything else? So damn different.

"I want you to promise me something."

I roll my eyes. "Seriously? You gave me condoms before we left."

He shakes his head and stares at his feet for two beats before looking up. "Promise you won't forget where you came from."

I hike a cocky brow that probably needs to be slapped off my face. "Okay."

"You're smart, you're skilled, and you work hard. I'm proud of you, but do me a favor and deflate that head of yours once a week. It'll keep you grounded. And it's worth repeating—don't forget where you came from."

"I won't, Red." *I stuff my hands in my pockets and pull in a big breath.* "Promise."

He rolls his eyes. "Quit calling me Red."

I shrug. "Whatever, Red."

Sighing, he moves across the miniscule room and doesn't stop. He wraps his arms around me as I stand here like a dumbass with my hands in my pockets.

He hugs me. Tight.

Finally, I hug him back.

"And call your mama. She's sick about leaving you here."

"I will."

"And don't knock anyone up. I'll drag you out back and beat you myself if you do anything to fuck up your life."

I nod. I don't want to fuck up my life, either.

"Love you, boy."

"Love you, too, Dad."

———

THERE AREN'T many people here. A majority of them are the ones who have taken time out of their lives to protect Bella, Abbott, and me.

And, for a short time, Red.

Sure, my dad had friends. I'll probably eat shit later for making this shindig private. But in the end, do I care?

No, I fucking do not.

Abbott is sitting sideways in my lap facing Bella, who's tucked to my side. Abbott is playing with my tie and has been since we sat down almost an hour ago. She's rolled and unrolled that sucker a billion times. Around her wrist, her arm, up to my neck, and in and out of her little fingers. I admire her focus, or lack thereof. Either way, she's committed to ignoring the show going on at the front of the church and I'm not about to make her pay attention. Abbott and Red had a special relationship. She's old enough ... she'll never forget him. I know it's not the typical parenting move since I probably rank in the bottom twenty percent of parents when it comes to doing the right thing.

But since Abbott does rank in the top of her class in

reading and math and got that from me, I'm counting on my good genes to get her through.

The pastor, who I do not know, starts to wrap things up and my gut twists.

"Well done, Isaac. You loved your family with all your heart. God rest your soul as you're reunited with the love of your life, Maggie. You raised your son with love."

Bella's hand on my thigh tightens.

"And you gave your heart to your little Abbott."

Abbott presses her face into my neck. Damn. She actually is paying attention. My throat tightens as her tears roll down my skin and disappear into my dress shirt.

I pull Bella in tighter and press my lips to the side of Abbott's head, fusing us together—fuck the being who tries to separate us.

After another few lines, the few people I've allowed to be here respond, "Amen."

Bella turns, lays a hand on Abbott's arm, and leans in to give me a kiss, but stops when the sound of guitar chords come over the shitty sound system of the old chapel. She frowns.

One side of my mouth tips and I lean in to take her lips—chastely, because of church and all—as Charlie Daniels starts to sing *Simple Man*. I stand, taking Abbott with me, holding her to my hip, and grab Bella's hand. She smiles and shakes her head before standing in the tight-ass black dress that hugs every curve.

I do my thing—thank the pastor and start shaking hands. When I get to Asa, he does not look like he's in funeral mode. He's all business.

He hands me his cell and speaks low. "Just got this.

The recruits are manning the control room and they're getting a lot of chatter. You need to see it."

I take the phone and scroll with Bella reading over my shoulder. When I reach the end, Bella asks, "Have you identified them?"

Asa shakes his head. "Not yet. Ozzy's working on it."

Bella looks at me. "I want to listen. Do you mind?"

"No. You go. I'll get Abbott settled with Addy and be over."

She looks to Asa. "Let's go. I'm ready for this to be done."

Bella

"They haven't spoken? It's only been text?"

"Yep." Ozzy is spinning whatever magic he creates in the back room of Crew's compound. More large screens cover old walls and makeshift desks have been set up with plywood on trestles. This was thrown into operation overnight and Addy told me yesterday Crew asked her to shop for more office furniture since no one else has time. "Whoever he's arguing with has their phone tied down so tight, I can't break it. They know their shit and are keeping it under wraps, which makes me think it's no terrorist. At least not an official one."

I look down and read over the transcripts again that have accumulated over the last day...

Randolph – The drop was made days ago and you've done nothing with it.

Unknown – I'll take care of it when I'm ready. Day job has been busy and my guy hasn't been able to get to it.

*Randolph – I'm **paying** for a timely service, not for when you can carve **time out** of your schedule.*

*Unknown – I'm at the airport. Making a quick trip to the States. Maybe I'll **run into** you.*

*Randolph – I told **you** to stay the fuck away. We don't need to be on the same continent right now. I need to keep this operation going through the end of the year when I announce my candidacy. After that, you're off the payroll.*

*Unknown – I **might be** on your payroll but you can't tell me where I can or cannot travel.*

Randolph – It better not have anything to do with me.

*Unknown – You **really** are the most self-centered SOB I've ever worked with. I have personal business.*

Randolph – This is your last warning—stay out of the U.S.

Unknown – Gotta go. Boarding. We'll share the same piece of land in less than seven hours.

I toss the papers on the plywood and kick off my heels. I didn't bother to stop at Crew and Addy's to change and now I'm regretting it. I'm definitely gaining my weight back and this dress is cutting off my circulation.

I look at Ozzy. "Have you exhausted all options of tracking that phone?"

He drags a hand down his handsome face. "I'm still working on it. This one is different. If I had my guess, it's been encrypted by someone who knows what they're doing. And by that, I mean someone like me."

Ozzy is a bit different from the rest of Crew's men. Is he a big, brute American? Of course. I assume it's a prerequisite. But the rest of the men have somewhat of a barbaric side they have to work to control—it's visible, simmering beneath their rugged surfaces. Cole is cut from the same cloth.

But not Ozzy.

I've gotten to know him over the last few days while I've had to sit for hours and stare at the mind-numbing screens while waiting for something to happen. Ozzy is different.

An engineer by trade, he doesn't have a background in the military or other type of enforcement—not your typical soldier of fortune. He is not a fly-by-the-seat-of-his-pants man. He's methodical in his risk-taking. Even so, he could snap the average human in half in a heartbeat and wouldn't think twice of it, which makes him scary on a whole other level.

I tip my head. "So you're saying there's still the teensiest chance?"

He hikes a brow and a ghost of a smile plays on his lips. "What the fuck, Bella? First you ruin my phone by sexting your long-lost lover and now you're busting my balls for not trying hard enough? I said I was working on it."

"Indeed, you did. I was only confirming."

"He hasn't figured it out yet?"

I turn to find Cole striding into the control room in a pair of athletic shorts and one of the few T-shirts he still owns. I need to do some online shopping for him.

Ozzy flips Cole off and turns away from both of us. "Your woman is giving me enough shit. I don't need more from you, Carson."

Cole slides his hand down my side and cups the side of my bum where I'm leaning on a makeshift desk. "Are you giving him shit?"

I turn to Cole. "I don't know what he's talking about. I've been a sweet, sugarplum fairy."

Cole lifts his chin to one of the screens. "Seems they're getting busy at the church."

I turn to take it in. It's the first sign of life since the men barged in and nabbed Gary and his minions. Gary is still enjoying his stay at the Vega B&B, but, lucky for him, he gets three delicious take-out meals a day, prepared by none other than the café at Whitetail. I doubt they know they're feeding our captive. Gary has complained, but not about the food.

At this point, we believe he's nothing more than a pawn in a much larger game. He is becoming more and more desperate and has given up information about other crimes he's committed for Wendy Sisson's organization over the last few years.

We're keeping him as a witness. When all is said and done, we'll need him since our illegal wiretaps will not be admissible in court. And quite honestly, given the drastic measures Randolph takes when someone dares to cross him, Gary is safer here. I have no trouble sleeping at night knowing there's a criminal being kept in the barn next door.

Well, I do have trouble sleeping but it has more to do with the hand on my bum and the man attached to it.

"I'm going to get out of this dress but I'll be back. I want to see what's going on there."

He stops me when I try to move away from him. "Do you need some help?"

"I'm trying to work over here," Ozzy complains.

As much as I would love that right now, I lean up to kiss Cole. "We shouldn't push him too far, love. I'll be right back and I'll bring food for everyone."

40

SHATTER

Cole

I love my job but that doesn't make me a workaholic. When I was active, I'd count down the minutes until Bella and I could steal precious hours together outside of our cases. Since I've been back at Langley, I can't wait to get home to Abbott. And when this shit is filed under *cases solved*, to Bella too. I work long hours. I don't need extra work on the side to keep me busy.

But today, on the day I had to say goodbye to Red, I'm over the damn moon to have this distraction.

And it's proving to be a doozy.

One car pulling into the scam of a church turns into two.

Two turn into three.

Something is going down because someone feels the need to meet.

Bella has been gone for at least forty-five minutes

and I just pulled out my phone to text her to hurry her ass back when car number three arrives.

But I force myself to put my phone down and frown as I lean in to get a better look. "Zoom in on the dark blue sedan."

Ozzy's fingers fly over the keyboard. Theoretically, I know the technology allows us to see anything larger than five inches off the ground in high resolution and cameras don't lie. But my fucking brain doesn't register what I'm seeing.

It can't be.

"Keep that camera on him," I demand. "This feed is being recorded?"

"Do I look like an idiot?"

I don't acknowledge that and hiss, "Fuck."

My blood churns and my heart races to catch up. If I didn't stick to a mostly clean diet and work out at least four times a week, I'd think I was experiencing what Red had four days ago.

This is not good. This is so far off the scales of bad, I'm not sure where we go from here. A heart attack might be a welcome event if it means diverting everyone's attention from the person walking up to the church located not far from where I stand.

"These ladies are the loveliest I've ever known. Do you know what they did?"

I turn and realize I was so overcome by what's playing out live on the screen, I hadn't heard her walk into the room. I'm not sure why she complained about the tight dress because her jeans look like a second skin and I'd bet my life she's not wearing a bra under that T-shirt.

I move to fully block her view. Her arms are full of containers stacked on top of containers, and from the smell, someone's been busy in the kitchen.

Her icy blues hit mine, innocent of what's going down behind me. I know I won't be able to keep it that way for long, if even a few more moments. But the need to throw myself at her, protect her, shield her heart, and her soul is overwhelming.

This will shatter her.

She lifts the containers in her arms. "I feel horrible we're here and not back at Crew and Addy's. They arranged a meal in honor of your father. Everyone is there and I told them I'd bring you back but they said they understood we need to be here. Still, I think you should make an appearance. They worked so hard—the food smells amazing."

"Baby." My voice doesn't sound like my own and I put my hands on her shoulders, turning us one-eighty so her back is to the screens. I look over her shoulder and Ozzy is frowning, wondering what the fuck is going on.

Bella gives her head a shake. "Why are you acting like an odd duck?"

I'm not sure I've ever been at a loss for words in my entire life. But I know the moment she learns the truth, her world will shift and never be the same again.

"Cole," she bites. "What in the ever-loving hell is wrong with you?"

I pull in a deep breath but make a mistake. It's instinctive and maybe even a form of self-preservation, but I glance at the screen that's zoomed in, displayed in the highest definition currently on the market. Internally, I curse Crew for having so much money he does not fuck around when it comes to quality.

I dip my head, cutting the few inches that separate us, and level my eyes on hers. I keep my tone even and calm. "I need to talk to you, but I need you to put the food down and sit."

She tries to pull away but my fingers flex on her biceps. Her eyes go big, sensing the difference in my touch, and she grits her teeth. "Dammit, Cole. Let go."

"No," I snap. "I need to talk to you first."

"What in the fuck is going on?" she demands, and for the first time ever I regret falling in love with a woman who's as tough as nails with a will as strong as steel. Because unlike every other woman I've ever had the displeasure of knowing, she doesn't panic. She's intense, all-business, and ready to kick someone's ass.

Right now, it looks like that ass might be mine.

"Sweetness." I try to calm her but her eyes narrow and I can see this is not going to fly. "Okay, at least put the food down."

Her pink, plump lips flatten, and before I know it, I catch her heel in my shin. It's enough for her to twist out of my hold and move away from me.

"What the hell is going on with you two?" Ozzy asks.

My hand is on her bicep again but I'm too late. She's already scanned every screen, her eyes settling on the one in the middle. I feel it under my touch when it sinks in. She freezes.

Her body goes totally and absolutely rigid.

I move in behind her. "Bella—"

She exhales on a whisper. "It can't be."

"There has to be an explanation," I try, praying there is but not sure how. "We'll figure it out."

Her breaths become labored. "Fuck me."

For once in my life, I have no smartass comment for that.

Ozzy still has no clue of the significance of what's happening but keeps the camera zeroed in on the man who's now standing in the gravel parking lot, openly talking with Wendy Sisson and Nick Peterson.

She shakes her head. "Why?"

"Baby, sit down—"

And that's when it happens.

Food hits the floor—the smell of fried chicken, baked beans, and rich, thick macaroni and cheese fill the command room like a greasy-spoon diner. Some remote part of my brain comprehends the combination of muck on the floor is an ode to my late father.

"What the—" Ozzy yells but I ignore him and reach for her.

She's around me and out the door before I can grab her hand. My foot slips on beans and melted cheese, putting me behind her at least four paces. By the time I catch up and get an arm around her waist, we're in the entryway of the old house.

I try to get her feet off the ground but she kicks, catching my bullet graze, causing me to buckle a knee. That's when her elbow catches my jaw.

Dammit—she knows my face is off limits.

"Fuck, Bella. Stop it," I growl.

"Let me go! I'm going to kick his fucking arse—"

She spins, flattens her hand, and smacks my temple. She's lost her mind.

"You're not going anywhere," I rumble and try to lift her to steal her footing.

The back of her head connects with my forehead

and I'm forced to blink away stars. "I bloody well am. I'm going to wrap my hands around his neck until he tells me what the hell he's done."

"For fuck's sake, I don't want to hurt you—"

"Then let me the hell go!"

I twist her in my arms and swipe my foot under her legs. We both hit the wood floor with a bang that echoes off the aged walls.

"I'm not letting you go anywhere, especially like this."

I roll on top between her legs but she already has a foot planted flat. She grabs my neck, arches, and pushes off the floor. We both go the other way and she rolls on top of me—her face flushed, her eyes wild.

She gets to her feet but I grab her wrist and put my feet to her hips, lifting her legs out from under her.

"Damn you—" she yells.

I kick one of her hips up, twisting her, and let gravity do the rest. I catch her between my legs before I roll and have her pinned, face to the floor.

"Cole!"

She struggles, but she's not getting up until I let her. Her wrists are grasped in my hands, her legs down to her ankles are pinned by mine, and my pelvis is pushed into her lower back and ass.

"You two are crazy." I look up and Ozzy is standing at the entrance to the hall, his stance wide and his arms crossed, taking in the freak show we're starring in.

"Leave us the fuck alone and call Crew," I demand, needing to be alone with Bella. "Tell him and anyone else who's free to get their asses here now! And get back in there to triangulate every phone in that building. I want to know every step that fucker takes when he leaves. Turn on the bugs we planted a few days ago."

We're both breathing like we crossed the finish line of an ironman race, or in her case, a badass-out-of-control race. The last thing I have time for is Ozzy. Nothing is more important than Bella's broken heart right now.

Every muscle in her body is tense.

I put my lips to her ear through her wild hair. "Baby, stop. Think. Just for a second. You cannot go over there. I can't, either. We need to do what we do best and figure out what the fuck is going on."

She shakes her head where she's pinned against the wood but says nothing.

"Calm. Let me help you."

Her chest convulses and she chokes out a sob.

Finally, her body goes limp.

Still, I brace. "Are you going to hit me again if I let you up?"

Tears leak from her eyes and I'm not sure my heart can take it. This might be worse than seeing her unconscious in the hospital.

I let go of one wrist at a time and twist to my ass. She doesn't get up, she doesn't run, and she doesn't give me an elbow to the eye socket. She folds into herself and her tears flow.

I drag her onto my lap, my woman who can overcome anything. She's endured time on her own—not only survived but thrived—working and doing what she loves even though it had to be in the shadows.

And *he* put her there.

"Baby."

She shakes her head where it's tucked in my neck, her hands fisting my shirt. "How did this happen? Why? Why would he do this?"

I tuck her in tighter, never wanting to let her go. "I don't know, but I'm going to find out."

41

COINCI-FUCKING-DENTALLY

Nine years ago

Bella

"I've made a decision."

My family turns their attention to me. It's our first night back together, all of us. We're on holiday and my first semester as a fresher at uni was fabulous. I loved my courses, my professors, and I even made some friends. Though, not many girlfriends.. They never much take to me.

Mum takes a sip of her wine. "What decision is that, love?"

"My course of study."

Devon laughs. "Weren't you supposed to decide before you started?"

I toss him a glare. "Maybe. But I wanted to be sure. It's a huge decision."

Dad stabs a piece of meat and dismisses my brother. "You're fine, Bella. What did you decide?"

I hike a brow at Devon before looking back to my parents. I don't have an apprehensive bone in my body but this … this is something different. I don't need their approval nor their blessing, but I can't lie, it would be nice. And my decision comes with enormous shoes to fill.

I pull in a big breath. "Criminology."

"Fuck," Devon chokes. "No way."

"Devon! You're never too old to watch your mouth at my table." Mum admonishes him before looking back to me with a smile. "I knew it. The day you took your first jiu jitsu lesson and kicked your instructor in the crotch, I knew!"

Archer picks up his beer. He was hired onto SIS as an MI6 like Dad and Grandpa before him. He's in training now. "Well, this is gonna be fun! The whole damn fam in the business."

"Proud of you, darling." Dad levels his eyes on me and has his serious-as-hell look about him. He's not trying to appease my latest whim, he truly believes in me. "I know you'll give it your all like you do everything."

Devon shakes his head.

"What?" I snip at him.

Devon is two years older than me—we're closer in age than he and Archer. Archer has always loved me the way one would love a puppy, because I'm merely a cute little girl in his eyes. But Devon and I were closer in school, competitive with grades and friends and basically everything.

Devon lifts his beer, tips it to me, his words dripping with sarcasm. "Congratulations. The princess has spoken and all approve."

I roll my eyes because this is nothing new. "Bite me."

"Devon, stop," Mum chides but can't keep the smile off her face. "I'm very proud. You'll be amazing."

"Thank you." I smile at Mum, and it doesn't matter how old I am, I stick my tongue out at Devon. "See you in class, big brother."

He grins—a shit-eating one at that. "Always the competitor. I'll take that challenge, Bella."

Archer raises his beer. "To Bella."

Dad picks up his high ball and corrects Archer. "To the Donnellys. May we carry on for generations, serving our country—in secret and with honor. We stick together, always." He looks to Mum and continues. "You gave me a good lot, love."

Mum picks up her wine and clicks it to his crystal. "Cheers. Couldn't be prouder of my family."

"WE'VE ALREADY IDENTIFIED Sisson's and Peterson's phone. Every other device in the building needs a tracker on it when they walk out of there. If he has one fucking app with the location services on, I want inside it," Cole growls.

In all the times we worked together, I'm not sure I've heard that tone fall from his lips. Cole's intensity is off the charts.

He's been barking orders since he stood me up in Crew's foyer, wiped the tears from my face, told me he loved me, and how he knew I had it in me to handle this. Then he informed me I needed to snap out of it because we had shit to do.

Time is of the essence. Professionally, I know what needs to be done.

But I can't get the picture out of my head of my brother standing there talking to the people who tried to kill Cole and his family ... and me.

Devon.

Yes, we squabbled when we were young, but not as adults. As adults, we were fine—normal. As normal as siblings can be from a family full of secret assets. As many ways as my mind has tried to spin this—to make it not true—I don't see how it can be any other way.

Cole dragged me back into the control room to find Ozzy simultaneously cleaning my mess off the floor while manning the satellite cameras.

"Who do you know that you can call?" Asa probes. "MI6 keeps their shit tight, no way can we get into their systems, which is why Ozzy couldn't break his phone. We need to know what cases he's been on and where he's been working."

Cole drags a hand through his hair and doesn't answer.

Asa keeps on. "You worked that part of the country for years. Surely you have a contact."

Then, something happens that never happens. My American, Cole Carson, is a lot of things ... arrogant, self-centered, brash ... yet always in control while working. However, today is a day of firsts because he and I are both teetering on the edge. "The Donnellys are my fucking contacts, Hollingsworth. And Devon is the one who met with the people who have been trying to kill us, blew my house up, and, oh, coinci-fucking-dentally, knew his sister was under my care and protection. So, no, I don't have any more Brits left in my arsenal besides the one I plan on spending the rest of my fucking life with!"

Papers fly across the room that were fisted in his hand moments ago.

"Fuck!" he bellows, a cherry to top off his very irate sundae.

I lean back in the office chair Cole sat me in after I semi-snapped out of it. I force myself to breathe. Everything is falling apart and Cole has lost control.

"Penn Simmons?" Grady asks.

Cole pauses for a second before pulling out his phone. "I'm not sure what he'll know, but he does know people all over. It's a long shot, but it's my only one."

"What the fuck are we waiting for?" Jarvis pipes in. "We can be in raid gear storming the place in less than fifteen minutes. We have the element of surprise. We need to take advantage."

"No." All eyes in the room turn to me. It's the first word I've spoken since my very uncharacteristic crying jag that the men walked in on. I focus on Cole. "The money hasn't moved. We need to see this through to the end."

Cole nods and turns back to the monitors, arms crossed, deliberating every earth-shattering problem raining down on us.

The room stills when sounds come over the speakers. Footsteps shuffle through a room at a quick clip. When the men busted in to take Gary and his helpers, they planted bugs but the church has been quiet until today.

"This is where you operate from?"

A shiver travels up my spine from hearing my brother's voice as if he were sitting right next to me.

"It's not exactly official business, Donnelly," Wendy chides.

"You don't say?"

I close my eyes. Devon was always the sarcastic one of the family.

Wendy keeps talking. "We know why you're here, but it isn't necessary. It was a mistake that won't happen again. You'll get your money's worth but it's going to take a couple days. We had some contractors disappear on us but should have someone else in line soon. We need the opportunity to arise for it to happen. The targets have been MIA."

"Maybe there's another way. Let me reach out to Carson," Nick Peterson butts in.

"There's no other way. I told you from the beginning when you agreed to join this effort," Wendy snaps.

"I know for a fact my sister is on our trail. It's only a matter of time before she and your CIA officer suss it out. And since I'm sitting at the end of the trail, that cannot happen. You were paid to make that go away and you fucked it up."

I'm physically ill. Cole turns to catch my eyes and bruises are forming on his handsome face from my freak out. Everything happening to him is because of *me*.

My throat thickens and I can't look at him any longer. The guilt is too heavy.

"Our contractors thought they were home," Wendy argues.

"Not quite sure how much more you can fuck up. You can't even get rid of the ex-Marine in Switzerland, for God's sake. How do you get anything done in your agency?"

"Penn Simmons..." Nick tries to explain how yet another soul is living and breathing that they've tried so hard to kill. "We couldn't get anyone to carry it out."

"He's been asking all over Europe about Spain. I'm not going down for that."

The more they argue, the more it goes back and forth, and the more it settles in my gut—I've been stabbed in the back by my own brother.

My own *blood*.

"I want my money back," Devon demands.

Silence blankets the audio feed and lingers so long, I shift in my chair for fear we've been cut off.

Wendy's lost her backbone when she finally responds, "That's not for us to decide."

"Then I want to meet with Randolph. If he insists on keeping his hands clean, he'll pay up. If not, he can come here and tell me his damn self."

"He won't come here," Nick insists and I hope he's wrong.

"Then tell the fancy-as-fuck Senator the money in my account is mine and there will be no action from his so-called terrorists. See how much funding his precious committee gets then. I came all this way and have a shit-load to take care of because you two can't carry out a simple fucking job."

I stand with a start, the office chair rolling away behind me. Cole's eyes zip to mine and I'm not sure if I have a headrush or am about to pass out.

"Baby—" he starts and reaches for me.

I put my hand up and look at the screen, muttering to no one, "Take the meet. Please, take the meet."

"I'll text him and let you know. Don't hold your breath." Wendy says.

"I'll be here as long as it takes for me to do what I have to do. Make sure the arsehole knows there will be no motivation for his troops to be spread around the world unless I get my money back."

Boots on concrete echo perfectly through the listening devices. They're so sharp, I'm surprised we can't hear Nick Peterson's heartbeat—he's that nervous.

Cole's heat presses into my back as I watch my brother stride nonchalantly out of the church, as if he didn't just admit to paying for murder to be carried out and threaten to finish me off himself. He climbs into a blue sedan and takes off like the nightmare this is turning out to be.

All of a sudden, the room becomes electric with activity. Crew and Ozzy move to keyboards. Asa is already on the phone. Grady and Jarvis are out the door and down the hall, chattering about guns and vests and night vision goggles...

But not us.

Cole's arm snakes around me and I'm turned, pressed to his chest with his big hand on the side of my head. His heart beats in my ear. I swear, it's the only thing giving me life at the moment.

His lips hit the top of my head. "I don't have the first clue what to say, sweetness."

I wrap my arms around him tighter. "However this ends ... my poor parents. They'll be devastated."

He tips my chin to look up at him. His eyes are not gentle nor are they guarded. "This is only going to end one way. Do you understand me? You'll be among the living and sleeping next to me every night in a home we rebuild together. I won't settle for anything less. Your brother has made his bed. I can't do anything about him, but I can take care of you."

I don't answer. I press my face into his chest as Crew

barks orders, Ozzy rattles off computer jargon, and Asa bosses the recruits.

"Baby," he calls for me.

I shake my head and look up to him. "I know what I need to do, Cole."

Bella

Randolph took the meeting.

"I don't like this."

"I don't care."

"We're not going to let anything happen to her."

"She took your ass down earlier—she'll be fine."

"Dammit, Bella. I've been fucking you without a condom. What about that?"

"Why is it we know every detail of their sex lives?"

This has been going on for the last thirty minutes.

Cole arguing.

Me not caring.

Crew reassuring Cole.

And Ozzy getting in every jab he can about my out-of-control tussle with Cole, as well as complaining about Cole oversharing. Ozzy is not wrong—my love is sporting two bruises on his beautiful face and we've thrown birth control out the window. I really do owe him a blowie for the bruises. I refuse to think of the consequences of the other right now.

I'm also not proud of the fact anyone—least of all Cole—had to tell me to *snap out of it*. Were the circumstances extenuating? Of course. I mean, Devon...

Shit.

Breathe, Bella.

Devon has done what he's done but I'm certainly not going to live in the shadows any longer. I had my moment but I've steeled my heart and am ready to do whatever the hell is necessary to end this.

Today.

I close my eyes and take a deep breath, willing that to happen, as Crew and his men plan, so I can spend the rest of my life with Cole and Abbott.

A magazine being snapped into place is enough to slap me back to reality.

My eyes fly open and Crew is standing in front of me with a sharpshooter rifle. "You'll have me at your back. I'll be closest. Ozzy will know your every move, but my goal is to not take my eyes off Devon."

I force myself to look away from the gun that will be aimed at my brother. "Okay."

"Let me go in," Cole insists. "It'll be better that way. You don't need to be put in this situation, not with Devon."

I shake my head. "It has to be me."

"It doesn't. However this goes, you don't need this in your head. Baby, you of all people understand—no one believes in you more than me. You do your job better than most. But that's a job. This is personal. If it comes down to it, you might not be able to do what you need to."

"I will."

"You don't know that," he argues. "In fact, there's no reason for either of us to go in. Let's regroup, let them hash it out, then we'll take everyone down."

I hop off the table I'm sitting on and move past Crew and Ozzy. I lift to my toes and close the distance to press my lips to his.

Cole stands stock still and doesn't return my kiss. He doesn't put his arms around me, nor does he reach for my bum.

I fist his shirt and pull him to me. "I have to look him in the eyes. I have to know why. If I don't do this, I'll never forgive myself."

His head falls back and he studies the ceiling. All I see is a clenched, stubbled jaw.

"Cole." I wait until he finally sighs and looks at me. He knows I don't need his permission. But I also know he loves me and had to say goodbye to his father today. It's asking a lot but I throw back the question he's pinned me with so many times. "Do you trust me?"

He shakes his head. "You know I do, but I have enough scars on my heart, baby. Don't give me another one."

I give him a small smile. "Never."

His face transforms into something I saw earlier— intense and probably downright scary to anyone besides me. "I know that fucker is your brother but he took you away from me. If he makes one move on you, I'll take him out myself."

The thought of that slays me but I understand. "I know you will."

He takes my face in his hands and pulls me to him. Kissing me long and hard and like no one is watching.

His fears dance with mine but his strength also fills me, giving me courage and, most importantly, the need to return to him above all else.

Even beyond my own blood.

He lets me go and takes a deep breath. "Okay. Let's do this."

Cole

WE'RE in the woods outside the church. They had surveillance all over this place. Ozzy picked up their signals with Crew's technology and killed it with a tap of his powerful mouse and some quick keystrokes.

Something I learned tonight about Ozzy—he might be a computer-engineering genius, but he likes staying behind about as much as he likes hearing about other people's sexcapades. He was green with envy as the rest of us left the compound in black tactical gear and armed into next week.

We all have our lane and mine is right beside Bella's. There's no way I'm letting her out of my sight until a shitload of people are under arrest or dead. At this point, I'm not particular how they end their night.

Grady's voice sounds in my ear. "They're lighting up Peterson three miles out."

I put a finger to my comm and press the button. "He's alone?"

"Yeah. We're still waiting on Wendy."

I exhale. Step one is underway.

Asa called in a favor who called in another and someone called another to have Peterson and Sisson stopped for driving with no license plates, which happen to be in the back of Jarvis's Explorer.

Grady laughs. "He's not happy."

"Let us know when you find her. They need to keep him for at least thirty minutes, maybe more. We'll keep you informed." I glance at the church and grit my teeth. "You're up, Bella."

Asa and Crew's recruits are situated around the building. I'm with Crew and he hasn't said a word since he set up. He's three feet from me, chest to the ground, laser focused with Devon in the sights of his rifle. He was a sharpshooter assigned to the White House when he worked for the Secret Service Uniformed Division. If Devon lifts an aggressive finger toward Bella, he's done.

She doesn't answer but the supersonic device she's wearing tells the tale. Every twig and leaf she steps on as she approaches the building breaks and cracks.

The door opens.

Her footsteps might as well be bricks dropping in my gut.

"Come back to me, sweetness."

———

Bella

I worked for a couple years as an operative before *someone* framed me for the terrorist attack. Those years are a blip compared to the career I was looking forward to. Nothing made me feel more alive than when I was working as a spy, pretending to be someone I wasn't, knowing the lies I lived were for good and not evil.

It was my high—a rush of adrenaline—and the

more I did it, the better I got. Cole might've had something to do with that.

Okay. A lot to do with that.

His cocky, all-knowing and self-assured persona
rubbed off on me. It didn't take me long to know when I
made the decision my first year at uni, I chose correctly.

I was good at what I did.

But now I'm a new me—a woman who's been
betrayed in the worst way by someone I love. If I were
walking into this sham of a church naked, I'm not sure I
could lay myself more bare than I am now.

I might as well be five again, getting picked on by my
big brother who I secretly idolized because he was
always the more cunning of the two. Archer, bless him,
is a teddy bear in comparison.

I watched Devon arrive alone on the cameras. He
came into the States on a commercial flight, though that
means nothing. Devon bleeds ingenuity. I'm sure
picking up a weapon was the first stop he made when
he landed.

Not that I'm into betting my life these days, but I'd
be shocked if he isn't armed.

I hold my head high with a pistol secured at the
small of my back and walk through the doors of the
building I've only seen the footprint of on fancy x-ray
sensors. The moment Devon hears me, he whips
around.

Pure and unadulterated shock takes over his
features, but only for a moment. My cunning brother
schools his eyes and smiles.

He smiles.

I've lost so much because of him and now he knows
I know.

And he fucking *smiles*.

"Haven't seen you in ages and now it's twice in the matter of, what ... a week? How many days has it been since our Caribbean rendezvous?"

He's at the old altar which isn't an altar any longer. Rows of pews separate us and I stop at the back, the long aisle leading to my lying, murderous brother.

I dread the moment my parents learn of his treacherous ways.

I lean a hip on the end of a pew and put my hand on the other. His eyes follow my movement, like the trained operative he is. He knows I'm one step closer to a battle. "I find your visit coincidental. There are only a few people on earth who know I'm in Virginia and you're one of them."

"I have a meeting, Bella. How did you know I was here?"

"You still think so little of me and my connections? I know a lot, Devon."

"You don't know shit."

I take a few steps, closing our distance by two pews. "That's where you're wrong. I know everything."

His brows pinch and his eyes narrow. They're angry and aggressive when he lifts his chin in a challenge and takes two steps closer to me. "You think you know so much? Enlighten me, little sister."

"Why? All those people in Spain ... your hands are soiled with their blood. Why would you conspire with anyone? For money, of all things. We were raised in the same home. Money was never coveted. What have you become?"

"Fuck you, Bella. Keep talking. It proves you're clueless."

I forget about the gun at my back or the likelihood he's armed, as well. This is personal.

"You killed them!" I scream. "Forty-three of them!" My words echo off the walls, bounce around the beamed ceiling, and back to the wood under our feet. "Seven of them were children! I don't even care about it being pinned on me right now. How did you become such a monster?"

"Bella!" Cole bellows in my ear and I stop halfway up the aisle where I've advanced on Devon.

This is not what I planned, not what any of us planned when we agreed I'd approach first, to try to persuade him to turn himself in for a peaceful ending. I begged for this opportunity, for my family and my parents.

"Bella, listen to me!" Cole growls.

I pause and Devon senses it, demanding, "What is it?"

Cole keeps talking. "You've got company we weren't expecting. Wendy Sisson's car just drove up. They didn't catch her, dammit."

Shit.

I steal more precious moments and press Devon. "Tell me. I need to know why."

"Baby, you need to get out of there. Let us finish it. You cannot be caught in the crosshairs. Not again," Cole says.

Devon and I both hear a car at the same moment. I stiffen but don't dare turn my back to him.

"Who's here?" Devon demands. "I know you know. Tell me, Bella."

"Fuck. Randolph is with her." Cole grits in my ear.

"I'll come in there and get you if I **have to**. Get the fuck out! Now!"

I ignore them both.

I don't take my eyes off Devon. "**Mum** and Dad ... you're going to break them, you know."

He shakes his head and looks past me. "Carson wouldn't let you come alone. He's **talking** to you? Is it Randolph?"

"They're walking up," Cole growls.

I step into a pew and make a **quarter** turn so no one is at my back.

Cole screeches, "Fuck me, Bella! **Get** out now!"

I turn to look at Devon.

He spears me with his eyes and **shakes** his head.

Now is not the time for pretenses. We're both trained by the same organization even though we haven't lived by the same oath.

I draw my weapon and it doesn't faze my brother one bit. He moves to the end of **my pew** and stands in front of me.

Sentry.

What the hell?

The door creaks open, and for **the** first time since the night at the Kennedy Center, I see Randolph in the flesh. But tonight, he's not talking **to me**. He points to my brother. "You have a lot of fucking nerve, Donnelly."

"Well, now," Wendy sing-songs **as she** steps up next to him, her eyes flitting between Devon and me. "This is an interesting turn of events."

43

DOUBLE

Cole

I f I hadn't lost so many damn phones in the last
few weeks, I'd have Crew sharp shoot this fucker
into a pile of dust.

My ass is well massaged from the vibrating it's taken
over the last fifteen minutes. Addy would never message
me now, she knows what we're in the middle of. She's
back at Whitetail taking care of Abbott with a recruit
standing guard. The only other person I care about in
the world is in jeopardy right now. If my sperm and her
egg had a rave in the last week, then I have even more at
stake.

As far as my priority list goes, Penn Simmons sits
right above my online grocery order. I do not have time
for him right now.

I'm about to take a chance and see if I can toss the
damn phone in the forest to come back for it tomorrow,
when I rip it out of my pocket and glance at the screen.

Penn - Answer your fucking phone!

Penn – It's about Spain.

Penn – What you thought is not what you thought. Fucking call me!

What the hell?

I press go on his name.

He answers in less than one ring. "It's not like we're golfing buddies. When I call, it's fucking important."

"I'm a little busy right now," I whisper.

"Then I'll be quick. Donnelly did not do Spain."

I sit back on my ass in the forest. "Which Donnelly?"

"Fucking Devon. I thought we both knew it wasn't the woman."

I did but I had to be sure he thought so too. "How do you know this?"

"Someone else from Vauxhall is behind the Spain job. They tried to pin it on the Donnelly woman. Devon went rogue to try and clear his sister's name."

What the fuck?

"Did you hear me?" Penn yells in my ear. "It wasn't Devon. He took an assignment with NSA to root out the real double agent because British Intelligence was fucking up the case."

"Devon works for NSA?"

This gets Crew's attention and he flinches for the first time all night. "What? The National Security Agency? You're sure?"

"You're sure?" I echo into the phone. "Time is of the essence and I cannot get this wrong."

"I'm sure enough that you can wait to kill him until after you vet my source," he bites.

"I'm not sure of anything," I say to Crew. "But for now, don't kill him."

Crew's finger immediately lifts from where it hovered over the trigger.

"Carson," Ozzy speaks into my other ear. "Man, some guy picked up the money in Amsterdam."

Crew and I look to each other and I ask, "Did you get a facial ID?"

"Running it now," Ozzy answers.

I multitask and listen to Penn in my other ear. "NSA knew BI had an internal problem. They were already tracking that shit when the bomb in Spain detonated. BI was pressured and it was easier for them to pin it on the young Donnelly. Devon reached out to NSA. He's been working as a double agent, but a good one."

Ozzy's voice comes through my other ear, blowing my mind. "Got an ID. Facial is turning up an Oliver Abram."

"Ollie?" I ask out loud and can't start to comprehend what this means. "Shit."

Crew turns to look at me, hearing the same feed from Ozzy. "I assume that's your Ollie."

"One and the same. We need to get Bella the fuck out of there."

Bella

COLE KEEPS BARKING ORDERS. "Get the fuck out. This is not what it seems and there's no gun trained on Devon —he's on your side and knows who he's dealing with. Let him take care of himself and finish this. Get. Out. Now."

I look at my brother but his eyes never waver from

the pair standing at the rear of the church where I was moments ago.

Wendy and Randolph are surveying the situation, studying us like we're some weird problem made with an array of numbers and symbols their simple brains can't compute. I'm holding my gun opposite them—there's no way they can see it.

Wendy reminds me of an ugly snake, slithering and slow but could pounce at any moment. "Interesting how you wanted her dead hours ago. Yet, here we are, interrupting your family reunion."

"Do I know you?" Randolph focuses on me and I wish I could put a bullet through his head. It would be for every woman he's ever wronged.

Since I trust every word Cole has ever uttered, I take my eyes off Devon and look at Randolph and Wendy. Devon's exhale doesn't go unheard.

He knows. At least for now. Because I would never allow him out of my sight if I thought he were a threat.

I'm trusting he isn't.

And look who has her own weapon—the snake herself.

"You're in too deep," Cole grits in my ear. "We're coming in. Be ready to hit the floor when I give you the word."

Devon takes a casual step forward and throws me a glance before shaking his head. Then he reaches out and grabs me by the arm opposite my gun. I feign a struggle, knowing full well I could break free in a heartbeat. If there's no gun trained on Devon right now, there's a good reason for it—I'm trusting what I don't have an explanation for.

"Told you she was on my trail." **Devon** tips his head to me before looking back at Wendy. "You're an embarrassment to your agency, Sisson. I wouldn't need to be here if you could carry out a simple operation. And you." Devon moves his gaze to the Senator. "These worthless pieces of shit reflect on you. If you can't cover my arse, find yourself another manager to fuck shit up around the world."

"We can't exactly make people disappear Stateside like we do in the field," Wendy defends herself and waves her gun around.

I try to pull my arm out of Devon's hold for show. His grip isn't angry or murderous, but protective. If I were anywhere else at the moment, I'd breathe a sigh of relief.

"I know you," Randolph doesn't take his eyes off me.

"You think?" I spout. "Maybe you should keep your willy tucked away long enough to worry about the fact Marie Kasey will soon be questioned by someone much higher than the D.C. police."

"Fuck." His face transforms into the murderous killer he is as he reaches into his jacket, producing his own weapon.

Devon flinches and angles me behind him.

"Hang tight, sweetness," Cole whispers in my ear. "We're almost in position."

Devon stares at Randolph and grits, "See what I mean? I told you to take care of her and you couldn't make it happen. I want my money back. I'm out."

Wendy shakes her head. "No one leaves once they're in. Not alive, anyway."

"You don't know who you're dealing with." Devon

grips my arm, giving me a shake before turning his attention back to Randolph. "How far do you plan to take this when your innocent attacks don't get any attention anymore? Will everything be like Spain?"

"Devon," I breathe as light as I can and try to flip my hair to cover my mouth. "They're coming."

Devon doesn't move a muscle and holds me close.

"Whatever it takes," Randolph confirms callously and I hold my breath. "Loss of life is a part of war—it can't be helped."

If I hold my words any longer, bile will rise in their place. "Your war is contrived for personal gain. You're a cold, calculating murderer."

Randolph has no reaction other than the tip of his head when a light hits his eyes. "You're the woman from the fundraiser. Couldn't get my mind off you for days. Got to say, like you better as a brunette."

"You'll suffer for what you've done," I spit back.

"You came to the wrong place, Ms. Donnelly." Wendy takes a few steps, the click, click, click of her low-heeled shoes might as well be a gong in the heavy air. "You see, we might not be able to do whatever we want in the States, but here—" she waves her gun around again "—in the privacy of this sanctuary, I can get away with a lot."

Randolph steps in next to her and pushes Wendy's arm down to lower her weapon. "I'll deal with her myself."

Devon pulls me tighter.

"Five seconds, baby," Cole gives me a warning.

I bring my hand holding the gun up and press the side of it to Devon's back. Then I take a deep breath.

"Say goodbye to your sister and move away, Devon.

That is, if you want to walk out of here with your head attached," Randolph drawls.

Cole counts. "*Three.*"

"I'm a Donnelly. You don't know who you're fucking with," Devon grits.

"*Two.*"

"It's no skin off my back." Randolph shrugs. "You think I can't buy someone else? Ollie's on his way to pick up the money. Maybe he needs a promotion to do the work himself."

"*One.*"

"You're wrong," Devon bites back. "But Ollie is finally going down and so are you, now that you just admitted everything to NSA."

Randolph's face contorts.

"Now," I whisper.

"*Go!*" Cole grits in my ear.

Cole

I'm first through the door.

Bullets fill the old building, ricocheting off walls and pews and bursting through stained glass that turn into exploding rainbows filling the night.

The only thing I see is Bella, flying into the pews, but not under her own accord.

Devon pushed her.

Or, more like threw her.

I don't see how she lands because Devon falls—flat to the ground from where he was standing.

Randolph dives the opposite way.

My eyes move to the side and there's Wendy Sisson. Her eyes land on me and she frowns.

Her gun shifts my way. I aim but don't have a chance to pull the trigger when her stunned eyes widen.

A bullet through the head.

I turn in time to see Bella tucking herself behind her pew from where she took out Wendy.

The men storm in behind me and I barely have time to yell for them to get down as bullets fly toward us.

Randolph.

Bella peers around the edge of the pew with her gun trained across the aisle. I stoop and make my way to the back of the church as the rest of the men scatter.

I press the button on my earpiece. "If someone draws him out, I can get a clear shot."

Bella's gun pops over the back of her pew.

"Dammit, Bella. Not you," I grit as she rapid fires toward the other side of the building.

I keep moving to the back of the church. It's the only way out and his only choice.

I take a knee, aim, and wait.

It only takes a few seconds as bullets continue to fly when Crew calls it.

Silence.

The senator has no choice but to escape. He comes crawling out like a dog and, I'm such an asshole, I whistle and call for him. "Randolph!"

His head jerks and he catches my eyes. I want him to know exactly how he dies before it happens. I'm making sure he'll never fuck with me, or my family, ever again. It's what he gets for even thinking about touching Bella.

I pull the trigger.

One shot.

Done.

I move to him and Wendy to kick their guns away from their lifeless bodies.

That's when I hear Bella, and this time she isn't calling for me, but rather her brother.

44

COCKY SELF

Bella

"**N**o!" It was all I could do to focus on the damn gunfight with Devon lying in the open aisle. I crawl to his crumpled body, blood creeping out from beneath him.

I can't find my breath and my heart twists.

"Devon," I call and grab his shoulder to roll him to his back. He blinks once, and in slow motion, his eyes shift to me. "Oh, thank God. Where are you hit?"

He tries to reach up but winces. "Shoulder."

"Bella!"

I look up and Cole is rushing toward us, ripping off his helmet and I demand, "Call an ambulance."

Cole doesn't go for his phone, but Crew does. Instead, Cole takes a knee and puts a hand to the side of my face. "Are you okay?"

"I only hit my head." I look back down to my brother. "He's losing blood."

"Ambulance is on its way," Crew announces.

Cole reaches for a utility knife in his belt and cuts Devon's shirt up the middle to find the wound. He wads up the material and presses it to Devon to stop the bleeding before lifting him. "Exit wound. This'll probably fuck up your shoulder but you should be okay. Man, this would've been way easier if you had given us a heads up."

I take Devon's hand in mine and squeeze it, happy tears pooling in my eyes. "I'm so mad at you right now, I'd take you down myself if you weren't already shot."

Devon's smile is not apologetic. He's damn proud of his cocky self.

"We flushed out Ollie last month but couldn't take him down until we found the money source. We knew it was coming from the States but nothing more. I've had eyes on you for months—you led us to Randolph. We didn't have solid evidence to put him away, it's why we let things carry on. Can't fucking believe that guy." He squeezes my hand before looking to Cole. "Sorry about your house, mate. We knew we were getting close and no one was home. It was my decision to let that IED blow." He looks back at me. "I took this gig to clear your name. But since Sisson and Peterson were in on it and Cole is CIA, we couldn't risk saying anything. The upper brass at Vauxhall are going to be shaking in their loafers when this hits the news."

"I hope they rot," I say. It's not a lie.

Asa walks up to us as he's sliding his cell into one of the many pockets on his vest. "Peterson is talking. Not only is he talking, he's singing like a jaybird. About Wendy, Randolph, the order put on Simmons. And Grady handed Gary off to the county Sheriff—he's ready to cooperate. With all the evidence, I think your time in Pakistan has come to an end, Bella."

He's right. My days living in hiding are over. I'm not going back.

"She wasn't going back anyway," Cole expresses my thoughts as if he were in charge of my future.

I glare at him. "No, I'm not, but by my own choice."

"Hey." Devon pulls at my hand and I look back down at my big brother. "This will teach them. No one fucks with a Donnelly."

I brush the hunk of hair away that always falls to his forehead. "No. No one fucks with us. Not anymore."

45

BLOODY

Cole

I pull my phone out of my pocket as I walk through the blackened forest. The number is unknown, but the most interesting calls I get on my work phone are. Sometimes the most exciting things begin with an unknown caller.

I'm not officially back at work yet. I'm on administrative leave until the people who police the police finalize their report. I'm good with it because I could use a fucking vacation. They told me things will be different when I return next week.

Different will be good.

It feels like an eternity, but it hasn't even been a week since Peterson was taken into custody, Bella killed Wendy, and I took down Randolph. From what I've heard, Marie Kasey has left the hospital but has a long road ahead of her. Not sure how an investigative reporter moves on from blackmailing a senator.

And Ollie, a man I trusted, has been charged with so

many counts of treason and terrorism, I've heard they had to put him in solitary. I don't even want to think about the grave he's dug himself.

And it's been almost a week since we had to say goodbye to Red.

Even with all that, the world is lighter on my shoulders, though life couldn't be more different. Bella's name has been cleared. She has free roam of the earth, can live as she wishes, and has given the intelligence community her proper middle finger, wishing them a holiday in hell. Now, she can go or do whatever she wishes—but I'm the lucky asshole she chooses to be with.

Not sure how I ended up with the best parents, the smartest child, and the most beautiful and cunning woman, but I'm not questioning that shit. I'm fisting them in my greedy hands and never letting go.

It seems my selfish ways know no bounds because I can't wait to see what my unknown caller might bring me. I put my phone to my ear as I make my way through the forest and vines on my way back to Whitetail where my family is waiting on me. "Carson."

"How's the gunshot wound?"

I pause but I don't stop walking because the patio light is on at the enormous farmhouse, with a tall, thin silhouette waiting for me.

"Who's this?" I ask even though I'm pretty sure I know.

He doesn't elaborate but he does start talking. "You and your girlfriend's mugs are everywhere, and not just the national news. You've made the BBC, Al Jazeera, and you're even popping all over news outlets in Africa."

I climb the hill, her light hair coming into view

before her blue eyes. "I only have a few minutes. Why are you calling me at this time of night?"

He proves to be as weird as he was the night our paths crossed. "You're famous and I can say I saw you in your underwear."

The tips of Bella's lips turn at the corners when I step out of the night. "It's late. Get to it."

"I need a favor."

Bella holds her hand out for me. The moment we touch, my cock jerks to life. I don't take my eyes off her as I continue with my unknown caller. "Don't we all."

"I'm making a move. Leaving the east coast for another position. Taking one of my cases with me. It's going to take some..."

Bella leads me through the dark house. It's late. Kids, babies, cats, cows, and assassins have been MIA for hours. I've been in Crew's command room with Ozzy going over some technology. "Spit it out."

"Ingenuity."

We walk up the first flight of stairs to the second story where our room connects to Abbott's. "Is that another word for *illegal activities*?"

I can almost hear him smile. "I would never."

The door clicks behind me and Bella continues into the room and shuts another, closing us off from the bathroom. "Why do I not believe that?"

"I need some covert help."

With her back to me, Bella unbuttons her shirt and shrugs it down her shoulders. "You must not've been paying attention at the academy. I'm CIA. I don't work cases in the U.S."

"You did last week."

Bella pushes her tight-ass jeans down her legs and I

can't take my eyes off her ass cheeks peeking at me through black lace. They're begging me to palm them and make them mine for however many hours I can stay awake. "Last week was different."

"So is this."

She turns to me and pops her bra. It lands on the floor and she comes to me. "I've got to go."

"Look, I know you push the boundaries and since I don't know the fucking meaning of boundaries, I thought we should become better acquainted. You can talk 'til you're blue about the rules and shit, but I have a case I think you'll find interesting."

My shirt hits the floor right before my jeans and boxers. A pair of panties is the only thing being worn in this room and I'm calling that a crime against humanity. It's also time I got rid of Brax Cruz, Special Agent for the DEA, no matter how special he thinks he is or how curious I am about his lack of boundaries. Nothing is as important right now as the mostly-naked woman standing in front of me. "Let's meet next week."

"Cool."

"Yeah," I barely agree. "Cool. Call me when the sun is up."

I don't say goodbye. I hang up on my new *friend* and toss the phone on the bed. What he has to say might be interesting tomorrow but, right now, my cock is running the show.

Bella

AFTER TOSSING HIS PHONE, Cole gives me a lazy smile. "For your information, when you suck me off, you'll do it naked."

I tip my head and smile at my tall, handsome, and very naked American. "So demanding. You act like you're in charge of this or something."

He tries to hide his smirk.

"Important call?"

He shakes his head. "Nothing is more important right now than your panties hitting the floor."

He knows I want this as much as he does. I tuck my thumbs into the hips of my panties and inch them down until gravity takes over. Stepping out with one foot, I use the other to send them airborne.

My flying panties are no challenge for Cole's quick reflexes. He never takes his eyes off mine as he reaches out and nabs them. But he does look down as he runs the thin silk through his fingers.

He gives me his eyes. "Wet."

Not only did Cole teach me the intricacies of managing a complex case, he also taught me to be brave in the bedroom. And he's right. I am wet. Because when I reach down to touch myself, my fingers slide easily through my sex.

Cole doesn't take his eyes off my hand.

I circle my clit and force myself to take a deep breath.

The whole time, he doesn't stop rubbing my panties between his thumb and fingers.

"Are you close?" he asks.

I bite my lip. I wasn't, but I might be now.

"Spread your legs."

Shit. I thought I was brave.

"Now," he demands.

I shift my legs and feel the cool air hit my very warm body, but don't stop circling.

"You're so fucking beautiful. There are moments I can't believe you're here. For good."

"I'm here," I whisper on an exhale. "Forever."

Not only am I here, I'm out in the open for all to know and see. I'm living free among society again. By necessity, I became accustomed to surviving on my own and being by myself.

I'm done with that lonely life and never want to experience it again. I'll miss living in England, but it wouldn't feel right any longer. Nothing feels right without Cole Carson.

My eyes fall shut and he bosses, "Don't stop until you're almost there."

My lids are heavy when I open them.

"I want you needy and on the edge when you suck me off."

I whimper and let my head fall back. I'm close and don't want to stop.

The next thing I know, my hand is ripped from between my legs and Cole's other arm circles my back. Our naked bodies are pressed tight and Cole is sucking my fingers that were between my legs.

He presses his hard cock to my belly and drags my fingers from his mouth with a pop before his lips land on mine.

By the time he ends the kiss, I'm breathless and rubbing my thighs together for relief.

"Love you, baby."

His arm tightens around me when I lean into him more. "I love you, too, Cole."

He smiles. "Okay. Now you can do whatever you want with my cock. He's excited as hell."

I shake my head but don't waste any time dropping to my knees. He's right. His cock is bobbing in front of me, long and hard and anxious.

I take him in my fist before running my tongue around his tip. He's smooth yet salty from precum. When I draw him into my mouth, chills run down my spine, knowing this is mine forever. Cole is mine forever.

I suck him in as far as I can, hollowing my cheeks, and use my tongue. In and out and in and out.

"Sweetness." Cole groans as he fists my hair. The sting at my roots make me suck harder and deeper and become wetter with need.

"Fuck," he hisses.

I peek up from where I'm kneeling. As my eyes pass over every toned and cut muscle, from his cock to the tips of his shoulders, I finally find his eyes, which isn't hard in the bright room.

Cole takes over and I've lost all purchase. Holding my head, he fucks my mouth, the tip of his cock touching the back of my throat with every thrust.

He stops unexpectedly and growls, "Don't want to come in your mouth. From now on when I come, it's only inside you with nothing between us."

Cole pulls out of my mouth and I'm in his arms, my legs wrapped around his waist. When we make it to the bed, I'm on my back and he's standing between my legs, wasting no time.

When he thrusts inside, all is right with my world.

But when he doesn't move, I open my eyes and frown. "What are you doing?"

Looking down at our connection, his fingers start to play.

"Oh," I whisper, remembering where we are, whose house we're in, and that there's only a bathroom between us and sweet, little Abbott.

"You like this?" Cole starts to move slowly as he works my clit.

I was close before and stopping was torture.

"Cole."

"Shh, baby."

I clamp my mouth shut and fist the sheets beneath me.

"But breathe," he adds.

Oh, for the love.

Two more circles of his fingers partnered with the delicious slow movements from his cock, I tip over the edge.

And it's all I can do not to wake the county.

I barely have a moment to catch my breath when Cole pulls out and flips me to my stomach. He kicks my legs apart and enters me from behind. I have to grip the bed to hold on. His fingers bite into my hips and ass, pulling me to him to meet his every thrust.

We haven't had many moments like this since we've been back together. Cole has been careful with me after surgery but not tonight. Tonight, he lets go and takes me the way he's meant to.

Solely.

Completely.

Making me his, the way he has since the first day we met.

And that will never change.

When he finally comes, my muscles are sore under

his grasp and I'm sure I'll be sensitive in other places too. His chest hits my back, pinning me to the bed, his breaths are so labored, I feel every move he makes.

He presses his lips to my forehead before they make their way to my mouth.

But what he says surprises me.

"It's been a month."

I open my eyes, seeing only him.

"Sorry?"

"Our bet," he breathes and goes on, speaking uncharacteristically like a caveman. "One month. Fixed your shit. You marry me."

It's been six days since everything went down at the church. Devon had to have surgery to repair his shoulder but it was a clean exit wound and won't do any lasting damage—nothing some physical therapy won't fix.

My name has been exonerated by British Intelligence, the CIA, and the rest of the western world—thanks to an army of people at my back. Vauxhall has contacted me countless times and I refuse to respond. I have also been contacted by my father's publisher, which I find interesting. I *did* take their call.

But for now, Vauxhall can kiss my free arse. Even though I haven't officially shut that door yet, I want nothing to do with them for now. They put me through hell. I have a right to some time to figure out what I want.

We said goodbye to Devon at the airport today. It was an especially emotional moment for me. The last few weeks have been nothing short of a roller coaster from hell. I didn't want Devon to leave. I spent every moment I could with him in the hospital and, after, when we squeezed him in here at Hotel Vega. Abbott slept on a pallet in our room and he took hers.

Family.

I was alone for too long.

Now I want nothing more than to be surrounded by the ones I love, whether I share their blood or not.

"I need you to say yes, Bella. If you don't, I might lose my shit."

A small smile plays on my lips. "*Might*?"

"Definitely. I will most certainly lose my *bloody* shit."

My smile grows. "If you're not going to use *bloody* so it sounds natural, please don't use it at all. I'm embarrassed for you when you do that."

My pet name is bitten out like a curse as he presses his still semi-hard cock into me. "Sweetness."

"You won your bet fair and square, Cole Carson. I don't renege on my agreements."

His dark brows pinch. "That's the lamest *yes* in the history of proposals."

"I'm sorry. I don't remember you proposing."

He doesn't try to hide his smile. "You got me there."

"Of course I do."

"It's happening. You marrying me will be the fastest way to your visa," he goes on. "How or where, I don't give a shit. But it has to be soon. I've lived long enough without you."

"I think I've lost my mind because this is strangely romantic."

He grins. "Uncle Sam takes the Queen. I feel like singing God Bless America."

I try not to laugh. "Please don't."

"Going to fuck you again to celebrate."

I sigh, happily. "Please."

"But I'll clean you up and eat you first."

I say nothing, but my expression says it all. I want that.

"Be right back, baby."

He walks into the bathroom. I hear the water running for a moment before he returns where I've curled into myself on my side.

He tosses a wet rag down on the nightstand and sits next to me on the edge of the bed. Instead of cleaning me like he said he would, he grabs my hand.

A thin ring appears on my left ring finger.

There's nothing astonishing or flamboyant about it. Its beauty is in its simplicity with a rather small, single round diamond perched in the middle. I'm sure there are a million in the world like it, but none of them were placed on my finger by Cole Carson.

"I dug and dug and dug. Finally found it in the rubble. Red gave this to my mom when she was eighteen." His voice is low and gravelly, emotion lying thick below the surface. "Wish I could've had you since you were eighteen. No amount of time with you will be enough."

My throat constricts and I climb to my knees next to him, holding my hand between us. I can't stop looking at it.

"I don't want to forget where I came from," he goes on. "Spent years trying to and it worked out like shit for me. Be with me, Bella. Be the mom Abbott needs. Build a family with me, here in BFE, Virginia. I know I'm a selfish prick to ask you to start over in a new country, away from a job you love, your family—"

I have to choke down my tears to interrupt. "Yes. Yes to Abbott, yes to BFE, and bloody yes to never forgetting where we came from." I press my lips to his. "Most of all, yes to you."

He wraps his arms around me and twists, flopping us both on the bed. "Okay. Now I'll eat you out."

I laugh as I finger the new ring at the base of my finger. It doesn't feel one bit foreign. Rather, it settles my heart.

As long as I'm with Cole, I'm home.

Two Months Later

Cole

I look through the house—literally through the house—since it's nothing but studs, to find Bella and Abbott twirling in circles in what will be the new sunroom off the back.

Plans are coming along ... fucking slow as hell.

At this point, if Jarvis finishes his Garage-Mahal and MacMansion before we can have a normal-ass house built, I won't be surprised.

Bombs don't exactly fit into the details of home-owners insurance. Normal paperwork turned into a ball of crimson duct tape. I thought we were going to end up being Crew and Addy's weird-ass step kids who never move out.

But tomorrow, sheetrock.

You know teenage boys and wet dreams? Yeah, well that's what sheetrock is to me right now.

I guess it makes me an official adult at the age of thirty-five.

"Daddy, let's go see my room! I have my own bathroom!"

"What are you?" I ask. "Fifteen?"

She skips by me and tags my hand in the process, dragging me up the stairs. I won't let her go by herself because of the lack of railings and walls and everything else to keep her safe. This place is a concussion waiting to happen.

"Not too long, love," Bella calls from what will be the kitchen. "I have to be back for a meeting soon."

Abbott pulls me into her room. Bella and I went round and round when we were designing the house. I wanted to stick with the budget we had from insurance. I'm no paid assassin with millions in the bank to build garages bigger than houses. But every time I went back to the plans, Bella was moving walls, adding a bathroom here, an extra closet there, and she's basically salivating for a pantry like Keelie's. She assured me we'll need these upgrades when Abbott is a teenager and our sperm-egg raves start to multiply. She then straddled my lap and told me she wanted to contribute to the house. How she worked hard, did nothing fun, and was sitting on a mountain of cash.

I just don't want to forget where I came from.

But if she wanted an extra bedroom, bath, bigger closets, and a pantry the size of a barn, who was my cock to disagree? Because when she straddles my lap, he makes all the decisions.

That's why we're on to bigger and way better things. But anything with Bella and Abbott is better.

Abbott tours me through the upstairs even though I know every square inch in my head—down to the light switches—before I carry her down to the main floor.

Bella beams. "It's going to be beautiful."

I smile back. "It's also going to be soundproof. Let's get you to your meeting."

Bella

I WALK UP the steps to Crew's headquarters. The old house has become a sentimental place for me. So many memories have been made here—both life-changing and heartbreaking.

Walking through the front door solo is monumental. Crew stands at the head of the dining room table. Asa flanks his left and Grady his right. Jarvis is next to Grady and I'm surprised to see Ozzy. He's been traveling the world on assignments for most of the last two months.

Everyone's eyes are on me.

Only me.

Crew is positioned in his normal weird stance that I find maddening at times—both casual and alert. He notes, "Carson's not here."

I join them in the dining room and stand at the opposite side of the table as Crew. "No. I'm sorry. He's made his decision."

Again, with no emotion, Crew lifts his chin.

I go on to explain. "Since he's not taking a position with you, he didn't feel he belonged here."

Crew barely narrows his eyes. "But you're here."

I pull in a breath. "Yes. I officially resigned from SIS. I'm a free agent."

It's small, but I don't miss it when Crew smiles.

I go on. "And Cole wanted me to express his gratitude. I'm sure he'll speak with you privately. He also wanted me to tell you that you now have a partner inside the CIA."

"I've always had him inside the CIA," Crew bounces back.

I shrug. "Yes, but now it will be like never before. Consider yourself upgraded to Platinum Status."

Crew nods. "That's good."

"He feels he can be of more use there, on the inside. Whatever you'll need, you'll get, Crew."

Grady glances at Crew. "That'll be helpful."

Crew nods. "It will. What does he want in return?"

I'd laugh but this meeting is too important. "Nothing. And since I'm here today and accepting your offer to work for your organization, and yours alone, I assume he simply wants you to keep me busy so I'll stay put. He won't admit that aloud but I know it's how he feels."

All male eyes dart around the room.

Wait. Did they not know Crew offered me a position among them?

I wipe the smile off my face.

Until Jarvis crosses his arms and grins, "Fuck, yeah. Welcome to the team, Spice Girl."

Then, I'm surrounded by manly smirks.

Well, now. That's better.

"I've been planning," Crew announces. "When I started this venture, I never meant for it to grow into anything else. We do what we do best—it's cut and dry and I liked it that way. But sometimes shit literally lands in front of you." He looks to me and then to Ozzy. "I might be a killer but I'm also an entrepreneur. I don't have to be smacked in the face with an opportunity to take advantage of it."

I've spoken privately with Crew over the last two months many times about how I might fit into his organization. I want to work but I'm also ready to start living my life, eager to find the balance Cole insists is waiting on me.

But I'm not an assassin and have no desire to be one.

And given the positive results of the test I took last week, running around the world chasing after bad guys isn't an option for me—at least for the next eight months.

There's also our wedding next month. I'm finding it easy to say goodbye to my former life. There's so much more to love about the one I'm living now.

Crew tosses a thick binder on the dining table in front of him.

Smack.

"It's time to diversify. Welcome to the team, Bella." Crew looks at me before settling his eyes on Ozzy. "This might get interesting, but I'm game."

Ozzy shrugs like it's no big deal. "Let's do it."

EPILOGUE

The next year

Cole

"Are you sure about this?"

I shift my weight from foot to foot and add a bounce every now and again. Sighing, I stuff my hands in my pockets and glance over at Grady. "What can I do? You've seen her. She's been in the gym every day for three months. She loves this shit. When she tries to spar with me, I'm forced to end it with sex. Better that than sport a new set of bruises."

"Why?" Ozzy bites. "Why can't you keep your fucking mouth shut?"

"He has no idea what he's in for." Jarvis takes his place next to me and lifts his chin toward the newb on the mat.

"Never thought I'd see anyone with a bigger chip on

their shoulder than you, Jarvis. But this guy gives the old you a run for your money," Crew adds. "Only you could find this big of an asshole who fits the bill. He's going to need some time."

Jarvis crosses his arms and doesn't take his eyes off the mat. "Remember when you humbled me on my first day?"

Crew lifts his chin. "It's one of my fondest memories."

Jarvis smirks. "He's about to get humbled by a blond chick who just had a baby. At least I got humiliated by you. He'll never live this down."

A huge fart comes from my chest and every man in the vicinity nods, impressed. I look down at my son strapped in his carrier and beam. "Good job, buddy."

Isaac Devon-brilliant-baby-Carson is six months old. He's a brute of a kid, but he would be from all the badass breastmilk he guzzles. He's a bigger, more masculine version of Abbott besides his eyes. His are so blue, they won't ever change and will no doubt melt cheerleaders' panties with a glance when he's older. I'm damned determined my kids will remember where they came from. I don't want them to wait until they're thirty-five to figure their shit out. Life is short—too fucking short—and my only regret on days like today is Red won't be able to meet his namesake. But if he were here, he'd bust my balls to give him more granddaughters.

We'll work on that next year.

"What kind of shit is this?" The recruit points to my wife, who's dressed in a pair of skin-tight leggings and a sports bra that teases me with the milky skin of her midriff. Her scar is still fading. "I am not fighting a chick."

"I know it's your first day, but don't be scared," Bella coos in a voice similar to the one she uses with Abbott. "If you need me to go easy on you, say the word."

Grady barks a laugh.

Despite being the best of his class at the Naval Academy where Jarvis found him, the recruit is young and stupid in many other ways. "Who the fuck are you and what game is this?" He looks at Crew and then Jarvis. "Is this a test? You're trying to get me to hit a woman so you can pummel my ass?"

"No trick, man," Jarvis assures him. "Carson works here and you'll answer to her as much as you will me. Pay attention, she's good."

"Would you like to start?" Bella asks.

"Fuck, no," the recruit throws back.

"Baby, do your thing," I call to her. "He'll catch up."

The recruit's eyes zip to me at the word *baby*.

"This is your last chance," Bella warns, shaking and flexing her fingers as she squares her shoulders.

He shakes his head and looks at his audience. We all nod, giving him the go ahead to try to kick my wife's ass.

Try being the operative word.

He turns to Bella.

Bella smiles ... so fucking beautiful. The glint in her eyes reminds me of the young woman I fell in love with years ago.

As instructed, he makes the first move.

Bella weaves.

He cuts.

Bella dodges.

They don't make contact and the recruit is surprised —frustrated and surprised.

Jarvis raises his voice. "Are you even trying?"

The recruit frowns before moving again. This time he goes for it. A punch comes so close to my wife's jaw, my insides tighten.

Then, she lets loose.

Kicks.

Strikes.

Jabs.

A leg sweep.

He gets her a couple times but she has no problem holding her own.

This goes on and the recruit realizes my wife is the real deal.

"Look at her go," I mutter.

Asa winces. "You are one crazy fuck, Carson."

"She's amazing," I add, not taking my eyes off her. "Makes me hard."

Ozzy sighs.

Bella spins one more time and takes him to the mat, his six foot-plus frame landing with a heavy thud. She pops up like a ninja jack-in-the-box and for the first time shows any sign of exertion. Her breaths come quicker as she brushes the dust off her black workout clothes and steps back, fixing her long, blond hair.

She walks off the mat and comes straight to me. I lean down and kiss her. "You know that turns me on, sweetness."

She smiles because she knows.

Now I can't wait for naptime. I'm going to put her in the shower and show her just how much.

Unbuckling Isaac from his carrier, she pulls him away from me as bubbles and drool run down his smiling chin, happy to see his mum, who we're both obsessed with.

"Mummy is done. Do you want to find Abbott and the cows? Moooo."

The recruit is bleeding from the lip and sweating his ass off as he climbs slowly to his feet, cursing under his breath.

"Don't worry," I call to him. "You'll get better. It's why you're here."

With our son in her arms, my wife agrees but doesn't look away from me. "Being here is a dream, isn't it, love?"

I put my arm around her shoulders and turn her to the open barn doors to find Abbott. I want to get back to our Saturday. "Being anywhere with you is a dream, sweetness."

Bella

I TAG my tea and move through the house to the back door. The weather took a turn tonight and Mother Nature has given us her first taste of fall. But I don't feel the nip in the air, I'm too emotional.

I settle myself into the thick cushions of the sofa in the sunroom, as I need to steal a second to myself.

I stare out at the sunset, past the shed, the garden, and to the thick foliage, now lit up in golds and reds. It's beyond the golden hour, the time of the day Cole and I usually have to ourselves. Abbott is in bed and, if the baby gods are in line, Isaac is winding down. This is our time together and we're rarely apart.

It's why I'm not surprised when the door opens behind me. Cole was on Isaac duty because Abbott and

I are lost in the world of child wizards—my funny accent coming in handy, she says.

"Did I piss you off?"

I choke out a huff and shake my head but don't look back. He'll know soon enough and I swipe at the damn tear that escapes.

"Hey." He walks around the sofa and frowns when he sees my expression. "Fuck. What did I do?"

I clutch my cup to my chest and wipe my cheek one more time. "Maybe I should ask you what you feel guilty about since you think you're the one who's made me stupid and emotional."

He hikes a thick brow. "I feel guilty for very little in life but when your face looks like this, I can't take it. If I caused it, I can fix it faster than I can anything else."

I smile through my bloodshot eyes. My fixer. And now I love him more than I did five minutes ago. I'm not sure my heart can take any more tonight.

"Move." He grabs my cup and places it on the side table before shoving me over far enough to flop down next to me. "Who do I need to hunt down and kill?"

I sigh and lean into his shoulder. "You're not a killer."

"I've killed people."

"Yes," I agree. "But only so they don't kill you first. Or me."

"True."

"I'm fine, Cole. I truly am. I'm not sure I remember the last time I was this happy."

His hand slides into my hair, angling my face to his. "Then I'm doing something wrong. You were pretty damn happy this morning before the kids woke up."

"I tucked Abbott in after we were done with our

chapter, kissed her nose, and told her I loved her. Like I do every night."

His sharp eyes soften the way they do when I speak of Abbott or Isaac.

I never expected Cole's daughter to blindly accept me as her mum. I wanted her to trust me because I love her as much as I do her father, and, now, her brother. I've made an extra effort with her since Isaac was born. It's been an honor to be in her life. But the child was abandoned by her birth mum. How does one heal from that kind of scar?

I hold his stare and tell him what has reduced me to a pile of mush. My voice is thick with emotion thinking of it and it only happened minutes ago. "Before I left, she said 'goodnight, *Mummy*'."

He sucks in a breath.

"I know," I agree with his unspoken sentiment. "It's huge. I'm so overcome, I can barely spit out the words."

He pulls me into his chest, almost suffocating me, his arms bound tight. "I knew she'd come around. She loves you. Hell, she adores you. But she's afraid. And I was afraid she'd always have *mommy issues*." He loosens his hold and pushes me back enough to look me in the eyes. "Love you, baby. Thank you for making life perfect."

"I don't know about that, but I love you too."

A smirk plays in the corner of his mouth. "I think it's time."

I settle into his chest farther. "Time for what, love?"

"Time to practice making babies again."

I reach for my cup. "Have we ever stopped?"

"Practice makes perfect." He grabs my cup and sets it back on the table before flipping me to my back, falling between my legs. "You're the one who wanted extra bedrooms. It's my job to make sure we fill them up."

I wrap my leg around his arse I love so much. "The bigger the family, the better."

"If I keep you pregnant, there'll be no more sparring for you."

I grin. "Today was fun, though. Like old times."

His lips press to the skin below my ear. "Come to bed and I'll spar with you. I'll give it to you good. You won't know what hit you."

I lift my hips to meet his cock. "Shall we race to bed?"

"So competitive. When it comes to bedroom brawls, I always win—like I do in everything."

I think back to his bet. "Your persistence has made me a happy woman."

"I can't help it. I'm the shit."

I shake my head. "Take me to bed, Cole. I'm emotional. You can take advantage of me."

"Mrs. Carson," he presses his hard cock between my legs. "I will not let you down."

No, he won't. My American—he's never let me down in anything. And I know he never will.

Thank you for reading. If you enjoyed *Scars*, I would appreciate a review on Amazon.

Read about Brax Cruz in *Possession,* the first book in the spinoff series, The Agents

Read Crew and Addy's story in *Vines*
Read Grady and Maya's story in *Paths*

Read Asa and Keelie's story in *Gifts*
Read Jarvis and Gracie's story in *Veils*
Read Ozzy and Liyah's story in *Souls*
Read Evan and Mary's story in *The Tequila – A Killers Novella*

The Next Generation
Read *Levi*, Asa's son

THOUGHTS AND ACKNOWLEDGEMENTS

Once upon a time, a character was born from nothing more than an author pondering, "I need a side character who will get very little screen time. Hey, let's make it interesting. Make *him* a *her*, and let *her* kick some ass."

Then the author fell completely and utterly in love and was forced at fictional gunpoint to create an entire backstory because that little character was screaming to have her story told.

Hello, Bella Donnelly.

Bella is also the most frustrating character the author has ever written. Neither English nor a badass, the author struggled. How does one create an alpha for Bella when she's a badass who can ninja anyone she pleases?

Hello, Cole Carson.

Only the most arrogant, lovable asshole around. It took a hero as over the top as him to balance someone as strong as Bella. Throw in the intelligence community, a nasty politician, and a tribe of favorite killers, and you've got yourself one wild rollercoaster.

Hello, I am that author.

Every book is a journey ... each one different from the rest. *Scars* challenged me in ways that left me frustrated while learning a great deal about how to push through writing struggles as well as environmental challenges (thank you very much, 2020).

I'm grateful to so many for the final product of this book. Michele, you're the first one to believe in me, have remained my biggest cheerleader, and accept me as your best friend no matter how scary I look daily on Marco Polo. I love you.

Kristan with edit llc, as always, you prettied up my words like a rock star. Thank you for not only being the perfect editing partner but a precious friend.

Layla Frost and Sarah Curtis, not only do you put up with my high-maintenance non-problems, but you beta read this book like badasses. And Layla, thank you for naming your baby after me. ;-)

Heather Stewart Soligo, you're a kickass alpha reader and didn't even know it. Thank you for your time and input exactly when I needed it. And, as always, thank you for your never-ending support.

Annette and Michelle with Book Nerd Services, you are my lifelines during releases. I'm so lucky I get to work with my friends.

Rebecca Arvieux with Bex Book Revieux and Sarah Poulton with Sarah Loves Reading Romance, when I needed special skill sets and knowledge on my characters, you both stepped up and saved the day. Thank you for your time and valuable input. Without you, *Scars* wouldn't be what it is.

Gi Paar with Gi's Spot Reviews, Carrie Marie with

Carrie's Bookshelf, thank you for **always** having my back and reading my words early. I **treasure** you both.

To Emoji, despite 2020, it's been a good year and I can't wait to see where the next twenty-five bring us. It's a gift to live life with you.

To my Street and Review Teams, you ladies are the shit! Quick on the draw to spread the word and unwavering support. It's an honor that you've chosen me to spend time with and support.

Lastly, to my Beauties. Every single one of you feels like my next-door neighbor. I could stand in the driveway for hours and chat with you. Thank you for spending time with me and helping to create one of the best spots on the Freakybook.

Humbled and grateful forever.

Thank you for reading.

BA xx

ALSO BY BRYNNE ASHER

Killers Series

Vines – A Killers Novel, Book 1

Paths – A Killers Novel, Book 2

Gifts – A Killers Novel, Book 3

Veils – A Killers Novel, Book 4

Scars – A Killers Novel, Book 5

Souls – A Killers Novel, Book 6

The Tequila – A Killers Novella

The Killers, The Next Generation

Levi, Asa's son

The Agents

Possession

Tapped

Exposed

Illicit

The Carpino Series

Overflow – The Carpino Series, Book 1

Beautiful Life – The Carpino Series, Book 2

Athica Lane – The Carpino Series, Book 3

Until Avery – A Carpino Series Crossover Novella

Force of Nature - A Carpino Christmas Novel

The Dillon Sisters

Deathly by Brynne Asher

Damaged by Layla Frost

The Montgomery Series

Bad Situation – The Montgomery Series, Book 1

Broken Halo – The Montgomery Series, Book 2

Betrayed Love - The Montgomery Series, Book 3

Standalones

Blackburn

ABOUT THE AUTHOR

Brynne Asher lives in the Midwest with her husband, three children, and her perfect dog. When she isn't creating pretend people and relationships in her head, she's running her kids around and doing laundry. She enjoys cooking, decorating, shopping at outlet malls and online, always seeking the best deal. A perfect day in Brynne World ends in front of an outdoor fire with family, friends, s'mores, and a delicious cocktail.

facebook.com/brynneasherauthor

instagram.com/brynneasher

amazon.com/Brynne-Asher/e/B00VRULS58/ref=dp_by-line_cont_pop_ebooks_1

bookbub.com/profile/brynne-asher

Made in United States
Troutdale, OR
12/07/2023